"A darn good series with vivid,
—*Mystery Sc*

"Will make you want to start knitting or weaving right away."
—ReviewingTheEvidence.com

Knit One, Kill Two

Agatha Award Nominee for Best First Novel

"A mystery with more twists and turns than the scrumptious yarns in the fictional shop of Lambspun. This is a clever, fast-paced plot, with a spunky sleuth and cast of fun, engaging characters. *Knit One, Kill Two* delivers the goods."
—Margaret Coel

"An intriguing mystery within a rich, colorful, tactile knitterly context."
—*Knitters Review*

"Well-drawn characters and a wickedly clever plot—you'll love unraveling this mystery!"
—Laura Childs, *New York Times* bestselling author of *The Teaberry Strangler*

Needled to Death

"Nonknitters and fiber fanatics alike will enjoy the yarn shop setting."
—*Romantic Times*

"Kelly is easy to like . . . A fun, quick read."   —*The Mystery Reader*

"As with the cleverly weaved *Knit One, Kill Two*, *Needled to Death* is a fine yarn that has cozy fans trying to unravel the threads of whodunit alongside of the heroine . . . [A] tightly stitched tale."
—*The Best Reviews*

continued . . .

A Deadly Yarn

"A terrific series with a heroine who grows more and more likable with each investigation."
—The Mystery Reader

"The whodunit is well crafted . . . A delightful mystery."
—The Best Reviews

A Killer Stitch

"Knitters will be pleased to add Sefton's series . . . to their knitting-related fiction shelf."
—Booklist

"Plenty to enjoy . . . Settle back in front of a cracking fire and enjoy the company of Kelly and co."
—MyShelf.com

"As light and fluffy as one of Kelly's balls of yarn . . . Readers may enjoy reading this book almost as much as they'll delight in knitting the cable knit scarf."
—Library Journal

Dyer Consequences

"Sure to please series fans."
—Publishers Weekly

"They just keep getting better . . . Each visit with Kelly and her friends becomes more enjoyable than the one before."
—Gumshoe Review

"Knitters will welcome the pattern for the same cloche hat that Kelly is knitting, and a recipe for pecan pie goes down easy, too."
—Booklist

Fleece Navidad

Dropped Dead Stitch

Double Knit Murders

Maggie Sefton

BERKLEY PRIME CRIME, NEW YORK

THE BERKLEY PUBLISHING GROUP
Published by the Penguin Group
Penguin Group (USA) Inc.
375 Hudson Street, New York, New York 10014, USA
Penguin Group (Canada), 90 Eglinton Avenue East, Suite 700, Toronto, Ontario M4P 2Y3, Canada
(a division of Pearson Penguin Canada Inc.)
Penguin Books Ltd., 80 Strand, London WC2R 0RL, England
Penguin Group Ireland, 25 St. Stephen's Green, Dublin 2, Ireland (a division of Penguin Books Ltd.)
Penguin Group (Australia), 250 Camberwell Road, Camberwell, Victoria 3124, Australia
(a division of Pearson Australia Group Pty. Ltd.)
Penguin Books India Pvt. Ltd., 11 Community Centre, Panchsheel Park, New Delhi—110 017, India
Penguin Group (NZ), 67 Apollo Drive, Rosedale, North Shore 0632, New Zealand
(a division of Pearson New Zealand Ltd.)
Penguin Books (South Africa) (Pty.) Ltd., 24 Sturdee Avenue, Rosebank, Johannesburg 2196,
South Africa

Penguin Books Ltd., Registered Offices: 80 Strand, London WC2R 0RL, England

This is a work of fiction. Names, characters, places, and incidents either are the product of the author's imagination or are used fictitiously, and any resemblance to actual persons, living or dead, business establishments, events, or locales is entirely coincidental. The publisher does not have any control over and does not assume any responsibility for author or third-party websites or their content.

PUBLISHER'S NOTE: The recipes contained in this book are to be followed exactly as written. The publisher is not responsible for your specific health or allergy needs that may require medical supervision. The publisher is not responsible for any adverse reaction to the recipes contained in this book.

PRINTING HISTORY
Berkley Prime Crime trade paperback edition / November 2010

Library of Congress Cataloging-in-Publication Data

Sefton, Maggie.
  [Knit one, kill two]
  Double knit murders / Maggie Sefton.—Berkley Prime Crime trade pbk. ed.
    p. cm.
  ISBN 978-0-425-23691-8
  1. Flynn, Kelly (Fictitious character)—Fiction. 2. Knitters (Persons)—Fiction. I. Sefton,
Maggie. Needled to death. II. Title.
  PS3619.E37K59 2011
  813'.6—dc22

                                       2010024897

PRINTED IN THE UNITED STATES OF AMERICA

10 9 8 7 6 5 4 3 2 1

Contents

Knit One, Kill Two

Acknowledgments

A thousand thanks to Shirley Ellsworth, the inspired owner of *Lambspun of Colorado* in Fort Collins, Colorado, the knitting shop I used as a model for this series and the place I first "fell down the rabbit hole" into this fascinating wonderland of color and texture. Shirley and her staff of gifted teachers and fiber artists never ran out of patience with my questions or encouragement for my beginning efforts. Thanks also to the Tuesday night knitting group for their rowdy and wonderful brainstorming of titles for this series of novels. And special thanks to Kristi for her last-minute artwork.

Thanks also to my agent, Jessica Faust, for her unceasing encouragement and support to write this knitting mystery. And special thanks to my wonderful editor, Samantha Mandor, for helping to bring Kelly and all her friends to life on the page.

Special thanks to my four daughters, my mom, and all my dear friends who've always believed in me and supported my writing dreams. And thanks to my ninety-two-year-old aunt, Ann, whose "quilt of memories" hangs on my bedroom wall.

And a special pat on the head to my dog, Carl, who's the model for Kelly's golf-ball chasing pet Rottweiler. I must admit that fictional Carl is much better behaved than real-life Carl, with or without golf balls.

One

Kelly Flynn nosed her car onto the gravel driveway and pulled to a stop in front of the familiar little house perched beside a golf course. Everything looked the same. Aunt Helen's beige stucco, red tile–roofed cottage looked as cozy and inviting as always. Golfers were scattered about the lush greens, doggedly working to improve their games. In the background the Colorado Rocky Mountains, still snowcapped in late spring, loomed over the entire scene. It was all picture-postcard pretty, just like Kelly remembered, except for one thing. Aunt Helen was dead—murdered a week ago in her picturesque cottage.

A "burglary gone bad," the police called it. Kelly's gut still twisted at the thought. Aunt Helen would have fought back. Kelly knew she would. Even though she was thin as a stick and a foot shorter than Kelly, she was wiry and tough. And she had spirit. Spunk. She'd never go down without a fight. Not Aunt Helen. No way.

Kelly felt tears rise to her eyes again as she remembered her aunt's favorite admonition: "Never give up, Kelly-girl. If you want something bad enough, don't you ever give up." The tears escaped, running down Kelly's cheeks, and she swiped them away with the back of her hand. She'd never even had the chance to say good-bye. At least with her dad, Kelly'd been able to tell him how much she loved him. Cancer might be an ugly way to die, but it was slower. Murder was a thief in the night, creeping in to steal away valuable loved ones. And this thief stole the only mother Kelly had ever known.

A cold, wet nose shoved against Kelly's neck, and she turned to pat the shiny black Rottweiler head resting beside her shoulder. Carl always sensed her moods. "Don't worry, boy, I haven't forgotten you. You're looking at that grass, right?" She pointed to the manicured golf course, stretching from her aunt's property all the way to the river that meandered diagonally through the scenic college town north of Denver.

Kelly let herself gaze. It had been six months since she'd returned to Fort Connor, where she spent her early childhood. Every time she returned, she wondered how she'd ever make herself leave again. The sky was bluer here, the air was cleaner, and the sun was brighter by a mile. "A mile high to be exact," as Aunt Helen used to say. What a gorgeous day. If her aunt was still alive, she and Kelly would take one of their favorite hikes along a trail in the nearby Poudre Canyon. How could it be so beautiful with Helen gone?

Carl whined to get her attention, clearly eager to explore. "Okay, boy, but you can't run on the course. The greenskeeper wouldn't appreciate your lifting a leg on every tee." Carl rolled his soft brown eyes to her in pleading mode.

"Nope. You'll just have to make do with the yard." Kelly opened the car door and slid out, grabbing a leash as she did.

Carl's ears perked up at the magic jingle, and he gave an excited yelp. That meant outside and play. Snapping the leash to his red collar, Kelly headed toward the small backyard. Tall cottonwood trees surrounded the property, shading both house and yard. Flower boxes were already planted, even though Kelly knew the frost date in northern Colorado was a yearly gamble. Somehow, Helen always won out. Her green thumb or gardener's luck could overcome even Colorado's capricious weather.

Kelly made a mental note to water the plants that evening. She wasn't about to let Helen's plants die with her. She swung the back gate open and ushered Carl inside. "It isn't the golf course, boy, but it's bigger than your yard for sure," she said, referring to her postage stamp–size townhouse yard on the outskirts of Washington, D.C. Carl didn't waste time. He took off the moment his leash was unsnapped, nose to the ground.

The sound of another car coming down the gravel driveway caught Kelly's attention, and she turned to see a red minivan drive up to the larger stucco and red tile–roofed house across the drive. A woman exited the van and entered the sprawling mirror-image of Helen's cottage.

Both houses and the assorted outbuildings nearby occupied a pie-shaped wedge of land that clung to the corner of a busy intersection. Kelly remembered when both streets were country roads cutting through fields of sugar beets and sheep farms. Now, a big box discount store swallowed the opposite corner and townhouses clustered across the street.

At least her aunt and uncle had sold their farmland to the city for a golf course and kept only the cottage and its yard. If she squinted her eyes hard enough, Kelly could block out the golfers and picture her uncle heading to the barn years ago when he was still alive.

"Kelly, is that you?" a woman's voice called.

Kelly shut the gate, knowing Carl would be occupied for hours identifying scents. She turned and recognized Mimi Shafer walking across the driveway. Mimi owned the knitting and needlework shop that now occupied what was once Aunt Helen's and Uncle Jim's farmhouse. Her aunt had been ecstatic about the arrangement, since she was an expert knitter and quilter, but Kelly had always felt vaguely resentful. She remembered when the house was filled with Aunt Helen and Uncle Jim—and memories. But Uncle Jim's long illness changed all that.

Now, Kelly felt nothing but gratitude. Mimi had been Aunt Helen's closest friend and had never left Kelly's side during yesterday's service. She gave names to faces and helped Kelly stand and sit through a liturgy that was no longer familiar.

Kelly straightened her white blouse and navy skirt. Not as tailored as her usual CPA firm attire, but sober enough for a lawyer meeting. She couldn't wait until she could change into a casual top and slacks, maybe even shorts if it stayed warm. Ever since she got back, she'd been dressed up and meeting people. Just like the office. But Colorado meant sunshine and mountains and freedom to Kelly. And that meant shorts, a T-shirt, and sneakers.

She brushed her chin-length dark-brown hair behind her ear and checked the barrette in back. Kelly'd rushed through her shower and dressing in order to fit in a morning run along the trail that ran beside the motel. She'd barely checked the mirror. After yesterday's tears, she needed to clear her head. Running always helped her think.

She waved to Mimi. "I just thought I'd let Carl use Helen's backyard today while I go to all those . . . you know, meetings. Lawyer, banker, and all that."

"That's a great idea. I'm sure he's tired of being cooped up in the motel room," Mimi said with a bright smile. Her sun-streaked brown hair feathered softly around her face. Fiftyish, slender, and pretty, she wore a powder-blue straight dress that accentuated her trim figure. But what really drew Kelly's attention was the open-weave vest she wore on top; the loosely fixed knots held the yarns together. Varying shades of blue traveled all the way to green and back again. The effect was stunning.

"Do you have time for a cup of tea or coffee?" Mimi asked, obviously hoping for a yes.

Kelly hesitated, running through her mental daytimer. That and the Greenwich Meridian time clock in her head kept Kelly on task. She depended on that clock. Back in the firm, everyone kept track of their time in tenths of an hour—six-minute intervals—billable hours. Consequently, Kelly was seldom late. "I have a few minutes. My appointment with the lawyer isn't until ten."

"Oh, darn, I was hoping we'd have more time," Mimi said, her smile momentarily missing. "I've been dying to show you the shop, but I guess it'll just have to wait until later today. Why don't we step over to the café?" She gestured toward the pathway leading around the farmhouse.

Kelly completely forgot that a bistro-style café had opened in the former kitchen and dining room of the farmhouse since her last visit. As they followed the flower beds and flagstone path, Kelly was astonished to see the café also spilled out into the shady back-yard. Surrounded by high stucco walls, the entire patio was private, secluded from the outside. The whole setting was delightful and charming, Kelly had to admit.

Mimi chose a table and sat down, motioning to a nearby waitress as Kelly settled into a wrought-iron chair. "This is really quite nice. I like what they've done here," Kelly surprised herself by saying. Noticing the many tables filled with customers lingering over late breakfasts and brunch, she asked, "How's it doing? Financially, I mean. I know how hard it is for small restaurants to make it." As a beginning accountant years ago, Kelly had had several restaurants to worry about. "Shoe box clients" she used to call them, because they always kept their accounts in shoe boxes for some reason.

"Actually, quite well, according to Pete," said Mimi. "He's the young man who had the idea of turning this whole area into a restaurant. Somehow, he managed to convince the management company that owns it to invest in used equipment, and he volunteered all the labor. He put his heart and soul into this place." She shook her head. "Let's hope all that hard work hasn't been wasted . . . for both of us."

Intrigued by the cryptic remark, Kelly was about to respond when the waitress appeared. She had shoulder-length reddish-brown hair that curved around a pretty face. "Hi, Mimi," she said with a bright smile, then turned a warm gaze to Kelly.

"Kelly, this is Jennifer Stroud," Mimi introduced. "She was also a friend of Helen's."

"Kelly, I just wanted to say how shocked we were at Helen's death. She was a wonderful lady. I used to see her over at the shop almost every day, and she was always so sweet and loving. We'll all miss her a lot."

The comments caught Kelly unprepared, and she felt her eyes grow suddenly moist. She glanced down at her napkin. "Thank you. You're very kind."

Jennifer reached out and patted Kelly's arm. "Hey, that's okay. Let me bring you something. I know Mimi's order already. Earl Grey, cream. How about you?"

"Coffee, black and strong," Kelly said with a smile, which helped chase away the tears.

"Down with decaf, right?" Jennifer winked as she flipped the notepad closed. "Be right back."

"I think she was at the funeral yesterday, but I really can't remember too much," Kelly said as she watched Jennifer skirt between tables, glad for the chance to compose herself.

"Oh, yes, she was there with the other knitting shop regulars."

"Regulars?" Kelly asked, "Who are they?"

"We've got lots of knitting and needlework groups that meet regularly at the shop during the week. Some are organized, some just happen, like Jennifer's group. They're a bunch of women, many of whom are around your age, who meet after work a couple of times a week or more. Of course, anybody who shows up is welcome to sit in with any group. That's how Helen met Jennifer and the others."

Kelly could easily picture that. Helen was always knitting, and loved nothing better than to share her passion. It was a shame Kelly had proven to be such an unwilling student. Now, she was sorry she'd always feigned impatience whenever her aunt had tried to coax her into learning to knit.

"I know Aunt Helen enjoyed that," Kelly mused. "She loved meeting new people. And living across from the shop, she could make new friends almost every day. Every week when I'd call her, she'd always tell me something funny she'd heard, usually from some friend." Kelly would miss those phone calls.

"Helen had lots of friends, as you saw yesterday at the service. Everyone loved her, and we want to help you in whatever way we can, Kelly. Several people have offered to help go through the house when you're ready."

Kelly groaned inwardly. That unpleasant chore had almost slipped her mind. Whenever it had appeared, she'd shoved it away. At least having people with her would make the task easier and less painful. "I confess I've deliberately not thought about that chore," she admitted. "I guess I'm avoiding going into the house after, well, you know."

"I understand, Kelly."

"Thanks so much. I really appreciate your help. I remember how hard it was going through my dad's things, and I'd been prepared for his death."

Mimi reached out and patted Kelly's arm. "Well, you're not alone this time, Kelly. We're here to help you."

Jennifer's cheerful bustle and the inviting tray of coffee and tea arrived just when Kelly felt her eyes grow moist again. After the funeral yesterday she thought she'd cried herself dry. Apparently there was a well inside her that ran deeper than she knew.

There was no one left anymore. Her dad, three years ago. Now, Aunt Helen. Her entire family was gone.

"Here you go," Jennifer announced as she set the tea and coffee in place. "Pete even threw in one of those wicked cinnamon rolls on the house."

"Ohhh, that's cruel," Mimi groaned. "He knows I can't have the sugar."

Kelly eyed the tempting coil of golden, flaky, sweet dough slathered with a sugary cream-cheese icing that drizzled down the sides. She'd forgotten Fort Connor's community weakness for these oversized breakfast buns. The bakery that specialized in making them kept the calorie count a secret.

"It's still warm," tempted Jennifer with a grin.

Her normal willpower was either sound asleep or stunned into silence at the sight of the huge pastry. So, with no nagging voice in her head, Kelly picked up the fork. "What the heck. I'll need it for all those meetings. Lawyers are depressing."

"Absolutely," Jennifer concurred, clearly enjoying Kelly's quick capitulation. "Besides, you're tall and slender. It'll never show. On me, it'd be on my hips in five minutes."

"Oh, right," Kelly retorted with a grin. "Why don't you share it with me?"

Jennifer rolled her eyes. "Don't tempt me. I was born with a sweet tooth."

"Seriously, I can't finish this monster all by myself." She sliced the bun in half and pushed one half to the side of her plate.

Jennifer glanced at the pastry. "We're not supposed to eat with customers."

Kelly sensed weakness. She took a big bite, closed her eyes, and let out a dramatic, *"Mmmmmmmmmmm!"*

"That's it. Priorities." Jennifer laughed and grabbed her portion.

"Which are?" Mimi teased.

Jennifer paused after swallowing. "Right now, sugar. It's gonna be a busy day."

Kelly polished off her share and reached for the coffee, which was surprisingly rich and dark. She drank in the blissful enjoyment of the strong brew. "Yum, this is really good for the plain stuff. My compliments."

"That's Eduardo's doing. He's our cook and insists on making the coffee every morning. I think he throws in espresso or chicory or shoelaces or who knows what. But it'll wake you up, for sure."

"Bless him, and tell him I'll be back." The timer went off inside her head, and Kelly drained the cup. "Speaking of that, I have to go. Lawyers get all pinched around the edges if you're late." She scooted back her chair and brushed telltale sugar flakes off her skirt. "Oh, Mimi, I almost forgot. Could you fill a bowl with water for Carl, please? I fed him this morning, but I forgot to grab his water dish."

"No problem. I'll give him some food come dinnertime, too, so don't rush. And make sure you stop in the shop when you return. I can't wait to show you everything we've done. You haven't been in since we opened four years ago." Mimi exuded pride. "You'll be surprised, I think."

"I look forward to it. Thanks, Mimi," Kelly said as she backed away from the table. Glancing at Jennifer as she headed for the pathway, Kelly waved. "Nice meeting you, Jennifer."

"Oh, you'll see me later at the shop. With the others. Good luck with the lawyer."

Kelly hastened to her car. She'd dutifully let Mimi show off her shop, for Aunt Helen's sake, if nothing else. Kelly couldn't knit her way out of a paper bag. So all that knitting stuff would be lost on her. Her aunt had tried several times to instruct Kelly when she was growing up and even as an adult, but it never seemed to take. Kelly would fumble the needles and drop the yarn—whatever it took to appear completely incompetent. There were so many more fun things to do outside on the farm, she just couldn't sit still long enough to learn.

Besides, all those different kinds of stitches looked complicated to Kelly. Knitting here, purling there. All that yarn, needles busily working away, stitch after stitch, row after row. Looked like a lot of work to Kelly. She just didn't have that kind of patience. The only patience she'd ever had was for numbers. Numbers stayed put on paper. They didn't fall off the end of the needles.

Oh yes, Kelly thought, as she backed her car out of the parking space, numbers were far less confusing than knitting.

Lawrence Chambers tapped his gold-rimmed pen against the leather desk pad as he scanned the documents before him. Kelly used the opportunity to study the lawyer, who was the same age as her aunt. His gray hair shone silver as a stray morning sunbeam crossed the desk. Chambers had been Aunt Helen's trusted lawyer and close friend for a lifetime.

"Thanks to Helen's foresight, you should have no problem handling any expense involved with the estate," he spoke up. "You're co-signer on both bank accounts, checking and savings, as well as the safe-deposit box. It was a smart move, considering you're her only heir."

"Aunt Helen told me four years ago what her wishes were. I've always tried to oblige her in whatever way I could."

Chambers glanced up from the papers in his hand and smiled across the large walnut desk. Kelly noticed his faded blue eyes were kind.

"Helen appreciated everything you did for her. She told me so many times."

Kelly glanced away. "She was like a mom to me, Mr. Chambers. You know that. Besides, when my dad died three years ago, I promised him I'd take care of her. She was his only living relative." Guilt twinged inside. She'd never broken a promise to her dad in her whole life.

Chambers set down the papers, watching Kelly, then gestured to the wall. "That's hers, you know."

Kelly studied the framed quilted scene that had caught her eye earlier. Deep, rich browns and greens portrayed a small house nestled in the mountains, surrounded by tall evergreens. "I thought that might be her work. It's so vibrant."

"Yes, she did that from a photograph of the mountain cabin our family has had for years." He smiled. "She surprised us with it on our anniversary. That was Helen. Always doing for others. If she wasn't stitching for someone she knew, she'd be knitting for the homeless shelter."

"Yes, I know. I'm the one who used to buy the yarn online to save her money." A spark of anger flared suddenly. "It doesn't seem right, does it, Mr. Chambers. My aunt was murdered by some vagrant, exactly the sort of person she tried to help. Where's the justice in that?"

Chambers clasped his hands on top of the documents. "There is none, Kelly. This is one of those horrible, awful acts of random violence."

Kelly stared at the floor-to-ceiling walnut bookcases that lined one wall. "The officer told me this was a 'burglary gone bad.' She said this guy came into Helen's house that night, saw her purse, and grabbed it. Then, supposedly Helen came out and saw him, screamed, and he strangled her. Then he ran off."

"Yes, that's exactly what the police told me. Apparently this man was a drunk and a vagrant and was always getting into trouble. He must have come into the house, grabbed her purse, and when Helen came out," his voice became strained, "he killed her for it." He sighed. "Thank goodness he was too drunk to be smart. The police saw him run away from the scene, so they caught him right away."

Kelly leaned forward in her chair and eyed Chambers. Something he'd said. "That's a little different from what the police told me. They said they'd seen this guy 'near the house,' not coming from it. Are you sure that's what they told you?"

Chambers pondered. "I'm fairly certain the detective who spoke with me said they captured the suspect fleeing the scene. Yes, that's exactly what he said. 'Fleeing the scene.' And I took that to mean he was coming from the house."

"Do you remember who you spoke with, Mr. Chambers? The woman who called me was a community relations officer and wasn't involved with the case."

"Oh, yes, I spoke with Lieutenant Morrison. He's in charge. A very experienced detective, from what I've heard. Very thorough."

Kelly opened her portfolio and wrote the name on a legal pad. "I'm sure you're right, Mr. Chambers. I mean, this guy had to be lurking around Aunt Helen's house before he came in. Looking in the windows or something." She closed the portfolio with a snap. "He must have been drunk. Why else would he have tried to steal from a woman who never carried more than twenty dollars in her purse?" A bitter note crept into her voice. It felt good to release it.

Chambers peered at Kelly over his glasses with a worried frown. "Well, uh, she may have had more in her purse—"

"Oh, no, sir," Kelly countered. "She never had more than twenty bucks and change at any one time. She always used her debit card because it kept her on a budget. And I should know, Mr. Chambers, because I drew up her budget and kept her accounts every month. She was still paying off some of Uncle Jim's medical bills, so she was very careful."

Chambers' lined face creased even more. "Didn't she tell you about the . . . the, uh, money she was borrowing?"

Kelly blinked. Surely she couldn't have heard the lawyer right. "Borrowing? Helen wasn't borrowing any money. Remember, I kept her accounts. I would know."

"I'm afraid she did. Just before she died."

Kelly stared back at him, incredulous. "*What?* Where . . . I mean, who . . . how much?"

"Twenty thousand dollars," Chambers said in a pained voice.

"Twenty thousand dollars!" Kelly sat bolt upright. "But why? And . . . and where would Helen borrow that kind of money, anyway? She was living on Jim's state pension and Social Security."

"The only place she could, Kelly. She refinanced her house. And went to one of those predatory lenders to do it." He shook his head, sadly. "I advised her against it, but she wouldn't listen. She said she needed it and would talk to me later. I assumed she was giving it to you, that you needed it for something."

"*Me?*" Kelly shot back. "I'd never ask Aunt Helen for money. I'd starve first."

Chambers sank back into his leather armchair. "Oh, my . . . oh, my," he said, clearly troubled. "I thought the money was for you, that's why I didn't worry too much when she said she needed it. After all, you're her only living relative."

Kelly stared at the diplomas that lined the wall behind Chambers' desk. This was impossible. It made no sense. Her aunt wouldn't even consider such a risky move without consulting Kelly. "This is crazy, Mr. Chambers. Aunt Helen was a sensible woman, you know that. She'd never do such a thing. Why . . . why, we just refinanced her house three years ago to pay off most of Uncle Jim's medical bills. We got a really low rate. Perfect for her. I was going to help her pay off the mortgage so she'd have it free and clear in ten years." Her hand shot out in frustration. "She wouldn't . . . she couldn't have done this stupid thing."

Chambers took off his glasses and rubbed his eyes but said nothing.

Anger flashed through Kelly, right up her spine. "Wait a minute. Do you think some sleazy con artist got his claws in Aunt Helen?

Tricked her into some wretched investment scheme? I'd told her not to even talk to those weasels if they called."

"No, no, Helen was too smart for that," he dismissed the threat with a wave. "She and I frequently discussed some of the scams out there for the unwary, especially vulnerable seniors."

"When did she talk to you? When did she tell you what she was going to do?"

"About three weeks ago. She called to tell me she was refinancing the house because she needed money and asked my recommendation for a lender. Apparently she'd already been turned down by her current mortgage company and two others. There was no more equity left."

"I know, we used it all three years ago."

"Well, I asked how much she needed, thinking I'd lend it to her myself. When she told me twenty thousand dollars, I was shocked and told her so. I asked what on earth she could need that much money for, and she refused to answer. Said she'd talk to me later and hung up. I didn't even hear from her again until last Friday, the very day she was killed."

"And what did she say then?" Kelly probed.

"That's when she told me she'd found some Denver mortgage company that was only too glad to write up an above-value mortgage. She wouldn't tell me the interest rate. It must have been awful. But she did say she got the check for twenty thousand dollars. It never occurred to me she'd cash it." Chambers leaned over his desk and sank his head in both hands. "Good Lord. That's what got her killed. All that money sitting in her purse. Oh, Helen, why? *Why?*" His voice cracked this time.

Kelly pondered for a moment, giving Chambers time to collect himself. She was still trying to make sense of everything she'd heard. Her logical mind didn't want to accept her aunt's illogical actions. It was totally out of character. Why would she put herself upside down in her mortgage at her age? Especially since she'd had to refinance only three years ago to pay off most of Uncle Jim's medical bills. And why on earth would she take all that cash home with her?

The shock of her aunt's murder had been enough to occupy Kelly's thoughts the entire two thousand–mile drive to Colorado.

But now that the funeral was over and she had more time to think, Kelly began to notice details. Details that didn't belong. After all, that's what she did for a living. In her consulting role with a large accounting firm, Kelly analyzed a corporation's financial statements looking for anything that jumped out and made her buzzer go off. She'd never imagined that she'd have to turn that same concentration on uglier matters so close to home.

Waiting another moment, Kelly gently asked, "Mr. Chambers, have you spoken to the police? Did you tell them all this, I mean about the money and all?"

He lifted his red-rimmed eyes and cleared his throat. "No. I would never divulge Helen's private business. That's privileged," he sniffled.

"Then I think they need to know there was a lot more money stolen than they originally thought. I'll call this Lieutenant Morrison as soon as I leave here." Picking up her portfolio, Kelly stood and deliberately let her voice assume the official business tone she used so often. That would give Chambers something to hang on to. "Thank you, Mr. Chambers, for everything you've done and everything you've tried to do to help my aunt. I'm going over to the bank right now and check the accounts. And I'll look into this new loan as well."

Chambers straightened and rose. "That's a good idea . . . oh, wait a minute. I think I wrote down the name." He paged through the daytimer on his desk, scanning the pages. "Yes, here it is. U-Can-Do-It Mortgage in Denver." He peered at the daytimer while Kelly wrote the information in her notebook. "Ohhh, yes . . . there *is* something else. Here's the note. Helen also said she was coming in soon to talk about her property. She wanted to make sure it all went to the city for gardens in case you didn't want to live in Fort Connor. But she didn't want to donate the land. It was to be sold, with you receiving all the proceeds."

Kelly stared blankly at him. Another surprise. "Gardens? Really? She never mentioned that."

"Yes, that surprised me, too." Chambers shook his head. "But, of course, she never got the chance to come in for the appointment. So you're free to sell the property if you choose."

"But that was her wish, apparently," Kelly mused out loud.

"Apparently so. She loved you very much, Kelly."

With that, Kelly knew she had to leave. If she misted up, Chambers would lose it again, and that would be embarrassing. Not so much for her, but for the older gentleman. "Thank you, again, Mr. Chambers," she said, and headed for the door.

"You're welcome, Kelly. And, I'm sure you'll find those mortgage papers in Helen's house. Take care, my dear."

Kelly waved and made a swift exit. She was sure she'd find the papers in the cottage, but the thought of going into the house where Aunt Helen was murdered still chilled her. Kelly hastened to the parking lot as she searched her cell phone's directory for the number of the Fort Connor police department.

Two

Carl was already at the fence waiting for Kelly when she pulled into the driveway. "Hey, boy," Kelly called out as she slammed the car door and headed for the yard. The sun angled over the mountains, or foothills as the locals called them, and a blazing ray of sunshine hit her right in the eyes. She always forgot how bright mile-high sunlight could be.

Kelly reached over the fence to pat Carl. He responded by placing both front paws on the fence so she could scratch his head. "I'll bet you had a better day than I did, Carl. Playing outside, chasing squirrels." At the mention of his newly discovered pastime, Carl glanced over his shoulder. "Remind me to take you to Denver and introduce you to that sleazy lender." She leaned over and let Carl lick her chin. "He was really sarcastic on the phone today. I'll bet he wouldn't be so rude sitting across from a Rottweiler." Carl obliged with a woof and Kelly laughed. The first time she'd laughed since, well, since this morning when she watched Jennifer snatch the cinnamon roll.

She turned toward the shop and checked her watch. It was after

6:00 p.m. Boy, she really didn't feel like having a tour right now. She was starving and hadn't eaten since she'd grabbed some chips on the way to the bank. And after this afternoon's bleak news from the lender, she'd lost her appetite entirely.

It was back in full force now, and Kelly's stomach growled on cue. She glanced at the shop's front door. It used to be the side door for Helen's and Jim's house, with a great shady patio right in front, facing the fields and barns. Kelly remembered Helen sitting in the shade on a summer day, yarn or needlework in her lap, watching Jim out in the distance.

Kelly shook off the memories and squared her shoulders. Time to tour. Hopefully it would be short so Kelly could keep up her enthusiasm. Mimi so obviously hoped Kelly would approve of the changes she'd made to the farmhouse. Kelly was determined not to disappoint her, even though she was sure each room would be a bittersweet reminder of happier days.

She strode to the front door, noticing for the first time the colorful flower beds everywhere, including the shady patio, which was still as inviting as ever. A sign spelled out the shop's name in the middle of the oak door. HOUSE OF LAMBSPUN. Kelly took a deep breath and yanked open the door, stepping inside.

That's as far as she got. She couldn't take another step. The assault on her senses held her in place. Color, color, everywhere she looked. Skeins of yarns in every hue imaginable spilled out of cupboards in tidy bundles, scattered across antique tables in twisted coils, and draped languorously in billowy soft bunches along white-painted walls. Azure blues blended into turquoise and sapphire. Lime greens skipped through spring grass to rest in deep forest emerald. And the reds—oh, the reds. Kelly's favorite. Cool raspberry sherbet, melting into vermilion, heating all the way to fire-engine red.

Kelly had to catch her breath. So used to the sober décor of the accounting and corporate world, Kelly felt her senses on momentary overload, adjusting. She stepped into the tiled entryway and immediately glanced up. A skylight opened above, allowing natural light to flood what used to be a dim foyer.

She slowly ventured inside. Up ahead, she saw the dining room. The old walnut floors had been polished smooth and shone with a deep, rich luster. Stacked wooden crates lined the walls, skeins of yarns tumbling out. A round maple table was in the midst of the room, piled high with baskets and open wooden crates spilling their colorful contents.

And that was just the yarn. Knitted, woven, and stitched creations were everywhere else—sweaters, vests, blouses, gloves, hats, purses, scarves, and shawls hung from the walls, dangled from cabinet doors, were thrown over shelves, were draped across antique dressers and desks, and were folded on tabletops. It was a riot of color everywhere she looked. Kelly remembered how each room opened and flowed into the other, giving the farmhouse a special warmth. Now, colors flowed from room to room, spilling over one another in a multihued torrent, and the warmth was still there.

Kelly glanced into what used to be the open, inviting family room and saw heads bent around a table, afternoon sunshine pouring through skylights and windows that bordered the brick fireplace. Quilters and other needlecrafters chatted quietly as they worked, their stitchery spread across their laps in various stages of completion.

Customers browsed everywhere, she noticed. The women varied in age. Teenagers sorted through egg crates of yarns with glittery metallic fibers. Young women in workout clothes knelt to explore huge chests overflowing with rainbow-hued skeins. Mothers balanced toddlers on their hips as they fondled tiny sweaters the color of English oatmeal. Gray-haired matrons murmured to each other beside tidy baskets of colorful embroidery and needlework thread. And was that a man she spied in the adjoining room? He was running his hand down the smooth wooden frame of a large weaving loom. A present for him or his wife? Kelly wondered.

Everything begged to be touched. Tags proudly proclaimed wool, alpaca, silk, mohair, cashmere, Yak down. Yak down? Softness beckoned everywhere as she slowly explored the still-familiar yet delightfully different rooms. Kelly's fingers itched to touch. As she wandered from room to room, she noticed customers succumb to the same urging she had. Touch. Touch. But unlike her, they didn't hesitate—fondling scarves, vests, knitted tops, sweaters, whatever they wished.

Kelly dove right in and touched everything in sight, reveling in the sensuousness of it all. Crisp mittens and nubbly scarves felt scrunchy and springy. She checked the label. Chunky natural wool from Chile. Her hand brushed a twisted coil of burnished copper, thick as a woman's braid, doubled over and tucked end to end. Hand-painted silk, she read, and nearly dropped it when she saw the price. Fat bundles of hand-dyed mohair beckoned next—magentas, periwinkle purple, teal blue.

And what was that confection draping in billowy soft bunches on the wall? It looked like cotton candy, but it was the color of seafoam. Kelly sank her hands into the greenish-blue billows, half expecting to smell the sugar. *Surely this couldn't be wool,* she thought, and checked the label. Wool and silk, shimmering sea, it declared. How could that be? It looked so different from the other skeins that purported to be the same. She ran her hands through the seafoam confection again. Maybe it was spun by fairies in the night.

A luscious raspberry knitted top dangling from an antique cupboard caught her attention. It looked as soft as, well, as silk. She checked the tag. Eighty percent silk, twenty percent cotton. *Oh yes,* she thought, as she fondled the top, letting it caress her skin, seductively soft. She noticed the light, open weave of the stitches. The pattern alternated open and closed sections running lengthwise down to the scalloped edge. For the first time in her life, Kelly wished she could create something like that. Sure enough, right at her feet was a bin brimming over with those same silk and cotton yarns, a rainbow of spring and summer colors. Kelly could swear she heard the silk whispering to her.

She was about to sink her hands into the bin when she heard Mimi call out behind her, "Kelly! You're here. And it looks like you've started your own tour." She laughed. "How do you like it so far?"

Kelly reluctantly left the tactile temptations at her feet. "Well, I stepped inside and kind of . . . got lost, I guess." She glanced around and smiled. "I can't believe what you've done here. Everything is so different, yet familiar. I can't get over it. I mean four years ago, all I saw were boxes really. You were just getting started. I had no idea it would turn out so . . . so . . . wow." She laughed, unable to find an adequate description.

Mimi beamed. "I'm so glad you like it. We've really tried to create a special world here."

"Boy, you sure did. I almost feel like Alice."

"Alice?"

"Yeah. I walked in the door and fell down the rabbit hole."

Mimi laughed loudly, the light of recognition in her eyes. "Well, we do think of it as our own wonderland. C'mon, let me take you into our main room to meet Jennifer and friends, then I'll show you the rest of the shop."

She gestured toward Kelly's favorite room, the homey living room with its Mexican tile fireplace, barn-paneled walls, and sunlight streaming through all the windows. The comfy sofas and worn end tables were gone, squeezed into Aunt Helen's smaller cottage across the driveway. Now, in the center of the room was a huge oval antique library table. Several young women were scattered around the edges, knitting, of course. Kelly felt a twinge of envy. One of them might be knitting that raspberry creation.

As she entered the room, she spied Jennifer. At least she knew someone. "Hi, Jennifer. How are you?" she said. Then her gaze landed on the casserole dishes in the center of the table, and the unmistakable aroma of food reached her nostrils. Kelly's stomach growled louder this time. Silk may be soft, but it sure wasn't edible.

"I'm doing great, Kelly. How were the meetings?" Jennifer asked.

Kelly momentarily pulled her attention away from the dishes. Was that pizza? Macaroni and cheese? Forget the diet. Childhood delights beckoned. "Well, it was kind of a tough day. You know, lawyers and all."

"Whoa. Hold it right there," Jennifer commanded, setting aside the forest-green wool in her lap. "You're hungry, aren't you? When's the last time you ate?"

"Uh . . ."

"That long. Okay, let's get you fed, then you can tell us all about the lawyers. We had a potluck tonight and there's plenty left." She jumped to her feet and grabbed a paper plate and began scooping up servings of macaroni and cheese, taco casserole, Feta cheese and tomato salad, curried chicken and rice, and a large slice of pepperoni pizza on top.

Kelly found herself demurring in a last effort at politeness. "Oh, I don't need that much."

"Don't lie. I saw you with the cinnamon roll this morning. Besides, I'm a waitress. I know hunger when I see it." Gesturing toward the table, she said, "There's a place beside Lisa." She handed the heaping plate to Kelly.

"Go ahead, Kelly. The tour can wait," Mimi said as she settled into a straight-backed rocker and picked up a frothy white shawl dangling from long, skinny needles.

Kelly dutifully complied, inhaling the aromas wafting off the plate. She sank into the chair and devoured the pizza.

The slender blonde to her left sent her a friendly smile and leaned over. "Kelly, I'm Lisa. I saw you yesterday, but I'm sure you don't remember. There were tons of people there."

Kelly managed to swallow long enough to reply. "Yes, it was a wonderful service, I thought. So many people . . ."

"Hey, don't interrupt her, Lisa," Jennifer instructed. "She's famished. Let her eat while we talk."

"I see you've already met the shiest one among us," Lisa nodded toward Jennifer. "Miss Mouth, we call her," she added with a grin.

A soft voice spoke up from the other side of the table, "Hi, Kelly. I'm Megan and I'm so glad to meet you. Helen talked about you all the time. We feel like we already know you . . . kind of."

Kelly noticed that Megan's fair skin and shoulder-length dark hair gave her face an almost porcelain quality, with classic, delicate features. Since her mouth was stuffed full of taco casserole that moment, Kelly nodded. "Boy, that's scary to hear," she said when she swallowed.

Megan smiled, revealing perfect little teeth. "No, it's good. She especially loved those trips you took with her. We must have looked at photos for weeks."

"Months," Jennifer corrected. "Boy, I could use some time lying in the sun in Provence. With some sexy Frenchman rubbing me with oil, of course."

"Olive oil, you mean," Lisa tweaked.

"Whoa," Megan protested with a laugh.

"Yesterday she begged me to help her stay on this new diet," Lisa said. "And did you see her go back for dessert tonight? Twice, yet," Lisa shook her head and gave Jennifer a wry smile. "I don't know why I try."

"Because you love fixing people," Megan tweaked.

"Hey, I tried, Lisa. Honest. But, c'mon, German chocolate cake? You know that's my favorite," Jennifer protested with a laugh that told Kelly the ribbing was all in fun.

"Every cake's your favorite."

"I'll get rid of those ten pounds, just watch."

"Not with cinnamon rolls, you won't," Lisa scolded.

"How'd you find out about that?"

Megan giggled. "Mimi let it slip."

Jennifer sent a dramatic scowl Mimi's way. "Snitch. Besides, it was only a half."

"You know, if you did one of Lisa's exercise workouts in the morning, you'd lose those pounds in a heartbeat," Megan offered, her fingers busily working a turquoise mohair-type creation that piled in her lap. "I do, and I can eat anything I want all day."

Jennifer eyed Megan sternly and paused working the needles. "Megan, you've got the metabolism of a Marine platoon on maneuvers. You could eat an entire buffet and still be your dainty, delicate, and disgustingly slender self." She went back to the dark green wool as Megan laughed. Was that a sleeve appearing in the wool, Kelly wondered?

Enjoying the friendly banter, Kelly decided to join in. "It was all my fault," she spoke up, balancing a forkful of curried chicken. "I tempted her. Practically shoved it in her mouth."

"Yeah, right," Lisa snickered.

"Of course, I plan to run an extra mile tomorrow morning," Kelly teased, winking at Jennifer.

"Traitor."

"You work out?" Lisa asked.

For the first time Kelly noticed Lisa was knitting a coral pink shade of that seductively soft silk and cotton yarn she'd seen earlier. Was that the same knitted top coming to life in her lap? "Heck, yes. Got to."

"See? Discipline," Lisa tweaked again.

"I get enough exercise running between the patio and the kitchen every day," Jennifer countered. "Besides, it's all I can do to throw myself in the shower every morning. No way could I get up earlier to work out."

"You're perfect just the way you are," offered Mimi, needles busily working the frothy white shawl.

"See? Mother Mimi thinks I'm perfect, so there." Jennifer poked out her tongue at Lisa.

"Each one of you is unique and lovely," Mimi continued with a maternal smile. "Lisa is statuesque and willowly. Megan is delicate and dainty, but tough as nails underneath," Mimi added.

"Boy, I sure hope you've got some adjectives left, Mimi, because you've used up all the good ones on them," Jennifer teased.

Kelly almost choked on a mouthful of mac 'n cheese, trying to suppress her laughter. Even the elderly lady browsing the bookshelves in the corner glanced over her shoulder with a smile.

"And Jennifer is voluptuous and sexy," Mimi decreed with a wicked grin.

Jennifer pumped the air. "Yes! Take that, you skinny Scandinavian."

Laughter burbled around the table and spilled out into the side rooms. Kelly felt the accumulated tension of the day release at last. She poured a glass of what looked like iced tea. The taste startled her. One of those herbals, probably. She drank out of thirst.

"Where are you working out while you're here?" Lisa asked, fingers moving quickly. "I use the gym on the west side of town if you need a place."

"I try to run every day if I can, so I've been using the river trail each morning. It's not far from the motel I'm staying in. Over near the interstate." Kelly leaned back in the chair, relaxing for the first time since she arrived in town.

Lisa gave Kelly's long-legged, slender frame a quick once-over. "You must play sports. You've got the look. Basketball?"

"Well, I used to play all of 'em back in school, but softball's my favorite. That and tennis." She brushed the wayward lock of dark hair off her forehead. "You get to be outside."

Lisa's eyes lit up. "Really? What position?"

"First base, usually."

Lisa beamed. "Boy, I sure wish you were staying around. We just lost a couple of players and really could use you. Megan and I play in a coed league in town. You'd like it, I can tell."

Kelly had to hide how much she liked the idea. But she had no time for softball. She was here to arrange her aunt's affairs, pay the bills, and get the cottage full of memories on the market. Something way down deep inside Kelly protested. She silenced it. Her job was waiting back in D.C. A very intense, demanding job with a very intense, demanding, important accounting firm. She had responsibilities. She had friends. Well, a few. She had a life. Yeah, right.

She deliberately glanced out the window toward the mountains to hide her thoughts. "Boy, I wish I could. But I can't be gone from my job that long. I told my boss I'd be taking care of my aunt's affairs and the house, and then I'd be back. A week or so. Others are handling my clients while I'm gone. I just couldn't . . ." Her voice trailed off.

"That's too bad," Megan said in her soft voice. "We're just getting to know you."

"What were you planning to do with the house, Kelly?" Mimi asked, her head bent over the shawl.

Kelly debated how to answer. This morning, she'd have responded quickly: fix up the house and put it on the market. But after talking with the Denver lender, she was no longer sure what to do. She needed to think. All of her aunt's neat financial arrangements had been thrown into disarray with the loan.

"Well, I'd planned to clean it up, then put it on the market," she offered. "But now . . ."

"Now, what?" Jennifer prodded after a moment.

Glancing around at the friendly faces and obvious interest, Kelly responded with honesty. "Things have changed. I just learned from the lawyer this morning that Aunt Helen refinanced the house only last week so she could pull out equity. Problem is, there was no equity left. I'd helped her refinance three years ago so she could pay off Uncle Jim's hospital bills. We got a great loan with low interest. And now I learn she just closed last week with some sleazy Denver lender so she could take out more money. I don't even want to tell you the interest rate."

Kelly closed her eyes and let out an exasperated sigh. "Of course, she's now upside down in her mortgage, and—"

"Upside down?" Lisa inquired.

"That means the loan is for a larger amount than the market value of the property," Jennifer explained, then glanced to Kelly. "I'm also a real estate agent. That's where I work every afternoon."

"Now it's not such an easy thing to sell the house. I'd have to bring all that extra money to closing." Kelly blew out a breath. "I've got some in savings, but my dad's death and medical bills three years ago wiped me out. There's no way I could bring that much to the table. Provided the house would sell, of course."

"Oh, it'd sell, trust me," Mimi said with authority.

"If you don't mind my asking, how much are we talking about here?" probed Jennifer.

For someone whose career meant being careful with financial information, Kelly hesitated only until two customers wandered from the room and out of earshot. Surprised at herself, Kelly felt comfortable, at ease, safe with these women. She leaned over the table and noticed the others did the same.

"Twenty thousand dollars," she whispered.

"*WHAT?*" Jennifer exclaimed. "Twenty *thousand?*"

"*Shhhhh!*" Lisa and Megan shushed loudly.

Megan's eyes were round as saucers, and Mimi's knitting had dropped, forgotten, to her lap as she stared with a worried frown.

Undeterred, Jennifer pressed. "That's crazy. Why would Helen need that much money?"

"That's precisely what concerns me. I took care of Aunt Helen's finances and advised her, and she never said a thing to me about doing this. She was a sensible woman. She'd never do something this financially irresponsible." Frustration seeped into her voice. "She had a real simple budget, and I kept her accounts every month. I mean, I knew where she spent her money. If she had some secret vice that took money, believe me, I'd know it."

"Yeah, like Helen was a secret gambler or something," Jennifer said with a snort. "Or closet addict."

"Helen? Never," Lisa agreed.

"Do you suppose she could have been one of those compulsive shoppers or something?" ventured Megan, fingers methodically working the turquoise yarn around the needles. "I mean, maybe she bought stuff out of her grocery money and gave it away. You know how she was always giving stuff away to the homeless shelter, Lisa."

Lisa nodded. "I dunno. Helen usually donated knitted mittens and scarves every year, not other stuff."

"Maybe she got hooked on one of those home shopping networks. You know, channel surfing one night," Jennifer offered. "Those things are lethal. It ought to be against the law to open the fridge door or use your credit card after midnight." Listening to everyone's laughter, she added, "I mean, I bought a set of exercise weights one night after one a.m., and I don't even exercise." She shook her head.

"Did you return them?" Kelly asked over the laughter.

"They wouldn't take 'em back. So they're in the back of the car for snowstorms."

"Well, I'm fairly certain Aunt Helen wasn't a compulsive shopper. And that's what worries me. I can't figure out why she'd need the money." Kelly dropped her voice. "Not to mention all that money was the reason she was killed. It had to be."

A somber mood settled over the table as all of them, save Kelly, concentrated on the yarns in their laps, needles working smoothly, adding row after row of stitches.

"Well, at least they've got the man who did it," Mimi offered finally.

"Tragic. If only Helen kept her door locked more. She was so trusting." Lisa shook her head.

"I heard he was drunk."

"Apparently he'd been arrested before."

"Threatened a woman in her yard near Old Town."

Kelly listened to their comments but said nothing. Finally, Mimi spoke up. "The police called me when they found Helen's door open and . . . and found her. Of course, I rushed over here. They asked me if there had been a disturbance at the shop earlier or if I'd seen anyone lurking around."

"Was there?" Kelly probed.

Mimi shook her head. "Nothing. And I'd never seen anyone hanging around here, ever. I was going to tell the policeman that but then they . . . they brought Helen out. They asked if I could come over to the medical examiner's and identify her."

"That must have been awful, Mimi," Megan ventured.

"It was." She bit her lip. "I'm sorry, Kelly, I didn't mean to—"

"That's okay, Mimi. I wish I'd been here instead." Guilt tugged inside.

"Have the police recovered any of the money?" asked Lisa.

"Nope. The detective I spoke with on the phone this morning said the vagrant had nothing with him when caught." Kelly paused. "I could tell the detective was surprised when I told him the large amount of money that was missing, but he tried not to let on."

"I heard they found her purse in the bushes near the river."

"Purse was empty, of course."

"Of course."

"I don't understand why they haven't found some of it," Megan ventured. "Twenty thousand dollars is a lot of bills."

"Exactly what I've been thinking," Kelly mused. "I asked the detective, and he assured me they thoroughly searched the river-bank area and the golf course."

"Maybe he hid it somewhere or buried it," Mimi offered.

"The bills were probably so scattered that the police never saw them," Jennifer volunteered, a forest-green sleeve definitely taking shape now. "I mean, they could have blown across town in the breeze. Or floated downstream. Heck, they could be in Greeley by now."

"More likely one or two people found the money, and they're keeping it. They're not about to reveal themselves," Lisa offered. "There're all sorts of people who wander that trail, you know. Some homeless guys sleep out there rather than go to the mission. I helped count them in the last census."

That comment aroused Kelly's suspicions. "Yes, but if someone like that suddenly found a bunch of money, they'd spend it, maybe in a convenience store. And that would draw attention, wouldn't it?"

"Maybe," Lisa agreed. "Unless they spent it at different stores. No one would notice."

Kelly's instincts still buzzed. "Maybe I'll go back and ask the detective in charge of the investigation that question. See what he says."

"Will you go tomorrow?" asked Jennifer.

"I'll try, but first I have to tackle the house. Got to do it. Besides, that's probably where the mortgage papers are since they're not in her bank box."

"Remember, we're going to help you with that chore, Kelly," Mimi instructed in a no-nonsense voice. "Several people here at the shop want to help. Me, Rosa, and Connie—"

"And us," spoke up Lisa, nodding to the others. "I can come over first thing in the morning. I'll switch clients around. I'm a physical therapist over at the Rocky Mountain Center, so we help each other out with schedule changes all the time."

"And I can come early, too," said Megan. "I'm a consultant, so I set my own hours." She grinned.

"I'll be over on my morning break," Jennifer piped up. "The closing documents should be in one of those vinyl folders or a file. Just pull them out, and I'll take them with me tomorrow afternoon if that's okay. I'm working over at a new home site south of town. Plenty of quiet time to peruse the file and give you a rundown after work."

"Hey, thanks, I appreciate it, Jennifer. I appreciate all of you and your help. I confess I've been reluctant to go into Helen's house. I dunno . . . I'm still uneasy about everything that happened." She looked around the table and saw reassurance. It felt good. Kelly hadn't felt that in a long time.

"That's understandable, Kelly," Mimi said with a warm smile. "Don't worry, we'll be there. In fact, I've got the key so we can start early even if you're not here. I mean with the cleaning and all. We wouldn't touch anything else."

Kelly felt a tightened muscle somewhere inside her chest let go. "Thanks, Mimi. That'd be fine."

"Maybe we'll finish early, and you can go to the police after that," suggested Lisa.

"Maybe, so," Kelly mused. "I'm hoping that detective in charge is as friendly as the one on the phone."

"Well, if you ever need some help, you can ask Burt," Mimi advised. "He's a retired police investigator who comes in here every day."

Kelly blinked. "To knit?"

"Don't look so surprised. We've got guys who knit *and* weave," Megan spoke up.

"Burt spins. In fact, he's gotten so good at it I pay him to spin some of my fleeces when they come in."

"Boy, big change from police work, huh?" Kelly joked.

"Well, his daughter kind of ordered him here. He had a heart attack after his wife died last year, and Ellen just panicked," Mimi went on. "She was afraid she'd lose her dad, too, so she gave him her own prescription to add to his new exercise routine." She grinned. "Ellen knew how relaxing knitting was, so she hoped he might like that, but Burt surprised her. He took to the wheel like a natural. He learned faster than anyone I've ever taught."

"So, if you need a friendly cop, Burt'll help you out," Jennifer suggested.

"Good. I'll remember that."

"I sense there's something that's bothering you, Kelly." Lisa peered at her. "Do you want to tell us or should we just mind our own business?"

"When have we ever done that?" Jennifer quipped.

Kelly paused a minute. "I guess it's this whole thing with the money that bothers me. I mean . . . my aunt does something totally out of character and gets this huge amount of money—well, huge for her, anyway. Not only that, but she cashes the check, takes the money home, then this guy just happens to stumble in that very night to rob her." Kelly's gaze narrowed as she stared at the shelves of knitting magazines. "It's all too coincidental to suit me. That makes my buzzer go off. And now, I'm remembering her last phone calls. She wasn't her normal, happy self."

"Really?" asked Mimi.

"Yes, she was more subdued, quieter, those last couple of weeks when I spoke with her on the phone. I didn't think much of it at the time, but now I'm convinced she was worried about something."

"About what?" Jennifer probed.

"That's what I'm going to find out. Whatever it was, it made my sixty-eight-year-old aunt borrow twenty thousand dollars in a hurry."

With that, Kelly pushed back her chair to leave, while the others exchanged worried glances around the table.

Three

Balancing a coffee mug with one hand, Kelly managed to unsnap Carl's leash with the other. Not easy, considering Carl had spotted a squirrel and was straining at the other end, ready to run. She opened the cottage's back gate and watched her dog take after the squirrel. The squirrel was ready, of course, and as fleet-footed as yesterday. "He's teasing you, Carl," Kelly warned with a laugh as she headed to the front door.

Mimi and the others had already started, she noticed. Bless them. She really hadn't wanted to be the first one inside the cottage. Through the open front door, Kelly spied Mimi, cleaning cloth in hand, and Lisa plugging in the vacuum. "Hey, you really did start without me, and it's only five after eight. I'm impressed," she said.

"Shop doesn't open till ten, so I figured I could get a lot done before then," Mimi said, not looking up from the coffee table she was polishing. The scent of orange floated on the air.

Kelly didn't even try catching Lisa's attention over the sound of the vacuum. Lisa was methodically working the carpet. Kelly stood for a moment in the doorway and looked around. The lacy white cottage curtains over the dining room window were shoved to the side, allowing bright rays of morning sunshine to pour into the rooms.

The cottage was a perfect miniature of Helen and Jim's farmhouse, including the sun room and mini–family room jutting to the side. They'd built the cottage as a home for Jim's mother years ago, and when she died, it became Helen's craft cottage. Kelly remembered the huge quilt frame that used to fill the mini–family room—yarns, fabrics, and needlework projects everywhere. Helen called it her sanctuary. When Jim was traveling across Colorado building state roads, Helen would nestle in here and pick up needles of varying sizes. Later, after Jim's death and most of the land was sold, the cottage became her home.

Would it feel different now, Kelly wondered? The cottage had always felt cozy and safe before. She entered the living room and headed toward Helen's antique desk in the corner, alert to any uneasiness. Setting her mug on the desk, Kelly stood for a moment and absorbed the sensations around her—the sunshine pouring through the windows, the dull growl of the vacuum nearby, and the delicious scent of orange floating in the air from Mimi's polishing cloth.

To her surprise, Kelly didn't feel uncomfortable at all. On the contrary, she swore she could feel a warmth around her that had nothing to do with the sunshine. Another part of her relaxed, and she started searching the papers that were spread on Helen's desk. After a thorough search, Kelly came up empty. No folder of loan papers.

Rats! They've got to be here, she thought as she headed toward the bookcases that lined one of the walls. At that moment, Mimi grabbed her polish and cloth and headed toward the sofa end tables. There, on the dining room table, Kelly spied a long black package.

Inside the black vinyl cover, Kelly found all the mortgage and closing documents. Flipping through some of the pages, she shuddered. She'd forgotten how long Colorado real estate contracts had become. She'd take Jennifer up on her offer to read through and decipher the essentials.

The vacuum shut off and Kelly heard a familiar voice behind her. "Hey, great, you found them," Jennifer called out as she came rushing into the cottage. "Let me take them and put them in my car, okay? No time for a break this morning. We're slammed. I'll see you after work at the shop. Bye." Within fifteen seconds, Jennifer was in the cottage, grabbed the document package, and was out again—talking the entire time. Words floated out the door in her wake.

Kelly was impressed. "I think that was Jennifer, but I'm not sure," she said to Lisa, who was attaching an extender arm to the vacuum cleaner.

"Yeah, she can really move when she wants to."

Just then, Kelly caught a movement outside the dining room windows. Rubber gloves up to her elbows, window cleaner and towels in hand, Megan was studiously polishing the glass. *Brother,* Kelly thought. *This house will be spotless by the time they finish.*

Hating herself for the reflex action, Kelly glanced at the carpet below and scanned for telltale bloodstains. She saw nothing, and heaved a huge sigh of relief.

It was time to join in the communal effort. After all, they were cleaning what was now Kelly's house. She reached for the mound of cleaning cloths Mimi had left on the sofa end table and was planning to start dusting bookshelves when something caught her eye. Actually, it was the absence of something. Kelly stared at the bare living room wall directly behind the sofa.

Where was the family quilt? The brass drapery rod and hardware were still on the wall, but the treasured family quilt was gone. Helen had stitched it more than thirty years ago from various bits and pieces of fabric that held meaning in her life. She'd included snatches of lace and crochet and needlework she'd done over the years, back to her childhood. There was even a lock of hair from their young son who died at age five. Priceless memories and bits of family history—all stitched with love. It was to be Kelly's after Helen's death. And it was gone.

"Mimi," she asked when the vacuum stopped. "Do you know where the family quilt is? Did Helen put it away in a closet or something?"

Mimi turned around and scanned the wall, her face registering surprise. "Oh, my, it's gone," she exclaimed.

"It's always hung on the wall as long as I remember. First in the farmhouse, then here when Helen moved. Why would she take it down?"

"I don't know. Maybe it's in the bedroom. Let me check." Mimi crossed the dining room, turned a corner, and peered into the bedroom. "No, it's not here, either."

Kelly stared at the drapery hardware. "Do you think she would have taken it to be cleaned or maybe preserved or something?"

Mimi shook her head. "No, Helen was an expert at caring for

fabrics. She'd do it herself. Maybe she's got it stored in a box in the closet." She gestured back to the bedroom. "I can go look."

"Would you, please?" Kelly asked, trying to ignore the uneasy feeling that crept into her gut. Why would Helen do that? She loved having the quilt there. It kept her family alive, she said. Why would she take it down and store all those memories in a box?

Lisa unplugged the vacuum and scooped up the cord. "What quilt are you talking about?"

"The one Helen made thirty years ago. She called it a family tapestry. She used pieces of fabric from clothes she'd made, bits of knitting and lace and crocheting she'd done. She even had her earliest needlework pieces she'd done when she was only four years old." Kelly continued to stare accusingly at the wall, as if it could speak.

"Was that what hung from the rod up there? I've never been in here before today."

"Yes, and I can't understand why she would take it down. Helen loved that quilt . . . and so did I."

Just then, Megan slipped in the glass patio door leading to the backyard. Carl immediately appeared behind the glass, watching them inside the house. "Well, all the windows are done, and the door, but that won't last long," Megan announced. "Not with big old Carl pressing his nose against the glass." She turned around. Carl responded by barking once and plopping both front feet against the glass. She grinned. "See what I mean? He's such a sweetie, big and goofy."

Mimi returned from the bedroom. "It's not in the closets, Kelly, nor under the bed. I even looked in the dresser drawers." She frowned. "Where would she put it?"

"Put what?" Megan asked.

"The quilt Helen had on the wall. It was a family piece, Kelly says," Lisa explained.

Megan's eyes popped wide as she stared at the wall. "You're right. It's gone. I remember seeing it when she took me here to help her quilt a piece last year. It was beautiful."

"When's the last time you saw it, can you remember?" Kelly probed.

Megan shrugged. "Gosh, probably months ago. I'd only come over here when Helen needed some extra hands to finish up something. You know how she was. Always setting herself deadlines and such."

"Did she ever mention taking it down or putting it away or having it cleaned or something?" Kelly tried again. That uneasy feeling in her stomach was still there.

"No, not a word." Megan picked up Kelly's worried tone. "Where would Helen put it, Mimi?"

Mimi stared at the wall with the same look of concern. "I have no idea, unless she'd store it in the garage, but I can't see her putting that heirloom in there with dusty boxes of Jim's old books."

"Neither do I," confessed Kelly, "but I'll take a look. This is really bothering me."

"Hey, we can do that," Lisa offered, wrapping the cord around the vacuum. "I'm finished with the vacuuming, Mimi's got the dusting, Megan's cleaning the kitchen, and—"

"And it's finished, so's the bathroom," Megan declared, peeling off her rubber gloves. "This house was already clean when we walked in here this morning, Kelly, so we're done. If Mimi doesn't need me in here, I'll go search the garage with Lisa for that quilt. Surely it's around here somewhere."

"Don't tell me you're all finished," another voice spoke from the doorway.

"Connie, perfect timing," Mimi invited in the plump middle-aged woman. "Is Rosa in the shop?"

"Yes, she just came in, so I thought I'd help out over here." She wagged a pair of yellow rubber gloves as she approached.

Mimi touched Kelly's arm. "You go over to the police department and ask those questions, Kelly. I know you've been anxious. We'll look for the quilt while you're gone." Gesturing around the bright, open rooms, she added, "As you can see, we're almost finished here, so there'll be plenty of eyes searching. Don't worry. We'll look in every corner of house and garage."

"Thanks, Mimi." Kelly gestured to the others. "All of you. I can't tell you how much I appreciate it. I . . . I . . ."

"Go on. We'll handle this," Lisa pointed to the door. "Go talk to the cops. And if anybody's rude to you, write down the name and Burt'll go beat 'em up."

"Lisa," Mimi scolded with a laugh. "Ellen'll kill us if we get Burt all riled up. He's here with us to relax, remember? Go on, shoo, Kelly. We've got it."

Kelly did as she was told, grateful once again for the outpouring of help and support Mimi and her "knitting shop regulars" had showered on her since her arrival. She wasn't used to such support. It felt good.

"I know how upset you must feel, Ms. Flynn," spoke the gray-haired matron with the familiar sad voice. Kelly remembered that voice from the many phone calls. "Families suffer so much when a tragedy like this happens. But rest assured, the investigation into your aunt's unfortunate murder is being handled with the utmost care."

Kelly glanced through the glass window of the small room she'd been ushered into when Officer Delahoy first greeted her. Outside, the main office of the police department looked no different from any business office, except that half the staff were in uniform, light-blue shirts and dark pants. Kelly wondered how many had worked on Helen's case. Glancing back to Officer Delahoy's kind brown-eyed gaze, she asked, "You said you weren't part of the investigation into my aunt's murder, right?"

Officer Delahoy smiled modestly. "No, Ms. Flynn, I wasn't. I'm a community liaison officer. I work with families who've been impacted by crimes, either directly or indirectly, like yourself. I direct them to grief counseling, therapy, whatever is needed. Did you want to see someone? I can arrange it."

"No, no," Kelly deliberately suppressed a smile. She hadn't come for counseling. She wanted answers. "No, I've got several questions about the suspect you've apprehended and—"

"Oh, well, I can answer that for you, Ms. Flynn. He's been a troublesome vagrant, an incorrigible drunk and disorderly for years. Been arrested for trespassing all over the Old Town area. He's been incarcerated more times than I can count." Her hand gave a dismissive wave. "He was seen near your aunt's house and ran when he saw police. Our officers caught him, of course," she said with a proud smile.

Kelly took a deep breath and gave Officer Delahoy her most affable smile. "Yes, Officer, thank you, I remember you telling me all that on the phone earlier. But now I have some different questions about the investigation itself. Could I speak with one of the detectives who was directly involved? Is one of them here?" She glanced through the glass again, then back to the crestfallen officer.

"Uh, well, I could check," she said, frowning a bit. Clearly Kelly's request was not a daily routine.

"Would you?" Kelly enthused. "I'd be *so* appreciative."

"Wait right here, and I'll see what I can do, okay?" Delahoy instructed as she turned to leave.

Kelly nodded and reached for the weak coffee she'd been nursing for the last half hour. Swishing the remains in the small foam cup, she downed the last of the weak brew. Ack! *How could people drink such stuff?* she wondered, and screwed up her face as she tossed the cup into the trash.

The tiny room was antiseptically clean, gray, and cold. Kelly wondered if they kept it that way on purpose. She shivered, as various scenes from movie police dramas started running through her head—interrogations, confessions, accusations—until the door opened and a tall, heavy-set man with bushy gray eyebrows entered. Kelly sat up straighter.

"Ms. Flynn? I'm Lieutenant Morrison." His deep voice seemed to resonate in the room. He sat down across from Kelly and leaned back into the metal chair, a black folder in his hand. "Officer Delahoy said you had some questions about the investigation. I was the lead investigator on the case. How can I help you?"

Kelly took a moment before she answered the imposing detective. "Thank you for giving me your time, Lieutenant Morrison," she started, flashing a charming smile. Morrison didn't return it. "My first question concerns this suspect you've arrested. Exactly why do you believe he was responsible for my aunt's murder?"

"Well, to start with, he was seen near your aunt's home by two officers and ran from them when they attempted to question him. He was intoxicated, well over the legal limit, and combative. Had to be restrained, in fact. This individual has been a particularly troublesome vagrant for a few years. Arrested for drunk and disorderly, trespassing, loitering, and public nuisance. So, we've had our eye on him." Morrison tapped the folder against his dark-blue trouser leg. "But last summer his behavior turned violent. He attacked an elderly woman who resides near Old Town. Only about a mile from your aunt's home. She walked out on her patio one summer night and saw him urinating on her rosebushes. She yelled at him, and he cussed her out."

Kelly wasn't sure, but something suspiciously like a smile tugged at Morrison's mouth. Surely not. It disappeared, and Kelly kept her rapt attention.

"Well, some old ladies would have been shocked and run inside and called us. But not this one. She cussed him back, then grabbed her broom and started to swat him. Well, he grabbed it and whacked her in the head. Knocked her down, but not out. Then he ran away, and she called us, which she should have done in the first place," Morrison said with a stern frown. "She was able to describe him well enough so that we recognized him. He denied it all, of course. Couldn't remember a thing. Liquor has fried most of his brain, no doubt. His memory, anyway. But she picked him out of a lineup."

"Wasn't he tried and sent to prison?" Kelly asked. "That sounds like assault."

Morrison's bushy eyebrows moved in agreement. "It is, but the judge decided to try intervention instead and placed the individual in an alternative treatment facility. Rehab, you might say." He flicked imaginary lint from his trouser.

Kelly could tell Morrison did not agree with the judge's decision, so she ventured, "Doesn't sound like it took."

The detective grunted. "You might say that. Unfortunately for your aunt. This might not have happened if this guy was still doing time."

Clearly, Lieutenant Morrison believed he'd found his man. "You know, I've got some other questions about the money, Lieutenant. Why hasn't more of it been found? I mean, I was shocked to learn from the lawyer that the amount was twenty thousand dollars, and yet none of it has been recovered."

"I'm afraid not, Ms. Flynn. Only her empty purse was found, thrown into the bushes beside the trail."

"You know, that doesn't make sense." She didn't bother to hide her skepticism. "This guy runs off with twenty thousand dollars.

That's a lot of money scattered beside the river. Someone should have noticed and reported it, don't you think? Some honest citizen, perhaps?"

Morrison observed her in silence for a moment before answering. Kelly got the impression he was assessing her. "There are a lot of people that use that trail, Ms. Flynn. Particularly late at night. And some of them aren't exactly what you'd called 'honest citizens.' Their first instinct if they found a bunch of money lying under the bushes would be to grab it and run like hell. In fact, that's what we think happened. One or two guys found the cash, grabbed it, and caught a bus out of town. There's a midnight bus to Denver, you know. They're long gone by now, I'm afraid."

"How would they even see the money? It was nighttime, right?"

"There was a full moon that night and a slight breeze. If those bills started blowing across someone's path, believe me, they'd notice."

Kelly deliberately stared at the wall behind him as she considered what he'd said. It made sense. Why then did something nag at her inside?

"I know this whole idea comes as a shock to you, Ms. Flynn, but we deal with individuals like this all the time. Some money comes into their lives suddenly, they grab it and disappear. Go wherever they think it's safe. Drink it up, gamble it away, usually get the rest stolen from them. It's sad, I know."

She let out an exasperated sigh. "It's all too coincidental, that's what bothers me."

"Coincidental?" Bushy eyebrows argued with each other.

"Yes. My aunt gets a loan from a sleazy lender even though we'd refinanced three years ago. Then goes to the bank and cashes the check for this huge amount of money. Huge to her, at least." Kelly lets the frustration into her voice. "And then, the very night she has all this money in her purse, a vagrant just happens to walk in and robs her. And kills her!" She shakes her head. "I don't know, Lieutenant Morrison. Helen lived in that house for the last four years, and I never heard her complain about prowlers or fear of someone even peeking in her windows, let alone robbing her. It's just all too . . . too . . ."

"Random?" Morrison supplied. "Crime often is, Ms. Flynn. I know that's no consolation, but I'm afraid it's all we've got to give you."

Kelly looked him in the eye. "Has this guy confessed yet?"

Morrison shook his head. "No. Claims he doesn't remember doing anything after he finished off the liquor. But that's exactly what he said last year after the other assault. I told you, he's fried his brain."

"Can you actually convict someone when they don't remember the crime? How does that work?"

"He'll get a fair trial, Ms. Flynn. Rest assured. Now, do you have any more questions?"

Not right now, Kelly thought to herself, but she knew when she was being dismissed. "I guess not, Lieutenant Morrison," she said as she started to stand up. Then she remembered something that had niggled in the back of her brain. "Oh yes, I was wondering if you'd discovered anything damaged or broken in the house when you, uh . . . when you found her."

Morrison flipped open the file at last and scanned it. Kelly stared covetously at the folder.

"There was an overturned chair near the dining room table, but no furnishings seemed to be damaged," he said, scanning the report. "Victim was found facedown on the living room carpet, about six feet from the table. Victim was still wearing rings and wristwatch. On the floor beside her was one broken knitting needle, another knitting needle with a single loop of purple yarn, and a bundle or skein, whatever you call it, of the same purple yarn. That's all we found near the body."

"A broken needle?" Kelly probed, her instinct buzzing. "Did you find the rest of what she was knitting? Knowing Helen, she was always knitting something."

"So we were told," he muttered as he turned the page and read. "We were curious as well, so we searched throughout the house and outside, but we never found any separate knitted item that matched the yarn."

"Now, that's strange, Lieutenant. Jewelry is left but Helen's knitting is stolen?" Kelly sharpened her skeptical tone.

Morrison flipped through the pages before answering. "When a person commits a violent criminal act, sometimes they do strange things, Ms. Flynn."

"I've also discovered my aunt's heirloom quilt missing. It hung on the wall for more than thirty years, and now it's gone. We can't find it anywhere. Why would the killer steal a quilt?"

"What makes you think it was stolen?" Morrison said. "She may have given it to someone."

"She wouldn't do that."

Morrison stared at her but made no reply, his skepticism obvious. Then, he placed the folder on the table and folded his arms. "Do you have any other questions?"

"Just one. Who was it that actually discovered my aunt's body? I think Officer Delahoy mentioned an off-duty policeman."

"Yes, two of our officers had just gotten a midnight meal from a nearby drive-thru and drove over to the driveway between your aunt's and the knitting shop to park and eat. They told me that driveway afforded them a good place to watch the shopping center across the street without being seen."

"And that's when they found her."

Morrison nodded. "Yes, they noticed the front door open and lights streaming out, and knew that was unusual. You see, our officers knew your aunt's habits, and they knew that an open door wasn't normal for her. So, they went to investigate. It's a good thing they did, too, because it was while they were checking around outside in the yard that they spotted this guy crossing the golf course, heading toward the river." Morrison nodded in apparent satisfaction at his men's efficiency. "They called out to him, and he took off."

Kelly, however, picked up a detail. "Golf course? I was told he was seen near my aunt's house."

Morrison scowled. "The golf course borders your aunt's property, Ms. Flynn."

"It's a big golf course, Lieutenant, and it also borders two streets and Old Town. This guy could have been weaving his way toward the river," she challenged.

"We think not, Ms. Flynn. Why do you doubt our officer's account?"

Kelly grabbed her purse and skirted from behind the table, glad she was as tall as the detective. "I don't necessarily doubt it, Lieutenant. I'm just concerned. I'm sure you understand. I want to make sure that my aunt's killer is caught and punished. That's all."

"So do we, Ms. Flynn."

"That's very reassuring, Lieutenant," she said as she opened the door to leave. "Thank you so much for your time. I'll stay in touch."

Four

Kelly caught sight of the moving shapes the moment she pulled in front of the cottage. Someone was in the backyard with Carl. *What th——?* she thought, slamming the car door. The sound of Carl's growling reached her eyes. Oh, no. What if someone jumped the fence and Carl decided to protect his newfound territory? Images of lawsuits flashed before her eyes.

Racing around the corner bushes, Kelly came to an abrupt stop. It couldn't be. No way. He was in San Francisco with his artist girlfriend. It was impossible, but the guy rolling around in the backyard with her Rottweiler bore a startling resemblance to Jeff, the Slime, her ex-boyfriend who'd dumped her after college.

Now that she was closer, Kelly recognized the familiar sounds of rough dog-play. Jeff used to play with Carl the exact same way— rolling on the ground, apparently unconcerned his hand was in a Rottweiler's mouth, laughing as if it were great fun. Kelly never quite captured that concept.

"Hey, mister! Who are you and what're you doing in Helen's, uh, my yard?" she yelled at the moving shapes. "Carl, stop! That's enough!"

Carl ignored her, obviously enjoying himself too much with the tussle. "Carl! Is that your name, fella?" the guy said, reaching around the dog's neck in a wrestling move. Carl responded with an excited yelp and more growling, as the guy laughed and rolled to the side. Carl darted after the rolling toy. For the first time, Kelly saw a glove in Carl's mouth.

Kelly noticed there was a big pile of dog poop not far away, and this idiot was headed right for it. What was it about rolling around with a dog on the ground that was fun? Gotta be a guy thing. "Hey, c'mon, mister!" she yelled again, heading toward the gate. "You may think it's fun now, but if he accidentally bites you, then you'll change your mind. And I can't afford a lawsuit right now."

"Whoa, Carl. Let me up," the guy protested, crawling to his knees. But Carl wasn't finished yet, and jumped from behind, sending the guy sprawling. The guy just laughed, but Kelly saw dog poop at three o'clock and closing fast.

"Carl, c'mon, let him up," she ordered in her stern attempt-at-dog-control voice. Didn't work. But this time, the guy was able to dodge Carl's lunge and scramble to his feet.

In his disappointment at game being over, Carl barked and dropped the glove, which the guy snatched. "Got it!" he crowed. "That's mine." He shoved the glove deep into his jeans pocket as he strolled toward Kelly and the gate. Carl responded by dancing in front of him, clearly hoping for more play.

"Did he grab your glove or something?" Kelly asked. "How did it get over here, anyway?"

Now that the guy was closer, she could see the resemblance to Jeff was faint. Tall and lean, this guy had brownish-blond short hair instead of carefully cut, sun-streaked blond. His face was different, too. His was a square jaw line, sharp nose, and blue eyes, not the Slime's almost too-handsome features. Although it was faint, the resemblance was close enough to stir old hurtful memories. She scowled at the guy out of aggravation at being reminded.

The guy responded with a big smile and extended his hand. Kelly hesitated for a moment then took it. His grip was firm, but then, so was hers. "I'm sorry if I scared you. My name's Steve Townsend, and Carl and I were just having a discussion over who owned the glove." He reached down and rubbed Carl's shiny black head. Carl barked twice and danced, hoping to incite more.

"Well, I could see that, but how'd the glove get over here in the first place?" Kelly kept her interrogative tone.

"Uh, yeah . . . well, I was practicing shots over at the greens," he said, pointing behind him. "And one of the guys walked by complaining real loud about losing his golf balls to some dog." He patted Carl, who obligingly stood beside him, just in case. "That caught my attention, because I'd noticed Carl in the yard when I drove by yesterday, so I volunteered to get the balls for him. That's how the big fella got my golf glove. Must have fallen out of my pocket when I climbed over the fence."

"You climbed into the yard with a Rottweiler for golf balls?" Kelly couldn't hide her shock. "You must be crazy, mister. Why would you do something like that?"

"It's Steve, and I introduced myself to him first." He smiled at Carl. "I can usually read animals pretty well. Believe me, I stay away from the unfriendly ones."

Kelly peered at the greens skeptically. "How'd those golf balls get all the way over here into the backyard?" she demanded, hands on her hips. This story sounded fishy to her. "You can't tell me those guys I see hacking away can hit a ball all the way over here."

Steve laughed. "Well, you're partly right. No way could they aim a shot over here, but some guys can't control their drives at all. And this one guy who was complaining so much has a wicked bad slice. Man, his balls go all over. I swear, he loses half the balls in the river." He jabbed his thumb in the riverbank's direction.

"You must spend a lot of time hanging around the greens if you recognize a guy's swing," Kelly barbed. She wasn't sure why she was still being combative. The guy had been nothing but friendly. "What are you, a caddy or something?"

A slow grin spread over Steve's face, and she thought she detected amusement in his eyes. "No. Years ago I spent a summer giving lessons, so I remember lots of the guys. Some improved, others didn't, like that one." The smile disappeared. "And this guy can also be a pain in the butt, so I didn't want you having any trouble right after Helen's death and all."

The sound of her aunt's name jolted Kelly and wiped the scowl away. "You knew my aunt?"

He nodded. "Yeah. She was a sweetheart. Real special." He glanced toward the cottage. "She'd invite me in for a cup of coffee and talk. I enjoyed spending time with her. She always had something good to say, you know what I mean?"

Kelly knew exactly what he meant, but the idea it would come from the mouth of this stranger was a total surprise. "How in the world did you meet her?" she probed. "Do you come over here to knit with the others or something?" Why she said that she didn't know.

This time he laughed out loud. "No, I come over whenever Mimi needs some repairs," he said, clearly enjoying her surprise. "Her son and I were best friends growing up, so she's like a second mom. I try to help her out any way I can. She's done a great job with that shop." He nodded in the direction.

His unfailing good humor and friendliness finally wore down Kelly's desire to be unpleasant. The faint resemblance was still an irritation, however. She removed the sharpness from her tone. "Yeah, I was amazed with everything she's done over there. She gave me a tour yesterday."

Steve extended his hand again. "Let's start over, okay? I'm Steve Townsend and you are Kelly, uh . . . is it Rosburg, like your aunt?"

She accepted his handshake. "Flynn. Kelly Flynn. My dad was Helen's brother. Rosburg was her married name."

"Good to meet you, Kelly Flynn. And good to meet you, too, big fella." He gave Carl a pat before he swung his long legs over the chain-link fence. "Listen, if you have any trouble from anyone over at the golf course, tell Mimi, okay? I'll be glad to run interference for you." He dug into his pocket and pulled out car keys and, with them, the wayward golf glove.

Carl started barking in anticipation. "That's enough, Carl," Kelly reprimanded.

"Might as well give it to him," Steve said, inspecting the ripped finger dangling.

"Hey, I'm sorry," Kelly said, suddenly contrite. "I'll be glad to buy you another pair."

"Nah. Not a problem. I've got lots of pairs," he said, tossing it to Carl who caught it midair. "Remember what I said about the golfers. Tell me if you have any complaints, okay?"

Her curiosity piqued. "Why do you think I might have complaints? Those were probably freak shots that landed in here."

"Well, let's just say those balls had some help getting all the way into the yard. But my lips are sealed." He pulled a golf ball from his other pocket, held it up, and winked at Carl before he walked away. "See you later, Kelly," Steve called over his shoulder.

Kelly stared after Steve for a second, aggravated all over again for some reason. Why would he see her later? And why was he calling her by her first name like he knew her? Just because he knew Mimi and Helen didn't mean he'd get to know her. Nope. That self-confident air of his put her off. It was all too familiar. The resemblance to the Slime was getting stronger.

"Carl?" Kelly dragged out the name in the did-you-do-something-you-shouldn't-have tone. Carl looked back with his "who me?" expression, glove dangling from his mouth. Remembering the ease with which Steve swung his long legs over the three-foot fence, Kelly's stare turned accusing. "Carl, did you jump over this fence? You'd better not have, or we'll both be in big trouble." She rubbed his head, and Carl dropped the glove and slurped her hand, all canine innocence. Kelly sighed loudly and glanced back at Steve's bright-red truck pull out into traffic.

"Oh, brother, this is worse than I thought," Kelly muttered, scowling at the loan documents before she drained the last of Eduardo's strong coffee. The carafe Jennifer had filled for her before leaving for the real estate office was empty. At least it lasted while Kelly sorted through Helen's bills and wrote checks that afternoon. Now, once again, it was after five and Kelly hadn't eaten since morning. The mortgage documents spread before her kept all hunger pangs away.

"I know, it's ugly. Not only would you have to bring twenty thousand dollars to the closing table, but there're penalty fees if you sell or refinance before two years." Jennifer gave a professional snort. "I've heard of this company and try to steer my clients away from lenders like this. But, bottom line, it's their money and their decision."

Kelly glanced around the cozy little bistro restaurant in what was once Helen and Jim's dining room and kitchen. Pete, the owner, was in the corner balancing out the cash register, ready to close for the day. She hunched over the table. "Jennifer, I don't have twenty thousand dollars, let alone money for penalties," she rasped. "But I have to sell the cottage. I've got to get back to Washington. My job's waiting, my townhouse," her hand shot out in frustration. "Everything's there. I've got to find a way to do this. But how?"

"I wish I could be more encouraging, Kelly," Jennifer said, her voice sympathetic. "But I've seen others try to get around these contracts, and it can't be done. Usually, they just have to wait out the two years, then sell."

"I can't do that," Kelly protested. "I have to get back to Washington and my job. I was going to call my boss tomorrow and tell him when I'd return. Now this." She dropped the documents and leaned back into the wooden chair. It creaked as she rubbed her forehead in a gesture from childhood. Thinking posture, her dad had called it.

Jennifer leaned back as well and swirled the last of her latte. "What about working from here? You know, telecommuting or whatever. For a while at least. Would your boss let you do that?"

Kelly stopped rubbing. Was that possible? She remembered when another accountant's wife had chemotherapy and he worked from home. Maybe . . . maybe she could buy some time that way. Just until she figured out this house problem. "You know, that's a good idea. I've got to have more time to solve this. I mean, Jennifer, I cannot afford a house payment AND my townhouse rent. No way." She shook her head.

"Could you find someone to sublet your place in Washington for a while?" Jennifer suggested. "I mean, just until you can find someone to rent this place."

Kelly stared in surprise. "Rent Helen's cottage?"

"It's your cottage now. And face it, that's what you'll have to do. If you can't sell it, then you can rent it. That will help with the mortgage payment, and you can get back to D.C. and your job." Jennifer smiled wryly. "Understand, I'd much prefer you could stay here with us, but my Realtor-self is trying to be helpful."

Kelly frowned at the thought of renting Helen's cottage with all the memories. Why was that different from selling? She didn't know, but it was. "How much would it rent for, do you think?" she forced herself to ask.

"Unfortunately, not enough to cover that big, nasty mortgage payment. But, maybe it would cover two thirds. It isn't a huge place."

"I know, that's what I like about it. It's cozy," Kelly mused.

Jennifer smiled. "Then I return to my original suggestion. Tell your boss you've absolutely got to telecommute for a couple of months or so and find someone to sublet your townhouse in D.C. I'll bet you wouldn't have as much problem renting that place, would you?"

Kelly pondered the idea, even though it was already resonating inside her. "You're right. There's a guy in my office who's been living with his sister in Maryland, and he's been dying to get a location like mine. I could give him a call."

"Do that," Jennifer prodded. "And call your boss. Pull out all the stops. Family and grief and all that."

Kelly caught the gleam in Jennifer's eyes. "You're shameless, you know that?"

"I know. I work at it, that's why I'm so good."

Scooping the documents from the table, Kelly slid them back into the portfolio. "I'll call first thing in the morning. It's already evening back east now. More importantly, I'm starving. Want to go out for pizza?"

"Better yet, we can have it delivered here," Jennifer suggested.

"You'll regret not ordering mine," Pete spoke up as he approached, coffeepot in hand.

"You're right," Jennifer said with a smile. "But Eduardo's closed up the kitchen, and he'd kill me if I rummaged through his refrigerator."

Kelly stared covetously at the coffeepot. "Hey, Pete, let me help you finish that off, okay?" she volunteered with a crooked grin, extending her cup. She'd grown comfortable with the café's owner in the last two days with her frequent coffee breaks.

"Man, that is one serious caffeine habit you've got there, Kelly," Pete joked, emptying the last of the dark brew into her cup.

Kelly's stomach growled. "Yeah, I know. But it's the only real vice I've got, so I treasure it."

"We're gonna have to work on that," Jennifer teased. "While you're here, we'll help you develop others."

"Watch out for her. She's dangerous," Pete warned as he reached to dim the lights. "See you tomorrow, Jen."

"Bye," Jennifer called over her shoulder.

Kelly shoved the portfolio into her briefcase as they both rose. "Any kind of pizza is fine with me, except sardine. Here, use my card." She offered Jennifer her credit card.

"Hey, thanks. I'll call this in while you go and catch up with Mimi and the others. It's Thursday, so Megan should be here." She pointed toward the doorway leading back into the knitting shop.

The murmur of voices beckoned through the shop doorway, and Kelly was struck again by the onslaught of color as soon as she entered the room leading from the restaurant. She also noticed something else. Three small weaving looms were set up along a cabinet-lined wall. Each loom had someone hunched over the intricate contraption.

Curious, Kelly watched the beginning weavers in fascination. She'd never seem looms that small before. The last time she'd seen anything resembling the ancient arts of weaving and spinning had been on a weekend tour to Mount Vernon, George Washington's Virginia plantation. *What do you know,* she thought. *Portable looms. Wouldn't Martha be pleased.*

Mimi glanced over one student's head. "Well, how'd it go, Kelly? Have you and Jennifer finished studying the loan papers?"

"Yeah, we're finished, and it's not good news."

"Why don't you go into the main room, I'll be over in a second." Nodding to one of her assistants, she gave the student beside her an encouraging pat on the arm. "You're doing great. Rosa is the best weaving instructor in town, so you'll be picking up speed before you know it."

"I hope so," the young woman said, staring at the shuttle skeptically.

Kelly took her time wandering through the adjoining rooms, feasting on color, fondling fabrics, stroking yarns along the way. When she reached the main room, she was surprised to see Megan was the only person there. Her dark head bent over the turquoise yarn bunching in her lap, needles appearing to move at warp speed. Kelly wondered how long it would take to learn to knit that fast.

Megan glanced up and grinned as Kelly sat down, dropping the briefcase at her feet.

"Hey, Kelly, how goes the mortgage discussions?"

"Not good," Kelly said and drained the last of the last of the coffee. She hoped the pizza delivery guy drove fast. "I'd have to bring more than twenty thousand dollars to the closing table. Jennifer estimates that with penalties and fees for early sale, it could be close to thirty thousand dollars! And that's approximately twenty-seven thousand more than I have in savings."

"Whoa . . ." Megan's eyes popped wide. "So what are you going to do?"

"Well, I can't sell, obviously, not for two years, Jennifer says. That's the only way to avoid penalties."

"That's good to hear," Mimi's voice chirped, as she pulled out the chair beside Kelly and sat down.

"I'm going to call my boss tomorrow and see if he'll let me work from here for a while, a couple of months maybe. Long enough for me to figure out how I'm going to pay my mortgage on the cottage and my townhouse rent." She let out an exasperated breath. "Jennifer made a good suggestion. Maybe I can find someone to sublet my place in D.C. until I can rent the cottage." Noticing Mimi's expression, she added, "I know, I don't want to, Mimi, but I'll have to. It's the only way I can pay the bills."

"You do whatever's necessary, Kelly," Mimi said, and gave her a reassuring pat on the arm like one of her novice weavers.

"Well, at least you'll get to stay here longer. That'll be great," Megan offered. "And you can move out of the motel and into the cottage tonight if you want to. It's spotless, and hey, Carl's already there." She grinned.

"That would be great," Kelly said, then remembered something. "Oh! Did you have a chance to look for the quilt?"

Mimi glanced down at the milk-white shawl in her lap, even her knitting slowed. "We looked everywhere, Kelly. The garage, all over the house a second time. We opened every box or container we could find. Nothing. I'm simply heartsick to think something has happened to that exquisite family piece."

The cold spot Kelly felt earlier returned to her chest. It gave a little squeeze. "Damn," she whispered. "Where could it be?"

"I'll ask everyone who comes in, Kelly, I swear I will," Mimi promised.

"It's too much to believe the drunken vagrant took the quilt *and* the money," Megan said.

Kelly was about to agree with her when Jennifer appeared, pizza box in hand. She set it on the table with a flourish. The aroma of pepperoni and cheese wafted from the cardboard box, and it wasn't even open yet. Kelly felt her hunger pangs go into hyperdrive.

"The delivery guy was backed up, so I went across the street to the pizza shop. There's enough for everyone," Jennifer announced and plopped down a large plastic bottle of soda. "I also picked up some diet drink."

Kelly hesitated long enough for Jennifer to grab a slice, then selected two gooey, cheesy slices for herself. She practically inhaled them both. Hunger retreated as the pizza disappeared. Even the knitting needles paused for a few moments as the women all talked and ate.

Now that hunger wasn't the first thing on her mind, Kelly remembered something else. "You know, I mentioned the missing quilt to the detective this morning, and he more or less dismissed it. He thinks Helen either gave it to someone or packed it away somewhere else." She let her voice convey her feelings about the ascerbic Lieutenant Morrison. "I could tell he didn't think it was important at all. And he thought I was real nosy for poking around in *his* investigation."

"You're going to keep poking, I take it," Jennifer said, pouring more soda.

"You bet. But he did tell me something I didn't know. Apparently a broken knitting needle was found next to Helen's body."

"Really?" Mimi asked. "It was broken?"

"Yes, and the other needle had only a single loop of purple-colored yarn on it. The bundle or skein or whatever was lying on the floor beside her. But there was no trace of the knitting itself, only a dangling strand of yarn and the one loop." Kelly saw their rapt attention. "Sounds like someone yanked it off the needles."

Megan's eyes got even wider. "I remember now! Helen was knitting a purple sweater. Some chunky new wool. She was halfway through the back by the time I saw her that afternoon."

"Yes, I remember, too," Mimi nodded. "She was making it for you, Kelly, if I remember correctly."

Kelly frowned. "Why would the killer steal Helen's knitting? It doesn't make sense. First, the quilt is missing, and now stolen knitting."

"Did the police notice it?" Jennifer asked.

"Yes, Lieutenant Morrison made a point of telling me they had searched around the house and outside but found nothing."

"Just like the money."

"Boy, they can't find anything."

"No way that drunk would grab Helen's purse and the quilt, then grab her knitting, too."

Kelly swished her soda in the plastic cup. "None of it makes sense. And things that don't make sense bother me." She glanced at her wristwatch. "I think I'll head back to the motel and grab a quick run before I check out. Running always helps me think. You know, sort things out." She grabbed her briefcase and rose.

"Okay, you run and think, and we'll stay here and knit and think," Jennifer said, pulling the forest-green yarn and half-finished sweater from her tote bag. "We can compare notes tomorrow."

"Do you need any help, Kelly?" Megan offered.

"No, thanks. I've got my suitcase and Carl's stuff, that's all." Smiling at them, she added, "I can't thank you enough for cleaning Helen's cottage this morning. I mean, you guys did all the work. I didn't do anything, really."

"There wasn't much to do," Mimi said, fingers swiftly working the white wool. Kelly wanted to sink her hand in it. The shawl piled in puffy billows in Mimi's lap, like mounds of white cotton. "The house was clean already."

"We simply touched it up," Megan added.

"Well, I wanted to tell you again how much I appreciate your help. Now, I can grab some dog food for Carl and settle in next door, not beside the interstate."

"Carl's staked his claim already."

Mimi chuckled. "He has the greatest time watching those squirrels. And, of course, they're not used to having a dog chasing them. They're giving him fits."

Kelly laughed and turned to leave. "Good for them. They'll keep him sharp. He's been bored silly in that little townhouse yard back home." Waving a good-bye, she headed toward the door, wondering why the phrase "back home" sounded strange when she said it.

Five

Kelly leaned against a huge cottonwood tree bordering the golf course and stretched her long legs behind her, finishing her runner's routine. This section of river trail was much prettier than the portion near the interstate. This morning she'd run through deep shade, past neighborhood parks, beside the winding river, and through tunnels beneath main thoroughfares. Her three miles had whizzed by, and she was back at the edge of the golf course before she knew it. Best of all, the weather had warmed enough for her to shed her sweats and run in shorts and a T-shirt.

Now for some of Eduardo's strong coffee before she jumped in the shower. Maybe she'd better fill a carafe. She'd need it for the phone call to her boss. Kelly edged around the golf course, heading toward the cottage, while she practiced some of the persuasive points she'd come up with last night.

Suddenly, a dark shape caught her eye. There was Carl, racing from the trees behind the cottage and onto the course. "What the . . . ?" Kelly stared and broke into a run.

Carl stopped briefly, nosed something on the ground, and headed back to the tree-lined yard. Kelly ran up behind just in time to see her dog climb over the three-foot chain-link fence and into the cottage backyard once more.

"Ah, *ha!* Gotcha!" Kelly shouted, finger pointing. "I saw that, Carl! No, no, *no!* Do not go over that fence! We'll get in big trouble if they—" She stopped midsentence.

A contrite Carl was lying down on the grass, head between his paws, staring at her with his I-know-I-did-something-wrong-but-I-couldn't-stop-myself expression. Right beside him was a cluster of five golf balls.

Kelly sucked in her breath. "Carl! You *did* steal those golf balls!"

Carl glanced toward his little stash of stolen treasure.

Kelly swung her legs over the fence in a swift motion—one of the benefits of being tall—and scooped up the balls. Carl jumped to his feet as if to protest ownership, then obviously thought better of it. He lay down again and stared at the flowerpots.

"You go ahead and sulk all you want. You cannot steal golf balls. Those golfers will complain about us, and we'll get in trouble," she scolded as she climbed over the fence again. "I'm going to take these balls back to the course, and don't you even think about getting them again, do you hear?"

Carl ignored her. Kelly raced to the edge of the course and threw each ball back onto the greens. She also threw a stern look toward Carl as she headed to the cottage. "I'm jumping into the shower, then talking to my boss. Don't even think about climbing over that fence," she warned, shaking her finger at her petulant Rottweiler. "I've got my eye on you, naughty boy."

Running up the back steps and into the cottage, Kelly tore off her T-shirt on the way to the shower. She'd get coffee later. Between the run and her confrontation with Carl, she had all the adrenaline she needed to plead her case to her boss.

Pete poured steaming coffee into the extra-large mug in Kelly's outstretched hand. The rich aroma of the dark brew tickled her nostrils. "Thanks, Pete. Can I run a tab? I might be here for a while."

"Works for me," Pete said, his round face crinkling into a grin. "And if you need anything to eat, let us know. We'll bring it to you right in the shop."

"Really? That's accommodating."

"It's good business." Pete winked.

Kelly took a long sip, feeling the familiar harsh-but-oh-so-good attack of a rich, strong coffee on her taste buds. Now she could handle anything—Carl and his golf ball habit, the cottage problem, whatever. She had her coffee and her boss's permission to work away from the office for "a couple of months or so." She didn't know why she'd added the "or so," but he agreed.

As she turned a corner into the shop, she spied Mimi straightening shelves. Fat spools of embroidery thread lined the shelves of two walls, floor to ceiling, in a rainbow of colors. More than a rainbow, every color imaginable, she guessed. "Wow. Look at the size of those spools," she said.

"Actually, they're called 'cones,'" Mimi said with a cheerful smile. "By the way, how'd you sleep last night? Were you comfortable at the cottage?"

"Actually, I slept surprisingly well. I forgot to set my alarm and slept longer than I have since I've been here."

"That's a good sign. Means you're settling in." She set the last cone of scarlet thread onto its shelf and gave it a pat. "How'd your phone call go with your boss? Were you able to convince him to let you stay for a while?"

"Yes, I was. Part of me was surprised, but I'm thankful he went along with it. I promised him I'd be able to keep up my account analysis. They can send me all the files I had on my desk, and I can download everything else I need from our secure corporate website." She took another long sip. "It's definitely doable."

"That's great. If you need to use a computer, you can use ours. It'll be busy during the day, but at night it's free," Mimi offered.

Kelly was touched. "Thanks, Mimi, that's sweet, but I brought my laptop, so I'll probably be working over at the cottage."

"Well, if you get lonely, you just bring it over here and work with us around the table, okay?"

For some reason that idea didn't sound as strange as it should to Kelly, and she didn't know why. She was about to make a joke when Steve Townsend suddenly appeared in the doorway. All trace of Kelly's smile disappeared.

"Hi, Mimi," Steve said, his friendly smile in place. "I had a little time this morning, so I thought I'd come over and talk about those cabinets you want." He glanced to Kelly. "Hey, Kelly, how's it going? I heard you're moving into the cottage. You settling in?"

"For a while," Kelly allowed, still finding it hard to return his smile. Did everyone know her business around here? This shop had a heckuva grapevine.

"I guess since you two have already met, I don't have to introduce you," Mimi said as she scurried down the hallway. "Let me get my notebook, Steve, so we can talk."

"What's Carl up to?" Steve asked with a grin.

"Actually, he's been up to no good," Kelly admitted. "If he had a doghouse, he'd definitely be in it."

Steve laughed. "Let me guess. Golf balls?"

"Yep. I caught him in the act. Jumping over the fence and snatching balls from the course then climbing back into the yard." A smile finally won out as she shook her head, remembering. "If it wasn't so serious, I'd laugh, but I don't want anyone lodging a complaint about us."

"Don't worry about that. You just make sure and tell me if some loud-mouthed golfer says anything to you or gives you a hard time, okay?"

Kelly eyed him. What was with this guy? Did he have some Sir Lancelot complex or something? "That's okay, but I don't think I'll need help. I've been handling guys like that for a long time."

Steve's grin spread. "Yeah, I can tell, and you're really good at it, too."

"Damn right."

"What'd you do with the balls?"

"Threw 'em back on the course. Then I gave Carl a stern lecture."

"Oh, that'll work."

"Yeah, that's what I'm afraid of," Kelly admitted. "I'd hate to have to put him on a leash, but I may have no choice."

"Well, before you do that, let me try something," Steve suggested. "I've got some old golf balls. Let me bring them over and give 'em to Carl. That might keep him happy."

Kelly stared at him. What a great idea. She wished she'd thought of it. "You know, that's a good idea. But do you still use them? I mean, I could buy new ones."

"Heck, no. They've lost their zing. I'll be glad to contribute them to the cause."

Mimi bustled into the room at that moment, open notebook in hand. Kelly took that as her cue. "Well, you folks get to work. I'll go enjoy my coffee in the main room." She raised her mug to Mimi and Steve.

"Do that, Kelly," Mimi called to her. "I think Lisa may be there."

Kelly made her way around the mid-morning customers browsing through the rooms. Lisa was the only one settled at the library table so far, but there were the distinct sounds of a class being taught in an adjoining room. She dropped her briefcase and sat down.

"Hey, good to see you," Lisa said with a smile that said she meant it. "Did your boss okay your staying here with us?"

Kelly noticed the "with us" felt good. "Yes, bless him. So, I've got some time to sort out how I'm going to manage this two-house situation." She drank deep from her mug.

"I'm so glad, Kelly. It's going to be great having you here longer," she said, concentrating on her knitting.

Kelly eyed the luscious coral sweater that was taking shape in Lisa's lap. *It was the color of spring azaleas back in Washington,* she thought, remembering the dark green bushes that lined so many walkways in the capital city and sprang forth with vibrant corals and pinks each April.

"That sweater you're knitting is gorgeous," she said enviously. "I saw a luscious raspberry one exactly like it hanging in the other room. I'm going to buy it."

"It's gone already. I saw a woman grab it yesterday."

Kelly's heart sank. "Darn it! I wanted that sweater. I've been thinking about it ever since I saw it."

Lisa caught her eye and smiled. "You can make one yourself. We'll teach you."

The idea tickled inside Kelly's brain, but old habits—and beliefs— die hard. "Oh, no way could I do that. I can't knit a lick. Helen tried teaching me several times over the years. Couldn't do it."

"Couldn't or wouldn't?" Lisa challenged.

Busted, Kelly thought to herself. "Okay, okay," she confessed with a sheepish grin. "You got me. I purposely made mistakes so Helen would think I was totally incompetent. But it wasn't hard. To make mistakes, I mean. Trying to hold those needles and the yarn at the same time," she observed, shaking her head. "Boy, it was tricky, and I kept forgetting what to do with the needles. I kept dropping them."

"Do you style your hair with the blow-dryer in the morning?"

Kelly blinked. What did that have to do with knitting? "Uh, yeah, but what—"

"Brush and blow-dryer, right?"

"Yeah, what does that have to—"

"Then you can knit."

"Okay, you're gonna have to explain that one. Somehow I missed the connection."

"Simple. You hold the dryer with one hand and make one motion, while you hold the brush with the other and make another motion, right?" Lisa said. "Same as knitting. But knitting is easier."

"Good point," Kelly conceded, but unwilling to surrender yet. "It's still large movements with the dryer, though, like in sports. I can do all those things really well. It's just the fine motor activities I find hard."

"Then I'm surprised you can put your lipstick on."

Lisa was good, Kelly had to admit, and much more tenacious than Helen. She cast around for a new excuse, but didn't get the chance.

"It only takes practice, like in sports," Lisa pointed out. "You probably couldn't throw a softball well the first time, either, but you learned. You can learn knitting the same way. With practice. Now, you won't start out with something like this sweater, but you can work up to it gradually. You can start with something simple, like a scarf."

"You're relentless." Kelly shook her head in admiration.

"I prefer 'determined,'" Lisa said with a grin. "Besides, I can see you really, really want to have that sweater. Face it, it's the only way you'll get it. We're not knitting it for you. But we'll teach you how."

Kelly sank back in her chair and swirled her coffee. The caffeine high had kicked in and she felt like she could leap tall mountains, or at least a skein of wool. "You don't know what you're getting into," she warned. "I can be real clumsy when I'm first learning how to do things. It even took me a while to learn to do my hair. Some girls are more, oh, I don't know, dextrous, I guess."

"Everyone feels clumsy when they first begin to knit. It feels strange, but that's normal. All it takes is doing it for a while, and the motions become more comfortable. Plus, you get an immediate reward. You see yourself creating something with every row of stitches."

That thought resonated somewhere inside Kelly. The idea was tempting. Lisa's persuasion (and the caffeine) were wearing down the years of resistance. Almost. "Well, I confess I'd really like to make that sweater."

"You can and will. Trust me."

"I may be too old to wear it by the time I do."

Lisa laughed, then added, "Do it for Helen."

Kelly grimaced, as the last of her resistance crumbled. Lisa truly was relentless. "You are shameless as well as relentless," she surrendered, hands in the air. "I give up. I'll give it my best shot, I promise. Will you be my teacher?"

"We all will, but I'll get you started. Right now, as a matter of fact." Lisa set her knitting aside quickly and stood up. "Come over here and pick out a yarn you like. Something you'd wear in a woolen scarf."

"Boy, I hope you really are patient, Lisa, because I get cranky when I can't do something. Don't take it—"

"Just come over here and pick out the yarn. Stop trying to weasel out of it."

Lisa stood beside several wooden crates that were piled artistically atop a corner table. Fat bundles of multihued yarns spilled from every crate. Charcoal shifted to lavender then violet then purple to burgundy, then abruptly to turquoise to lime with a pause on emerald. The next crate held brighter, lighter springtime colors, all traveling from muted to vibrant hues.

Kelly stood and savored it all for a long moment, trying to picture a long woolen scarf of many colors. "Decisions, decisions," she mused, reaching out to stroke the bundles. She fingered different strands of yarn until she found the colors and texture she wanted, while Lisa waited patiently.

Choosing the maroon, turquoise, and charcoal bundle, she held
it out. "How about this? I like these colors."

"That'll make a beautiful scarf, and those yarns are good to work
with," Lisa said as she took the bundle and read the label. "Let
me grab some number-eight needles, and we'll get started." She
snatched a second matching skein from the bin and headed toward
the front.

"You need my credit card?" Kelly called.

"I'll tell them to put it on your tab," Lisa called over her
shoulder.

First she was running a tab for her coffee, now it was knitting
supplies. Kelly couldn't believe everyone was so accommodating
here. Clearly, she'd been in the Big City Back East too long. She'd
forgotten how to move at a slower pace. She could get used to this.

Kelly settled back into her chair and sipped her coffee as she
looked through the window toward the cottage. The trees bordering
the golf course blocked her vision of the greens, so Kelly couldn't
tell if Carl was behaving himself or not.

"Kelly, Lisa tells me you're learning to knit. That's wonderful,"
Mimi said as she sped through the room, heading for the office.
Steve followed in her wake and tossed Kelly a grin as he passed. She
didn't return it.

"Okay, here we go," Lisa announced, pulling out the chair next
to Kelly. She opened a fat bundle of yarn and shook it so that one
dangling strand separated itself from the others. Lisa snapped the
two long wooden needles from their plastic cover. "I bought you
birch needles. I sensed you'd like wood. It's warmer and natural. I'll
cast on some stitches and get you started."

Kelly watched in fascination as Lisa pulled the dangling yarn
free and draped it around the fingers of her left hand, then taking a
knitting needle, Lisa began an intricate maneuver of yarn and needle that resulted in several loops suddenly appearing on the needle
in her right hand.

"Now, see? That's the sort of magic thing that knitters do that
tells me I'll never learn," Kelly complained. "I don't even understand what you just did."

Lisa grinned. "It's called 'casting on,' and there's almost as many ways to do it as there are knitters. Don't worry about it now. You'll learn later. I just wanted to get you started with the basic, simple knit stitch. Now, watch what I do." Lisa scooted her chair closer to Kelly.

Kelly obliged and leaned over, watching Lisa's fingers intently as Lisa talked her way through the movements. "Right needle slides under the stitch on the left needle, wrap the yarn back to front, and slip the stitch from left needle to right. Under the needle, wrap the yarn, slip the stitch." Over and over Kelly watched Lisa's fingers do the maneuvers as she finished a row.

"Okay, now you try," Lisa held out the needles to Kelly.

Kelly stared at them suspiciously.

"Go on, take them. They won't bite."

"If you say so. Let's see how patient you really are."

"Quit stalling."

Kelly took a deep breath and accepted the needles, trying to hold them the way Lisa did. "Okay, now you're gonna have to talk me through this. Right needle goes here . . ." She tentatively aimed the needle's tip toward a stitch.

"Under, under."

"Under, like this?"

"Yes. Now, take the yarn and wrap it around the needles back to front."

Kelly hesitantly did as she was told. "Now what?"

"You slip the stitch off the left needle and onto the right."

Kelly stared at the stitch, then poked at it with the right needle. It didn't move. "It won't go."

"Not by itself it won't. You have to slip it off."

"What if it doesn't want to?"

Lisa snickered. "Trust me, it wants to. You just have to convince it."

"You mean argue with it? I've never argued with wool before."

Lisa laughed out loud this time. "No wonder Helen gave up on you. You're so stubborn."

"Hey, that's one of my few virtues."

"Yeah? Well, guess what? I'm the queen of stubborn. I'll outlast you."

Kelly gave in with a sigh. She believed her. Lisa gave new meaning to determined. "Okay, convince it to leave, convince it to leave." She tentatively slipped the needle beneath the stitch and pushed. "You want to leave the left needle, yes, you want to leave . . ."

Lisa laughed as the stitch finally slipped off the left needle and onto the right. "Alright! See? That's all there is to it."

Kelly stared at her. "All? *All?* That was like the labors of Hercules, for Pete's sake. And that was just one stitch." She held up the beginnings of the scarf—one row of stitches, all Lisa's, and one stitch of hers. "Most scarves are four feet long. I can't argue with yarn for that long. A couple of inches, maybe, but not four feet. I'm exhausted."

"It gets easier with each row. Just sit here and relax and knit. In a couple of hours you'll be surprised how much smoother the motion will be."

Kelly feigned a look of horror. "A couple of hours! You've got to be kidding. I can't sit here and do this for two hours. I've got errands to do."

"Do them in the afternoon."

"Carl needs me."

"He's got the squirrels."

"I'll get bored."

"No, you won't. Someone is always here at the table to talk to. Besides, it's a challenge. And I'll bet you've never resisted a challenge in your life."

Rats. Lisa spotted her weakness. Kelly was all out of excuses.

"True enough, but give me a minute, and I'll come up with something else."

Lisa shook her head, her eyes twinkling. "You are something else. But you've met your match, this time, Kelly. You're not getting out of this. You're learning to knit today if it takes all morning." She reached around Kelly's chair and snatched her briefcase. "And to make sure, I'll take your briefcase and keys to Mimi's office," she teased and sprang from the chair before Kelly could respond.

Kelly burst out laughing. "Hey, no fair!"

"What's not fair?" Jennifer asked as she approached the table and sat down. "Hey, you're knitting!" she exclaimed, pointing to the beginning effort. "Good job. Helen would be proud."

"Boy, you guys work together, don't you?" Kelly said, feeling that little tug inside at the mention of her aunt.

"You bet," Jennifer agreed, pulling the green sweater from her tote bag. "How'd you get her started?" she asked Lisa.

"Coercion, intimidation . . ."

"And guilt," Lisa added. "I used Helen."

"Good job," Jennifer nodded. "How far have you gotten?"

Kelly held up the needles. "One stitch, and it was excruciating."

"See what I mean?"

"Oh, yeah. Listen, Kelly, make it easy on yourself and do what Lisa says. She'll nag you to death otherwise."

Lisa grabbed the nearly completed coral silk sweater and dangled it between her hands. "Just keep telling yourself raspberry sweater, raspberry sweater . . ." she taunted.

Kelly had to laugh. "Okay, I'll keep trying, but I'll be on Medicare before I finish." She stared at the needles again. "Now, where was I? Oh, yeah, arguing with the wool." She slipped the needle beneath another stitch, wound the yarn, and pushed at the stitch. "You want to leave, you want to leave."

"What the heck?" Jennifer peered at Lisa.

"Don't go there."

Accompanied by much mumbling, Kelly cajoled another stitch off the left needle and onto the right, then another, and another. But it was slow going. Great, she thought glumly, she really would be on Medicare before she finished this sweater.

Just then, voices bubbled through the doorway of the adjoining room. "Burt's class must have finished," Lisa observed.

Kelly glanced up and spotted Megan in the midst of the others filing past, all chatting eagerly and pointing to a picture-filled booklet. She grabbed the chance to cease her labors. "Hey, Megan," she called. "How was the class? What did you learn, spinning?"

"Yes, Burt's beginning class," Megan replied as she approached. She dropped her tote bag and started to pull out a chair, then stopped and stared at Kelly. A big grin spread. "Hey! You're knitting! That's great! Did Lisa teach you?"

"I'm not sure *teach* is the word. Coerce, browbeat, punish, annoy—"

"And guilt," Jennifer added. "She used Helen."

Megan laughed, settling in herself and pulling out the turquoise sweater and skinny circular needles. "Well, whatever works."

"A-hem!" Lisa prodded, pointing to Kelly's motionless hands. "Speaking of working. Get busy."

Kelly heaved an exaggerated sigh. "Slave driver." She slowly began the maneuvers again, without mumbling this time. She decided to actually try the motions without complaining and see if they became smoother. Sometimes, yes. But sometimes, a strange knot would appear in the yarn out of nowhere. Other times, Kelly felt like she was forcing the needle through the stitches. The yarn seemed to bunch around the needle, tighter and tighter. It was like the wool had a mind of its own, and it was tired of cooperating. Now it was fighting her.

She was tempted to stop and ask for help, but stubbornness raised its head and urged her to keep going. It should get easier. Alas, it did not. She glanced around the table at the others, their hands moving deftly, creating row after row of stitches. All the while they talked and laughed and, it seemed to Kelly, barely paid attention to the yarn and needles.

"Hello, everyone," a girlish voice chirped. "I was hoping there'd be someone here after class."

Kelly looked up and stared. She couldn't help it. Bright pink-and-white lace flounced into the room as the older woman, barely five feet tall and as round and plump as a dumpling, settled into a chair beside Kelly. Her silver hair was pulled back into a neat twist and anchored with—what else—matching pink ribbon. Kelly blinked. She doubted Helen's kitchen curtains had that much lace.

"Hi, Lizzie, how are you?" Megan greeted her.

"Oh, I'm fine, dear," Lizzie said and withdrew a pastel blue baby blanket from her bag. "Burt is such a good teacher. I'm almost convinced I can spin when I listen to him. But then I go home," she sighed, "and I seem to forget what he said and get so confused."

Ah, a kindred spirit, Kelly thought. Perhaps we can sit and mumble at the wool together. Then, Kelly peered at the baby blanket. Row upon row of beautiful, even stitches, with a pattern woven into the design. Small holes outlined the shapes of flowers throughout.

Kelly examined the rows of laborious stitches she'd created. They certainly looked different from Lisa's smooth even row that started the scarf. There were holes in her piece, too. Unfortunately, they were not part of any recognizable design. Instead, they appeared at random. Boy, if this was the best she could do, it didn't matter if she finished a sweater or not. She wouldn't wear it. It'd be too ugly. Better to bury it in the garden and hope it didn't kill the flowers.

She heaved another dramatic sigh and returned to her labors, hoping that someone would notice and take pity. Maybe they'd let her stop. Admit that she was a failure at this. But the others were studiously ignoring her.

Lizzie, however, leaned over and gave her a dimpled smile. "Hello, Kelly. We met briefly at Helen's service the other day. I'm Lizzie Von Steuben. My sister, Hilda, and I were friends of Helen since . . . well, since forever, it seems. We all grew up in Fort Connor, you see." Her round face saddened. "It was such a tragic loss for us all. My condolences to you and your family. I hope you're holding up under all this stress."

Kelly was touched by Lizzie's obvious concern. "Yes, thank you, Miss, uh, Mrs. Von Steuben. Everyone has been so very kind and helpful."

Lizzie dimpled again and blushed, fluttering a hand. "Oh, it's still Miss, my dear. But you can call me Lizzie. Everyone does." Glancing at Kelly's endeavors, her eyes went round. "Ah, what, uh, exactly what are you knitting, dear?"

"She's just started on her very first scarf," Lisa piped up. "I convinced her it was a fitting tribute to Helen."

"Ah, yes," Lizzie said, intently watching Kelly's studied movements. "A scarf, very good. How's it going, dear?"

"Agonizingly," Kelly complained loudly.

Megan giggled and bent her head over her knitting but said nothing.

"Don't pay attention to her complaints, Lizzie," Lisa warned. "She's trying to play dumb and incompetent. But we're not buying it."

"I see," Lizzie observed with a smile, then glanced to her own stitches, needles moving swiftly in the baby blue yarn. She'd glance at Kelly, then back to her own knitting. Again and again.

Kelly pushed another stitch off the needle, forcing it. Arguing was out of the question. The wool wasn't listening. "Whoever said this was relaxing was *nuts*," she declared loudly. Jennifer snickered but said nothing.

Noticing Lizzie's continued interest, Kelly waited until Lisa and Jennifer started talking again, then she leaned closer to Lizzie.

"You know, sometimes the stitches slip off easier, and other times I have to force them off," she whispered. "Why is that? I'm doing the same movements Lisa taught me."

Lizzie leaned over and whispered conspiratorially, "That's because you're strangling the wool, dear."

Six

Strangling the wool? *How'd she manage that?* Kelly wondered. She'd started out arguing with it and wound up killing it. She stared blankly at Lizzie. "How'd I do that?"

"Oh, it's easy, dear. All beginners do it," Lizzie said with an airy wave of her hand, barely missing a stitch. "Here, let me show you how to loosen the stitches." She set down her own yarn and reached for Kelly's.

Kelly clutched hers tighter. "I have to do it, or I don't learn. Show me on yours," she bargained.

"Very well, dear." Lizzie picked up her needles once again. Kelly noticed they were about the same size as hers. "Now, just watch how I loosen each stitch, just a little. Give it room to breathe."

Kelly watched Lizzie's hands slowly move through the familiar motions. But this time, Kelly noticed something different. Lizzie worked the right needle forward somewhat in a smooth motion, and sure enough, the yarn looped between the needles was looser and moved easily over the needles.

"Wow, that does make a difference," Kelly admired. "No wonder mine were so tight."

"Now, you try," Lizzie encouraged. "You'll be surprised how much easier it will be. I promise."

Somehow, Kelly believed her. Lizzie's gentle manner was encouraging. She picked up her needles and concentrated on emulating Lizzie's movements. To her amazement, the yarn cooperated. "Look at that," she said, slipping one, two, three stitches off the needle. "Thanks, Lizzie. You're a doll."

Lizzie dimpled again. "Oh, it's nothing, dear. We were all novices once."

Kelly concentrated on the new movements, watching the stitches move from the left needle to the right. Before she knew it, she'd finished an entire row—and it hadn't been excruciating at all like her previous efforts. She examined the inch or so of scarf she'd created. Pretty homely. Maybe if she kept going she wouldn't notice the ugly inch once she finished. After all, this last row looked a lot better.

A loud contralto voice boomed across the room, "Lizzie, come here. You simply must see this piece." A tall, large-boned woman beckoned in the doorway to the classroom near Mimi's office.

"Yes, dear, I'm coming," Lizzie said and popped from her perch on the chair in a flutter of pink and lace.

"Hey, Hilda," Jennifer called to the woman.

"Hello, my dear. I see you have taught Helen's niece to knit. Excellent. Helen would be pleased," Hilda decreed before disappearing into the classroom again.

Kelly didn't even bother to reply this time. But Mimi did, as she bustled into the room, Steve still in her wake. "I agree, Kelly. Helen is probably smiling at you right now."

Not if she takes a good look at my first rows of knitting, Kelly thought, but kept it to herself. Thanks to Lizzie's helpful encouragement, the motions were finally becoming smoother. Another row finished, then another. Her stitches finally started to resemble knitting. Amazing.

"Oh, Lisa, I just heard from Trish," Megan spoke up. "She can't make it to the game tomorrow morning. She sprained her ankle working out yesterday. Poor thing. That'll really throw off her schedule."

"Is she training for a race or something?" Kelly asked, curious.

"Yeah, triathalon." Lisa stopped her knitting and frowned. "Darn! It's Friday night. Where are we going to find another first baseman."

"Hey, that's okay," Steve spoke from across the room where he was measuring wall space. "You're playing us tomorrow. We'd love you to show up one short."

"Yeah, I'll bet," Megan taunted. "No way, Steve."

Suddenly Lisa zeroed in on Kelly. Kelly could almost feel the red laser light dancing on her forehead. Uh oh. She knew what was coming from the smile on Lisa's face.

"Hey, Kelly, I know how you can repay me for teaching you how to knit," she teased.

"You mean I have to pay for all that abuse?" Kelly challenged, hoping to head her off. "I refuse."

"C'mon. We need a first baseman. That's your position, right?" she cajoled. "Plus you said you wanted to but you didn't have the time. Now, you do."

Kelly sorted through various excuses, but the idea was already resonating inside with an emphatic *yes*. However, she wasn't going to give in that easily. "I can't. I'm busy tomorrow morning."

"Doing what? It can wait a couple of hours."

"Knitting. You said I had to practice."

"Yeah, right, like that's gonna happen," Jennifer said with a snicker. Lisa and Megan laughed out loud.

"Why don't you ask Jennifer, instead?" Kelly ventured. This time Lisa and Megan nearly fell off their chairs laughing. Even Steve laughed as he measured. "Hey, what's so funny?" she demanded.

Jennifer grunted. "Sweating in the sun is not my idea of fun. I prefer indoor sports." She gave a sly wink.

"C'mon, Kelly," Lisa said when she stopped laughing. "You know you want to."

"Yeah, I do," Kelly admitted with a grin. "But I haven't played in so long, I'm gonna be pretty bad."

"Somehow, I doubt that," Lisa replied. "Look, meet us tomorrow at Moore Park on the west side of town. Eight o'clock sharp. We'll warm you up, won't we, Megan?"

"Oh yeah."

"See? That's why I don't like sports," Jennifer decreed. "You're always playing them at some ungodly hour of the morning." She gave a dramatic shudder.

Kelly noticed Steve approach, tape measure in one hand, notepad and pencil in the other, and assumed he was headed to measure another wall. Instead, he stopped by her chair.

"They trapped you pretty good, Kelly," he teased with his engaging grin. "First the knitting, now the softball."

Kelly was forming a retort, when Lisa piped up. "You're up to something, Steve. I can tell from your tone of voice."

Steve chuckled. "I noticed yesterday Kelly has a pretty short fuse. I was hoping if I annoyed her enough, she wouldn't show up tomorrow."

"All right, 'fess up," Jennifer prodded. "What happened yesterday, Kelly?"

Again, Kelly didn't get a chance to reply. "She chewed me out for playing with her dog," Steve said innocently.

"That's all?" Megan tweaked.

Kelly knew Steve was goading her, but just like Carl, she couldn't stop herself. "He left out the part about climbing into my backyard . . . without permission." She assumed an aggrieved air.

Jennifer drew back in mock shock, hand to her breast. Megan giggled. Lisa simply smiled.

"See?" Steve grinned. "If I try hard enough, I can make her mad. Then maybe she won't show up. I mean, if she's any good, we don't want her playing with you guys."

Kelly had to bite the inside of her cheek to keep from opening her mouth. She started to count to a thousand but only made it to ten. "You can leave anytime now," she said archly.

"I was just about to," Steve said, clearly unfazed by her hostility. "See you folks on the field tomorrow." He gave a wave as he left.

Not two seconds passed before Jennifer spoke up, "My, oh my. That little backyard confrontation must have really fired up Steve's interest."

"Yeah, Kelly. He really likes you. I can tell," Lisa said.

"Well, that's too bad," Kelly retorted vehemently, "because I don't like him."

"Why?" Megan peered at her.

"He annoys the daylights out of me."

"*Steve?*" Jennifer asked, incredulous. "Why? You don't like good-looking guys or something?"

"He's too good-looking," Kelly shot back, more forcefully than necessary. "I don't like that. And he's too smart-mouthed and has that arrogant, easy way about him." Kelly tightened her grip on the needles, jabbing at a stitch.

The others exchanged glances before Megan ventured softly, "Methinks the lady doth protest too much." She quickly ducked her chin and concentrated on the turquoise wool.

"Ah, yeah," Lisa said. "I sense there's more to this reaction than meets the eye. Am I right?"

Kelly jabbed another stitch and yanked the yarn between the needles, scowling at the wool now. "He reminds me too much of the Slime," she confessed finally.

"The Slime?" Lisa lifted a brow.

"Got to be a guy," Jennifer decreed.

Kelly dragged that stitch off the needle and jabbed at another. The stitches had tightened once more. "Jeff was my boyfriend all through college. Love of my life, actually. I thought we were soul mates. Boy, was I wrong."

"Tell," prodded Lisa.

"Nothing to tell, except he dumped me right after graduation. Bastard. If it hadn't been for me, Jeff wouldn't have made it through business school." Yank went the yarn. The wool was fighting her now. Her grip tightened even more with the memories. "I mean, I studied with him, tutored him, practically did his homework as well as my own."

"Men are scum," Jennifer intoned. Megan giggled.

"Well, this one was. He told me he was rethinking his life and our relationship." She snorted. "Rethinking, my ass. I found out later he'd been sneaking around with another girl. Some art student."

"Really?" Megan sounded horrified.

"I told you. Scum." Unfortunately, Jennifer couldn't keep a straight face any longer.

Kelly noticed and relaxed her death grip on the needles. The wool positively sighed in relief. "So, that's why he's the Slime."

"And Steve resembles him?"

"Well, yeah, a little. Tiny bit, I guess. But it's that attitude I can't stand." Kelly scowled again. The yarn practically trembled in fear.

Lisa glanced at her watch and immediately gathered sweater, yarn, and needles into her bag. "Oops, I've gotta get to the clinic. I have clients scheduled from noon to five. See you in the morning," she said as she rushed from the room.

Jennifer checked her watch as well. "Yeah, I'd better get back to the café. Pete's real lenient with my break time, but I don't want to abuse it." She shoved the green wool back into her bag as she rose. "I'll stop in for a few minutes this afternoon late, in case anyone's here. See ya." She waved and left.

Kelly glanced at Megan. She was curious about Megan's consulting business, since that had always been a dream of Kelly's. Leave the corporate grind behind and strike out on her own. Now, with the cottage and its huge mortgage, that dream looked farther and farther away.

"Their schedules seem to work out for them," she ventured as she continued her knitting. Now that she'd relaxed once again, the wool cooperated as well. "I'm curious. How does your schedule work, Megan? I've actually thought about consulting one of these days."

"My schedule varies every day. That's why I like it," Megan offered. "I spent four years in corporate IT and couldn't take the stress anymore. So, I checked into independent consulting and discovered that I could develop my own client list and not compete with the big guys." She eyed Kelly. "There's a lot of opportunity out there, Kelly. You should look into it during these months you've got here. You might be surprised at what you find."

Something in what Megan said resonated inside and Kelly nodded. "Maybe I will."

A burly, middle-aged man appeared from the spinning room. Kelly guessed he was Burt, since he was carrying what must be a modern-day spinning wheel. It sure didn't look like anything George and Martha had at Mount Vernon.

"Hey, Burt," Megan spoke up. "Have you met Kelly?"

"No, I haven't, and I've meant to." Burt set the wheel in the corner and approached, hand outstretched. "I'm Burt Parker, Kelly. Pleased to meet you."

Kelly took his large hand, felt the roughness, and smiled back into Burt's suntanned, lined face. It was a good face. "Nice to meet you, too, Burt. I've heard a lot about you."

"And we've heard a lot about you, too, Kelly. You were the light of Helen's life, you know."

Kelly almost choked up on that but swallowed it down. "Yeah, she was pretty special to me, too."

Burt reached out a large paw and gave Kelly's shoulder a fatherly pat. "That's okay. Listen, I look forward to talking with you some more, Kelly, but I've gotta run right now. See you later." He gave a friendly wave and left.

Darn, Kelly mused. She was anxious to talk to Burt, since he was a former police investigator. Lieutenant Morrison had brushed aside several of Kelly's questions about Helen's murder. Morrison seemed to have ready answers for everything—finding no trace of the loan money, the vagrant showing up right after Helen cashed the large loan check. Only the missing purple knitting seemed to puzzle him.

Kelly, however, didn't like coincidences. They set off her warning buzzer. She was hoping to run all of it past Burt and get his professional opinion. Maybe she was worrying over nothing. If so, maybe Burt could tell her.

"Hey, good timing," Jennifer called out from the knitting shop's front door. "Finished your errands?"

"Yeah," Kelly said as she exited her parked car and headed across the driveway. "I've got my Internet service provider, got everything fired up and ready to go, even bought office supplies. Now, all I need are my account files."

Jennifer pushed open the oak door. "You deserve a break. I'm meeting friends in Old Town tonight, want to join us?"

"I'd love to, but I've got so much e-mail waiting for me, it's unreal." Kelly shook her head. "I'd better spend tonight clearing it up. Ask me again next time, okay?"

"Depend on it," Jennifer said as they made their way through the shop.

Customers always seemed to be browsing, Kelly noticed, no

matter what time of day. She glanced toward the counter in the far room and hoped they were buying as well. Mimi scurried through the room then, pencil behind one ear, notebook in her hand.

"Hey, Mimi, how're those cabinets coming?" Jennifer asked as she paused in front of a whole wall of yarns. Fat yarns and skinny yarns tumbled out of the artistically arranged wooden crates, tempting Kelly with their texture and colors.

"Steve's going to pick out some I can choose from tomorrow. I'm hoping he'll be able to get them installed next week. Of course, that depends on his schedule." Mimi said all this as she passed through the room and out again.

"I guess he's a pretty busy handyman," Kelly ventured, squeezing several pudgy skeins.

"Who?" Jennifer asked, squeezing some herself as she moved among the crates.

"This Steve guy."

Jennifer stopped and turned to Kelly with a laugh. "Steve? Trust me, the only person he does handyman jobs for is Mimi. And that's because he and her son were friends growing up." She grinned. "Steve's actually a builder. Pretty successful, too. He's been involved in some big projects off the interstate lately."

"Oh," Kelly said, clearly surprised. "Then why is he always hanging around here and the golf course next door?"

"Installing cabinets and playing golf, probably." Jennifer gave her an enigmatic smile before she returned to the yarn. "Take a look at these yarns and picture a winter scarf," she said, holding up a fat multicolored bundle.

"I'm already knitting a scarf," Kelly countered.

"Yes, and a beautiful one it will be when it's finished. But right now I sense you need a boost of confidence that only comes with finishing something. Something really pretty." She fingered the colorful strands. "These wools knit up fast because they're big and bulky and you use large needles. You can knit one up in a weekend. See?" She pointed to a chunky wool scarf of mottled cream and chocolate that hung beside the crates.

"Wow," Kelly breathed, fingering the soft fibers, the huge stitches. "That's the same wool?"

"Yep. And all you use is the knit stitch. You already know that. So, which one do you like?"

The idea of completing something fast was as appealing as the yarns. She grabbed the fat bundle from Jennifer's hand. "This'll be beautiful."

"I agree," Jennifer said and grabbed a matching bundle. "You'll need two. Go grab a chair while I get the needles and put these on your tab." She raced off.

Kelly was surprised to see Burt sitting at the table, several books spread open before him. "Hi, Burt. Preparing for your spinning class?"

Burt smiled. "Yeah, I try to give everyone lots of references so they can learn from the experts, too." He went back to scribbling on a pad.

Kelly glanced around and saw that they were alone in the room and decided to grab the quiet moment. She settled into the chair nearest Burt and leaned over the table. "Burt, do you mind if I ask you a couple of questions?" she asked in a soft voice.

Burt looked up. "Sure, Kelly. Have you started to spin, too? I heard you're learning to knit."

"Ah, not exactly," Kelly had to laugh at the image. "No, I have some questions about some of the, uh . . . the details surrounding Helen's death. Several things are bothering me, and, well, I just wanted to run some of them past you if I could. Mimi told me you were a retired police investigator."

The relaxed expression on Burt's face faded and another one appeared. He settled back into his chair. "Sure, Kelly. But the person you should be asking is the lead investigator. Lieutenant Vern Morrison. He's in charge."

"I've already spoken with him, and he's, well, he's not all that forthcoming," Kelly said, gesturing. "I get the feeling that I'm almost bothering him."

"Did he answer your questions?"

"Yes, but his answers left me with more questions."

Burt peered at her for a moment. "Why don't you give me an example. I'm not sure I know what you mean."

"Okay. I told him that I thought it was just too coincidental that this dangerous vagrant happened to show up at Helen's house right after she'd cashed a check for twenty thousand dollars."

Burt's eyes widened. "Twenty thousand dollars?"

Encouraged that she'd actually gotten a reaction from a police investigator, even a retired one, Kelly explained. "Helen's lawyer told me the other day that she'd recently refinanced the cottage so she could withdraw a large amount of money. She cashed the loan company check that afternoon, and that evening she was killed." Kelly shook her head. "Coincidences like that make me suspicious. But Morrison simply stared at me and said nothing. Like it wasn't important." She sat back and watched Burt.

He examined the calluses on his right hand for a few seconds. "I'm sure he was thinking the same thing, Kelly, only he didn't show it. Morrison is a good cop. Close-mouthed, yes. But he doesn't miss much."

"Well, I'm afraid he may be missing something here. I don't believe that drunk just happened to stumble into Helen's house that night." Kelly's hand jerked out in irritation. "The lawyer called it a 'senseless act of random violence.' I don't buy that."

"I'm afraid it does happen, Kelly," Burt offered, his face revealing traces of the tragic scenes he'd witnessed.

Kelly made a disgusted sound. "Why is there no trace of that money? Helen got twenty thousand dollars in cash, and yet there wasn't one bill found floating on the river or in the bushes." Kelly scowled. "Morrison said there were all sorts of people who could have found the money and grabbed it, then gotten out of town before the police ever searched."

"Well, that is true. It would be easy for some troublemaker to make off with the money. Grab it, run down the trail past the river, then hop over to the bus station, and get out of town."

Kelly sighed. Darn it. She was hearing the same scenario from Burt that Morrison gave her. Was she the only one who saw things differently?

"But what I'm curious about, Kelly, is why Helen would need twenty thousand dollars. What was happening?"

A huge sigh of relief shot through Kelly. At last. Someone had picked up on her primary concern. "Now, that's the biggest puzzle of all, Burt," she confessed. "I took care of Helen's affairs, and she never indicated anything was wrong. It was totally out of character for her, and I'm clueless as to why she'd do it." She watched Burt process her answer as well as her concern.

"That's interesting, Kelly," he said after a moment. "I can understand why you're concerned."

"Oh, goodness me, Burt, are you still here?" Lizzie chirped as she fluttered into the room.

Kelly concealed her disappointment at being interrupted. At least Burt had validated one of her concerns. She wished he'd say something more. "Have you been here all day, Lizzie?" she asked.

"Well, I've been in and out," Lizzie said as she settled at the end of the table. "Hilda is teaching one of the advanced knitting classes. I wanted to watch. And help, of course." She dug into her bag and removed the beautiful blue blanket.

"Okay," Jennifer announced as she bustled into the room. "Here are the needles and yarn. I've got enough time to cast on some stitches and get you started." She plopped into the chair beside Kelly.

"Well, you ladies have a good evening," Burt instructed as he stood and gathered his books and notepad. "I'll see you folks next week." Before leaving, however, he patted Kelly on the shoulder again. "Nice talking to you, Kelly. I'm sure we'll have another chance to chat."

"I hope so, Burt. Nice meeting you," she said as he waved goodbye. Turning her attention back to Jennifer, she saw her casting on loopy, loose multicolored stitches onto the biggest needles Kelly had ever seen in her life. She blinked. "Whoa! Those look like something out of a cartoon. Are they really needles?"

"Sure are, and you use them with these great chunky yarns. That's why the scarf knits up so fast. Watch." Jennifer proceeded to slowly do the knit stitch and suddenly big stitches appeared in a chunky row.

"Well, I'll be darned," Kelly observed.

"Here. You can take over. I've got to go home and get ready for tonight." She handed over the huge needles and ball of yarn. "Enjoy." She grabbed her tote bag as if to leave.

"Hey, don't leave yet," Kelly pleaded. "I want to make sure I can do this."

Kelly stared at the needles, then fondled the beautiful soft yarn. Yummy. This could be fun. Did she simply jump in?

"Start knitting like you've been doing," Jennifer coaxed. "Same motions."

"Okay," Kelly said, still dubious. She pushed the big clumsy needle beneath a stitch, wrapped the springy yarn over the needles, and slipped the stitch. It certainly did look strange. Not neat and tidy and even like her stitches were starting to look like in the smaller yarn.

"Keep going. Finish the row."

Kelly did as instructed and stared at the row. It still looked strange. Colorful, but strange.

"Now do another."

She did and was amazed how far apart these rows were from each other. She held up her efforts. "You sure it's supposed to look like this?"

"Absolutely," Jennifer reassured. "Just keep knitting row after row and trust in the process. I guarantee that you'll love it after ten rows. I'll stay till then." She checked her watch.

"If you say so." Kelly went back to her stitches. After a couple more rows, Kelly found she was liking the way the part chunky, part skinny yarn looked. The stitches were all different. Springy and soft, soft, soft.

"Kelly, dear," Lizzie spoke up after a moment. "I've been wondering if you've heard from Helen's cousin since you've been here? I spotted her at the service. But she's such a shy person, she didn't stay like everyone else. Has she given you a call?"

Kelly stared at the colorful wool in her lap, but this time she didn't see it. *Cousin?* What *cousin,* she wondered. *Helen never mentioned any other living relatives. Neither did her dad.*

She peered at Lizzie. "I wasn't aware Helen had any other living relatives. She always told me she was the last one left in her family."

Lizzie paused her knitting and pondered for a second. "Well, perhaps she's a distant cousin or something. I think she used to live in Wyoming. At least that's what Helen said when I asked her a couple of years ago."

Knitting forgotten in her lap, Kelly continued to probe. "Does she still live in Wyoming? What else did Helen say?"

"Well, that's about all," Lizzie replied. "Helen seemed reluctant to talk about her for some reason, so I didn't press it. I do remember asking if her cousin would like to be contacted by the Altar Guild. I was serving as chairwoman that year, you see. But Helen was quite adamant about saying no. She said her cousin was terribly, terribly shy. That's why she never stayed after church and introduced herself, apparently." Lizzie gave a little sigh as if it was hard to believe that anyone would not enjoy the company of others.

"What's her name?" Jennifer prodded. Kelly noticed she no longer looked anxious to leave.

"Ummm, let me see, I think she said it was Martha. Yes, that's it. Martha. I'm afraid Helen neglected to tell me the last name." Lizzie smiled. "Maybe she was afraid the Altar Guild would come calling."

Martha. Martha. She had a distant relative named Martha. "Thank you for telling me, Lizzie," Kelly said. "I had no idea there was another family member in the area."

"Helen never mentioned another soul in the three years I knew her," Jennifer volunteered.

Kelly's mind started racing. Obviously this Martha was someone Helen felt close to or she wouldn't have been so protective of her. Shy cousin Martha. Kelly had to find her. But how without a last name? Then, an idea tickled.

"Lizzie, does that church—"

"St. Mark's, you mean?"

"Yes, St. Mark's, does it have a directory of members or something like that? Maybe I can go through the entire directory checking out all the Martha's until I find her."

"Oh, that won't be necessary, dear," Lizzie said with a wave of her hand. "I'm fairly certain you can find her at the weekday mass. I think she comes nearly every day. I notice her every Monday when I go to Guild meetings."

Kelly couldn't believe what a gold mine of information Lizzie turned out to be. "There's only one problem, Lizzie. I don't know what she looks like. Can you describe her a little, so I can recognize her?"

Again, the airy little wave. "Oh, I can do better than that, dear. Why don't you come to church with Hilda and me this Sunday, and I'll point her out to you. I'm fairly certain she comes to Sunday service as well. And if you can't speak with her in all the crowd, then you surely could on a weekday."

Jennifer turned her head and gave Kelly a sly grin and a wink. "Boy, she trapped you on that one," she whispered.

She did, indeed. Kelly had to admire Lizzie's style. But that didn't stop her from trying to get out of it. She hadn't been to church in years, since before her dad died. Holidays and Helen's service didn't count.

"Jennifer, I think it would be ever so lovely if you could join us, too," Lizzie continued with her dimpled smile. "Hilda and I would simply love to have your company."

Kelly couldn't resist. She turned to Jennifer with a wicked grin of her own. "Yes, Jennifer, I'd just love to have you join us. Please do."

Jennifer waved away the double assault. "Ladies, thanks so much, but you'll enjoy the service much more without me. I haven't been to church in so long, I'm sure the walls would shake. You wouldn't want to lose all that stained glass, now would you?"

"Don't be silly, dear. It'll be fine, and Hilda and I will take you both to the Jefferson Hotel for their special Sunday brunch afterward. We like to treat ourselves every Sunday. They have those cinnamon rolls you like so much, dear." She eyed Jennifer, the invitation dangling.

"Lizzie, you truly are wicked," Jennifer gave in with a sigh. "You know I can resist anything except those."

"Wonderful!" Lizzie enthused. "Now, I suggest we come early for the nine o'clock service. That way we can make sure we don't miss Martha." Lizzie's knitting picked up speed.

Kelly caught Jennifer's eye. "Give me your address and phone number and I'll pick you up Sunday morning. I'll even bring coffee."

"Please. Lots of it," Jennifer said with a resigned shake of her head as she withdrew a business card from her bag.

Seven

Kelly bent over, hands above her knees, and squinted at the batter hunched over home plate. The sky was that brilliant Colorado blue she remembered so well, and the mile-high sunlight was brutal. She adjusted her *USS Kitty Hawk* baseball cap. Its brim was frayed, but it was her good luck charm. It was also her dad's. She couldn't play without it.

Her right knee was skinned from her slide into second base in the last inning. There was dirt and grit imbedded in her left knee from an earlier slide. Her knees stung, her back ached from first basemen's crouch, and her right shoulder was sore from throwing—and she couldn't be happier.

The batter swung at Lisa's curve ball and missed. Kelly's foot reached out for first base instinctively. Why had she deprived herself of this simple pleasure these last few years? She loved playing ball. She'd played it her whole life. In fact, softball had been the one thing she could depend on when her dad took a new job and they had to move again. Every time she'd come to a new school, that's how she found friends.

The batter swung and cut the air. Strike two. Lisa's got some stuff, Kelly had to admit. She glanced over her shoulder at the varied group on the field. Coed leagues were always a melting pot of twenty- and thirty-somethings. It reminded her of the accounting firm's team she used to play on before . . . well, before her dad got sick. She'd let a lot of things go when Dad got sick.

Yeah, like your life, a voice nagged inside.

Over in left field, Megan was swaying side to side, her fielder's glove at the ready and her face smeared with enough sunscreen to shut down a solar array. Kelly grinned. What a contradiction Megan was. Shy, geeky tech writer, hardware-software guru, and, according to Lisa, a passionate fashion designer at heart. Kelly was surprised that Megan played softball. Kelly would never have imagined quiet, dainty Megan running down a ball. But there she was, playing her heart out and getting dirty.

"Hey . . . batter-batter-batter-batter-batter!" yelled a grinning middle-aged guy from the bleachers. Memories surfaced as Kelly recalled hearing the familiar parental chant, called out to children still learning the game.

A woman's movement caught her eye, and Kelly stifled a laugh. There was Jennifer, hiding her hangover behind sunglasses and a hat that would have done Scarlett proud, sipping a double espresso latte.

"Too many tequila shooters last night," was all she muttered as she passed Kelly on the way to the bleachers. The fact that Jennifer was even here at ten o'clock on a Saturday morning was amazing.

The batter swung again, and this time she connected, then headed down the baseline as the ball landed fair. Old instincts took over then, muscles long trained into movements that were second nature. Kelly didn't even have to think. Lisa snatched the ball in a nanosecond and whipped it to Kelly. It hit her glove with a satisfying *whap*. Oh, yeah. Kelly reached out to tag the girl as she slid into base. *Gotcha,* she said inside.

"Way to go, Lisa!" she called out as she threw the ball back to the pitching mound. Lisa snagged it with her graceful long-armed movement. Kelly rubbed her right shoulder. Even sore, it felt good. In fact, she felt good—until she spied the next batter.

Steve Townsend strolled to the plate with the easy assurance of someone who knows he can hit anything the pitcher sends across. Not a problem. Kelly frowned at him out of habit. Of course, he'd probably hit it out of the park. Everyone said he was a baseball star in high school and college. It was too much to hope for that he'd play down a notch.

She was right. Steve connected on Lisa's first pitch, a low-dropping slider that seemed to hang over the plate, just waiting for Steve to hit it. He obliged. Kelly winced at the satisfying *smack* of ball meeting bat—the reverberation that carries on the wind when wood meets force and sends it back again. She watched the ball sail over everyone's head and far into the outfield.

A homer, of course, she thought glumly and debated whether she should trip the smug bastard as he rounded her base.

* * *

Kelly pulled in front of Jennifer's condo and grabbed her cell phone. When she'd called five minutes ago to let Jennifer know she was on the way, Jennifer said she was straggling out of the shower. Punching in the numbers, Kelly was surprised to see Jennifer coming down the concrete steps.

"Wow, that was fast," Kelly commented as Jennifer climbed into the car. "I'm impressed. I thought you'd still be getting dressed."

"Old memories returned. I could swear I heard Sister Josephine's voice nagging me to hurry up or I'd be late for mass." Jennifer looked around. "Where's that coffee?"

"Right here." Kelly reached in the back and brought out the tall cup with familiar green logo. "Drink up."

Jennifer complied without a word.

"I guess you went to parochial school, then?" Kelly asked as she headed through the early morning Sunday traffic.

"Yeah, until eighth grade. You can imagine how happy the nuns were to see me go."

Kelly laughed. "I'll bet you gave them fits."

"I did my best. How about you?"

"I went to public schools, everywhere we lived. My dad was a district manager for a large automotive chain, so we moved around a lot."

"Boy, I sure would have liked moving around as a kid," Jennifer said between sips. "I was bored out of my skull back in the Midwest."

"Where?"

"Indianapolis."

Memories triggered. "We lived in Fort Wayne for about a year, before we went to Detroit, then on to Newark, New Jersey, for two years, then finally settled in northern Virginia for my last three years of high school."

"I thought you grew up here."

"I did, but when I was ten my dad got promoted and we went on the road. Actually we went to Saint Louis for a year before Indiana."

"Boy, you really did move around. Was it hard making friends? In school and all?"

"Yeah, it was always kind of scary at first. But playing ball helped. Maybe that's why I love it so much. That's how I made friends in every new school." She shook her head at the flood of memories coming back as she drove. "It was still hard though," she said wistfully. "Sometimes I'd make up all these fantastic stories about why my dad and I had to move around so much."

She turned onto a large avenue, bordered on both sides by older gracious homes, but Kelly didn't even notice. "One of my favorites was that my dad was this notorious and untouchable card shark who roamed about the country making his living in shadowy back rooms of fancy casinos. I'd sit next to him and pour his whiskey, and count cards, of course."

"Of course."

"Then afterward, we'd sneak away in the early morning light. In a red convertible, too." Kelly laughed. Where had that memory come from? "I'd daydream out the window of our old yellow Plymouth station wagon. Dad called it beige, but it looked dog-barf yellow to me."

Jennifer raised her hand. "Had one of those." She upended her cup then pointed. "St. Mark's is up ahead."

"Oh my gosh, is that Lizzie out front?" Kelly said as she slowed the car, spying pink-and-white fabric fluttering in the spring breeze.

"Sure is." Jennifer waved through the window, then pointed to the right. "You can park in this lot on Sunday."

Kelly pulled in and grabbed the first space she spotted. "Boy, she really likes pink, doesn't she?" Kelly said with a chuckle as they both headed through the lot and across the street.

"Oh, yeah."

Lizzie stood on the church steps waiting, a huge grin on her face. "Good morning, girls! You're bright and early, too," she announced.

"Don't remind me how early it is, Lizzie. I'm barely awake now," Jennifer teased. "I hope the priests are as boring as I remember, so I can go back to sleep. We are sitting in the back, I hope?"

Lizzie's musical little laugh ran up the scale as she settled herself between the two of them. "Jennifer, you're such a caution. Yes, we are sitting in the back. In fact, I've got our places already saved.

Come along." And she encircled her arms around theirs and guided them through the open doorway and into St. Mark's.

They paused at the entrance to the sanctuary, and Kelly's gaze swept over the graceful vaulted ceiling, the tall marble columns, and walls of stained glass—window after window. Poignant memories surfaced. The last time she'd been here with Helen was Christmas Eve mass.

Jennifer deliberately walked over to the sconce of holy water and peered into it. "Well, I don't see any ripples, so the walls aren't shaking. Yet. The Heavenly Powers must not know I'm here."

"Come, dears," Lizzie indicated the last pew in the center.

Kelly settled between Lizzie and Jennifer and noticed that they could watch both entrances from this vantage point. Good job, Lizzie.

Lizzie straightened her pink flounces and whispered. "I've already explained to Hilda why we're sitting back here. Now, I suggest we start our prayers. That way no one will notice our surveillance." She pulled out the cushioned kneelers and settled herself.

"Okay," Kelly went along and gingerly knelt. Both knees complained, still sore from yesterday's game. Glancing over her shoulder, she noticed Jennifer had already cuddled into a cozy position against the side of the pew, arms folded, eyes closed. "I take it you're praying," Kelly whispered.

"Repenting is more like it," she replied without opening her eyes.

Kelly leaned her arms on the pew in front and watched the church slowly fill with people. Pastel spring colors were everywhere, and Lizzie was not the only lover of pink. The overcast sky must have cleared, because Kelly noticed brilliant colors splashed across a side wall. Sun painting through stained glass.

Since she'd been going to the shop, Kelly seemed to notice colors more, vibrant colors everywhere she went. *How come everything looked different to her now?* she wondered.

Her knees sent a painful message, and Kelly eased herself off the kneeler and onto the seat. Clasping her hands, she still kept her reverent pose. Lizzie was actually saying prayers, Kelly observed, a pearl rosary dangling between her fingers.

Kelly didn't pray anymore. It didn't work. She'd prayed a lot when her dad was first diagnosed with cancer and all through his treatment. All those prayers, and none of them worked. He died anyway.

Lizzie's voice broke through Kelly's painful memories. "Don't make a stir, dear, but I believe I see her. She just passed us. The woman in the navy blue dress." Lizzie nodded toward the left aisle.

Kelly focused on the parishioners in the aisle. A slight, gray-haired woman in a navy blue dress slowly walked toward the front of the sanctuary. Choosing a side pew, she settled in and immediately sank to her knees, head lowered, hands clasped. Kelly wished she could have seen her features. From the back she looked like half the older women in church.

As if reading her mind, Lizzie spoke up. "We'll get a better look at her when she leaves, dear. She'll pass right by us again. I suggest you wait for a weekday service to introduce yourself. Not so many people around, you see. She appears easily startled."

Kelly suppressed a smile. Lizzie was turning out to be quite the stake-out queen. But she'd made a good point. The church was filled with people. They'd be standing in the aisles by nine o'clock when the service began. If this Martha was as easily startled as Lizzie suggested, she might panic when Kelly introduced herself. If she chose to run rather than talk, she could disappear into the crowd of departing parishioners. Not the ideal way to begin a relationship, Kelly decided.

"Thanks, Lizzie, that's a good suggestion," Kelly leaned over and whispered.

Kelly flicked the tiny speck off her dark blue skirt and recrossed her legs for the fourth time in the last thirty minutes. She leaned back into the empty pew and observed the nearly empty church. Only a handful of people sat in the front two pews for Monday morning mass. Kelly had shown up early and chosen a spot mid-church for her vantage point. She figured when she introduced herself, Martha would be too far from the door to make a run for it. Meanwhile, Kelly did her best to appear absorbed in prayer so the priest wouldn't include her in the proceedings.

Her planning paid off. Martha arrived alone, five minutes before the service began. All Kelly had to do was wait for the service to end. While the priest's voice rose and fell in the familiar ritual, Kelly pondered the best way to greet Martha. She wanted to appear friendly and nonthreatening, but she wasn't sure what that looked like.

Instead, her mind kept bringing back scenes from the night before when she'd joined Lisa, Megan and the rest of their team for dinner and drinks in a cozy Old Town café. Kelly hadn't laughed that much in a long time. It felt good. It also felt good to hear everyone ask her to continue to play with them.

"Please, Kelly," the shortstop, Sherrie, pleaded across the table. "You're awesome, girl. We need you."

The effusive praise and encouragement had stroked something deep down inside that Kelly hadn't felt in a very long time. That felt better than good. She was really glad she'd gotten her boss's commitment for a couple of months "or so." The "or so" might be stretched.

The sudden movement of the prayerful few in the front captured her attention, as they stood and held out their hands for the blessing that ended each service. Kelly straightened her businesslike attire and grabbed her shoulder bag. Most of the attendees were older, but not all, she noticed as they headed down the aisle.

Martha was near the end of the group, so Kelly rose, genuflected, and crossed herself out of habit. Then she stood quietly, waiting for Martha to approach, hoping no one else would strike up a conversation with her.

As Martha drew closer, head bent, hands still clasped as if in prayer, Kelly tried to study her features but couldn't get a good look. Finally, the older woman was only a few feet from the pew, and Kelly stepped into the aisle to face her.

"Martha?" she asked in a soft voice which she hoped was non-threatening.

The older woman stopped abruptly, her head jerking up in obvious surprise. She stared back into Kelly's face, her eyes wide with concern, as if she wasn't used to being spoken to by strangers. Kelly stared into huge blue eyes, made even bluer by Martha's white face. Kelly sincerely hoped Martha didn't have a heart condition, because she looked scared to death.

"Yes?" she answered barely above a whisper.

"Martha, I'm sorry if I startled you, but I wanted to introduce myself. I'm Helen Rosburg's niece, Kelly Flynn, from Washington, D.C."

The startled blue gaze changed. Fear changed to wary observation. "Ahhh, yes. Kelly." She nodded. "I can see the resemblance now."

Relieved and a bit surprised at Martha's acknowledgment, Kelly continued. "Someone from the knitting shop had seen you at Helen's service last week and mentioned you attended this church. So I thought I'd come by and meet you." She attempted a bright smile. "I was surprised to learn Helen had any other relatives in the area. She always said she was the last one in the family."

Martha's pale face had regained some color and a tiny smile as well. "Well, that's almost true. I'm one of her distant cousins from Wyoming, so we never saw you folks down here that often. My father had a sheep ranch way up near Lander. I didn't even move here until a few years ago."

Kelly noticed Martha seemed to cradle her left arm with her right. *Perhaps she has a handicap,* Kelly thought. *That could be why Helen was so protective of her.* All manner of questions bubbled up inside Kelly now about this extended family she never knew. "Martha, I'd really like to find a time to chat with you about the family and Aunt Helen, if I could?" she ventured. "Is there a time I could come and visit you? Do you live here in Fort Connor?"

Martha glanced toward the stained-glass windows, morning sun beginning to heat up the glass and send colorful shards of light across the pews. Kelly could feel her hesitation, but when Martha turned back, she said, "Yes, of course. Why don't you come by this afternoon about two?"

Delighted Martha was so obliging, Kelly beamed. "That would be wonderful! I'll look forward to it. Where do you live?"

"I'm in a small house in Landport, just north of town. On Maple Drive—"

A woman's voice interrupted, calling from the back of the church. "Martha, are you coming, dear?"

Martha waved to the other woman. "I'll be right there, Myrtle," then turned back to Kelly. "My house is a small white frame, two-eleven Maple. I'll expect you at two, Kelly."

With that, Martha hastened down the aisle to join her friend, leaving Kelly grateful for the invitation and a bit startled at Martha's speedy departure. "Good-bye, thank you," Kelly called as the two women left the church.

Eight

Kelly glanced at her watch as she closed her car door. If the mail had brought her office files, she'd have a couple of hours to get them set up before her visit with Martha. She was headed toward the mailbox until she heard the sound of an increasingly familiar voice in her backyard. Sure enough, there was Steve playing with *her* dog. Didn't this guy have a dog at home?

"Here you go, boy. All yours," Steve called and threw several golf balls into the yard. Carl responded with an excited bark and raced off to catch them as Steve approached Kelly. "Maybe these old balls will keep him off the course."

Kelly had already forgotten. "Yeah, thanks. Let's hope it works."

"Let's hope," Steve said with a grin as he reached into his jeans pocket and withdrew a golf ball. "I rescued these a minute ago. Carl had six of them."

Kelly winced. "Darn it! I was hoping—"

"What? That he'd heed your lecture?"

Kelly scowled at him, which seemed to amuse Steve to no end. He actually grinned wider. Brother, this guy annoyed her on purpose. What was with him, anyway? She took a deep breath. "Noooo, I was hoping he'd get bored and stop, I guess."

"Why would he? It's a fun game. He steals balls. You fuss at him. Do you scowl at him the same way? I mean, like you are right now?" Steve laughed. "Face it, Kelly. You're fun to tease."

Of course, that only made Kelly scowl more, which made Steve laugh even more. "Don't you have something better to do than stand here and be annoying?" She challenged.

"Matter of fact, yes. I'm going to throw these balls back onto the course so the golfers can find them, then go take Mimi to see some cabinets," Steve said as he turned to leave, then stopped. "Uh oh. Too late. I think Carl's busted."

To Kelly's dismay she spied three male golfers striding off the edge of the greens and headed right toward them. One man, in plaid slacks, pointed at them with his golf club. When he drew closer, Kelly could see he didn't look happy.

"Hey! Are those my golf balls? Dammit! I've been looking for them," he yelled as he strode up.

"No, Mr. Houston, those are some old balls of mine," Steve answered congenially, pointing toward the balls scattered about the yard. "I was about to place yours on the greens now. The dog's new to the neighborhood, and I'm sure the balls were just too tempting. He'll settle down."

"Settle down, my ass!" Houston yelled, clearly furious. "I've been losing balls all week because of him."

Kelly noticed his two middle-aged golfing companions hung back from the fray a few feet and stared at the ground. The balding man shook his head and grinned at his taller, better-dressed companion.

"It's your lousy slice, Frank, that's been losing the balls," Baldie taunted. "The dog's just doing what comes naturally. Chasing balls." Then he and his natty friend snickered in unison.

Watching Houston's face flush even redder, Kelly spoke up. "Mister, I apologize for my dog—"

Houston cut her off, jabbing his club toward Carl. "That mangy hound has no business stealing my golf balls just because they roll over here. I'm going to report him!"

Watching the club's movement, Carl burst into a ferocious, snarling bark, glaring right at Houston. Houston jumped back.

"See? He's vicious! Look at him!" he yelled, which only made Carl bark more.

"Carl, easy!" Kelly commanded, hand raised, as she stepped between Houston and her dog.

"For God's sake, Frank, put the club down!" Well-Dressed yelled. "You're deliberately provoking him."

"Yeah, Frank," Baldie interjected. "You're on *his* turf now. If you wanta discuss territorial imperative with a Rottweiler, go ahead. We'll pick up the pieces."

Oh, great, Kelly worried. They've already put Carl into the killer Rottie category.

"Carl has never attacked anyone before, I assure you," she swore, hoping to convince them.

"He's vicious, I tell you! Vicious, and I'm gonna report him—"

"Look, Mr. Houston," Steve interrupted, stepping forward. "I can vouch for the dog myself. He's not vicious, are you, Carl?" Steve placed one hand on the fence and gestured to Carl. Carl obliged instantly by standing up, paws on fence, so Steve could rub his head. Steve patted Carl with one hand and reached into his pocket with the other, withdrawing the stolen golf balls. "Here you go," he offered them to Houston. "Now, I've got a much better way to solve this. Why don't—"

"Look at that!" Houston exclaimed, staring at the balls. "Tooth marks on my new Titleists! I just bought these." His companions snickered behind their golf gloves.

"I've got a better way to solve this, Mr. Houston," Steve offered. "Let me help with that slice of yours. See if we can reduce the angle a little. You're almost on the green now—"

"By about fifty yards," Baldie said with a derisive snort.

"And with a little tweaking, we can get you straightened out, I'm positive," Steve continued, barely missing a beat.

"You giving free lessons, Steve?" Well-Dressed inquired with a smile. "If so, sign me up."

"On special occasions, Alan," Steve replied.

"What's so special about this?"

Steve shrugged. "I like the dog and don't want to see him get a bad rep."

Kelly watched this exchange with fascination. The older men were paying careful attention to Steve, as if his offer of golf lessons was a big deal. Even Houston had calmed down. Brother, Steve must be one heckuva golf instructor.

"You serious about those lessons?" Houston peered at Steve.

"Absolutely."

"What if it takes more than one lesson?" he bargained with an oily smile.

"Then it takes more than one."

"Jeez, Frank, don't push it," Baldie jabbed. "Take the lessons and leave the dog alone."

Houston scowled at Carl, who returned the favor. "Okay, I'll take you up on the offer. When can we start?"

"I'll check my schedule and give you a call," Steve said. "Got a card?" Houston searched his pocket and obliged.

Kelly felt the ball of tension in her stomach start to recede, until she heard a woman's voice call out.

"Hallloo! Excuse me? Are you gentlemen searching for golf balls, I hope?"

Oh, no, Kelly thought as she watched a very pretty blonde, attired completely in pink shirt, shorts, and tennis shoes, walk up, dangling a golf club side to side.

"I seem to have lost mine," she declared. "It's so embarrassing. I've just started lessons, and I'm absolutely awful! I declare, I'll never master this game. I don't know how I hit one all the way over here."

"Frank, why don't you check those," Baldie ordered, pointing to Houston's toothmarked balls. "Maybe one of them is hers."

"Oh, no," she shook her golden head. "Mine are specially marked, and they're pink. That's so I can't lose them."

"Good idea, ma'am," Steve said with a lazy smile. Well-Dressed hid his laughter behind a sudden cough.

"I'll be sure to look for it, ma'am," Kelly offered. "I'm afraid my dog has been tempted by the flying balls and—" She paused, watching Carl suddenly bound over to the corner of the yard and nose behind the flowerpots, then trot back to the fence.

"What the—?" she said, staring at the object in Carl's mouth. "Carl, what have you got?" She held out her hand. Carl obediently dropped a pink golf ball into her palm.

"Oh, my!" Pinkie exclaimed. "He found my ball. What a nice doggie." And she reached out to pat Carl on the head. Carl slurped her hand while everyone except Frank Houston laughed out loud.

Kelly walked up the narrow sidewalk leading to Martha's front porch. The concrete was cracked and broken in places, she noticed, and the little frame house was badly in need of paint. However, the gardens were immaculately tidy and filled with blooming plants. Splashy bright tulips—red, yellow, purple—reached for the sun. She glanced about the older neighborhood streets. Kelly hadn't been in Landport for years, usually passing straight through on the way into the canyons. As a small, northern bedroom community for Fort Connor, the pace was slower and appealed to many who wanted out of the traffic and ever-increasing development to the south.

As Kelly started up the creaky wooden steps, she heard the squeak of a screen door opening. Martha appeared in the doorway, in a pale-blue cotton housedress and bedroom slippers.

"Hello, Kelly, come in. I've made us a pot of tea," she greeted and held the screen door wide.

"Thanks, Martha, that's sweet of you," Kelly said as she entered. Then she held out a slim rectangular box. "I brought these. They're from that fancy chocolate shop in Old Town."

"Oh, aren't you sweet, Kelly. Thank you." Martha's thin face brightened with a smile. "You settle into a comfy chair, and I'll bring our tea." She placed the chocolates on the dining room table as she walked past.

Kelly glanced about the sparsely furnished living room and dining room and noticed a familiar chair beside the floor lamp. She headed straight for it and sat down, immediately sinking another two inches lower. She remembered this chair. It was Uncle Jim's and was one of Kelly's favorite spots to read when she was a child. She ran her fingers over the worn upholstery with fond recollection of enjoyable hours spent there.

Helen must have given it to Martha years ago, she mused, scrutinizing the other furniture as well. By the time Martha emerged with a small tea tray in one hand, Kelly had identified three chairs and two end tables that once resided at her aunt's. She wondered if Helen had provided all the furniture. Didn't Martha have furniture of her own? Kelly also couldn't help noticing the definite absence of a common item in most elderly women's homes: knickknacks.

There were none on the fireplace mantel or on the shelves. Lacy crocheted doilies adorned the backs of chairs and shelves instead. As for framed pictures, there was only one hanging on the wall. It looked to be an enlarged photo of Helen and Jim. Every older home of this vintage that Kelly had visited over the years had its walls covered with family portraits and modern photos. Memories recaptured. Where were Martha's family photos? Where were Martha's memories?

Martha crossed the living room, teacup in hand. "Here you go, my dear." She offered the cup to Kelly. "I've put some cream and sugar in it already. Is that all right?"

Not really, but Kelly would bite her tongue before saying so. "That's fine, Martha," she lied as she accepted the cup. "Come, sit. Stop fussing about me."

Martha took her cup and settled into a high-backed maple rocking chair. Kelly noticed she steadied the saucer against her left hand while she held the cup with her right and wondered how she'd injured her arm. But then, Kelly had so many questions she didn't know where to begin. Meanwhile, Martha rocked quietly and sipped her tea, studying Kelly.

"I can see you've got a lot of questions, Kelly," Martha spoke up. "Foremost, you're probably wondering why Helen never told you about me."

"Ahhh, yes," Kelly said, relieved Martha initiated the subject. "I have to admit I'm curious. Helen always said she was the only one left in Colorado."

A smile sparked briefly on Martha's thin face, then was gone. "Well, I guess that's technically true. I lived my whole life in Wyoming."

Kelly gestured toward the empty walls. "I was actually hoping you had some photos or family albums. It would be wonderful to see some of these relatives. Do you have any photos at all?"

A cloud passed across Martha's face. "Yes, I had many albums and pictures, Kelly. A lifetime's worth. But they're all back in Wyoming. Back in what was once my home." She sipped her tea.

"What happened? Did you lose your home?" Kelly asked, intrigued by the cryptic reply.

Martha set her empty teacup on an end table and folded her hands in her lap before she settled a somber gaze on Kelly. "No, I walked away from it. Ran, actually. In the middle of the night.

I literally took the clothes on my back and my purse, that's all. You see, my husband's drinking had increased over the years, and he started hitting me. Just a slap at first, but it got worse each time. I won't go into the details, they're still too painful. But one night, four years ago, he broke my arm, then he passed out on the sofa, drunk. That night, I knew I had to escape, or he might kill me the next time. I ran five miles down the road to the closest neighbor and begged them to drive me to Cheyenne. There, I called Helen. She'd always said to call if I ever needed her. Bless her soul, she drove up to get me that very night."

Kelly sat mute, stunned by what she heard.

Martha continued. "Helen took me to the hospital in Fort Connor, then helped me find this place, and even paid the rent until I got my Social Security checks again. She asked her lawyer, Mr. Chambers, to help me. You see, I was deathly afraid of my husband discovering where I was. So, Mr. Chambers handled everything, dear man." She rocked silently, staring ahead.

Kelly sat in silence, questions bombarding her inside. "Martha, I'm so sorry," she said finally. "Trust me, I will never divulge your whereabouts to a living soul, I swear."

Martha's thin face relaxed visibly. "Thank you, Kelly. You're truly as caring as Helen always said you were. But we no longer have to worry. I read in the Wyoming papers last January that my husband had died. Drinking, of course. He ran his truck off the road and crashed into some boulders one night. He died instantly, the paper said." Her voice trailed off wistfully. "It was so very sad and such a waste. He really was a good man at heart. It was the drink that did it."

Kelly held her tongue and decided to turn the conversation toward the future, not the past. "Has Mr. Chambers checked into your inheritance rights, Martha? You and your husband were still married, right?"

A smile played with the corners of Martha's mouth. "Ever the accountant, aren't you, Kelly? Helen depended on your cool head and sharp mind. Yes, Mr. Chambers is looking into the estate for me. Again, for free. I can never repay that man."

"Are your children in Wyoming?"

Martha's smile vanished. "In a matter of speaking. Our only child, our son, Ronald, died when he was only seventeen. He was driving too fast on one of the country roads. He's buried there on our land." Her voice faded away.

Kelly sat and sipped the sugary tea, choosing her words. She hadn't expected to hear a story such as this. "Martha, I will be happy to help you in any way I can," she said finally. "When Mr. Chambers finishes with the estate settlement, I'll do your taxes, if you'd like."

"Oh, would you? That would be so helpful. I confess I've never had a head for business. Ralph always handled that, including our taxes."

Kelly paused, forming her next question. The possibility that Helen had intended the loan money for Martha had been niggling in her mind ever since she'd learned of Martha's existence. Maybe she could work into it.

"How is your health, Martha?" she ventured. "I mean, does your arm give you any trouble? I notice you favor it."

In affirmation, Martha stroked her left arm gently. "It twinges when the weather changes. And of course, I no longer have the same use of it that I used to. But I've adjusted. I've even learned how to open jars." She lifted her chin a bit, Kelly noticed.

"So, your health is good, then," she continued to probe. "I mean, your heart and everything?"

Martha almost looked amused. "Yes, indeed, it is. I know I look frail, and the arm adds to that, but inside I'm strong as an ox, Kelly. I used to work sunup to sundown on the farm years ago. Kept me healthy, I guess. Why do you ask?"

Kelly let out a sigh. "Well, to be honest, I was wondering if you held the answer to something that's puzzling me. You see, I learned last week that Helen had refinanced the mortgage on her cottage and withdrawn a large amount of money. She never told me she planned to do that. So I was trying to figure out why she'd need the money and not tell me." Kelly stared through the tall living room window, not really seeing the trees outside. "When I heard about you and met you briefly in church, I confess, I thought perhaps she'd intended the money for you. And maybe you needed it for . . . for something." She gestured in an attempt to explain. "Maybe you needed an operation or surgery . . . I don't know."

"Money? H-how much m-money?" Martha whispered, her face completely drained of color.

Kelly glanced back at the sound of concern and set her teacup on the table immediately. It was a good thing Martha had said she was healthy, because she looked as if she was about to pass out that minute. "Martha, are you alright?"

"Yes, yes," she said, dismissing the question with a wave of her hand. "Tell me about this money again. When did Helen withdraw it?"

That cold feeling returned to Kelly's gut. Clearly, Martha knew nothing about Helen's large withdrawal. The neat and tidy answer to the money puzzle had been eliminated, leaving Kelly once again with her nagging doubts. "Helen never told you she was taking out another mortgage and withdrawing cash?" she probed.

"Never. When did this occur?"

"Chambers said she called him the very day of her death and told him she'd just received the check from the loan company. He also said he never dreamed she'd cash it that afternoon."

"That was the day she was murdered?" Martha looked truly horrified now.

"Yes. That's the thing that bothers me the most. The very day she cashes a check for twenty thousand dollars, someone just happens to break into her house and kills her." Kelly deliberately let the lingering resentment seep into her voice.

Martha sat bolt upright in the rocking chair. "*Twenty thousand dollars!*" she exclaimed, eyes as round as saucers.

"That was my reaction, too," Kelly declared. "Frankly, I was hoping you were the answer. Now, I'm left with all my nagging doubts about her death."

"What do you mean, Kelly?" Martha asked, concern evident on her face. "The police have the wretched man responsible for her death. He's in jail, I thought."

"The man in jail is a vagrant the police saw running away from the vicinity that night. They're convinced he's the killer because he has a history of drunken violence." She screwed up her face. "He has no recollection, of course. And on top of that, all the money is missing. Not a single bill was found at the house or near the river. And that doesn't make sense to me, Martha. The police have all sorts of theories for how the money disappeared, but—"

At that, Martha sprang from her rocker and began to pace the worn oak floor. "Oh, dear . . . oh, dear . . . oh, dear . . ." she muttered as she walked, fingers plucking at her left arm.

"What is it, Martha? What's the matter?"

"I had this feeling, a bad feeling," Martha said, so softly Kelly wasn't sure if she was talking to her or not.

"What feeling, Martha? Please tell me," Kelly coaxed. "It might be important."

Martha made one more turn about the small room before stopping in front of Kelly's chair. "Helen was worried about something, and she wouldn't tell me what. But I knew something was wrong. When I questioned her, all she said was, 'Our sins come back to haunt us, don't they?'"

Kelly sank back into the familiar cushioned chair. Sins? Aunt Helen? Surely not. That made no sense. "What did she mean, Martha? Do you have any idea?"

Martha's brief glance answered Kelly's question. "Yes, I'm afraid I do," she said as she returned to her rocker. She rocked quietly for a full minute before speaking. "I'm sure she meant her youthful indiscretion years ago."

With great effort, Kelly kept her jaw from dropping and waited for Martha to continue.

Martha observed Kelly's rapt attention. "Years ago, when Helen was still in high school, she had a . . . well, she conceived a child. This was nineteen fifty-five, so things were very different than they are now. Oh, my, yes. Her parents were stricken, of course, especially when she refused to name the father." Martha's voice got softer as she stared toward the windows. "Her father and mine were brothers, and even though our families didn't see each other often, we stayed in touch. Helen and I were only a year apart. Her father insisted she come to our farm in Wyoming to spend the rest of her pregnancy and have the baby. He also insisted she put the baby up for adoption, or she couldn't return home."

Kelly sat in shocked silence, stunned by what she heard.

"Naturally, Helen and I grew very close during those months. My mother and I both were with her at the birth. And when she gave up the baby." She paused.

"That must have been so hard," Kelly whispered, feeling an anguished tug inside.

"It was," Martha replied. "But we placed him with a local agency, the Sisters of Charity, and they assured us he'd have a wonderful home. A healthy baby boy. Blond and blue-eyed."

"When was he born?" Kelly asked.

"December eleventh, nineteen fifty-five. I remember it was snowing the night he was born. Helen stayed with us through Christmas, then returned to Fort Connor after New Year's. That next year was much happier for her. She met Jim Rosburg that spring, and they were married in late fall." Martha's expression softened. "They had a good marriage."

"Did Helen ever get curious about the child? Or try to look for him in later years?"

Martha shook her head. "Not to my knowledge. Helen and I never spoke of that particular bit of shared history again."

"But you think her comment last month referred to that?" Kelly pried.

"I'm afraid so," she said, rubbing her arm. "I had this bad feeling come over me when she said it. And I asked her straight out if she meant the child, but she wouldn't answer. Of course, that worried me even more."

"Do you think the child learned of her identity and contacted her?"

Martha shook her head. "I don't know if it was the child or perhaps the father who had come back to 'haunt' her, as she said. I wish I knew."

So did Kelly. Hundreds of questions were buzzing inside now, but Kelly had no answers. "And she never revealed the name of the father?"

"Never."

"Did she ever say anything about him?"

Martha sighed. "Only that he 'couldn't marry her.' That's all she ever said."

Hmmmm, Kelly thought. *Couldn't or wouldn't?* she wondered. And who was he? Maybe Helen kept the birth certificate or something. Something with the father's name on it. Kelly had yet to really search the desk or dressers in the cottage. Perhaps Helen left a clue to this man's identity.

Had the baby's father reentered her life? Had the child found out his true mother and contacted her? Which was it?

Kelly pulled herself out of the comfy chair. "Martha, I cannot thank you enough for trusting me with all this. I'm going back to the cottage to start searching right now. Helen may have saved some memento or something from the past that might tell me more."

"Do you really think her death is connected to all of that in the past?" Martha asked, face puckering with concern again.

"I don't know, Martha. But like you, I've got a bad feeling about all of this. Something's not right about the police version of Helen's death, and I intend to find out what it is."

Nine

Kelly snapped on the miniature Victorian desk lamp, and a golden circle of light spilled across Helen's maple desk and onto the floor. Dusk had settled, and she didn't even notice. If it hadn't been for Carl barking for supper in the yard, she wouldn't have known it was dark outside. Her stomach growled, and she checked her watch. No wonder she was hungry. At least Carl was smart enough to know dinnertime when it arrived.

She'd been so absorbed in searching that she'd lost all track of time. Checking her stainless steel mug came up empty. Just like her search. She'd gone through every drawer in Helen's house—desk, bedroom dressers, dining room cabinets, china closet, kitchen drawers, even the tool drawers in the garage. Nothing. Kelly had even checked the undersides of each drawer and cabinet in case Helen had hidden a document in the cracks. There was no paper, no picture, no record of any kind that indicated this child existed.

Kelly stood up and indulged in a long stretch. Food would help. She always ran dry of ideas on an empty stomach. On the way to the kitchen, she noticed that the knitting shop was already closed and dark. It seemed like only a few minutes ago that she'd called Mimi and asked about the boxes in the garage. Now, it was nearly night.

Mimi had confirmed that the boxes contained only books. No papers or folders of any kind. *Darn,* Kelly thought, *every place turned up nothing.* Helen must have eliminated every trace of that event in her life.

Kelly surveyed the fridge's meager contents and chose a peach yogurt. She really needed to buy groceries. At least there was some coffee left, and she drained the last of the pot into her mug. Snagging a spoon, she wandered back into the cozy living room and sat in the middle of the old Oriental rug to enjoy what passed for dinner. Was there any place she hadn't looked, she wondered?

She surveyed the room and consumed the yogurt in two minutes flat. Her glance traveled over the bookshelves, drifted away, then abruptly returned. She'd noticed on the lower shelf some varying size volumes, not the neat and tidy rows of novels and handyman and history books. Curious, she settled beside the bookcase and removed one. It was an atlas. Just to be sure, she riffled the pages, then replaced it and withdrew the black leather volume beside it. The leather felt smooth and warm to the touch. On the front was an American flag inlay and the name of Helen's high school and the date—1955.

Helen's high school yearbook. Kelly felt a little buzz inside, and it wasn't connected to caffeine. Helen was eighteen when she gave birth, that meant she was seventeen when she became pregnant and still in high school. The baby was born in December, after her graduation. *Maybe the father was a fellow student,* Kelly thought as she turned the pages.

Black-and-white photos of young women in white blouses and impossibly full skirts, crinolines peeking from beneath. Clean-shaven young men with crew cuts. Every page, it seemed, had a signature. That didn't surprise Kelly, knowing her aunt's vivacious nature. Helen probably had lots of friends. Loopy, swirling script recorded best wishes. And spare, cramped signatures wrote across photos.

There was Lawrence Chambers, she noticed. Younger-looking but somber even then. He stared out with wide eyes. "To Helen—the brightest girl in class!" he wrote beside his picture. Kelly paged through the class snapshots and into the activities section of the yearbook. Greetings and best wishes adorned nearly every page.

Kelly was about to riffle through the last pages, when she spotted another signature. This one wasn't childish scribble or loopy swirls, but bold, heavy strokes of a black ink pen. "Yours, always. Curt," the jagged script read. Above was a photo of a lean and lanky young cowboy holding a horse's reins and staring right into the camera, as if daring the photographer to capture his image. Kelly leaned over the photo, fascinated by the young cowboy. All trace of boyhood was gone from his face. Only the slightly cocky lift to his chin hinted at youth. Something about the photo made Kelly's antennae buzz. Maybe she'd hit pay dirt after all.

She scanned the credits for his name. Curtis Stackhouse. Flipping to the back, she scanned the index and found two more photos. One a blurry shot of Curtis on the football squad and the formal graduation "mug shot." Kelly noticed that the dare-you look in Stackhouse's eye was evident even there.

Kelly stood up and headed for the dining room and her laptop computer. Thank goodness her office files hadn't arrived yet. That way she wouldn't feel guilty spending the rest of the evening tracking Curtis Stackhouse on the Web.

"Hey, good morning," Rosa called out when Kelly made the turn from the restaurant doorway into the knitting shop.

"It's a great morning, Rosa," Kelly declared as she made her way around a weaving loom. "Are those all knitting magazines?" she asked when she noticed Rosa's armload.

"Well, some are. Others are pattern magazines, and weaving magazines, and spinning magazines, and designer magazines." She smiled over her shoulder. "You name it, we've got it."

"I'll have to check those later," Kelly promised and headed for the main room, balancing briefcase, knitting tote bag, and coffee mug. She almost got there, but the changing display in the middle room captured her first.

The fat multicolored bundles of chunky yarn she chose for her new scarf were now replaced by solid pastels—pink, lime, coral, tangerine—all just as pudgy and soft and begging to be touched. Kelly freed up one hand and started squeezing the plump bundles, unable to resist. New skeins in different colors had been added to the other displays as well. Naturally, she had to examine those, indulging the irresistible desire to sink her fingers into the softness.

Another new display on the center table caught her attention next. It was a little girl's coat in a rich burgundy. She leaned over the table and fingered the fabric. It resembled an old-fashioned bathrobe and felt even softer. What was it, she wondered?

"It's French chenille," Rosa spoke up beside her. "It comes on one of those big cones, see?" She pointed to the corner, and sure enough, there was a huge cone of burgundy chenille.

"It feels like an old-fashioned bathrobe," Kelly joked. "But softer."

"Oh, yeah. It's yummy soft and knits up like a dream. You should see how fast this little coat knits up."

Kelly stared in awe. It had tiny sleeves and a collar and buttons. "Easy for you to say. I'm just learning. No way could I do that."

Rosa tossed her long dark braid behind her back and laughed. "You'll be surprised how quickly you'll learn. I made one of those for my little girl in January. She turned five, and it was absolutely adorable on her. Meanwhile, you could start with something really easy, like those trendy washcloths."

"Washcloths?"

"Yes, for the bath. They're all the rage. People are knitting those up like crazy. They sell for $30 in the boutique shops."

Kelly's mouth almost dropped open. She was about to comment when Megan came through the foyer and into the shop. Like Kelly, she had a mug in one hand and her tote bag in the other.

"Hey, Kelly. You missed all the excitement yesterday afternoon. The police came over with some yarn they found by the riverbank. They wanted Mimi to identify it to see if it was Helen's."

"What?!" Kelly exclaimed as she followed Megan to the library table where she deposited her things and sat down. "Darn! I wish I'd been here. Was it that Lieutenant Morrison?"

"No, it was a regular uniformed officer," Megan replied as she settled into a chair. "I only got a glimpse of the wool. He had it in a plastic bag. But Mimi could tell you more, after all, he was talking to . . . oh, there you are, Mimi. Tell Kelly what happened yesterday with the purple wool."

Mimi appeared from the office area. "Hi, Kelly," she greeted and started straightening books on the shelves, glancing briefly over her shoulder. "One of the police officers investigating the case came by with a plastic bag with charred pieces of purple wool inside. He wanted to know if it was the same wool Helen was using for the sweater."

"Was it?"

"It appeared to be the same." Mimi continued to move among the shelves, patting books into place. "There was a small section of sweater that hadn't been charred, and I could tell from that."

Kelly frowned. "And he said they found it near the riverbank recently?"

"Yes. I believe he told me they found it yesterday. And they wanted me to identify it before they sent it to the criminal investigative lab in Denver."

"I wonder why they didn't find it the first time they searched the riverbank," Kelly mused out loud, swirling her coffee. "Lieutenant Morrison swore they searched every inch of that trail by the river. And now, a week later, a piece of Helen's sweater shows up."

"Burned, too," Megan contributed, head bent over the turquoise sweater she was completing. Two sleeves had appeared.

"Why would he burn it?" Kelly speculated as she reached into her tote bag and brought out the colorful chunky wool scarf she'd started two days ago. Hopefully, she'd remember what she was doing. "That makes no sense. Here's this drunken vagrant with a purse full of money and he takes time to burn a half-finished sweater."

"I agree, it makes no sense," Megan concurred. "I mean, according to the police he tried to hide the money near the riverbank. If so, then why would he start a fire and draw attention there?" She shook her head.

"Why, indeed?" Mimi spoke softly as she approached.

Kelly glanced into Mimi's worried face. "There are too many

things about Helen's death that don't make sense to me, Mimi. I don't like it."

Mimi reached out and patted Kelly's shoulder. "I know you don't, dear. I don't, either. Why don't we knit on it."

"Knit on it?" Kelly repeated with a smile. "What do you mean?"

"Well, whenever I need to think things over, I sit down and knit quietly for a while. It calms my mind, so my thoughts become more ordered or something. Anyway, that's how I work through problems." She smiled then headed toward her office.

"Works for me, too, Mimi," Megan piped up. "Even software code unravels as I knit."

Kelly picked up the oversized needles and half-finished scarf. "Okay, if you say so. Now, let's see, where was I?" She slowly attempted a knit stitch and it cooperated perfectly. Good, she hadn't forgotten and continued the stitches. After a few rows of colorful chunky stitches, Kelly did notice herself relaxing, just a little. She glanced up at Megan, who was intently working an edge. Strange. She didn't feel the desire to talk. It was kind of peaceful just sitting there, knitting in the comfortable room with the morning sun pouring through the windows. It really was peaceful . . . until a man's voice shattered the quiet.

"Well, hello there, Ms. Flynn. The girl at the counter told me I could find you here."

Kelly jerked around and saw a man who looked vaguely familiar. "Yes, I'm Kelly Flynn. And you are . . . ?"

The well-dressed man flashed Kelly a big smile and strode forward. "You probably don't recall, but I was in the threesome that came looking for golf balls the other day. But I wasn't the one acting like a horse's behind." A wicked smile claimed his face.

It was a nice face, Kelly noticed. Tanned, ruddy complexion, topped off with wavy graying hair. Recognition sparked inside. He was one of the golfers, the well-dressed one, and he was even better dressed now. Kelly could tell a hand-tailored suit when she saw one.

"Oh, yes, I remember now." She peered at him, suddenly worried. "Carl didn't steal your golf balls, did he?"

The man threw back his head and laughed out loud for a second.

"No, Ms. Flynn, he didn't. Mainly because I don't have a slice like Frank's. So Carl shouldn't see any of my golf balls. I wanted to introduce myself to you professionally." He reached inside his jacket and withdrew a card, handing it to Kelly. "I'm Alan Gretsky. I'm a real estate broker with Metropolitan Realty. We're the biggest in the area now."

Kelly relaxed as she read the card. Thank goodness. He was a Realtor. Realtors she could deal with a lot better than irate golfers. "Ahh, thank you, Mr. Gretsky. I'll keep your card."

"Well, Ms. Flynn, I was hoping we could schedule a few minutes to talk. I'm sure you've noticed all the new retail development that's come to this area recently."

"It's hard to miss, Mr. Gretsky." Kelly relaxed against her chair, bracing for the pitch she could feel coming.

"All that new building has made your property even more valuable, Ms. Flynn," Gretsky said, shoving one hand into his pocket in a relaxed pose. "I spoke to your aunt about selling her place last year, but she wasn't interested. And, believe me, I totally understood her position, Ms. Flynn." He placed his other hand on his heart in apparent empathy. "At her age, moving would be a very traumatic experience. But you, I understand, already reside in another state, am I right?"

He'd done his homework. Kelly nodded. "Yes, I do, Mr. Gretsky. I live in Washington, D.C."

"So, selling this property wouldn't be out of the question, would it?" He cocked his head with studied casualness.

Kelly decided to cut to the chase, so Gretsky would leave and she could get back to her knitting. "Normally, that would be true. However, I learned my aunt recently refinanced and the mortgage terms include very heavy penalties if the property is sold within two years. So, I'm afraid I'll be renting the property instead of selling, Mr. Gretsky. But I'll be sure to keep your card for the future."

Gretsky's disappointment was clearly evident. "I'm, well, I'm sorry to hear that, Ms. Flynn. There are some clients of mine who were most interested in this location." He shook his head and frowned. "Listen, let me check into some things, and I'll get back to you, all right?"

Not really, Kelly thought, but replied, "If you wish, Mr. Gretsky, but I'm afraid it's a waste of your time."

"Maybe not," he said as he turned to leave. "Maybe there's a way to work things out. Meanwhile, you have a good day now." He flashed another bright smile and a wave as he left.

Kelly exhaled a loud sigh as she returned to her knitting. "You gotta love salesmen. If there's a breath left in a corpse, they'll revive it to get a sale."

Megan giggled. "Well, at least he wasn't too pushy."

"Give him time. I sense he won't give up."

After a few quiet minutes, Megan asked, "Have you looked into the consulting ideas yet?"

"No, not yet. I've been so involved in . . . in . . ." Kelly hesitated. How much should she reveal of Helen's past? Would she be disloyal to Helen's memory if she told her friends? Helen was dead. Murdered. And Kelly sensed the real killer was not the man in jail. Perhaps Megan and the others could help in her search for answers.

"You don't have to explain, Kelly. You've been up to your neck in trying to sort through Helen's things and get yourself settled since you got here. Don't worry. You'll have plenty of time to check into the possibilities. Then maybe you won't need Mr. Smiley's services after all." Megan looked up with a wicked grin.

"Yeah, maybe you're right. Meanwhile, there're some other things I need—"

"Hey, there! Missed you yesterday," Jennifer declared as she breezed in and plopped into a chair beside Kelly. She pulled out the nearly finished emerald green sweater. "I'm on break so let's do some quick catch-up. I assume Megan has already told you about the wool found by the river, right?"

"Yes, I did, and Kelly is just as suspicious as we were that it hadn't been found before."

"Okay then," Jennifer's needles began moving quickly. "What I want to know now is how was your meeting with Helen's cousin, yesterday? Was she as timid as she looked?"

Kelly watched Jennifer's needles and wondered if they could keep up with Jennifer's quick tongue. "Actually, yes. She clearly doesn't do well with strangers, but once I told her I was Helen's niece, she relaxed. Sort of."

"Helen has a cousin?" Megan asked in surprise. "I never knew."

"Neither did I. So you can imagine my surprise when Lizzie told me last Friday. Helen never mentioned her."

"Lizzie was kind enough to show us this cousin for a price," Jennifer added.

Megan laughed. "Let me guess. She invited you to church."

"Yep. And brunch afterward at the Jefferson Hotel. Believe me, only the thought of those cinnamon rolls got me through the sermon." Jennifer gave an aggrieved sigh.

"Thanks to Lizzie, I was able to recognize Martha at the Monday morning service. There weren't many people around, so she didn't run away when I approached her. In fact, she invited me to her house in Landport yesterday afternoon for a visit."

"Really? That's great. Did she know anything about why Helen needed money?" Jennifer probed.

"Not a thing. In fact, when I told her, she was visibly upset." Kelly saw their rapt expressions and leaned forward, lowering her voice, even though no one else was near. "She told me Helen had been bothered recently by something or someone from her past."

"Someone from her past had been bothering Helen?" Megan whispered, eyes wide.

"What kind of someone?" Jennifer pried. "A good someone or a not-so-good someone?"

"That's what bothers Martha, and me, too. Especially now that she's told me the rest." She purposefully paused. Both Jennifer and Megan leaned forward simultaneously, obviously waiting.

"Well?" Jennifer demanded. "You can't tease us with this Helen-has-a-past tidbit, then drop us. You know we'll pry it out of you eventually."

"You have to promise me you will absolutely keep it to yourselves, no one else. Except Lisa. I'll tell Mimi and Burt this afternoon. Okay? I feel disloyal enough as it is."

"Disloyal? Why?" Jennifer challenged. "Helen's been murdered. Maybe this someone knows something that can trap the killer. Heck, maybe he *is* the killer. Or she."

"That's what I told myself," Kelly admitted. "Okay, here goes. Martha confided that Helen had an illegitimate child right after high school. Her father sent her to Wyoming to live with Martha's family until the baby was born and placed for adoption. Helen and Martha became real close during that time, because they were both the same age. Anyway, Helen's father said she couldn't come home unless she gave up the baby. So, she did as she was ordered and afterward, returned to Fort Connor. According to Martha, Helen met Uncle Jim that next spring and married him in the fall."

"Wow," Megan breathed softly. Even her knitting needles slowed.

"Do you think your uncle Jim was the father?" Jennifer offered. "Maybe they couldn't marry until they were eighteen or something like that."

Kelly shook her head. "No. I remember Uncle Jim telling me he'd just come into town after getting out of the army, and he bought this piece of land for a sheep farm. Then he met Helen on a blind date. One of his army buddies introduced them." She went back to her own knitting as she continued. "Martha said Helen never mentioned the baby again. Or anything about that episode in her life, until last month. Helen came over and looked really worried, according to Martha. She asked Helen what was wrong, and all Helen would say was 'our sins come back to haunt us, don't they?'"

"Uh oh."

"Sounds like the kid found out who his mother was and showed up." Jennifer said. "I've heard of that happening."

"Or the father came back into her life, maybe," Megan suggested.

"Yeah, I figured it had to be one or the other. Or both. Who knows? So I spent all yesterday afternoon going through every drawer and storage cabinet in the cottage, searching for some clues to this child's identity. Or the father's."

"Did you find anything?"

"Nothing about the child. No documents, birth records, nothing. But I did find something interesting in her senior yearbook."

"Ahhh, yes, those god-awful records of our socially challenged years. I burned mine."

Kelly had to smile. "Well, I'm glad Helen didn't. Because I saw a great photo and personal inscription from this hunky cowboy, and I'm going to see what I can find out about him. Seems he still lives in the area. He's a rancher, from what I found on the Web."

Megan grinned. "Let me guess. You Googled him."

"Sure did. None of us can hide anymore. A simple Web search can track us down," Kelly joked.

"Forget the Web. I want to see the photo," Jennifer demanded. "A hunky cowboy from Helen's past. Sounds promising." She glanced at her watch, then shoved her knitting into the tote bag. "Gotta get back to work. Talk to you folks later. And I expect to see that photo."

"Will do," Kelly promised as Jennifer sped away.

"Wow . . ." Megan said again. "This is all so surprising. I mean, it doesn't change my feelings about Helen at all. If anything, it deepens my respect for her that she'd make that kind of sacrifice."

"That's how I feel," Kelly said, relieved to see her faith in her friends was justified.

Rosa leaned around the doorway to the classroom area. "Megan, did you want to see the new designer magazines before I put them on display?" she asked.

Megan nearly leaped from her chair. "You bet," she exclaimed and dropped her knitting on the table as she sped from the room. "Be back in a minute, Kelly," she called.

Kelly continued knitting in silence, adding row after colorful row to her scarf, surprised how peaceful it felt. Soon, she'd finish this first skein and have to start the second. Now, how did Jennifer say to join those ends, she searched her memory?

"Well, good morning, Kelly, I was hoping to see you here," Burt's deep voice cut through the quiet.

"Hi, Burt," Kelly said with a warm smile. "You here to teach a class?"

"Naw, I'm here for my morning constitutional," he joked. "Mimi probably told you I come every morning to spin some of her fleeces. Hafta confess I enjoy the spinning a heckuva lot more than that exercise regimen the doc's got me on."

"I bet. Hey, can you do it out here? I'd love to watch. I've heard those classes going on in the background, but I haven't had a chance to watch yet."

"Sure thing. Actually, this spot by the windows is my favorite. All the sunlight sure feels good," he said as he grasped the spinning wheel in the opposite corner and carried it closer to the windows. "There, now," he said, settling the interesting-looking contraption next to a rocker.

"Boy, it sure doesn't look like Martha Washington's spinning wheel at Mount Vernon," Kelly observed as she watched Burt open a bottom cupboard and pull out a large plastic bag. "Is that what you spin?"

Burt settled into the rocker and grabbed two handfuls of the creamy white fibers in the bag. "Yes, this is a fleece. Straight from the sheep. Cleaned and carded, of course."

Searching her memory for Mount Vernon trivia, she found one. "Carding, that's done on those square things with teeth?"

Burt grinned. "Yep, you have to remove all the unwanted particles and stuff before you can spin it." All the time he spoke, his fingers were pulling the puffy white cloud of fibers apart. "What I'm doing now is to get the fibers separated into what's called *roving* so they're easier to spin. Now, just watch," he instructed.

Kelly was already watching, fascinated by the intricate movements. Burt's fingers wound the roving around a slender spool, then held it taut as his feet started the wheel turning. Slowly the fibers started twisting into a strand of yarn, which fed onto the wheel and wound onto a wooden bobbin.

"Wow," she said after watching the rhythmic motions for a few moments. "Look at how much you've done already," pointing to the bobbin filling with yarn.

"Yeah, and look how much is still in the bag," Burt joked.

Kelly settled back with her knitting, listening to the soft hum of the wheel, and sorted through the competing questions in her head. Which to ask first?

"I guess you heard that the police brought some wool over here for Mimi to identify," she ventured. "Apparently Helen was knitting a purple sweater when she was killed. And the killer stole it. Broke a knitting needle, too. Lieutenant Morrison told me they found the needles and remaining skein of yarn lying beside her body."

She watched Burt for a reaction, but didn't see any. He continued to concentrate on his spinning for a moment before he spoke. "What else did Morrison say?"

"Nothing. Other than they never found the sweater when they were searching the house or vicinity. I asked him straight out why would the killer steal a half-finished sweater? Morrison simply stared back and said he didn't know." Kelly shook her head. "He also told me they made an exhaustive search of the riverbank area at the time. But now, only yesterday, they find some pieces of Helen's wool, burned no less." She deliberately infused the last words with skepticism, hoping to incite a comment.

Burt continued to spin without a word, so Kelly decided to simply pour out her concerns. She was tired of keeping it inside. "You know, Burt, that makes no sense at all. If this drunk really was the killer, why would he take time to steal Helen's knitting? I mean, he'd already grabbed her purse full of money, right?"

"That's a good question," Burt replied, minding the wool.

Encouraged by the positive response, Kelly kept on. "Something else is missing from the cottage, Burt. Helen's heirloom quilt is no longer on the wall where it's always been. Mimi and the others searched every nook and cranny in the house and garage and never found it. I told Lieutenant Morrison, and he simply said Helen probably gave it to someone." She gave a dismissive sound. "But Helen would never do that, Burt. She made the quilt and meant it for me. It's a personal record of her family. No way would she give it away."

"Hmmmm," was all Burt said.

"And there's no way I'll believe that drunken vagrant stole it. After all, he's got Helen's purse in one hand and her knitting in the other. I mean, according to Lieutenant Morrison, that's what happened."

Burt smiled. "Boy, I'll bet Morrison's ears are really burning about now."

"Well, they should be." Kelly gave an indignant sniff. "It's so illogical, it's ludicrous. This guy is drunk and staggering, yet he's able to do all these intriguing complex maneuvers. I don't buy it, Burt."

"What do you believe happened?" Burt asked after a minute.

Kelly took a deep breath and plunged in. "I don't think that vagrant killed Helen. I think someone else did. And that someone else planted the burned wool near the river because that's where the vagrant slept. Making him look more guilty. But I think someone else murdered Helen for the money. Someone either found out about the money or asked her to get it for them. Why else would she take out that loan? And why would she keep it secret from me?"

The wheel finally stopped turning as Burt met Kelly's gaze. "Do you have any idea who that someone might be, Kelly?" he asked, voice somber.

"Not yet, Burt, but I'm going to find out," Kelly swore. "Helen's cousin told me yesterday that several weeks ago, Helen had been contacted by someone from her past, and she was very upset about it. She wouldn't tell her cousin who it was. I think this person contacted Helen and wanted money."

"Then why kill her?" Burt countered. "She had the money right there."

Kelly glanced toward the sunshine. "I don't know, Burt. Maybe something went wrong. Or maybe, it wasn't enough money. Something happened, and Helen wound up dead. The money was stolen. And the quilt, too."

Burt frowned. "The quilt doesn't make sense. Neither does the knitted sweater. Money, yes. Those things, no."

"I know, I know," Kelly gestured impatiently. "There are too many loose ends. That's what drives me crazy."

Burt started the wheel again, his fingers returning to their rhythmic movements as the bobbin filled. "I'll make a couple of phone calls. On the quiet. Don't want to step on any toes, but I still have my contacts in the department. I'll let you know what I find out, okay?"

An immense burden seemed to lift from her shoulders. At last, her suspicions were taken seriously. "Thank you, Burt, I cannot tell you how much I appreciate your help."

"Don't get your hopes up, I'm only going to ask a few questions."

Kelly was about to thank him again, when she spotted a familiar white truck with red and blue stripes come down the driveway. Her office files had arrived at last.

Ten

Mimi toyed with the teaspoon. She'd stirred her cup of Earl Grey tea so much, Kelly was sure it was cold as a stone by now. "This is so very disturbing, Kelly," she said after a moment. "In a way, it was almost comforting to believe that Helen's death was a random act of violence. But now . . ."

"I know," Kelly picked up the thought. "Now, there's a real possibility that the killer knew her, and that's a very scary thought."

"Frightening," Mimi agreed and shivered. "I cannot imagine who this person from her past might be, can you?"

Kelly glanced around the empty café. Pete didn't mind if Mimi's staff entered after closing. Sometimes it was the only private spot available. She leaned back into the wooden chair and swirled the dregs of her coffee. She'd deliberately waited until nearly closing to speak with Mimi, not only to avoid the afternoon customer rush, but also so she could make progress on her office accounts.

Responsibilities had landed with the delivery of her corporate client files. Kelly was amazed how foreign these accounts looked to her after nearly three weeks away from them. Her mind had drifted so far from corporate accounting issues, she wondered at first if she could lasso it back. That image made her laugh. Coming back home to the West was affecting her in more ways than she knew.

"I'm guessing either the child found out his birth mother's identity and approached Helen, or the father reentered her life. I searched every place I could in the cottage but found nothing about the child. However, I may have found a clue about the father in Helen's high school yearbook."

"Really? What was it?"

"There's a very personal inscription on one of the photos. It's not much, but it's something." Kelly drained the last drops, grounds and all, and screwed up her face at the bitter taste. "His name's Curtis Stackhouse, and he's a rancher in northern Colorado apparently. Unfortunately, I couldn't find much personal information on the Web. I've found notations of land sales, he's listed as a livestock breeder, both sheep and steers. There's a photo of him judging sheep at a state fair years ago. Calves, too. He's a member of various organizations but they didn't list addresses or phone numbers. And he's not listed in the phone directory at all. In fact, there're no Stackhouses listed."

"Hmmm, Stackhouse," Mimi pondered, staring off into the darkened café. "I don't recall that name. But Steve would probably know."

"Steve? Why would he know?"

Mimi smiled. "Steve's family has been in Fort Connor for generations. I think his great-grandfather farmed here in the 1880s or some such. His father used to be one of the biggest ranchers and landowners in northern Colorado. Over the years, of course, he's sold most of it, but his father knew just about every ranching family that ever lived here. And Steve has probably met most of them growing up. His mom and dad used to throw big barbeques every summer." Mimi's expression grew wistful. "I remember going to those parties. There was music and great food outside in the summertime. Oh my, they were nice."

Kelly deliberately said nothing, not wanting to disturb Mimi's memory. She wondered how she could pump Steve for information without revealing Helen's past. Immersed in her thoughts, she was startled at the sound of Rosa's voice.

"Connie's on the phone. She doesn't think she can help Megan with the trip to the wool festival tomorrow. She's home sick with stomach flu. Do you want to talk with her?" Rosa asked as she leaned around the archway into the café.

"Ohhh, no!" Mimi exclaimed. "Poor girl. Let me talk with her," she said and left to grab the white portable in Rosa's hand. "Don't leave yet, Kelly."

Kelly grabbed her empty mug, wishing Pete left some coffee, and headed back into the bright lights of the shop. Checking her watch, she realized Carl was probably visualizing roast squirrel for dinner. It was dusk outside already. If she left now, she could run by the shopping center and buy groceries. She didn't think she could face peach yogurt again.

Rosa was going through the familiar closing routine. Kelly grabbed her tote bag and was about to leave when Mimi called out, "Wait, Kelly. I need to ask you a favor."

"Sure, what is it?" Kelly answered as Mimi hastened toward her.

"I was counting on Connie to help out Megan tomorrow morning. We're taking a group of our senior knitters to a wool festival up near Rocky Mountain National Park. We've got five ladies signed up, and Megan will need help driving them over and back. Would you be able to go with them tomorrow?" she asked. "It would take the whole morning and early afternoon, probably. I know that's asking a lot, Kelly. After all, you just got your files and you're working—"

Kelly held up her hand. "I'll be happy to help out, Mimi. No problem. I can work ahead tonight, so I can take off tomorrow morning," she said with a reassuring smile. "Besides, it'll be good to get up in the mountains."

Mimi beamed. "Ohhh, thank you, Kelly. That's so sweet. You'll enjoy the festival, too. There are sheep and alpaca and llamas and demonstrations and vendors. Goodness, if it has to do with wool, it's there."

"Sounds like fun," Kelly said, heading toward the door. "I'm going to the grocery store already, so I'll gas up the car for tomorrow."

"Oh, don't worry about that. We won't need your car. Steve's taking his truck. As a matter of fact, you can ask him about that rancher while you're riding into the mountains."

That caught Kelly by surprise. "Steve? Why's he going?"

"He volunteered to pick up this loom that I ordered," Mimi said over her shoulder as she headed toward her office. Rosa was already turning off lights. "The craftsman will be at the festival, and I simply don't have a vehicle big enough to carry that thing. Thanks, again, Kelly. See you in the morning. Nine o'clock would be great." She turned a corner and was gone.

Kelly frowned after her. Sneaky, Mimi. Very sneaky.

* * *

"I'll let you ladies out here," Steve said and aimed the truck to the side of a huge exhibition building, away from the packed parking areas. "That way you won't have to walk far. The entrance is right around the corner." He pointed toward the crowd of people milling around the front.

Kelly was amazed at how many people were already at the festival, and it was only mid-morning. She couldn't remember being at these fairgrounds before. Maybe they were new, she thought, as she read the signs hanging over several of the barns spread out in a horseshoe. Sheep. Alpaca. Llamas.

"Oh, thank you, Steve, dear. You're such a gentleman," Lizzie said. "Isn't he, Kelly?"

"Oh, indeed, he is, Lizzie," Kelly agreed, trying not to smile as she shouldered open the passenger door of Steve's big red truck. Glad she'd worn sneakers and jeans, Kelly easily hopped to the ground and offered her hand to Lizzie. Even with the built-in step below the running board, the petite little knitter would need help making it to the ground.

Now that she was back in the West, Kelly reacquainted herself quickly with the oversized vehicles that filled city streets and county roads as well as interstates—the Serious Trucks, or as her dad used to say, "trucks with attitude." Kelly wondered if every owner needed a whole cavalry worth of horsepower and towing capacity, especially when she saw most of them parked outside grocery stores, garden centers, and fast food restaurants—sparkling clean with nary a speck of dirt of them. She checked out the huge tires on Steve's truck. They were caked with mud.

She wasn't surprised. Thanks to Lizzie, Kelly had heard about Steve's latest building project, his next development planned north of town, how he started his business, his college career, all the academic as well as athletic honors, why he chose getting his hands dirty building houses after obtaining his architect's degree rather than working in an office, his family's connections to Fort Connor, and on and on. Kelly was truly impressed at Lizzie's grilling techniques. She'd put any corporate interviewer to shame. Kelly half-expected Lizzie to ask Steve his bank balance.

To Steve's credit, he'd tried several times on the hour-long ride into the mountains to change the conversation. Kelly would pick up his lead and Lizzie would cooperate for a few minutes. Or until one of them stopped for a breath. Then, straight as any marksman who's found his target, she'd return to probing Steve.

Steve would catch Kelly's eye overtop Lizzie's immaculately coiffed silver-gray hair and grin, then politely, good-naturedly answer her questions.

"Grab hold, and I'll help you down, Lizzie," Kelly offered.

Lizzie scooted herself to the edge of the seat, which was difficult because she was wearing yards of rose pink cotton, gathered fetchingly with, what else, but white lace. "Oh my," she declared, eyes wide. "It's so far down."

"Don't worry, Lizzie. Let me help you." Steve stepped up and in one smooth movement had picked up Lizzie and deposited her safely on the ground.

"Ohhhh, thank you, you're *so* considerate," Lizzie chirped, hand fluttering at her breast. "Isn't he, dear?"

"To a fault," Kelly concurred obediently, watching Steve turn to hide his grin.

The unmistakable whine of bagpipes sounded suddenly, and Kelly was about to ask who they were, when Megan strode up.

"I've found them, ladies," she called over her shoulder to the little gaggle following in her wake. "I almost lost you guys when you went right past the parking lot."

"It'll be easier for me to load the loom here. The builder said I could use his space," Steve explained.

"Ladies! I hear bagpipes. Hurry up, or we'll miss them," Lizzie called to Megan's charges.

"Okay," Megan glanced at the ladies, then Kelly. "Let's get them all inside together, pick a meeting place, then let them scatter."

"Sounds like you've done this before," Steve said with a chuckle.

"Oh, yeah." Megan nodded, waving her charges forward. Lizzie was already heading toward the entrance. "Steve, I'll call you on your cell when we're ready to round 'em up and leave. Will you be here the whole time?"

"Yeah, I've gotta track down this guy and load the loom and

secure it for the ride back." He glanced around. "Don't worry. I'll amuse myself. I already recognize some people I know, plus I'll check out the vendors. Good luck, you two," he added before he strode off.

"Anything I should know? I've never chaperoned seniors or knitters before," Kelly teased as they fell in behind the ladies.

"Yeah, matter of fact," Megan said, pulling the entrance tickets from her jeans pocket. "Keep an eye on Lizzie, okay? She's prone to mischief sometimes—"

The rest of her sentence was drowned out by the bagpipers' nasal hum and whine. As the little group rounded the corner, there were the pipers—bagpipes wailing and plaids fluttering in the mountain spring breeze—cutting a swath through the crowds. Kelly felt her blood stir as it always did at the sound of the pipes. Her dad used to say it was "the Irish" stirring in her. The pipers, twelve in all, headed toward the livestock barns, while spectators paused at food stands and llama lectures to watch. Kelly noticed a young boy bringing up the rear with a placard proclaiming the upcoming Battle of the Bagpipes that weekend.

"Okay, ladies, here're your tickets," Megan waved the packet in the air. "Let's get inside and find a meeting place, then you ladies are on your own." The ladies flocked around, accepting their tickets and obediently handing them to the door attendant.

All except one, Kelly noticed. Lizzie stood, staring after the departing pipers as if mesmerized, the pipes fading into the distance. "Come on, Lizzie," Kelly encouraged, taking her arm and guiding her to the door. "Let's go inside and see the wonderful world of wool."

"Very well, dear," Lizzie acquiesced with an audible sigh. "Those pipers were magnificent, weren't they? Such strapping men, too. Don't you think? I especially noticed the tallest one in the back with the gray beard. My, my, he was a handsome devil."

"Uh, yes, I suppose they were," Kelly agreed, a little surprised at Lizzie's turn of thought.

"I wonder if they're real Scotsmen. What do you think?"

"Ahhh, gee, Lizzie, I really don't know," Kelly admitted, shepherding her through the doorway and into the cavernous hall.

"I've always wondered what a Scotsman wears beneath his kilt," Lizzie said, as causally as if she were describing a new yarn. "Do you know, dear?"

Kelly barely heard her, her attention was already captivated by the myriad variety of vendors' booths and stalls that stretched almost as far as she could see. "Uhhh, no, Lizzie, not really," she replied, absently.

Megan's voice cut through Kelly's fascination long enough to imprint where and when they were all to meet for the return trip. Sorting that tidbit away, Kelly felt the pull of the colors and textures all calling out to her at once—come and touch. She gave an offhand wave to Lizzie as she merged with the clusters of people moving between booths. "See you later, Lizzie. Enjoy yourself."

"Oh, I will, dear. Don't worry about me."

With that, Kelly dove into the colorful sea surrounding her, floating from stall to stall—fingering lace so delicate she was sure it was cobwebs, not thread at all, knitted sweaters and shawls in every color and texture imaginable, and weaving like she'd never seen before. Nubbly and patterned. Fabric so fine and soft, she was sure it was woven by fairies. Kelly was amazed at the designs. Some were worn, others were hung as art. And, indeed it was. Dazzling colors and designs that tempted you to touch as well as admire.

Kelly immersed herself in the sensation of it all, drifting happily through the busy aisles, stroking fabrics and squeezing twisted coils of wool and mohair and alpaca in every hue, brazen and demure. The silk vendors' stalls held her captive as she caressed the sinfully soft selections. Hand-painted or blended with fibers less regal, Kelly swore it whispered her name, just as it did in the shop every time she passed. Perhaps she'd become good enough to knit that sweater after all. Maybe. She was nearly finished with the chunky scarf.

It was only when she caught sight of a food vendor's hot dogs and her stomach growled did Kelly notice the time. Whoa. She'd been wandering for over two hours. Only an hour and a half left to sightsee. Indulging the sudden craving for a hot dog with all the trimmings, Kelly also grabbed a soda and left the exhibition hall. She really owed it to herself to visit the animals that provided the luxurious fibers for all those glorious creations.

Walking toward the livestock barns, Kelly glanced at the mountains and took in her breath. She hadn't been up here to the national park in years. She'd forgotten how gorgeous it was. The views of the Rockies were stunning, as sun glinted off the glacier-tipped peaks.

She lingered at the llama lecture, as a man explained the varied abilities the stately animals possessed. The llama stood patiently, clearly used to being ogled and examined, while the handler pointed out the animal's qualities to a cluster of listeners.

From there she wandered toward the barn with the alpacas, similar to llamas but a bit smaller. There, the breeders were holding forth as eager owners-to-be gathered around and asked questions. Kelly noticed all the blue and red ribbons adorning the stalls. Here, the alpacas watched *her* and came up to the fence as if posing for a photo. Kelly was convinced they looked disappointed she didn't have a camera.

She also couldn't help noticing the heightened level of care and nurturing lavished on these interesting animals. Most stalls had carpets covering the dirt. And the owners were quick to clean up any of nature's occurrences, lest their expensive animals step in anything. Perusing a newspaper article on the growing alpaca business with the title, "Have You Hugged Your Investment Today?" she could see why the owners were so solicitous. Each animal was worth tens of thousands of dollars.

Kelly was pondering why until she spotted the spinners with their wheels. There, she sank her hands into a loose skein of one hundred percent alpaca wool and understood at last. Soft, soft, luxuriously soft. Unbelievably soft. Creams, grays, browns, combinations of all, even a stunning tweed.

She began to notice the intricate patterns on the animals' bodies and saw that the spun wool often varied in color as well. Before leaving the barn, Kelly glanced over her shoulder once more and could have sworn she spied an alpaca smirking at her, as if to say, "Told you."

Draining the last of her soda, Kelly tossed the can into a handy trash barrel and headed toward the sheep barn. Here, the familiar sound of bleating filled the air, and she realized another alpaca bonus. They were quiet.

Lambs prodded into an unruly judging line protested each maneuver. Some were as docile as their reputation. Others were unrepentant troublemakers and made Kelly laugh out loud with their antics.

"He's having none of this," Steve observed as he drew beside her.

Kelly chuckled. "You know, it's been ages since I've been around farm animals. I'd forgotten how much fun it was."

"It's fun to watch, all right. But if you have to clean up after them, that's another story." Steve shoved his hands in his back pockets. "Helen told me they had sheep in the early days, until it cost them more to raise than they fetched at market."

Kelly closed her eyes to recall. "You know, I can still remember the sheep. It was when I was real little. Then they sold them off." She shook her head. "It just didn't pay in those days. If Uncle Jim hadn't had his job with the state highway department, they never would have made it. Finally, he started boarding peoples' horses, and that helped a lot. At least it allowed them to keep the farm."

"Let's go over there," Steve said, pointing across the barn. "That's the best of breed awards."

They skirted around the younger animals, and Kelly spotted the huge adult sheep. Wow. She'd forgotten how big the woolly creatures could get. A huge black ram strutted past them, head high, clearly lord of the realm. Kelly had to agree. He was magnificent.

As she and Steve strolled slowly around the fenced judging area, Kelly noticed three men standing and talking. Two were dressed in corporate attire—suits, ties, and shiny shoes—definitely out of place in a barn where one could, and frequently did, step in something. The other man, taller than his companions, was dressed appropriately in Colorado Cowboy Modern—jeans, boots, denim shirt, and a Stetson. Something about the man was familiar, and Kelly found herself staring. Fortunately, the man was actively listening to his companions and didn't notice her.

"I thought we'd spy Lizzie here," Steve spoke up. "She was headed down toward the livestock barns a little while ago."

"Lizzie was heading to the livestock barns?" Kelly repeated, surprised for some reason. Dainty little Lizzie didn't strike her as a budding alpaca breeder. Of course, she could have been after the wool.

Steve shrugged. "Well, that's where I assumed she was going. She was actually talking to one of the Scottish bagpipers when I saw her, but they were close to the barns, so I figured—"

Kelly grabbed his arm. "Wha-what did you say?"

"I said she was talking to one of the bagpipers." Steve peered at her. "Anything wrong?"

The memory of Lizzie's curiosity about the Scotsman's undergarments suddenly flashed through Kelly's mind, along with Megan's earlier warning: "Keep an eye on Lizzie. She's prone to mischief."

"Oh my gosh," breathed Kelly. "We'd better find her. *Now!*" She turned and raced from the barn.

"Why? Hey, where're—?" Steve called out then hastened after her. "What's the matter?" he demanded when he caught up.

"Megan warned me to keep an eye on Lizzie before we split," Kelly explained while they threaded their way through masses of people. The crowds had increased since morning. "She said Lizzie could get into mischief. I didn't know what she meant until now."

"What kind of mischief is she talking about? I mean, she's nearly seventy, isn't she?"

"That may be, but Lizzie was transfixed by the bagpipers earlier, particularly one of them she described as 'a handsome devil.'" Hearing Steve's laughter, Kelly shot him a look. "It's not funny."

"Yeah, it is."

"Not when her last question to me when we entered the hall was, 'What do Scotsmen wear beneath their kilts?'" Kelly noticed heads turning on that one, and the crowd seemed to part around her. She felt Steve's hand on her arm.

"Wait a minute," he said between spurts of laughter. "You can't seriously think that sweet little old lady would . . ." He gestured aimlessly.

"I don't know, but I don't want to find out, either. Megan will kill me when she finds out," Kelly declared.

"Kill you when I find out what?" Megan asked, drawing beside them. She took a big bite of a chili dog.

Kelly decided she'd better wait until Megan swallowed or they'd have to stop the Lizzie search and administer the Heimlich maneuver on Megan. "Uhhh, we're just looking for Lizzie. Steve saw her around the barns. We don't want her to get lost."

Megan gulped. "Lizzie? Where is she? What's she doing?" She peered around the crowds.

"Well, you said to keep an eye on her." Kelly angled toward the sheep barn once more, craning her neck to see around the crowds. "Where did you see her, Steve?"

"Actually, she was right beside the barn when—" He stopped and pointed. "Wait a minute, isn't that her right over there?"

Kelly followed the line of sight and caught a glimpse of an unmistakable pink cotton skirt fluttering in the spring breeze. People were still blocking her view, but it had to be Lizzie, she thought with a sigh of relief. "Oh, good, there she is," she said and hastened to shepherd the wayward little knitter back into the fold. Until Steve reached out and caught her arm.

"Wait, hold on," Steve said as he peered above the crowds. "Uh oh . . ."

"What? What's the matter?" Megan demanded, weaving side to side, trying to see around people. "What's she doing?"

Steve started to laugh. "You . . . you don't wanta know," he managed before he bent over double, laughing.

Kelly's heart skipped a beat, and she shouldered her way between two husky men so she could see what Steve was talking about. When she did, she came to an abrupt halt and stared, mouth open.

There was Lizzie, all right, but she wasn't alone. She was still talking with the tall, handsome-devil Scotsman. Talking and looking. The Scotsman stood, hands on hips, while Lizzie demurely held up his plaid kilt, observed for a few seconds, then lowered it once again.

Kelly saw a slight movement to her left. Megan's chili dog dropped to the dirt. She stared horrified, face beet-red. Steve, meanwhile, was still bent over with silent laughter, hands on his knees. Obviously, it would be up to her to handle the situation, Kelly decided, and snapped out of shock mode. She cleared her throat and yelled, "*Lizzie!* We need you back with the others *now!*"

Lizzie turned and waved, smiling brightly. "Coming, dears," she chirped as if nothing unusual had just occurred.

"Oh . . . my . . . God . . ." Megan whispered. "I don't believe she did that."

"Believe it. Now I know what you mean by mischief," Kelly said, shaking her head.

Meanwhile, Lizzie was bidding farewell to the grinning bagpiper, who kissed her hand before she rejoined them. That seemed to delight her no end. "What an adorable and obliging gentleman," she cooed, when she rejoined them.

Kelly grabbed Lizzie's elbow and steered her back toward the exhibition hall. "That's an understatement," she muttered to Megan, who still had a slightly glazed look.

Steve had finally stopped laughing, out loud at least. "Folks, I've got the loom all loaded and tied down, so whenever you want or need to head back into town, let me know."

"Ohhh, thank you, dear," Lizzie said. "But I haven't even seen the wool exhibits yet."

Kelly shot Steve an I-don't-believe-she-said-that look, and he turned his head to hide more laughter.

When they approached the hall entrance, Megan stepped up and encircled Lizzie's arm possessively. "Now, Lizzie, you're going to stay with me while we see the exhibits, okay? No disappearing allowed, understand?" She leveled a stern gaze at Lizzie.

Clearly unflappable and unfazed, Lizzie beamed. "Of course, dear. We'll see everything together. Oh, do you think we might have a spot of lunch, first? I'm simply famished."

"Let's meet the others first. Then we'll all go together," Megan agreed, then turned to Steve. "Listen, Peggy is staying here with a weaver she knows, so I'll be able to take everyone back with me, Steve. You and Kelly can go on back into town. Kelly, I know you've just gotten your accounts, so you're probably swamped."

"You sure you won't need any more help?" Kelly gestured, adding pointedly, "I mean, can you handle everything?"

Megan nodded in schoolmarm fashion. "Oh, yes. We're meeting the others in ten minutes. I'll have some help then. Don't worry. We're fine now. Ready, Lizzie?"

"Oh my, yes," she enthused. "I'm so excited."

Megan refrained from comment, instead guiding Lizzie through the entrance.

Kelly stood, hands on hips, and shook her head, watching the little round knitter wave good-bye before she disappeared inside the hall. "But, I haven't seen the wool exhibits, dear," she said, in a breathless imitation of Lizzie.

"I think she's seen enough," Steve said with a laugh.

It was contagious, and Kelly joined in, laughing at the bizarre scene they'd just witnessed. No one at the shop would believe it. Or maybe they would. After all, they've known Lizzie longer. How on earth would she explain it to Mimi?

"My truck is parked on the other side of the building," Steve said, looking over the crowd. "We can stop for some coffee on the way out if you want to leave now."

Kelly's taste buds tingled in anticipation. She was about to reply when a man's voice caught her attention, and she turned around. There were the men she'd noticed from the sheep barn, standing only a few feet behind them. City Suit was introducing a fourth man to Colorado Cowboy. Something he'd said caught her attention, what was it?

"What are—" Steve started then paused, when she held up her hand. She focused on the group, blatantly eavesdropping.

"Jeff," City Suit said to the newcomer. "I want you to meet Curt Stackhouse. He's been good enough to guide us through this land deal."

Kelly drew in a deep breath, observing Colorado Cowboy as he smiled and shook hands all around. Of course, she thought. That's why he looked familiar earlier. He's got the same smile. The same face. Older, of course.

"Do you know them?" Steve asked in a low voice.

"Well, not really, but . . ." she hesitated, wondering how she would explain. More importantly, now that she found Stackhouse, how would she introduce herself, let alone ask him questions?

"Well, you're sure acting funny," Steve observed.

Suddenly Kelly got a wild idea. She'd need Steve's cooperation, though. It was crazy, but it was the only chance she had. Now that she'd found Stackhouse, she wasn't about to lose him until she knew where he lived. "Uh, Steve, would you be willing to . . . to . . . uh, take a ride with me?" she ventured.

"We're already planning to take a ride back into town, remember?" he joked.

"I mean another ride. Before we go home."

"I guess that depends on where."

She exhaled a breath. "I don't know yet. Wherever that tall guy in the Stetson is going. Once he splits from the city guys, I mean." She gestured behind her.

Steve peered first at the men then at her. "And why do you want to follow him?"

"Well . . . it's a long story," she confessed, glancing over her shoulder to make sure they were still there. "Let's just say I need to know where this guy lives, so I can talk with him. Ask him some questions."

"Why don't you talk with him now? He's right behind you." Steve was observing her very carefully.

"Uhhh, it's kinda hard to explain—"

"Try."

"Too many people around. It . . . it has to do with Helen," she admitted finally.

"With Helen or with what happened?" he probed.

Kelly met his level gaze. "He's a link to her past. And I'm hoping he knows something or someone. I'll . . . I'll explain later."

Steve stared at the men again for a long moment. "It'll be tricky. We don't know where he's parked or what he's driving."

Kelly pondered that for a minute. "Well, I could follow him while you get the truck, but we'd have to meet . . ."

"I know. Give me your cell phone," he said, hand outstretched.

Kelly dug into her pocket and withdrew the phone. Steve took it, punched in numbers, then returned it. "That's my cell number. You follow this guy while I get the truck. I'll park along the side of the road over there and wait." He pointed past the gates. "Call me when you've seen him getting into his vehicle, then come out to the road where I can pick you up, okay?"

Great idea, Kelly had to admit. "Okay, got it." She nodded, then teased, "You sound like you've done this before."

"Just don't lose him," Steve advised, turning back into the crowd. "This better be good, Kelly," he called over his shoulder.

Eleven

"Mimi thought you might know this guy or his family," Kelly said, observing the new spring grass that stood a foot tall beside the winding road. "She said your father knew all the ranchers in the area."

"Stackhouse, Curtis Stackhouse," Steve repeated as he guided the truck around a curve. "That name is vaguely familiar, so I must have heard of him or met him once. Heck, it could have been years ago or last month. I meet a lot of landowners in my business. Some are ranchers, others want to be. And those guys definitely looked like buyers."

"You mean the 'suits'?"

Steve grinned. "Yeah, the city suits. They're buying land. You can smell it. Either for themselves or for a developer. I'll bet on the developer."

"Well, one guy said Stackhouse was 'guiding' them through a deal, so maybe you're right." Kelly focused on the big black truck farther ahead.

Their plan had worked perfectly, much to Kelly's relief. She'd merged with the crowd behind Stackhouse and companions and followed him all the way from their good-byes to his meandering stroll past the wool barns and a quick striding search for his parked truck. Once she'd glimpsed the mud-splattered vehicle and memorized the license plate, she phoned Steve and hastened to find him. They only had to wait a few minutes before Stackhouse's truck appeared, and they followed a safe distance behind. Now they were nearly out of the canyon leading from the national park and approaching the outskirts of the smaller towns surrounding Fort Connor.

"Should you speed up? We don't want to lose him when he gets to the edge of town," she urged.

"We're fine, relax. Besides, I've got some questions. You spent a lot of time explaining about this cousin Martha and how she got here from Wyoming and how close she was with Helen and how she was worried that someone from Helen's past came back to 'haunt' her. Then you searched the cottage and found the yearbook and Stackhouse's photo."

Kelly watched the mouth of the canyon open wide as the road straightened onto a rock-rimmed meadow. She sensed Steve zeroing in on the pertinent details she'd left unsaid. He didn't miss much, she'd noticed. "That's right."

"There's something you're not saying, I can tell. It makes no sense that a sweet lady like Helen would have done anything to cause a successful rancher like this Stackhouse to threaten her. Unless they were both involved in something illegal, like running drugs. But I kind of doubt Helen was a drug dealer." Steve glanced at Kelly. "So finish the story. Tell me what you're holding back. If you're worrying about Helen's privacy, don't. I promise I won't repeat what you say to a soul. Helen was pretty special to me, too."

Kelly believed him. "Yeah, you're right," she admitted with a sigh. "Sorry, it's hard to explain. That's why I'm being so closed-mouthed. I've only told my friends at the shop, because I don't want anyone to think less of Helen."

"That would be impossible. Unless she really was a drug dealer," he joked.

Steve's laughter helped Kelly let go. She proceeded to tell him the story.

"Wow," Steve said softly. "Any chance your uncle Jim could be the father?"

"Nope," Kelly said with a shake of her head. "He told me he met Helen on a blind date when he arrived in town and bought the farm."

"Hmmm."

"Yeah, that's what I said, too."

"And Helen was worried about this person?"

"She was worried about something, according to Martha."

"And no trace of the child's records?"

"None. I went through every drawer and cabinet and crevice, believe me. The only clue I found was that yearbook photo and the inscription from Stackhouse."

Steve shook his head. "I gotta tell you, Kelly, that's pretty slim."

"Don't I know it, but it's all I've got," Kelly admitted.

"How does the money play into it?"

Kelly shrugged. "I don't know. Maybe this person was blackmailing her or threatened her somehow. Maybe she tried to pay him off to leave her alone."

"Have you thought about what kinds of questions you're going to ask this guy? I mean, how're you going to approach him?"

"I'm still working on that," Kelly confessed.

"Well, work on it faster, because Stackhouse just put on his turn signal," Steve warned. "Bet he's taking that county road on the left."

Kelly felt her throat tighten. What *would* she say? She had to be careful not to arouse his suspicions. "Oh boy, well, I know I have to ease into it. I mean, I can't make him suspicious." She watched the huge black truck ahead and, sure enough, it turned left on the next road.

Steve slowed down, too. "I'm going to drop back a little so we won't be right on his tail."

It was all Kelly could do to hold her impatience in check while Steve deliberately waited for a long line of cars to pass in the opposite lane before he turned onto the county road. As they crested the hilly road, she relaxed. There, farther ahead, was the truck. "Thank goodness," she breathed.

"Okay, we've gotta have a cover story to explain why we're driving up on this guy's property."

"*We?*" Kelly shot him a quizzical look. "I don't need help asking questions."

"What were you expecting to do?" Steve countered. "Drive up his mile-long driveway, step out of the truck, and go ring his doorbell? Don't you think that would look a little strange? Who am I supposed to be, the taxi?"

Hmmm. He was right. That would definitely look strange. Rats. She hated it when he was right.

"Listen, I've got an idea," he said. "We've got a loom in the back, so why don't we say we're new to the area, just settling in, and you're a weaver."

"I can barely knit, now you want me to weave?"

Steve grinned. "Work with me, okay? We're newcomers, and we're buying land north of town. And we've been thinking about adding some sheep or alpaca—"

"I just saw an alpaca for the first time today. What if he asks me a question?"

"Just hand off to me, I'll answer. You're the weaver, and I want to start breeding alpaca—whoa, there he goes." Steve pointed ahead as the black truck turned onto a private road.

Kelly watched a dust cloud kick up in the truck's wake as they passed. There was a large, two-story white house in the distance and a sprawling red barn. She also noticed the fencing around Stackhouse's ranch was in good condition. Black and reddish brown cattle dotted one pasture, and she thought she spied sheep in a far meadow backing up to the foothills.

"We'll go down to the crossing then turn around," Steve suggested.

"Okay, I'm a weaver, and we want alpaca, and we're ignorant. But how do we explain why we're there?"

"We can say someone at the shop told us that he'd be a good person to give advice about this business."

Kelly nodded. It might not be great but it was better than what she had, which was nothing. "Okay, let's go with it. Let's just get him talking. I'll take it from there."

Steve slowed at the intersection of the two county roads and turned the truck around. "Good luck. Any idea how you're going to ease into it?"

"Not a clue," she replied as they approached the private road to Stackhouse's ranch. "I'll play it by ear. See what happens."

They turned onto the road and slowed, a cloud of dust billowing around the truck. "This'll be interesting," he said.

It certainly will be, Kelly thought, her mind sorting through and discarding one question after another as they followed the driveway all the way to the barnyard. To her surprise, Stackhouse emerged from the barn and, seeing them, walked to the side of the split rail fence bordering his pasture as they drove up.

"Okay," Steve advised, parking the truck. "Just keep that great smile, and we're halfway there."

If only a smile would do it. Kelly jumped from the truck to the ground, straightened her T-shirt, and forced her brightest "meet the client" smile. Corporate life had its benefits. She could talk to anyone now without showing the emotion within. But this was not the corporate world, and she'd need a folksy, just-starting-out innocence to appear natural. She took a deep breath. That would be harder to pull off. Kelly hadn't felt innocent in so long, she'd forgotten how.

Steve met her beside the truck. "Okay, here goes," he said, smile already in place.

Kelly fixed the brightest smile she could find as they started across the barnyard. Stackhouse stood waiting, hands on hips, Stetson pulled low. "Hi there!" Kelly chirped loudly, waving her hand as they drew nearer.

"Good afternoon, sir," Steve called out. "I hope we found the right ranch. Are you Curt Stackhouse?"

"Yes, I am. What can I do for you folks?" Stackhouse replied as Kelly and Steve paused a few feet from him.

"Well, then, we found the right place, honey," Steve said, glancing to her before he reached out to shake Stackhouse's hand. Kelly bit her cheek to keep from frowning at the familiarity. "I'm Steve Townsend, Mr. Stackhouse, and this—"

"Kelly Flynn, sir," she said, offering her hand to the tall rancher, who was observing them closely. Stackhouse shook her hand firmly. His hand was big and warm and calloused, a working rancher's hand.

"We're gonna be married this summer, and we'll be buying some land north of town pretty soon, maybe thirty acres or so," Steve said, then put his arm around Kelly's shoulders, drawing her closer. Kelly nearly bit her lip in two this time. Steve knew she wouldn't blow their cover by pushing him away.

"Really?" Stackhouse said, brow quirking. "Whereabouts?"

"We've been looking at some acreage near Wellesly. I'm renting in Fort Connor now because it's close to my job at Advanced Tech. I'm an engineer there. I came to the university years ago, well, and I haven't been able to leave since." Steve glanced around with a guile-less look. "It's so beautiful, I had to stay."

A smile tugged at the corners of Stackhouse's mouth. "I've heard that story a lot over the years," he said.

"And I've *always* wanted to come back," Kelly did her best to gush. "I grew up here when I was a little girl, until my dad had to take a job out of town. But I've always wanted to return. I've been working back East since college." She gestured, keeping her eyes Barbie-doll wide. "And then I met Stevie on a cruise, and it's just *so* wonderful! Now, I can come back home!" Her voice ran up a whole octave at the end of that sentence.

Stackhouse observed them both for a few seconds. Kelly held her Barbie pose, even though she felt her cheek start to twitch. "Well, that's a real nice story, folks, but I have to wonder why you're telling it to me."

Steve gave a chuckle. "Well, you see, Mr. Stackhouse, Kelly here is a weaver. In fact, that's a new loom in the back of the truck. We bought it from Sam Gepardson today. And—"

"You know Sam Gepardson?" Stackhouse asked. "He's a fine craftsman. A real artist."

"Yes sir, that he is, sir. We met him when we picked up the loom, but he was highly recommended by the folks at Kelly's favor-ite shop in town, House of Lambspun."

"Ohhh, yes!" Kelly jumped in, gesturing again. "They're *so* helpful. You see I'm new at all of this, and they tell me everything to do."

Stackhouse nodded, the skeptical expression Kelly first noticed no longer present. "They're good people. My wife's a spinner, so she knows the woman who runs the place, uhh . . ."

"Mimi?" Kelly supplied with another exuberant gesture. "Oh, yes, she's been *so* much help. And all the other people there, too. That's why we're here! It was one of them who suggested we come see you." She turned to her accomplice, Barbie still in place. "Stevie has alpaca questions." She could tell Steve was trying his best not to laugh.

"That's right," he went along with an agreeable nod. "You see, we were thinking we might add some alpaca once we move in, and this woman in the shop, right, honey? She said you'd give us good advice on the business. Even told us how to get to your ranch."

Stackhouse peered at them. "What was her name?"

At this, Kelly called up a Lizzie mannerism. Hand to her breast, she exclaimed, "Oh, my goodness, I simply *cannot* remember. But she was tall and blonde and very, very pretty," she volunteered Lisa's description.

Stackhouse shook his head and folded his arms across his chest. "Well, I wish I knew who it was, because that's kind of strange advice. You see, I don't have any alpacas. I've got a few hundred sheep, though. My wife has a small milling business in addition to her spinning."

"You don't?" Kelly squeaked, eyes wide. If they got any wider they'd pop out.

"Whoa . . ." Steve exclaimed, guileless still. "Well, I'm sorry we disturbed you, Mr. Stackhouse. I guess the lady was mistaken, honey."

"I'm sorry you folks wasted your time." Stackhouse removed his hat, running his hand through his pewter gray hair. "Listen, let me give you a couple of phone numbers to call—" At that, a familiar cell phone jangle sounded. "Uhhh, excuse me, folks," he said, then slipped the phone from his jeans and stepped away a few paces.

Kelly grabbed the moment. She turned to Steve with her most formidable frown. "You are *so* out of line, mister."

"Who, me?" Steve declared, all innocence. "What're you talking about?"

"You know what I mean. Move the arm. Now."

"Hey, I was just getting into the role," he teased.

"Sure, you were. Move it."

"But we're engaged, remember?"

"Move it or lose a rib. Your choice."

Steve backed away, laughing, arms in the air "hands up" style. "Hey, who was that a minute ago? I've never seen her."

"That was Barbie, and she's just your type," Kelly said, unable to suppress her own laughter.

"Sorry for the interruption, folks," Stackhouse said as he approached. "Let me give you a couple of names of breeders here in town. They can answer all your alpaca questions."

"That would be great, sir. Thank you," Steve said.

Stackhouse started to dig in his pocket, and Kelly realized she'd better act fast if she wanted more from Stackhouse than friendly conversation. Grabbing the most plausible line she could think of, Kelly plunged in. "Did you grow up here your whole life, Mr. Stackhouse?"

"Sure did." Stackhouse found his pen then withdrew a card from his back pocket. "So'd my father. We've ranched here since 1910."

"Oh, goodness," Kelly said. "My aunt grew up here, too. What year did you graduate from high school?"

Stackhouse smiled. "In 1955. A long time ago."

"Oh, my!" Kelly chirped, hand to breast again. "That's when my aunt graduated, too. What high school?"

"Fort Connor High."

"Goodness, what a coincidence. She went there, too. Maybe you knew her. She was Helen Flynn, then. Her parents had a small sugar beet farm east of town."

The change in Stackhouse's expression was barely noticeable, but immediate. Kelly would have missed it if she hadn't been staring at him intently with her wide-eyed pose. Barbie was useful after all. A light appeared in his eyes for a split second, then was gone.

He glanced down and wrote on the card. "You know, that name does sound familiar. But I can't bring back a face."

"Ohhhh, she was really pretty back then, I've seen her pictures," Kelly gushed. "She was petite with dark brown hair and bright blue eyes. And I'll bet she had a lot of friends!"

Stackhouse looked up and gave Kelly a guarded smile. "I'm sure she did, Miss Flynn. But I just can't place her. Sorry." He turned to Steve and handed him the card. "Here, you go. These folks will tell you all you want to know about the alpaca business."

"Hey, thank you, sir," Steve said, shaking Stackhouse's hand again before he turned to Kelly. "You ready to go, honey?"

"Thank you so much," she said, letting Steve take her arm as they started to leave. "You've been very helpful, Mr. Stackhouse."

"I'm sorry I didn't remember your aunt." Stackhouse caught her gaze for a second.

Yes, you did, Kelly said to herself. But to Stackhouse, she simply waved and called out, "That's okay, thanks so much for helping."

Steve waved as well as they headed toward the truck. "He's lying," he said softly.

"You betcha," Kelly concurred with a vigorous nod.

Steve opened her door, and Kelly scrambled in." Hey, can Barbie come back for the trip home?" he asked.

"Not on a bet," she said and slammed the truck door shut.

Twelve

"**You** split the yarn into fourths, like this," Mimi directed, slowly pulling the strand of yarn apart. "Then, you'll use a darning needle and thread each little tail under and around and into the stitches to hide it."

"I don't have a darning needle," Kelly said, feeling deficient somehow.

"It's okay. We keep a supply right there in that little cedar box." She pointed to the center of the library table. "Megan, would you please hand me a needle? I'll get you started, Kelly, then you can finish."

Megan retrieved a needle. "Here you go. That's a great scarf, Kelly. I love those colors."

Kelly beamed with the pride of accomplishment. Considering how rocky her introduction to knitting had been, she was still amazed she'd created something so beautiful. She ran her hands over the colorful chunky-knit scarf. Now all she had to do was wait until autumn so she could use it. Or maybe not. April brought springtime temperatures and flowers, but springtime in Colorado was a fickle suitor. As likely to drop several inches of snow and freezing cold as seductively warm days that hinted of summer.

"There, now weave it in and around until there's only a little bit of yarn left, then tie a knot," Mimi said, demonstrating each step. "And snip, you're done."

"Wow. That's the first easy thing I've learned. Even I can do that," Kelly declared, taking the scarf and needle.

Slowly she replicated Mimi's movements. This step certainly

was easier than the binding-off process when her scarf was finished. Kelly wasn't sure how pulling one stitch over another would result in a finished edge, but darned if it didn't. Only a few maneuvers and she had a finished scarf in her lap. Except for the two dangling tails of yarn on each end and in the middle.

Mimi sank back into her chair and sipped her Earl Grey. "Thank you again, Megan, and you, too, Kelly, for what you did yesterday," she said, shaking her head. "Goodness, I had no idea it would become so . . . uh, challenging, shall we say?"

Jennifer snickered at the end of the table as she worked the emerald yard. "You gotta love Lizzie. She knows no shame. A woman after my own heart."

Megan scowled across from her. "Stop that, Jen. Don't you dare encourage her. Lizzie doesn't need any more ideas."

"Who, me?" Jennifer said, all innocence. "Never."

Laughter sounded over the hum of the wheel in the corner, as Burt interrupted his spinning long enough to tease. "You're incorrigible, Jennifer."

"I know, it's one of my finer traits."

"I still cannot believe Lizzie did that," Mimi said, smile winning out.

"Believe it," Kelly intoned, tucking in the fourth strand, only one dangling tail to go. Changing the subject, she added, "But the best thing that happened was our trip to the rancher's place after the festival."

"*Our?*" Lisa teased across the table.

This time it was Kelly's turn to scowl. "Well, I had no car, so I persuaded Steve to follow this rancher, Stackhouse."

"The hunky cowboy in the yearbook?" Jennifer pried.

Kelly nodded. "One and the same."

"Steve didn't know the family?" Mimi asked.

"No, he said the name was familiar, that's all." Kelly jabbed a tuft of red wool through the needle's aperture. "And to tell the truth, it worked better because there were two of us. We pretended we were ignorant alpaca breeders-to-be and were sent to him for information. He bought it, thank goodness, otherwise I wouldn't have been able to ask him questions."

"What kind of questions?" Megan ventured, binding off the edge of her turquoise sweater.

"Well, I wanted to see his response when I mentioned Helen's name, so I worked up to it. Asking him if he grew up here, where he'd gone to school, stuff like that. Then, I slipped Helen in."

"What'd he say?" Lisa prodded, examining the stitches on her coral sweater.

"He said he couldn't remember her even though the name was familiar, but the expression on his face said different. Even Steve saw it. It was subtle, but you could tell he knew Helen." Kelly gave a mission-accomplished nod.

"Kelly, I hope you're not suspecting this rancher on the basis of a facial expression," Mimi cautioned.

Kelly exhaled a sigh, listening to the rhythmic hum of the wheel behind her. She and Steve had discussed the same thing when they drove back to Fort Connor yesterday. It was obvious Stackhouse knew more than he was saying. He'd recognized Helen's name. He remembered her, but he wasn't admitting it. Kelly thought she saw a flicker of something else in his eyes. But nothing else was visible on that suntanned and weather-beaten face. "I know," she admitted. "A guilty expression proves nothing."

"Yeah, it might not be guilt at all. It could be heartburn," Jennifer joked, causing a ripple of laughter.

Lizzie popped into the room then and bustled over to the bookshelves. "Mimi, we have those spring sweater patterns you showed me last week, don't we? Hilda is finishing her class and wants to show them the next project. Now, where are they?" she worried out loud as she removed a large three-ring binder and started paging through it.

"They should be there, Lizzie, I checked yesterday," Mimi advised, rising from her chair.

"Ohhh, here they are, dear," Lizzie declared, familiar smile returning. "Don't get up, I'll copy them."

"Hey, Lizzie, I hear you had a little field trip of your own yesterday," Jennifer tweaked.

"What do you mean, dear?" Lizzie replied as she slipped the plastic-encased patterns from the binder.

"Jennifer . . ." Megan warned ominously.

Jennifer continued, unfazed. "To visit the bonny lads of Scotland. A piper, too, I heard."

Lizzie beamed, hand to breast. "Ohhhhh, yes. He was an exceptionally handsome gentleman, tall and broad, with full gray beard."

"Tell me, Lizzie—"

"Jennifer!" Megan tried again.

Kelly knew exactly where this was going. So did Lisa and Mimi, she could tell from their smiles. Megan was wasting her time trying to divert Jennifer.

"Tell me, Lizzie, was he regimental or not?"

"Regimental, dear? Whatever do you mean?" Lizzie glanced over her shoulder as she headed toward the classroom.

"I've heard that when a Scotsmen is in regimental dress, he wears nothing beneath his kilt," Jennifer explained with a devilish smile.

Lizzie paused halfway to the doorway. "Oh, really? I shall have to remember that."

"Why do I even try?" Megan muttered.

"Beats me," Lisa said with a grin.

"Well? Was he, Lizzie?"

A light rose blush colored the little knitter's round cheek. Kelly spied a distinct twinkle in her eye as well. "It was green, dear," she said simply and headed for the doorway.

Kelly dropped her scarf. Mimi choked on her tea. Unflappable Lisa's mouth fell open, while Megan sank her head into her hand. Even Jennifer appeared at a loss for words, for a split second.

"*Green?*" she called out. "Lizzie, get back here!"

"Make her stop," Megan pleaded.

"Can't be done."

Kelly turned at the strangled sound of laughter behind her and saw Burt, red-faced, bent over his wheel, wiping his eyes. "You okay back there, Burt?"

"Oh . . . yeah . . ." he rasped and coughed. "But I spun a knot in my yarn."

"You asked something, dear?" Lizzie leaned around the corner.

"Did you say green?" Jennifer said, eyes alight.

"Yes, dear. His underwear was shamrock green." And she disappeared around the corner again.

Soft laughter bubbled around the table, as Kelly tucked away the last tiny strand of yarn. She held up her new creation and admired it all over again.

"I can't follow a great line like that," Jennifer said, stuffing her nearly finished sweater into the tote bag. "Time for me to get back to work. See you guys later."

Megan checked her watch. "Me, too. I've got to finish a tech article for this new client. I'm really trying to impress them so I can snag that account." She grabbed her knitting and shoved it into her bag as she rose to leave. "See you later."

Mimi rose as well, balancing her empty teacup. "I'll check in with Hilda and see if her students need any help." Glancing to Kelly, she added, "Kelly, now that you know how to knit, you can sign up for Hilda's next sweater class. She's a wonderful teacher."

"Whoa, I don't know if I'm ready for that," Kelly hedged. "Sweaters look a lot harder than my easy scarf."

"You can do it," Lisa declared. "Pull out that first piece you were working on and start knitting. Get used to the smaller needles again. Then, we'll teach you how to do the stockinette. That's what you'll need for Hilda's beginning class."

"Stockinette? Is it hard?" Kelly asked, dubious already.

"No, not after you learn to purl," Mimi said as she headed toward the classroom. "I'll teach you how in just a minute. Let me check on Hilda first."

"Purl? I have to purl? Why can't I just knit?"

"Because that's how you do stockinette," Lisa explained. "You knit one row, then purl the next. And that makes this nice pattern, see?" She placed the scrumptious coral sweater on the table and pointed to the pattern. "That's called *stockinette,* and it's great for sweaters."

Kelly ran her fingers over the silk and cotton yarn, admiring the smooth interlocking stitches. "That is pretty. At least yours is pretty. I'm not sure mine will be."

"Hey, you'll do fine. You're a fast learner," Lisa encouraged and sat down again. "Now, take out your first piece and start knitting."

Digging into her own tote bag, Kelly found her homely first

effort. She nearly flinched when she saw it. Compared to her pretty scarf, it was downright ugly. "Boy, these needles feel small now," she said.

"Start knitting. It'll come back. You were doing fine before."

Kelly did as she was told and proceeded to knit, slowly at first until the smaller needles and yarn started to feel familiar once more. Soon, she'd finished a row, then another. That peaceful feeling she remembered returned as well, heightened by the warmth of the morning sunlight streaming through the windows and the hum of Burt's spinning wheel.

"They're all doing a great job in there," Mimi announced when she returned. "Oh, good, you've gone back to your knitting."

"Oh Lisa's orders," Kelly joked.

Mimi sat beside her and scooted her chair closer. "Oh, good, you're at the end of a row. Now, if you'll give it to me for a moment, I'll show you the purl stitch."

Kelly handed it over and leaned forward to watch. "Go slowly, please."

"I will. Now, with the knit stitch you slid the right needle to the left of the stitch. Well, purling is the opposite."

"Opposite?" Kelly complained. "That'll mix me up, won't it?"

Mimi smiled. "You'll get the hang of it. First, the yarn goes in front of the needle, not behind as it did with the knit stitch. Then, the needle goes to the right of the stitch. Then, you wrap the yarn and slip the stitch like before." She moved slowly through each of the maneuvers over and over.

Kelly peered suspiciously as the new stitches moved from the left needle to the right. The whole maneuver was backward. Great. She had enough trouble going forward. And just when she thought she was getting the hang of knitting.

"And you'll have to tighten the stitches a little, too," Mimi continued. "Now, you try." She held out the yarn.

"Oh, brother, backward knitting," Kelly muttered as she reluctantly took the needles.

"You want that sweater?" Lisa challenged.

"You'll be able to do it," Mimi reassured. "It's easier than you think."

"Easy for you," Kelly joked as she started to replicate Mimi's movements—very slowly. Once again, the needles felt clumsy and awkward as she completed the new movements. But gradually the motions got smoother. Somehow she completed one row. Amazing.

"Great," Mimi enthused, rising from her chair again. "See? I knew you could do it. You were the only one doubting yourself. I'll check on you in a little bit." And she scurried from the room, heading toward the front of the shop.

Noticing the increase in customers browsing through the adjacent room, Kelly figured the sweater class had ended and now everyone was shopping. She glanced toward two young women, conferring beside the crates of wool, silk, and mohair. They squeezed the bundles as much as she did, Kelly noticed.

"Lisa, that's a particularly fetching color for you," a woman's deep voice boomed.

Kelly saw Lizzie's older sister, Hilda, stride into the room. As tall and broad as Lizzie was diminutive and plump, Hilda's rawboned features were in sharp contrast to Lizzie's delicate ones. It always startled Kelly to see them side by side; they were so different, yet they were sisters.

"Thank you, Hilda. I'm finishing up now," Lisa said, then glanced toward Kelly. "Kelly wants to join your next sweater class. She's dying to make the same sweater." Lisa held up the gorgeous coral creation. It was beautiful. Short-sleeved, pretty pattern. *Perfect for spring and summer, too,* Kelly thought enviously.

"Excellent," Hilda decreed, approaching Kelly. "I see you've finished your scarf, Kelly. It's lovely. You've obviously mastered the knit stitch."

"Well, I don't know if *mastered* is an accurate term, but I am better than I was," Kelly admitted, purling away.

"Hmmm, what exactly are you knitting now?" Hilda asked, peering suspiciously at Kelly's practice piece.

Kelly glanced up, unable to stop the feeling she'd been called to the front of the class by the teacher for doing something wrong. "It's my practice piece," she admitted, a little embarrassed. "Mimi just taught me to purl."

"Ahhhhh," Hilda replied. "That explains it. Keep going, my girl. Practice stockinette next, and you'll be ready for my class."

She gathered up the binder she'd placed on the table and turned as if to leave. Kelly was actually relieved. Hilda's presence was a bit overwhelming.

Suddenly Hilda spun about and boomed in her loud almost basso voice, "I almost forgot, Kelly. How is Helen's cousin, Martha, doing? She ran away like a little mouse after the services. I never had the chance to inquire after her."

"She's doing well," Kelly ventured, carefully choosing her words to protect Martha's privacy. "She doesn't really feel comfortable with strangers, that's why she avoids people. But, she's actually quite nice. I got to spend some time with her last week."

"That was thoughtful of you, Kelly. You're a good girl. Helen would be grateful, I'm sure," Hilda declared. "If you see Martha again, please tell her to call us if she needs help of any kind."

Kelly looked into Hilda's rugged stern face with its strong craggy features. A masculine face, really. She imagined Hilda must have found it hard to be the ungainly, almost ugly, sister of delicate, demure, and pretty little Lizzie.

"Why, thank you, Hilda. I'll tell Martha. In fact, I thought I'd drop over there tonight and check on her. See if she needs anything. Her left arm is somewhat paralyzed, and she has trouble doing things. I plan to help her when I can."

Hilda walked over and gave Kelly a strong pat on her shoulder. More like a good thump than a pat. "Good girl," she repeated. "Well, I must be off. Good day, everyone." And she swept from the room.

"Are you going over after dinner?" Lisa inquired.

"Probably. I have to finish this one account first. Hopefully, I'll finish by dinnertime." The clock insider her head prodded Kelly to check her watch. "Which reminds me, I'd better get back to work. I'll see you tomorrow," she added as she stuffed her practice piece into her bag and rose.

"Not tomorrow. I'm swamped with appointments all day. But, we've got practice tomorrow night at the ball field. I'll see you then."

Practice. Kelly hadn't heard that word in a long time. It felt good. Outside. Sun setting over the foothills. Oh, yeah. She'd be there. "At the same field?" she asked, wrapping her new scarf around her neck despite the warm temperatures.

"No, actually, we're practicing on the junior high fields at the corner of Stover and Perkins. On the east side of town. Seven o'clock. And we usually go into Old Town afterward." Lisa said. "It's gonna be summer before you know it."

Summer. Kelly felt the word run all the way through her, leaving a warmth like a ray of sunshine. "Sounds good. I'll see you there."

Suppressing all desire to touch and squeeze fibers and fabrics, Kelly hurried from the shop. Nearly eleven. She needed to get on task. This telecommuting was fine as long as she kept track of her time. Tick tock inside her head.

As she scampered down the steps toward the driveway, she noticed a man step out of his car and wave. "Well, hello, Ms. Flynn. I just stopped by to see you," Alan Gretsky called out and headed toward her, bright smile in place.

Great, Kelly thought, suppressing a frown. She wanted to get back to work, but she owed it to herself to hear what the Realtor had to say. After all, she would be selling the cottage someday, wouldn't she? That question niggled in the back of her mind, then darted away. "Hello, Mr. Gretsky," she managed.

"Ms. Flynn, I've got great news for you," Gretsky declared, clapping his hands together. "I've been discussing your property with my out-of-town client, and they are extremely interested in purchasing. And when I told them the particulars of the present loan arrangement, they were undeterred, Ms. Flynn. Undeterred," he repeated as if it were a new word.

Gretsky fairly reeked with enthusiasm. His eyes danced with excitement, his suntanned face glowed, and he looked ready to dance in place. Kelly couldn't help but smile. It was hard not to like such a friendly fellow, especially when he wanted to give you money. "What exactly does that mean, Mr. Gretsky?" she asked.

"My clients want to make you an above-market offer on your property, Ms. Flynn. *Above* market," he said, emphasizing the repeated word this time.

Kelly held her smile in check. "How much above market?"

Gretsky folded his arms across his chest and grinned wider, if that was possible. "Thirty thousand above market, Ms. Flynn. That should more than cover your expanded loan plus penalties and fees. More than enough."

Her mouth dropped open. Kelly couldn't help it. The amount shocked her. "What? Why would anyone pay that much money for this little piece of land and the cottage?"

Clearly enjoying her reaction, Gretsky rocked back on his heels. "The buyers have their reasons, Ms. Flynn. This land would be perfect for some high-end townhomes beside the golf course. Those are very popular nowadays."

Kelly stared across to the quaint little cottage. Thirty thousand over market. That meant she could pay off the entire loan, including the extra twenty thousand Helen had borrowed. And pay off the penalties, too. She wouldn't even have to dip into her meager savings. The idea was tempting, she had to admit.

"And, I believe they can be persuaded to pay your closing costs, too, Ms. Flynn," Gretsky added. "I took the liberty of mentioning the unfortunate situation with your aunt's demise and, well, they said they'd help you any way they could."

"Boy, that's a lot to think about, Mr. Gretsky," she said, shaking her head. "I hope they're not in a hurry for a decision."

"I think they're willing to wait for a while. Shall I tell them you would seriously consider their purchase offer?"

Even though part of her fought the idea, the accountant in Kelly responded, "An offer like that is definitely worth consideration, Mr. Gretsky."

She'd be a fool not to. All of the financial concerns that had bedeviled her for the last few weeks would be gone in a twinkling. She could return to her former life. Everything would be back to normal. Why didn't that feel better?

Gretsky nodded knowingly. "I was hoping you'd say that, Ms. Flynn. I'll tell my buyers. You have a good day now." He tipped his fingers to his forehead in a mini-salute and returned to his shiny black Lexus.

Kelly watched him drive away and wondered why such good news didn't feel better. Why didn't *she* feel better?

Thirteen

"**Are** you sure I can't do anything for you while I'm here?" Kelly asked, succumbing to the familiarity of Uncle Jim's overstuffed armchair. She let herself sink in.

"No, dear, but thank you for asking," Martha replied, rocking in her straight-backed rocker. "I may take you up on the offer later, though. Mr. Chambers notified me the other day that my late husband's estate was nearly finished probate. And when it is, I'll be able to retrieve some of my treasured family possessions." She sipped her tea as a worried frown pinched her face. "I can't imagine Ralph would've sold my family keepsakes. Lord, I hope not. They're of no value, except to me."

Glancing about Martha's tidy but sparsely furnished living room, Kelly tried not to slosh the tea in her cup. "Did you have a large house in Wyoming? If so, we can bring back some of the furniture." Giving in to a smile, she added, "It's a little Spartan here, Martha. I'm sure you'd feel more comfortable with your family keepsakes on the shelves."

Martha nodded. "You're right, it is, and I *would* like to see my family pictures on the mantel once again. And my china." Her eyes lit up. "Oh my, Kelly, I had some beautiful pieces I'd collected over the years. Goodness knows if they're still there. And my quilts. Oh my, yes. Mustn't forget those. Wedding ring, Dresden plate, little Dutch girl," she murmured as she rocked.

"Don't worry, Martha," Kelly reassured. "We'll retrieve them all as soon as Mr. Chambers says we can. How far away is it? Were you in Cheyenne?"

"No, we were farther west, almost to Laramie."

"Is it a large house? We may need to rent a moving van."

"Oh my, I can't imagine needing that much, really. I've learned to do with a lot less these past few years." Her gaze shifted toward the lace-curtained windows. "It's a good-sized house, Kelly, indeed it is. We can probably give most of the furniture to the church. Or, the Sisters of Charity. Yes, they could sell what they don't need and keep the proceeds. Now, as for the equipment outside, well, I guess we'll just have to have an auction?"

"Equipment? What kind of equipment?"

"Why, all the ranch equipment, naturally. We had seven thousand acres when I left. And about three hundred head of cattle. Mr. Chambers said he'd hired on some folks to manage the place until all this is settled. I don't know what I'd do without that man." She shook her head. "Mr. Chambers has handled every little detail so I don't have to. Even drew up a will for me. Goodness, I've never had a will."

"He certainly is thorough," Kelly agreed. "You said he'd hired ranch hands?"

"Oh my, yes. Livestock can't be left unattended. They have to be fed and watered and looked after, especially in the winter. We'd get snowdrifts six feet deep out there sometimes. I imagine our neighbors, the Simpsons, did it after Ralph died. I'll have to thank them." Martha closed her eyes, as if picturing. "Cattle will have to be sold at auction this summer, I imagine."

"No desire to continue ranching?" Kelly probed, wondering if Martha's desire to sell off everything from her former life stemmed from unpleasant memories or a genuine desire to continue her new, simpler life.

Kelly felt protective of Martha already, and she'd only known her for a week. But it was enough for Kelly to feel drawn to help the wiry little woman. She recognized the same feelings she'd had for her aunt's well-being surface within. Their connection might be slight and only recently formed, but it was there. Kelly could feel it resonate inside herself.

"No, Kelly, I truly don't. In fact, I want to do something different with the land. I'd like it to stay open and wild. No houses. We're losing too much of our open space to development, nowadays."

Kelly was surprised at her response. "Wow, that's a great idea, Martha."

A tiny smile tugged at the corners of her mouth. "I've been thinking about this ever since Mr. Chambers said I'd inherit everything.

And I've decided I want to donate the land to the Nature Conservancy, so it'll remain a natural area forever."

"That sounds wonderful. Is Mr. Chambers working on that, too?" Kelly asked, admiring Lawrence Chambers' thoroughness and attention to detail. He'd not only taken great care with Helen's legal affairs, but he was now aiding Martha.

Martha reached to the table beside her and poured herself another cup of tea. "Not yet. He has to have some tests done on the land first. More tea, Kelly?" she offered.

"No, thanks, I'm good," Kelly chirped, holding the half-finished cup of tea. Oh, what she wouldn't give for a cup of coffee right now. "What kind of tests?"

"Mineral tests, to see what may be out there. Ralph never had it done. Wanted to run cattle and that was that. But Mr. Chambers says there may be oil or gas out there, and we need to find out before it's donated. That would change the arrangement."

It would, indeed, Kelly thought, impressed again with Chambers' thoroughness. "Absolutely, Martha. You could section off any income-producing acres from the rest of the natural space. And that income could be placed in a trust for your lifetime, then pass on to the conservancy."

Martha's face brightened with the broadest smile Kelly had seen so far. She didn't know Martha could look that happy.

"Ever the accountant, aren't you, Kelly? You're going to be such a help when I have to handle all those details."

"Don't you worry about a thing, I'll be right there," Kelly promised.

"I appreciate that more than you know."

Noticing the darkness outside the windows, Kelly decided now was as good a time as any to ask the other questions she'd brought with her. "Uh, Martha, if you don't mind, there're some questions I'd like to ask you. About Helen."

Martha leaned back into her rocker, teacup nestled against her injured arm. "I could tell there was something else on your mind, Kelly. Go ahead. Ask me anything."

"Could you think back to those months Helen lived with your family in Wyoming and you two grew so close? Do you remember anything, any detail at all, that Helen may have mentioned about who the father might be? Did she ever let something slip in a wistful reminiscence?"

Martha closed her eyes and was silent for several minutes, her rocking slowed as well. Kelly held her tongue so as not to disturb Martha's reflections.

"I recall she said they always had to slip away to see each other. Once, she mentioned their favorite hideaway was a cabin up in Poudre Canyon. They'd pretend to be hiking with a church group, then go off by themselves instead. Helen said that cabin was her favorite place on earth."

Kelly pondered that for a moment. "Whose cabin was it? I know Helen's family was poor, so it definitely wasn't theirs."

"She wouldn't say, but I sensed it belonged to him or his family." She glanced toward the darkened windows. "I always felt that he was from a wealthy family that wouldn't have approved their relationship. Even though Helen never said so, I just sensed it."

"Hmmmmmm." Kelly tapped her teacup, causing the cold tea to slosh. "You could be right. Or, there's another possibility, even though it's one I don't like to entertain. Helen could have been seeing a married man. Perhaps that's the reason for her secrecy."

Martha frowned. "I never allowed myself to consider that possibility. It wouldn't be Helen. But I suppose anything can happen. And in those days, reputations could still be ruined by a messy affair, especially in a small town. Marriages certainly were."

Pausing for a second, Kelly tried to find the right words to ask the next question. It was definitely ugly, but she had to ask. "Is there any possibility that Helen had more than one boyfriend? I remember her telling me once that she 'used to keep the boys guessing' when she was in high school. I know this sounds awful, but do you think Helen might have had, uhhh, relationships with several boys?"

Shock claimed Martha's face. "You knew your aunt better than that, Kelly!"

Embarrassed and a little ashamed for having asked, Kelly apologized. "I know, Martha, she wasn't like that. Please forgive me for saying such things, but I'm simply trying to look at her murder from every angle I can."

"I know you are, Kelly. It's just . . . it would be unlike her to do that."

"Did she ever mention knowing some handsome young cowboy?" Kelly probed in her last effort.

Martha's bright smile returned. "They were all handsome young cowboys back then, Kelly. Every boy in my high school class was determined he'd go on to be a rodeo star and win that big silver belt buckle." She laughed softly.

Kelly gave up with a sigh, remembering the top prize at Cheyenne Frontier Days, awarded to the best rodeo cowboy each year. "You're probably right. I'd just found an inscription in her high school yearbook that looked promising. Some young wrangler-type wrote over his picture, 'Yours, always. Curt.' I was hoping maybe Helen had let something slip about him."

"Curt, Curt," Martha murmured, eyes closed. "No, Kelly. I would have remembered that name. Sorry."

"That's okay, Martha," Kelly said with a loud sigh. Setting the teacup aside, she pulled herself from the comfy chair. If she left now, she could still run over some account totals before bedtime.

"Don't try to take this on your shoulders, Kelly. It's not your burden, you know." Martha said, rising from her rocker as well. "You've done more than enough as it is."

"I wish I believed that, Martha, I truly do. But thanks for saying it anyway," she said, then kissed Martha's thin cheek and waved good-bye.

Balancing her oversized metal mug of Eduardo's coffee, Kelly dropped her tote bag and several plastic binders on the library table. They landed with a solid thump. "The new girl, Suzie, asked me to bring these to you," Kelly said as she sank into the chair beside Mimi. She'd been surprised, actually, to see Mimi alone, rocking quietly in the shop's main room instead of bustling about, managing. A peacock-blue skein of yarn lay in her lap and was slowly coming to life on Mimi's expert needles.

"Thank you, Kelly. I'll get to them in a few moments. After I knit awhile longer." She sent Kelly a quick smile and then returned her attention to the yarn.

"What are you making?" Kelly asked, reaching out to touch the brilliant blue. Was it wool? Silk? Cotton?—A combination? She rubbed the strands. "Hmmm, feels like . . . silk?"

"Very good. Silk and cotton. Exactly what you'll use for that sweater you're dying to make. And I'm making one of our popular sweater designs to put out in the store. We've sold every one of these. Incidentally, how's the purling?"

"Better." Kelly sipped her coffee. "And I've started the stockinette. Knitting one row, purling the next. I have to admit, it looks halfway decent."

Mimi laughed softly as she rocked, fingers working the yarn. "Are you always so hard on yourself, Kelly? Give yourself credit. You're doing quite well."

"Thanks. Coming from you, that's a compliment." Kelly pulled out her practice piece, which was growing to the size of a lopsided placemat. That idea was ludicrous, though. Kelly was certain the sight of it would put off her appetite.

Checking her stitches, Kelly started the new row. After she and Mimi had spent several tranquil moments in silence, knitting, Kelly spoke up. She sensed Mimi was worrying about something.

"Mimi, are you all right? You're awfully quiet this morning."

"I'm fine, Kelly. Something's on my mind, and I wanted to think about it for a while, I guess."

"Knit on it for a while?" Kelly offered Mimi's word for unraveling problems. "What sort of problem are you unraveling? Is it something you can talk about or would you rather not? I'll understand, either way."

Mimi chuckled. "You've got a good memory, Kelly. No, I haven't unraveled anything, and yes, I can talk about it." She took a deep breath and kept knitting for another minute before she continued. "I heard from my landlord yesterday, and the news isn't good."

"Raising your rent?"

"I wish that were it. No, it's more serious. He sold the property this week. His health deteriorated so last year, he simply had to cut back and is closing his property management business. Selling all his properties."

It was impossible to miss the worry on Mimi's face, as if an invisible cloud darkened. "Whoa, what does that mean for you and the shop?"

"That's what has me worried, Kelly," she admitted. "There's no guarantee the new owner/landlord would renew the shop's lease this fall. Mr. Jeffers, the former owner, tried to reassure me on the phone, but I could tell he wasn't sure what the new owner will do."

"Have you heard from the new landlord yet?"

Mimi shook her head. "And that's what concerns me. This all happened so quickly. Usually, when there's to be a transfer, the tenant receives a letter advising them of change of ownership. Not that they can stop the sale or anything, but as a courtesy. I received no notification until yesterday with Mr. Jeffers' phone call."

"Hmmm," Kelly thought. "Is that breaking any terms in your contract? Have you checked?"

"Yes, and all it says is 'notice will be given' but no time frame." She chewed her lip. "I guess I'll be smarter with the next contract I sign. But Mr. Jeffers was an old family company and they had an excellent reputation in town."

"Mimi, now it's your turn to stop being hard on yourself. Most people wouldn't have caught that, either. Tell me, who's the new owner?"

"Some company called A&G Management. That's another thing that bothers me. It's not listed in the phone directory, so I'm wondering if it's an out-of-state company that's trying to buy up land. Rumor has it the Big Box discounter is looking for more land parcels."

Kelly wondered if Big Box was also the buyer who was interested in her property. Gretsky said his clients wanted to build townhomes. "What does Big Box want to build?"

"Companion stores, an upscale restaurant, some office space, boutique shops."

"Hey, Mimi, you're 'boutique,'" she teased. "The shop is definitely trendy. Maybe they'd give you prime space."

"I don't think so, Kelly. The word is that Big Box has lots of plans for Fort Connor. Somehow I don't think my little shop is part of it."

Mimi's poignant tone stole Kelly's smile. "Worst case scenario, if you had to move, where would you go?"

Mimi's busy fingers stilled and sank into the peacock blue yarn in her lap. She stared toward the wood-trimmed paneled windows, morning sunshine pouring through. "That's what I've been trying to sort through, Kelly. I made a few calls and was startled at the rental prices I've been quoted. I knew Mr. Jeffers was reasonable in his pricing, but, goodness, I had no idea he was beneath market."

"Would you be able to afford the new rent? Is your profit margin able to handle that increase?" Kelly pried, unable to stop being an accountant.

"Yes, but it'll take all the extra I'd planned to use for investing in more new looms. And, of course, my retirement plan will have to wait. Again." She exhaled a long sigh.

"Mimi, I will help you with your new accounts. No problem. I'm really good at that. Don't worry, I won't let you fall through the cracks," Kelly promised and patted Mimi's arm. After weeks of receiving reassurances on all things large and small, it felt good to be able to give it as well. Completing the circle.

The new part-time helper, Suzie, hurried into the room. "Mimi, that pattern company is on the phone," she announced. "Can you talk with them now, or should I take a message?"

Mimi nearly sprang from her chair, tossing the yarn to the table. "Now! I'll talk now. I've been trying to reach them for over a week and the phone is always busy," she complained. Hurrying from the room, she nearly ran into Burt. "Oooops, sorry, Burt," she apologized before she headed for the front.

"Looks like she's busier than usual today," Burt observed to Kelly, placing a can of diet soda on the table.

"You might say that," was all Kelly said. Mimi could announce the news in her own time. "How're you doing, Burt?"

"Fine, fine," Burt answered and surprised Kelly by taking the chair beside her instead of setting up the spinning wheel in his favorite sunny window. He clasped his hands together and leaned toward her. "Actually, I'm glad I found you alone, Kelly. My contacts in the department shared what they could with me, and I thought you'd be interested."

Kelly stopped mid-purl, dropping the knitting needles to her lap. "What'd they say?" she whispered, leaning closer.

Burt glanced over both shoulders before he spoke. "I talked with the coroner and judging from the marks on Helen's neck, she was probably seated when she was strangled."

"Seated?" Kelly asked, incredulous. "That doesn't make sense. Why would she be sitting when this drunken vagrant invades her house?" Burt looked her in the eye, and suddenly Kelly understood. "She must have known the killer. Otherwise, she wouldn't be sitting down, would she?" Kelly's heart beat faster at this new information.

"It's unlikely," Burt replied.

"Did the coroner tell Morrison? I mean, are they paying attention to this new information?" she demanded, voice rising.

Burt placed his finger to his lips and glanced over his shoulder again. "I'm sure they are, Kelly. Morrison is sharp."

Kelly held her tongue, even though she disagreed with his assessment of the lead investigator.

"And you'll be relieved to know they're doing extensive tests on the yarn that was found beside the river. Apparently, there were tiny specks of blood on the yarn. That caught their interest because they also found blood droplets on some of the carpet fibers they took from the cottage."

Kelly caught her breath. Now here was news. Bless the crime scene investigators. "Whose blood was it? Helen's?"

Burt shook his head. "Nope. My crime lab informant told me she was type A. The blood was type O. Same as the suspect."

The elation Kelly felt evaporated. "Darn it! I was hoping we'd find something that proved he wasn't the killer."

"Don't give up yet," Burt advised. "Only blood typing was done so far. DNA tests are still pending."

Kelly sank back in her chair, the new information swirling inside her head, sending up one new theory after another. "When will they be done, Burt?"

"In a few days, so be patient," Burt said and gave her a fatherly pat as he rose. "Now, I'd better check on the new fleece Mimi mentioned yesterday." He headed toward Mimi's office until Kelly's voice stopped him.

"Thanks, Burt," she called after him. "You're a prince."

Fourteen

Lisa poured the tawny ale into her glass and took a sip. "How's your shoulder doing?" she asked Kelly.

Kelly leaned back into a wicker chair and stretched her legs, enjoying the warm spring night. Midnight, and the outdoor cafés sprawling through the heart of Old Town were still filled with customers. They spilled out into the historic plaza.

"It's sore, but it's a good sore, you know?"

"Oh yeah," Lisa grinned. "I know what you mean. With me, it's my elbow. When I don't pitch regularly, it stiffens up. Sounds like your shoulder was ready for some action."

"I'd forgotten how much throwing helps." Kelly sipped the most famous of the local microbrewed boutique beers. "And I'd also forgotten how good this tastes. Yum." She ran her tongue over her upper lip, licking off the creamy foam.

Lisa motioned her boyfriend, Greg, to the table. "Did you talk to Sully? Can he make it this weekend?"

Greg, tall, blond, and marathon-runner lean, sauntered to their table and leaned over Lisa's chair. "Nope. He's gotta work in Denver." Glancing to Kelly, he gave her a bright smile. "You wouldn't be up for a three-day trek to Diamond Peak, would you? We need an eighth person to even it out."

Kelly stared wide-eyed for a second, letting her expression answer for her.

Lisa laughed out loud. "Okay, I guess not. Wait a month, and you'll change your mind. It's great up in the canyon on a summer night, lying under the stars, staring up, counting—"

"Mosquitoes," Greg teased and kissed the top of Lisa's head.

"Hey, there weren't that many last year. Not at that altitude."

"They were all in our tent, then." He laughed. "You ready to leave?"

Lisa nodded, drained her glass, grabbed her bag, and rose. "Good practice tonight, Kelly," she said, sliding her arm around Greg's waist. He did the same. "See you at the shop."

"Night," Kelly said, raising her glass. They both waved as they walked off.

She felt an old familiar twinge inside, watching Lisa and Greg together. Both tall, blond, slender, and handsome. Two nice people. They made a nice couple. She wondered if that might be in store for her someday. The last time she thought it was right, it proved wrong, and she had her heart broken.

Draining her beer, Kelly grabbed her wallet, shoved it in her jacket pocket, and rose to leave. The sound of salsa music spilling from a nearby club captured her attention, and she turned to see several couples moving to the beat near the outdoor fountain. One of the girls looked a lot like Jennifer. Kelly wove a path through the outdoor tables, eyeing the girl.

Sure enough, it was Jennifer—margarita in one hand and dancing her heart out. Kelly scrutinized the guy pulsating to the music beside Jennifer. Tall, spiked black hair, and hotter-than-hot looks. If ever a guy had Bad Boy written all over him, he was it. Kelly smiled to herself as she walked out into the soft spring night, the seductive Latin rhythms floating after her.

Kelly placed Carl's food dish on the cement patio as the doorbell rang. *Darn,* she thought, heading inside the house. She was about to start her early morning run. Sunshine streamed through the cottage's lacy white curtains. A perfect day.

Yanking open the front door, she was surprised to see Mimi standing there, newspaper in hand. "Hey, good morning. What brings you over so early? Is the shop opening at six a.m. now?" Kelly joked.

Mimi didn't return Kelly's smile. In fact, the worry lines crossing her attractive face deepened. "Kelly, there's something in the paper you need to read. I've been hoping and praying I'm mistaken, but . . ." Her voice trailed off.

"What is it?"

Mimi didn't reply, but handed over the newspaper instead. Kelly took it and could not miss the front page lead article: "Second elderly woman slain in home."

She caught her breath and read on. Was this a copycat murder? the reporter speculated. Victim was found strangled in her modest Landport home. Kelly's heart skipped a beat. Oh, no. Please, no. She poured over the article, searching for some identifying detail that would confirm what Kelly already feared inside.

And then it jumped out at her. At the end of the article, the reporter mentioned the "bright red, yellow, and purple tulips" lining the walk to the victim's white frame house on Maple Street. Kelly's heart sank. It had to be Martha. Kelly'd noticed the glorious display of tulips lining Martha's walk the last time she'd visited. And the absence of such a colorful arrangement at the neighboring homes along the street.

"Oh my God," she breathed. "It's Martha."

"Ohhhh, no," Mimi whispered, wrapping both arms around herself. "I was hoping it wasn't true, hoping—" She shut her eyes and turned away.

Kelly felt sick to her stomach. She sank down on the front step, the newspaper dropping to her feet. She had done this. She was responsible for Martha's death. It was her questions and search for answers that got Martha killed. No one in town even knew about Martha, not even her church. Helen had protected her cousin well—until Kelly came along. All those years of carefully protecting Martha's whereabouts from an abusive husband, all for nothing. Kelly managed to blow Martha's cover in a few days. She led the killer right to Martha's door.

Kelly's gut wrenched, and the tears started to flow. Damn. There were still tears left. She'd never run out of tears, would she? She sank her face in her hands and let them fall.

"I'm so sorry, Kelly," Mimi soothed, voice beside her which indicated that Mimi had joined her on the concrete step. "I could tell you'd grown fond of Martha in the short time you knew her." She rubbed Kelly's shoulder comfortingly.

"I killed her, Mimi. I'm responsible," Kelly said through the tears.

"What? Don't be ridiculous, Kelly—"

"The killer must have been watching and followed me to her house. I got her killed. It was me . . ." Kelly choked on the last words as another flood of tears washed over her.

Mimi kept rubbing Kelly's shoulder without speaking, all the while Kelly wept softly. Grief for Martha mingled with the still-raw grief for Helen. And her dad, even though that was three years ago. Everyone was gone. She'd just found a new family connection in Martha, only to have it yanked away before she'd even gotten to enjoy it. Why was it loved ones didn't stay in her life? Was it her? Was she poisonous, or something? Even her old boyfriend left.

Now that she was waist-deep in the swamp of recrimination and guilt, more hurt bubbled to the surface. Old, old wounds. *Don't forget your mother,* an ugly voice whispered. *She left you, too. And you were only a baby.* The well that ran deep opened then, and tears continued to pour forth hot on Kelly's cheeks.

"Kelly, Kelly . . ." Mimi said. "You are not responsible for some-one else's actions. Least of all, this vicious killer who committed these crimes. Maybe he learned of Martha from Helen. Maybe there's some connection between them all. Who knows? And we certainly don't know what's going on inside that sick mind."

Cried out at last, Kelly lifted her T-shirt and wiped her face, dry-ing her eyes, wiping her nose. She had to move. Run. She couldn't sit still anymore. She needed to chase away the dull ache inside. Push it back way down deep where she didn't have to look at it or feel it. She pulled herself to her feet.

"I've got to run, Mimi. I . . . I need time to think," she said, brushing grit from the back of her latex shorts.

"I understand," Mimi said as she rose. "I'll tell the others when they come into the shop, if you want me to."

"Yes, please. I don't want to have to say it." She reached over and gave Mimi a quick hug. Mimi squeezed back. "Thanks for every-thing, Mimi," she said, breaking off before the tears returned.

"I'll tell Burt, too, when he comes in this morning," Mimi called as Kelly started off.

Kelly waved, heading for the edge of the golf course, which she followed until she picked up the river trail. Once on the paved pathway, Kelly decided to forego the scenic route she usually took. She wasn't in the mood for too much beauty this morning. Instead, she went the opposite direction, knowing it would lead through an open, almost barren wilderness area, then skirt past an abandoned industrial site before winding through a deeply wooded and shaded passage beside the river once more. Traffic on this section of trail was sparser, which suited Kelly just fine. She wanted to think. Needed to think.

She settled into her running rhythm and picked up her pace, early sun at her face. The sun felt good, and so did the rhythm. Dense trees started to thin and traffic sounds grew fainter as she ran. Each stride, each breath helping to ease the ache. Like rubbing a cramped muscle slowly, slowly, walking it out. Running it out.

Who did this? Who killed these sweet women? Who was that vicious? And why? What threat could they be to the killer? What did Helen and Martha know that caused their death? Kelly sorted through one idea after another, discarding them right and left. None made sense. Trees thinned to disappearance, open grassland now. Three ravens, obsidian black, cried their complaint at being disturbed and took to the sky. What leftover feast had they found in the brush?

Helen withdrew money to ward off the threat. It hadn't worked. Was Martha lying when she said she didn't know who the money was for? Kelly rounded a curve, startling more birds, flushing them into the air. No, no, that wasn't right. Martha's concern about the money withdrawal was too real.

Maybe . . . maybe it wasn't about the money. Maybe it was something else that made Helen and Martha a threat. Perhaps they knew something about someone. Information that could harm that person. Kelly let the thought simmer for a while as she headed out of the grassy area and toward the old factory site. Broken windows gaped in the concrete block walls like gouged out eyes, staring without seeing.

It had to be about the baby and Helen's hidden love affair, Kelly mused. Who would be threatened by that? Someone who had a position of respect in the community, perhaps? Someone who had secrets to hide. A face surfaced. A furtive glance that hinted at secrets. Stackhouse. Kelly's breath quickened, even in the midst of her stride. She remembered Curt Stackhouse's guilty denials about Helen. He was lying. Why would he lie unless he was trying to hide something?

Kelly picked up her pace, rounding another curve that bordered the abandoned site. Far from the highway, no sounds of people or cars carried on the breeze. No one around for miles. Was Stackhouse the one? He was certainly a successful rancher. Land buyers and sellers courting him long distance even. Real estate deals right and left, Kelly surmised, caught up in this scenario. He mentioned his wife owning a business. Maybe he was afraid she'd divorce him if the truth came out. Maybe that would destroy his investment business, maybe—

A raven's shrill cry overhead startled Kelly from her creative imaginings. Suddenly, she felt a warning chill ripple through her. *Turn. Turn now,* her instinct said. Still running, Kelly whipped her head around to look over her shoulder and was shocked to see a hooded cyclist bearing down on her—only a few yards away.

Kelly leaped to the side of the trail with a surprised yelp as the cyclist whizzed by, a blur of gray sweatshirt and sweatpants. She couldn't even see his face, it happened so fast. Or was it partially covered? Sunglasses. Yes, he wore sunglasses. And the gray hood covered everything else.

Breath coming fast now, the workout's disciplined breathing was gone, replaced by an adrenaline rush. Thanks to all those years of softball and sports, Kelly's reflexes were razor sharp. She stood, hands on hips, wondering how any responsible cyclist would ignore the basic courtesies of the trail. The normal calling out of "coming up on the left" that one heard so regularly it was as familiar as early morning birdsong.

Kelly already knew the answer. That was no ordinary cyclist. And he deliberately did not call out a warning because his intent was to run right into her. At the speed he was going, she'd have been knocked unconscious on the side of the road. Who knows how long she might have lain there in this desolate section before she was found?

Something caused Kelly to look up then, and she swore she saw the raven perched on the roof of the gutted building. "Thank you," Kelly said out loud to the bird. Its warning cry had brought her back from deep reverie in the nick of time.

Kelly peered down both directions of the trail, comprehending for the first time how isolated she was right now. A cold chill ran up her spine. *Get off the trail now,* her instinct warned. Kelly glanced at her watch. She'd been running for more than thirty minutes. It was a long, desolate run back on the trail. What if the cyclist returned?

The realization that the cyclist and the murderer may be one and the same resonated inside. It had to be Martha's killer come back for Kelly. After all, the vagrant suspect was still locked up. Who else but Martha's killer would come looking for her?

Kelly didn't need any more convincing. She took off into the scrubby, rutted terrain beside the trail, heading north. The trail ran diagonally through Fort Connor from the foothills northwest of the city to the southeast edge of the county, following the river most of the time. Kelly knew the highway lay to the north of the river at this point, and highway meant cars and people. She might have to hike a few more miles to the shop and home, but she'd be surrounded by traffic. Who would have thought she'd ever welcome traffic?

The ruts became crevices and filled with prickly bushes. Kelly plunged through them all, keeping the morning sun on her right shoulder as a compass. She felt the thorny branches tear at her legs but didn't even look down. Blood would wash off. At least the cyclist couldn't ride out here. Heck, she could barely walk out here.

At that moment, her left foot sank into some oozing ground, more muck than mud. *Yuck,* Kelly thought, as she yanked her foot free and tested for drier ground across the barren area. *Up ahead,* she thought she spied barbed wire. Instead of trepidation, it brought elation. Barbed wire meant boundaries. Fences. And probably the highway.

Sure enough, Kelly heard the glorious sound of trucks, the *whoosh* and the rumble of heavy rigs on asphalt. Amen, she breathed, right before she tripped over a rock and tumbled forward. Splat. Face-first into the dirt and grit. Muttering some of her dad's favorite curses from his "navy days," Kelly scrambled to her feet again. Brushing grit off her filthy T-shirt, she bent over to brush her knees and stopped. Why bother? Long bloody scratches marked her legs from knees to ankle. Might as well add skinned knees to the mess.

Climbing the incline to the highway's edge, Kelly released a huge sigh of relief. Yes. She was only a couple of miles from home. All that was left was the barbed wire. Kelly scanned the expanse of rusty wire, then took a deep breath, and gritted her teeth as she grabbed hold. Yanking two of the wires in opposite directions, she struggled through, feeling her expensive running shorts catch, then rip, as she yanked herself free—on the other side at last. Thank God her tetanus shot was up to date.

Not wasting a moment, Kelly set off running alongside the highway. The thought of Eduardo's strong coffee was enough to bring back her strength and her stride as she headed home.

"Oh my gosh! What happened to you?" Megan exclaimed when Kelly finally stumbled into the shop.

"Coffee . . . please," was all Kelly said as she leaned over, hands on bloody knees, to catch her breath.

Megan snapped into action. "Suzie, would you get Kelly a mug of Eduardo's strongest? Put it on my tab," she directed, gesturing toward the front of the shop. "And tell Mimi to come quick, if you see her." Approaching Kelly, she offered, "We need to get you cleaned up."

"No, it's okay," Kelly said when she caught her breath. She'd sprinted the last half mile to the shop, dodging cars at intersections. "I'm going home to . . . to shower in a minute."

Mimi raced into the foyer and her mouth fell open at the sight of Kelly. "Oh, no! Kelly, did you fall down? What happened?"

"I've been climbing through scrub brush and barbed wire to reach the highway," Kelly said, straightening at the sight of Eduardo's coffee headed her way. She reached out both hands as Suzie delivered the treasure into her grasp. "Ohhhh, Suzie, you're a lifesaver." With that, Kelly took a big drink, causing teenaged Suzie to flinch.

"Oooooo, watch out, it's hot," she warned.

Kelly didn't care. What was a burned tongue compared to all the other scrapes and bruises she'd received this morning? Another big swallow and she'd begin to recover, she was sure.

"Why were you climbing through brush?" Mimi demanded, concern still evident. "I thought you were running on the trail."

"I was, but I got chased away." She had to have another long drink before she could tell this story. But before she could begin, another voice interrupted from the adjoining room.

"Mimi, do you want to take a look at this first cabinet and tell me if you like the angle?" Steve said as he rounded the corner. "I can move it another inch—whoa! What happened to you?" He stared at Kelly.

"Someone chased her on the trail," Megan announced.

"What?" Steve cried. "Did he hurt you, Kelly?"

"Look at her," Suzie interjected, eyes round. "She's all torn up."

Kelly held up her hand, quieting the speculation. "I wasn't actually chased. Some guy on a bicycle nearly ran into me on the trail. And I decided it wasn't an accident, so I got out of there the best way I could. Unfortunately, I was in the section down by the abandoned beet processing plant, and the trail veers pretty far from the highway at that point. So, I had to hike through some nasty brush to get out. Plus, barbed wire."

"Oh, Kelly," Mimi's voice trembled. "Was he actually following you?"

"Probably," she nodded. "I don't think it was by chance he caught up with me in that deserted stretch." She took another sustaining drink of the rich dark brew and felt strength returning to her strained legs.

"Did you get a look at him?" Steve asked in a low voice.

"I did, but he was all covered up in a hooded gray sweatshirt and sunglasses, so I couldn't tell features. Plus, he was going so fast, he was just a blur." Her mouth hardened. "Bastard. He was headed right for me. No warning, nothing. If I hadn't turned when I did and saw him coming, I'd be lying unconscious beside the trail right now."

Mimi shuddered, Megan's pale face got even paler, while Steve's features darkened into a scowl.

"Kelly, you have to tell the police," Megan insisted.

Kelly made a dismissive noise. "And listen to Lieutenant Morrison tell me it was my overactive imagination. No thanks. I'll tell Burt. He'll believe me, then maybe he can get the message to Morrison." She drained the cup.

"Burt should be in shortly, Kelly," Mimi said. "I was planning on telling him about Martha, too."

"Yes, please do, and ask him to make sure the information gets to Morrison, would you?" Kelly placed the empty mug on a table spilling over with tidy bundles of yarn. Her bloodied hand looked garish among the bright spring colors. "I'm going home to shower and clean up all these scrapes. I'm a mess." She brushed her hands down her filthy shirt and shorts.

"You're coming back over here afterward, right? I mean, Burt will want to talk with you, I know he will," Mimi declared.

Kelly nodded. "I'll come back later. I've got to log on to my office site and get some work done. Ask Burt if he'll hang around till lunch."

Without another word, she was out the door and down the steps. She'd come back all right. Check with Burt, get his opinion, and grab some more of Eduardo's coffee before she took the long drive out to Stackhouse's ranch.

Fifteen

Kelly shifted her coffee mug and tote bag to one hand and yanked open the shop's front door. Smoothing her lightweight sweater over her jeans, she stood for a moment and let the familiar surroundings sink in. It always felt so good here. Everytime she stepped inside, she could feel the difference immediately. Soothing, relaxing, she couldn't quite put it into words. But it felt good.

Recognizing Jennifer's voice, Kelly headed toward the main room. Jennifer and Lisa both sat at the library table, knitting as usual. Lisa was offering assistance to a woman twice her age beside her. And Jennifer had something other than emerald-green yarn in her lap.

"Hey, are you finished with the sweater?" Kelly asked as she settled into a nearby chair.

Jennifer looked up at Kelly with a concerned expression. "Yeah,

I finished yesterday. Listen, how are you? Mimi told us all about your . . . your . . ." Jennifer paused, watching Kelly's finger to lips then pointing to the new knitter across the table.

"I'm fine," Kelly said brightly. "My legs are a mess and they sting like crazy from the alcohol, but they'll heal. I'm gonna have new scars to join the ones from softball."

Jennifer clearly wanted to hear more, but Kelly shook her head no and mouthed "later." Steve rounded the corner from the classroom area, hammer in one hand and a cabinet door in the other. Spying Kelly, he immediately came over.

"How're you doing?" he asked quietly when Kelly gestured to the newcomer with Lisa.

"I'm okay," Kelly said, noticing the worried look. Everyone was worried. She almost felt guilty for causing such concern. "I used every bandage in Helen's cabinet. But I'm okay. Now I'm getting mad."

"At the guy?"

"Ohhhh yeah."

"That's good. But maybe you'd better run on the creekside trail from now on. There're lots more people all the time on that trail." He motioned around the table and toward Mimi's office. "We all think you'd be safer there. You don't want to give Mimi heart failure." He smiled wryly.

Kelly could tell he was forcing a smile for her sake. "I think that's a good idea," she agreed, reaching for her tote bag. "I don't feel like scrambling through brush again any time soon."

Steve turned back to the half-finished cabinets hanging against the wall. "Promise me you won't do anything crazy, okay?" he said over his shoulder.

Kelly hesitated. *Define crazy,* she thought, but answered, "No plans to. But I will find out who he is. Depend on it."

Just then Burt strode into the main room and headed for Kelly. "Ahhh, there you are. Are you okay?" he asked as he drew up a chair.

Another concerned face, Kelly observed. Now, she was really starting to feel guilty. Everyone in the shop was worried about her. She wasn't used to that. "Yeah, a little scratched up, but that's okay."

Burt glanced to the newcomer who was gathering her things together and thanking Lisa for her help. "I called my old partner and asked him to get the message to Morrison about Martha. And about your encounter on the trail this morning," he said softly.

Kelly noticed Jennifer leaning closer to hear. "Thanks, Burt. Let's hope Morrison doesn't dismiss Martha's death as a copycat or try to explain it as another robbery gone bad," she said with a sarcastic tone.

Burt smiled at that. "Cut him some slack, Kelly. He's a good man. He'll figure it out."

Kelly didn't need to register her doubts at that comment. Jennifer gave a disdainful snort. "I don't know who this guy is, but he sounds like he couldn't find his you-know-what with a flashlight."

Burt ducked his head, clearly trying to hide his grin. "Ohhh brother, you girls are brutal. Time for me to leave, before you pick on me."

Noticing Lisa's student waving good-bye, Kelly brought her voice back to normal. "We'd never pick on you, Burt."

"Yeah," Jennifer said with a grin. "You're one of us."

"Thanks, Jennifer. Coming from you, that's a compliment," Burt said as he rose to leave. "Kelly, take care of yourself, okay? Take it easy the rest of today, why don't you?"

"Will do, Burt," Kelly lied, picking up her knitting where she left off. "I'm going to sit here and knit."

"Good girl." Burt nodded in satisfaction and waved as he left.

True to her word, Kelly sat and knitted one row, then purled the next, getting her rhythm back, watching the neat rows of stockinette stitch appear.

She'd sit here and knit—for a while. Long enough to lull everyone in the shop into relaxing. Then, she'd slip away and head to Stackhouse's ranch while it was still afternoon. That's when she and Steve found him there last week.

Glancing to the side, she noticed Steve immersed in cabinetry. Jennifer concentrated on the scarlet bulky knit yarn she was knitting. Her needles were almost as large as the ones Kelly used for her scarf.

"What're you making?" she asked, purling easily now.

"I thought I'd try that open-weave vest Megan showed me."

"We were all worried about you, Kelly," Lisa's voice interrupted across the table. "Megan told us all about it." She shivered. "You really think it was, you know, the . . ."

"Killer?" Jennifer finished the sentence. "Had to be. Who else would follow her out there?"

A cell phone's melodious jangle sounded. Lisa finished winding her long blonde ponytail and secured it with a rubber band before she grabbed her phone.

Kelly waited until Lisa was absorbed in conversation before she leaned toward Jennifer. Instinct told her she should tell someone where she was going, just in case. Kelly deliberately didn't think about the "in case" part.

"Jen," she whispered, glad Steve had left the room. "I'm going to run an errand, but I don't want you to freak out when I tell you what it is, all right?"

Jennifer's large brown eyes widened even more. "Oh brother. This doesn't sound good."

"It'll be okay," she said as much to convince herself as Jennifer. "I'm driving out to Stackhouse's ranch in a few minutes. I'll be back by dinner."

"Why? I thought you guys talked to him already."

"We did, but both Steve and I could tell he was lying when he said he really didn't remember Helen. I think he remembered her a lot, judging from the look in his eyes."

"So?"

"So, I want to ask him some more questions. Maybe he remembers something from the past that might help."

"There's something you're not saying. I can tell."

"Yeah," Kelly admitted. "I want to see the expression on his face when I ask him about Martha."

"Are you crazy?" Jennifer retorted, clearly horrified by Kelly's plan. "What if he's the killer?"

"Well, I'll play stupid and jump in my car and drive home fast," Kelly joked, hoping to deflect Jennifer's objections and ease her own fears.

Jennifer glanced over her shoulder and lowered her voice. "Yeah?

And what if he doesn't let you? What if he attacks *you* this time? Face it, Kelly, somebody was out to hurt you this morning."

The overwhelming sense of Jennifer's objections began to override Kelly's bravado. Frustration and anger and determination had all boiled together this morning while she'd showered and dressed. Adrenalin kicked in as well as she formulated her scheme. Perhaps it was crazy, but at least it had helped bury the grief and guilt over Martha's death. Now, they were shoved down deep where Kelly couldn't feel them.

She let out a long sigh. "Yeah, I've thought of that, too," she admitted.

"Good. Now I know you didn't get stupid overnight. You'd be crazy to go over there alone. If you want me to, I'll go with you."

"No, he'd probably clam up—" Suddenly Kelly got a new idea. "Wait a minute, I know! I'll take Carl with me. I'll have him on his leash. Nobody in his right mind would try to attack me in front of my dog."

Jennifer opened her mouth as if to object, then closed it again. "Okay. But he's gotta be on his leash right beside you. Promise?"

"Promise," Kelly agreed with a grin and put her knitting back into its tote bag.

Carl shoved his smooth black head right beside Kelly's as she headed down the road to Stackhouse's ranch. She reached up and stroked a smooth ear. "Hold on, boy, we're almost there," she promised her excited dog. Carl had been pacing the backseat since they left. Pacing and falling flat, of course. Every time she turned a corner, he'd slip on the upholstery and lose his footing. Doggie wipeout.

Approaching the open barnyard area, Kelly scanned the outbuildings for Stackhouse. His huge black truck was parked on the graveled spot, so she figured he was home. But what if he wasn't? Would she turn around and head back into town? Kelly admitted she didn't have an alternate plan.

Fortunately, that wasn't necessary. Stackhouse appeared in the barn door, watching Kelly bring the car to a stop nearby. Parking swiftly, she grabbed the dangling end of Carl's chain lease. With a dog as strong as Carl, she used an industrial-strength metal leash.

"You have to behave, Carl," she admonished him as she stepped out and opened the door for her dog. Carl bounded from the car, yanking Kelly at least two feet. She reined him in, glad she was strong, otherwise she'd be lying face-first in the dirt right now.

Kelly saw Stackhouse slowly approaching, so she went into the routine she'd practiced on the drive over. She hoped it sounded convincing.

"Hello, Mr. Stackhouse," she called cheerfully, waving her hand as she went to meet him.

"Afternoon, Miss, uh, Ms. Flynn, isn't it?" he replied, stopping a few feet away. "Nice dog. What's his name?"

Kelly noticed a wary expression on the rancher's weather-beaten face, so she ramped up the wattage of her smile. "This is Carl, and I wanted to bring him out so he could see this gorgeous place you've got here. I can't wait till Stevie and I can have some acreage of our own like this." She glanced around appreciatively. Carl took one look at Stackhouse and pulled forward, clearly anxious to do a meet-and-sniff.

Stackhouse smiled, just a little. "Hey, fella, how're you doin'?" He held out his hand close enough for Carl to sniff.

Carl sniffed thoroughly, then slurped with his long pink tongue. Stackhouse chuckled. Kelly took note that he'd passed her dog's test. Carl was a good judge of character.

"Don't slobber on Mr. Stackhouse, Carl."

"That's okay, Ms. Flynn." Stackhouse caught her gaze. "Surely you didn't drive all the way out here to show your dog the scenery. Is there something else, Ms. Flynn?"

Kelly took a breath and plunged in, hoping she'd find her way. "Well, yes, Mr. Stackhouse, I, uh, well . . . I wanted to ask you again about my aunt, Helen Flynn Rosburg. You see, I kind of got the impression when we spoke last week that you really did remember her. But something was holding you back. Or maybe you were embarrassed or something."

She was desperately hoping Stackhouse would volunteer a comment at that point, which she could use to bounce off of, but he didn't. He stood there, observing her with his Stetson pulled low over his eyes, shading his face. He said nothing. So Kelly stumbled on.

"You see . . . I'm trying to find anyone that might have known my aunt all those years ago. I've got this . . . this strong feeling that her death was caused by something in her past. Perhaps something that happened."

Still no reply from Stackhouse. He stood like a cowboy statue, staring at her. Kelly felt the sweat start to bead on her forehead. She distracted herself by patting Carl's side. He was busily checking out ground smells. A lot more than squirrels lived in these pastures.

To her immense relief, Stackhouse finally spoke. "That was a long time ago, Ms. Flynn. What makes you think I know anything?"

Kelly met his steady gaze and gambled. "Instinct, Mr. Stackhouse. My gut tells me you did know Helen. I saw it in your eyes," she said, hoping blatant honesty might earn her a few points.

Stackhouse held her gaze for an excruciating minute, then glanced toward the forest edging his pastures. "You've got good instincts, Ms. Flynn. I'll give you that."

Kelly blinked, surprised that her honesty had been matched. "You knew Helen, didn't you?"

"Yes, Ms. Flynn, I knew her. In fact, I'll never forget her. She was the first girl I ever fell in love with. And the only one to break my heart."

This time, Kelly couldn't contain her surprise. Stackhouse clearly noticed, and a wry smile tugged at the rancher's mouth. "Why don't we take a walk," he suggested, pointing toward the pasture. "That way Carl can chase what he's smelling."

He led the way into his open pasture, Kelly and Carl following. Now that she was knee-high in the spring grass, she noticed the varied shadings of early green, from chartreuse to lime. Approaching a small clearing, Stackhouse stopped and grabbed a stick at his feet. He held it up to Carl. Carl was already two steps ahead of him and began to yelp, eager to play.

"You want this, Carl?" Stackhouse tempted. "Go get it." And he tossed the stick in an arching throw.

Not a bad throw, Kelly had to admit, and released the leash just as Carl lunged forward. Watching her "protection" race off into the high grass, Kelly hoped this new feeling she had about Stackhouse was correct. There was an honesty coming off the man, and she didn't think he was faking it. Her antennae were sharp, and she had yet to pick up any uneasiness or deception on his part.

That surprised her. She'd convinced herself all morning that Stackhouse's wary expression last week signaled something dark. Now that she was here, she felt no threat whatsoever. She'd better be right, because Carl had disappeared into the grass now. If Stackhouse really was a clever killer, he could dispose of her out here in the pasture. No one would find her in the grass, save Carl and the ravens. The memory of the huge bird's warning caused a secondary pause.

She decided to break the ice, hoping Stackhouse would explain his tantalizing comment. "That sounds like you and my aunt had some, uhh, shared history together."

"Yeah," he said with a nod. "We shared a few moments of history, you might say. I wanted a lot more than that, but Helen didn't."

This time it was Kelly's turn to stare silently, waiting for Stackhouse to continue.

"We went through high school together." He stared off into the grass, where Carl's head bobbed occasionally. "And I had a crush on her the whole four years. I must have asked her out a thousand times. Helen would laugh and tease me, but never say yes to a date. In fact, I don't think she dated anyone. I never saw her with any other boys, either."

Kelly kept her silence, not wanting to interrupt the reminiscence. Obviously, Aunt Helen had cleverly concealed her real affections from everyone.

"But, I sensed there was someone else. I'd swear to it."

"What made you think so?"

He turned to Kelly with a wide smile. "Instinct, Ms. Flynn. Same as you."

"Did she drop any clues about this person?"

He shook his head. "Nope, not a one. But I got the feeling that she was protecting him for some reason. Can't explain it. Just a hunch."

"And you never saw her dating any of the other boys?"

"Nope. She'd flirt with some of them, but nothing more. Hell, she wouldn't even talk to most of the boys. I felt kind of special.

Helen liked to talk to me. She'd let me walk her to and from class. I don't know why she picked me and none of the others."

"I do," Kelly declared with a grin. "I saw your photo in the high school yearbook. You were a handsome devil, Mr. Stackhouse." She figured Lizzie's vocabulary would come in handy about now. "Matter of fact, you're still handsome."

Stackhouse slanted a look her way. "You've got your aunt's charm, that's for sure. And you can call me Curt. I don't stand on much formality."

"Kelly," she offered in kind.

"You even resemble her, you know? There's a look that comes in your eye that's pure Helen." He grinned. "Maybe that's why I'm talking like a damn fool right now."

"It's never foolish to admit falling in love, Mister, uhh, Curt. And I find your honesty refreshing. Some boys would have dropped a girl like Helen once she turned them down. Yet, you two stayed friends."

Stackhouse gazed past Kelly's shoulder toward the sprawling ranch house in the distance. "We were close until summer of our senior year, then she stopped talking to me."

Kelly did some mental arithmetic. Early spring would have been when Helen conceived the child she later gave up. "What happened to change your friendship?" she probed.

Stackhouse stared into the pasture for a long moment. The only thing that broke the silence were the cries of annoyed birds that Carl had unwittingly flushed. "I guess it won't be disloyal to talk about it," he said in a subdued voice. He drew in a breath. "We . . . well, we became intimate one night. The night after graduation, in fact." He shook his head. "I still remember as if it were yesterday. It was a warm spring night in late May." He gazed off toward the mountains this time, clearly reminiscing.

Kelly, meanwhile, was making an effort not to let her jaw drop. She hadn't expected to hear this, especially after he'd emphasized that Helen refused to even date him. Waiting as politely as she could while Stackhouse enjoyed his memories, Kelly couldn't hold her curiosity a moment longer. "Wow. That's quite a bombshell,

Curt. I trust you're planning to explain Helen's sudden change in behavior. You can't just leave me hanging like this."

He looked up and grinned sheepishly. "Well, I reckon I owe you an explanation."

"Damn right."

He laughed. "You get more and more like Helen the longer I talk to you. She didn't mince words, either."

Remembering her aunt's occasional "salty" language, Kelly smiled. "Thanks, but get back to explaining. What made Helen change her mind? She wouldn't even date you before. Did something happen at graduation?"

"Not that I remember. It was just all us kids surrounded by our families, posing in those caps and gowns, feeling awkward and proud at the same time."

"Did you see her there with her family?"

"Yep, she looked happy like everyone else, posing for pictures."

"How'd you get together that night, then? Did you call her or meet her?" Kelly prodded.

"Nope," he said with a bemused expression. "That was the strangest part. She came over to see me. Drove over in her father's old Ford truck. My family had just returned from the high school as I recall. Then, there's Helen ringing our doorbell. You could have knocked me over with a feather."

"What'd she say?"

"She didn't say much. It was her face that did the talking. I could tell she was angry. And she'd been crying, because her eyes were red. She never admitted what was bothering her, but I could tell it was something really important. To her, at least." He paused. "She wanted to go out for a drive and talk, so we did."

"What'd you talk about?" Kelly probed, hoping to keep Stackhouse remembering the pictures inside his head.

"You know, she didn't say much. Just kept asking me questions the whole time she drove. What was I going to do after school? What kind of summer job? Had I decided which college? I wound up doing most of the talking, as I recall."

It was clear to Kelly that Stackhouse had enshrined these

memories of Helen, otherwise he wouldn't have such clear recollections. "Where'd you drive?" she continued to probe.

"Up into Poudre Canyon late at night." He shook his head, as if still amazed by the youthful bravado. "We drove past Rustic, then she pulled off the road. Wanted to take a walk, she said. It occurred to me then that she was headed somewhere."

"Was she?"

"Yep." He nodded. "Up through the trees there was a clearing and a cabin that just happened to be unlocked. It was a beautiful place, it truly was." He smiled ruefully. "We stayed the rest of the night. Came back at dawn. I lied to my parents and told them Helen had dropped me off with some of my buddies after midnight. Didn't want to add to the trouble I was sure she'd be getting when she got home."

"Were her parents upset? Did you ask her?"

He shook his head. "Didn't need to. Nice girls didn't stay out all night in those days. It was a different time. I'm sure she caught hell from her dad. He was pretty strict." Stackhouse stared past Kelly's shoulder. "I thought that evening was a whole new beginning for Helen and me. Turned out to be the end."

"Why? What'd she say?"

"Not much. In fact, she barely spoke to me after that. Acted like there was nothing between us, like nothing had happened. Even when I proposed to her, she'd just look away and say no, she couldn't. Or wouldn't." He sighed heavily. "I must have asked her to marry me at least a hundred times."

Kelly puzzled over the scene he'd painted. What was going through Helen's mind for such erratic behavior?

"She was working at a soda fountain that summer, and I came over every afternoon after I finished working the fields. Must have consumed several gallons of cherry limeade talking to her." The memory brought back his smile. "I'd go over, talk to Helen if she'd let me, drink cherry limeades, and propose. Just like clockwork every day. Until July."

"What happened in July?"

"Suddenly one day, she was gone. The owner of the drugstore said she had to go to Wyoming to help take care of her sick aunt and cousin. Her dad's brother owned a cattle spread up there. I figured she'd be back pretty soon, so I waited all summer and fall. When she didn't return, I went to ask her family. They weren't too friendly, and they said Helen was staying in Wyoming 'indefinitely.' That's when I finally gave up. I realized she couldn't really care for me, or she'd have tried to contact me. Write or something. But I never heard from her, so . . . I let her go. Had to."

Kelly watched his face and the remembered emotions register there. His sincerity appeared genuine. Kelly swore she could feel it. But her skeptical side roused itself from the remembrances and shook awake with a question.

Was it possible Stackhouse was faking? Was he inventing this whole story to lead her astray and away from suspecting him from complicity in Helen's death? That thought didn't resonate inside, but Kelly felt compelled to follow it up, anyway. There was only one thing she had left to test Stackhouse, but she had to work up to it.

"When did you learn she was back in town?" she asked.

"When a friend told me she saw an engagement announcement in the paper that next year. I didn't even contact her. By then, I'd finished my freshman year at the university. I was glad she'd found someone who made her happy. That made it easier for me, too." He smiled. "I met my Ruth that fall."

"You know, Helen's cousin, Martha, came to live in Fort Conner a few years ago. Helen helped her start over after she left her abusive husband back in Wyoming."

"Sounds like something Helen would do. How's she taking Helen's death?"

"Pretty hard," Kelly answered. "That is, while she was still alive. She was the elderly woman who was just murdered in Landport the other day."

Stackhouse stared at Kelly, shock written on his face. The last doubts Kelly had about his guilt disappeared. He couldn't fake that reaction.

"My God," he breathed. "What do the police say?"

"They're looking into a connection between the deaths," Kelly said, fervently hoping Morrison was doing exactly that.

Stackhouse scowled. "I thought police caught the man who killed Helen."

"They have a suspect in jail. He's a drunken vagrant who's been causing trouble in Old Town for years. The police saw him on the golf course near Helen's house that night, and they're convinced he did it."

He peered at Kelly. "But you're not."

"Nope. It's too easy and doesn't explain everything. There were some personal items and money stolen from the house that night, yet the drunk didn't have a thing with him except a hangover."

"Hmmmmm."

"Yeah, exactly."

"What do you think happened?"

Kelly paused, choosing her words carefully. "I don't know, but I'm going to find out. That's why I'm poking around in Helen's past. Sorry about all the questions, but I was hoping you'd know something."

She broke off her sentence when she spied a familiar red truck barreling down the road to the ranch. Her cover was about to be blown.

"Here comes your fiancé. How're his alpaca plans coming?"

Kelly made a quick decision. "He's . . . he's not my fiancé. He's just a guy I know from the wool shop. We thought it might be easier to come out here and ask you questions if we looked like a nice young couple moving into town." She gave him a wry smile, as the truck drove into the barnyard.

Stackhouse eyed her carefully, sizing her up all over again, Kelly sensed. "Soooo, you came out here to ask me questions because you thought I might have something to do with Helen's murder, right?"

Kelly took a deep breath. "Initially, yes," she confessed. "But our conversation has convinced me you had nothing to do with Helen's death."

"How can you be sure, Ms. Flynn?" he challenged.

She met his steady gaze. "Instinct, Mr. Stackhouse." Then, she gambled and gave him a wink.

Stackhouse's smile returned and he chuckled then nodded toward Steve, who'd leaped from the truck and was crossing the barnyard. "So, you and Stevie aren't engaged?"

"Lord, no, I barely know him."

"Could've fooled me. You two look like a couple."

Kelly did her best to look appalled, which seemed to amuse Stackhouse. "No way. My friend at the shop must have told Steve where I was going. He was there building cabinets for Mimi."

"So he doesn't work for a computer company?"

"Nope," she said, watching Steve head through the pasture.

"Building cabinets? Is he a carpenter?"

"Actually an architect, but he's a developer now. Likes building houses."

"Thought you said you hardly knew him."

"People at the shop talk."

"Uh huh."

Kelly eyed Stackhouse and saw the amusement. Surprisingly, she didn't mind his teasing.

Steve was coming closer. However, Carl also noticed and was headed straight for him, galumphing through the grass in huge leaps. Steve spotted Carl coming at him, and they both disappeared down into the grass. Doing the slobber and roll, no doubt, Kelly decided. Had to be a guy thing.

"Well, your dog sure likes him."

"He bribes him with golf balls. Carl can be bought."

"Well, he's a good judge of character. He liked me," Stackhouse said with a laugh.

Kelly had to join him as they watched Steve distract Carl by throwing a stick, then head their way.

"Good afternoon, Mr. Stackhouse," Steve called as he drew nearer. "How're you doing, sir?"

"Real fine, now that Kelly explained why she's here," he replied.

Kelly watched Steve's reaction. Relief was still mixed with concern. "It's okay, Steve. I've grilled him already, and he's off the hook," she deliberately joked.

Steve visibly relaxed. He advanced toward Stackhouse and extended his hand. "Well, in that case, Mr. Stackhouse, let me re-introduce myself. Steve Townsend."

Stackhouse clasped his hand. "Call me Curt. And I gather it's not Stevie. I'll bet Kelly does that just to annoy you."

"Sounds like her." Steve agreed with a grin.

"Hey, payback for the arm," Kelly retorted, unwilling to let the jibe stand.

"I hear you're a builder. Now I know where I heard your name," Stackhouse said. "One of the Wellesley town council told me about your new site out near county road sixty-four. Smart move. We need more affordable houses. Keep it up, son." Checking his watch, he glanced back at the ranch house. "Well, folks, once again I've really enjoyed chatting with you, but I've gotta get back. I promised Ruth I'd take her to dinner in town tonight, and I'd better get cleaned up." He started walking toward the sprawling frame house, Kelly and Steve falling in step behind. "Ruth and I'd love to have you two over for dinner some time. Why don't you stay in touch, okay?"

Surprised by his kind offer, Kelly agreed quickly as did Steve. "I'd like that, Curt," she said. "You've been really polite with my, uh, investigation."

"Wish I could have helped more, Kelly. Keep on asking questions," he said over his shoulder. "And keep in touch." He picked up the pace, heading for the ranch house.

Instead of returning to his truck, Steve leaned on the hood of Kelly's sporty sedan. "Don't give Jen a hard time when you get back to the shop, okay? She didn't want to tell me, but I sensed you were going to do something like this. So, I made her talk."

Kelly laughed. "What'd you do? Bribe her with a cinnamon roll?"

"That works? I'll use it next time." His smile disappeared. "You had us all worried. I had to swear Lisa and Megan to secrecy so they wouldn't tell Mimi. She would've called the cops. And I guarantee Curt wouldn't be so friendly if the cops came racing up his road."

Feeling prickly and defensive, Kelly retorted, "I'm perfectly capable of taking care of myself."

Steve glanced away. "Listen, I wanted to talk to you about something else. Something serious."

Caught off guard, Kelly stared at him. And in a moment of complete honesty confessed, "Steve, I'm about to choke on serious. It's been nothing but serious since I returned to Colorado. Helen's death, now Martha's. I can't take any more. Honest to God."

Steve looked out over the pasture. Carl's head bobbed up at a crow's angry caw then disappeared into the grass again. "Don't worry. It isn't about you or Helen or anyone you know. It's a story about my best friend and me when we were growing up here years ago."

"Is it short?" she asked.

He didn't smile, simply folded his arms and leaned back against her car, still staring out into the grass and trees in the distance. "Yeah, it's short. Bill and I were best buddies all through junior and senior high. We were gonna be roommates at the university our freshman year. We'd party together, hike, take our girlfriends camping up in the canyon, all that."

Kelly leaned against the car as well, listening, deliberately not interrupting. Sounded good to her.

"Our plans were all set. Until that June, right after high school graduation," Steve continued. "Some guy was having a party at his folks' place up in Estes Park. Bill really wanted to go. I had an early call at my summer job that next morning, so I didn't want to. No way would I get back home till three a.m. from their place. My job at the golf course required me to be there at six a.m. every Sunday."

"Wow, that must have put a crimp in your social life," Kelly interjected, hoping to dispel this cloud that seemed to settle over Steve as he talked.

"Yeah, kinda. My girlfriend was pretty understanding, though. Anyway, Bill begged me to drive him up there, even if I had to leave early. His car was in the shop. He'd broken up with his girl-friend, Lauren, and really had it for this girl he'd just met. She'd asked him to show up, since it was her cousin who was throwing the party. So, I agreed. Told Bill I'd drive him up, stay for a while, then he'd have to find another way home. Or, stay with the new girl, whatever." He paused.

"Did he stay?"

"Yeah," Steve said, then drew a deep breath. "He was having a great time dancing with this girl when I left about eleven. So, I waved good-bye, and that was the last time I saw him alive."

Kelly held her breath. She'd sensed this story was not going to have a happy ending.

"Seems after midnight, the host brings out his own little stash of designer drugs, and Bill joined in. Most of them don't even remember much after that, they were all so wasted. But the parents returned the next day and found Bill lying dead on the rocks below the cliff. Who knows what happened. He either walked out onto the cliff and fell off or was pushed or whatever. Hell, maybe at that point he thought he could fly."

Steve's face darkened with the memories, Kelly noticed. She held a respectful silence for several long minutes, then gently offered, "I'm so sorry, Steve. That was an awful way to lose your best friend."

"Yeah. It was."

"I'm curious, though. Why did you want to share it with me? And why now?"

"Because I don't want you to make the same mistake I did after Bill's death. I blamed myself for years, convinced that if I'd been there, he never would have died. He'd have gone home with me like he always did when we partied late. And he'd be alive today."

He turned to face her. "And I can tell you're blaming yourself for Martha's death. Thinking you're responsible. None of us is responsible for someone else's actions, Kelly. I know now that Bill would've stayed at the party no matter what I did. He was crazy about that girl. It was his choice to stay. I couldn't have stopped him. And you couldn't know there was a killer lurking around Martha, watching and waiting. It's not your fault."

Kelly met his direct gaze and stared back, saying nothing. She could feel the truth in what he said, but part of her still didn't want to accept it. Not yet, anyway. She looked away, twisting the leash into a coil. "Yeah," she admitted. "Part of me knows that. And part of me doesn't accept it."

"I know. It takes time. Enough said." Steve shoved away from the car and put his fingers to his lips and let out an ear-piercing whistle.

Carl's head popped up from the grass, and he started galumphing toward them. Kelly wished she could whistle like that. She'd tried but it never worked.

"C'mon, big fella," Steve said as Carl broke through the grass and headed their way. "I'm heading back to the shop to finish up some adjustment on the cabinets. I'll tell Mimi and the others you're okay. Hey, how're ya doing, boy?" he said, bending over an exuberant Carl.

"Thanks, I appreciate it," Kelly said, attaching Carl's leash. "I've got to get some work done on my accounts before nightfall. C'mon, Carl. We've gotta go home." She yanked Carl's leash and opened the door.

Steve was already walking to his truck. "See you, Kelly," he called over his shoulder.

Kelly jumped in her car, revved the engine, and headed down the ranch road, noticing the sun was about to kiss the tops of the foothills. Dusk would settle soon. Steve had already turned his truck in the same direction but waited for her to pull ahead of him.

Kelly stopped as she came parallel with his truck. Something was niggling in the back of her mind. She signaled him to lower the passenger window and when he did, she spoke up. "Listen, I really appreciate your confiding in me. I could tell it was a hard story to tell. It was a hard story to listen to. But I'm curious about something. Have you ever told that story to anyone else?"

Steve waited a moment before answering. "Only one other person. That was Mimi. Bill was her son." With that, the window closed and Steve's big red truck moved down the road.

Kelly opened the sliding glass patio door and Carl raced outside into the darkened backyard. Night creatures surely must be afoot. Kelly leaned against the doorframe and gazed up into the silky blue-black sky. Now that it was nearly midnight, much of the surrounding commercial lighting had gone dark. The stars were brighter, she noticed as she sipped a hot chocolate. As die-hard a caffeine addict as she was, coffee and midnight did not go together.

Arching her back, she indulged in a long satisfying stretch, grateful to be off the computer at last. These investigative excursions were taking quite a toll on her work schedule. So far, she'd juggled both.

Drawing the blinds, she stepped out into the patio, enjoying the blanket of total darkness that enveloped her. Looking past the golf course, she could see the shadowed mountains in the distance, looming. Silent and protective. She stared at them for a long while, in hopes their silence would calm her restless mind.

She'd overlooked something. She must have. Stackhouse wasn't involved in these murders. And Kelly was still convinced the vagrant wasn't guilty, either, even though he'd been charged with Helen's. Was Morrison going to try and explain away Martha's death as well? She had to find something, some information somewhere that would convince him the real killer was still lurking about. Kelly wasn't about to spend the rest of her time in Fort Connor looking over her shoulder whenever she found herself alone on a trail or roadway.

Swirling the last of the hot chocolate, Kelly sorted through the ideas churning inside her head. She needed to ask more questions. Maybe . . . maybe she could find someone from Helen's high school who knew Helen all those years ago. Someone who still lived in Fort Connor. There had to be some clue as to who Helen's mystery lover was. Was he really some wealthy son of an important family like Martha suspected? And what happened on graduation night that upset Helen so she'd run to Curt for consolation? Did the rich boy reject his poor girlfriend now that he was headed to college? Did Helen tell him about the baby? Did he reject her?

Kelly visually traced the Big Dipper, letting the stars' vastness calm her. Then the image of Helen's high school yearbook came to mind. That was a good place to search. Perhaps she could tell from some of the messages who Helen's close friends were. It might not be much, but it was all she had.

Draining the hot chocolate, she went back inside and grabbed the yearbook off its bottom shelf. She plopped down on the Oriental carpet like before and began paging through the book. Scanning the written messages, deciphering swirls and cramped scrawls, Kelly slowly perused the pages until she came to what she and her friends had always called the "mug shots," those stiff, lookalike photos that revealed every flaw.

Starting with the A's, Kelly scrutinized page after page until she reached the end. There she paused, and studied one photo. She leaned closer, examining it, then she smiled. Closing the yearbook with a satisfied snap, she shoved it back onto the lower shelf and headed to bed.

Sixteen

"**Kelly,** how are you?" Mimi asked, peering over a box of crinkly, lacy yarns.

Must be a new shipment, Kelly guessed, since the brilliant colors and textures didn't look familiar. "I'm fine. A little tired from having to work so late last night, but okay. What kind of yarns are they?" she asked, pointing to the blaze orange, fire-engine red, and bubble-gum pink brimming from the box. "I don't recognize them."

"Probably because they don't last long enough for you to even see them," Mimi said. "It's called 'eyelash' because it's got all these little fibers that knit up into these great trendy scarves and tops, whatever." She started arranging the profusion in a crate along the wall. "Girls just love these yarns. They'll be gone in two weeks."

"Wow," Kelly said, sinking her hand into the pile. "They're soft and yet they look spiky."

"I know. They're such fun," Mimi said with a youthful giggle. "I whipped up a scarf for my thirteen-year-old niece last week for her birthday. 'Electric limeade' was the color. Then I knit little strands of crimson silk through it as well. I called it cherry limeade." She grinned, pleased with herself.

Remembering Curt's comment about his summer of cherry limeades, Kelly had to smile. "Great idea, Mimi. Why don't you make another and wear it so we can see."

"Maybe I will," she said as she headed back toward the checkout area.

Kelly stroked the eyelash once more, then headed to the main room. Megan was already there, knitting with a neon pink cotton that nearly glowed it was so bright. "Wow, that's a great shade for you, Megan," she said, dropping her tote bag and settling in. "What are you making?"

"I thought I'd make the shell that's hanging over there." She pointed to a red sleeveless top dangling from the ceiling of the other room.

It was almost as pretty as the top Kelly would make someday. She wasn't sure when "someday" would arrive. Maybe she could actually start now. After all, she finally felt comfortable doing the stockinette stitch, she thought, as she pulled out her practice piece and started knitting. Maybe.

"You know, we were all worried about you yesterday," Megan said softly without looking up.

Kelly let out an audible sigh. This would take some getting used to. "I know, and I'm sorry. I didn't mean to concern anyone. After all, I had Carl, and he'd be more than enough protection."

"Steve told us about Carl."

Busted. "Okay," Kelly admitted with a laugh. "He was a little distracted by, well, by everything. But it turns out I didn't need protection. Trust me, if I felt anything questionable about Stackhouse, Carl would never have gotten off his leash. I swear."

Megan glanced up, and Kelly was surprised to see so much concern still. "I believe you. Just promise you'll take one of us along next time you're sleuthing. We can lurk in the background while you're asking questions, so we won't cramp your style."

Kelly laughed out loud, picturing Megan lurking, as well as herself 'sleuthing about' à la Sherlock Holmes. "I'll think about it, I promise."

"You don't have to do everything alone, Kelly," Megan said as she returned to the neon pink rows of stitches.

Letting that thought play through her mind, Kelly kept up her knitting and purling, row after row of stockinette forming in the variegated wool. After a few minutes, she checked her watch. Lizzie should be arriving with Hilda any minute. Hilda's advanced knitting class began at eleven.

Just then, she heard the front door's jangle and Lizzie's birdlike soprano voice and Hilda's rich contralto in the foyer. *Right on time,* she thought. Sure enough, Hilda sailed into the room like a cruise liner—tall, substantial, impressive bulk. Lizzie followed in her wake, skimming the water like a sailboat, darting and quick to respond to the wind's whim. "Good morning, ladies," Kelly greeted them both.

"Ah, good morning, Megan, Kelly. Still laboring on that practice piece, I see," Hilda observed as she steamed past.

"Good morning, dears," Lizzie chirped as she floated by.

"Morning, Hilda, Lizzie," Megan replied.

"Lizzie, when you have a minute, could you help me with some of my stitches?" Kelly asked.

"Surely, dear," Lizzie agreed. "Let me get Hilda settled, and—"

"I'm fine, Lizzie," Hilda decreed. "Go help Kelly."

"Well, if you're sure, dear." Lizzie set her knitting bag, fabric bag, and purse on top of the library table and started to draw up a chair.

"Why don't we go into the café and have some tea, all right? That way we won't be distracted by Hilda's class. Megan, you'll excuse us, won't you?" She deliberately caught Megan's gaze and winked.

Megan glanced to Lizzie then said, "Absolutely. I have to go back and work as well. See you later."

"What particular problem were you having, dear?" Lizzie asked as Kelly led her to the café.

Choosing a quiet table in an empty corner, Kelly offered Lizzie a chair and settled in herself. "Well, to be honest, Lizzie, I think I'm doing pretty well with my stockinette. Take a look and tell me what you think." She handed over her misshapen practice piece.

Lizzie observed the stitches with a professional eye, checking both sides of the piece—knitting and purling sides. "Very good, dear. I can see where you got the hang of it, so to speak, and your stitches improved."

"Thank you," Kelly said, feeling the flush of accomplishment. "Coming from you that's high praise."

"Flattery, flattery," Lizzie dimpled.

Kelly signaled a waitress over. Jennifer was scouting property this morning for her real estate office, apparently. *Just as well,* Kelly thought. She wanted privacy for this chat. "Tea, Lizzie?"

"Oh, yes, thank you, with cream and sugar," she told the waitress, showing another dimple.

When the waitress scurried off, Kelly set her knitting aside and leaned forward slightly. "Actually, Lizzie, I have other questions I'd like to ask you. Not about knitting at all, if you don't mind?"

"Why, certainly, dear. What is it?"

"I was paging through Aunt Helen's yearbook last night, and I couldn't help noticing your picture there, too. You were in the same class, right?"

Lizzie beamed. "Yes, we were. We both were graduated the same year. In fact, Helen and I shared several classes together. She was clever with math like I was. Sometimes we were the only girls in the class." Her eyes lit up in amusement.

Better and better, Kelly thought. "That's wonderful, Lizzie, because I'm trying to find out everything I can about Helen's last year in high school. The people she knew, what groups she joined, who were her friends, and all that."

Lizzie cocked her head. "Why are you asking, dear? Do you think it has something to do with her death?"

Kelly smiled at Lizzie's perceptiveness. "Perhaps," she hedged. "I'm simply trying to look everywhere I can for information."

"Well, of course, I'll be glad to help. What would you like to know?"

"Did she have a lot of girlfriends? Anyone close to her?"

Lizzie closed her eyes. "Not really. Helen always kept to herself. Almost aloof. I admired that quality in her. She always looked so . . . so self-contained." She gave a wry smile. "And of course, that quality never sits well with the popular girls. They like to think every other girl is jealous of them. So when they see someone who isn't, well . . . they tend to get mean-spirited."

"So, Helen wasn't one of those popular girls you're talking about?" Kelly moved her arm so the waitress could serve their tea and coffee.

"No, indeed. Helen seemed in her own little world most of the time."

"You two were friends, weren't you?" she asked when the waitress left.

"I'd say we were acquaintances. We went to the same church, so our families knew each other, but Helen and I didn't really even talk much until high school. That's when we shared classes together."

"Were you one of those popular girls, Lizzie?" Kelly ventured with a smile.

Lizzie dimpled and blushed at the same time, clearly delighted to be considered. "Oh, my gracious, no! I was never one of them. Why, Hilda and I weren't even allowed to date. Oh, no. Papa was much too strict for that. And having boyfriends was absolutely required for those other girls. They were always whispering and giggling and telling tales about all the boys and each other, of course."

"Did they talk about Helen?"

A devilish smile teased Lizzie's mouth. "Oh, yes. It used to infuriate them that the boys paid so much attention to Helen when she didn't pay attention to them. Helen had this way about her. Ohhhh, it was hard to define . . . she was saucy without actually flirting. But it was fascinating to watch her. She didn't lead them on, like the other girls. Helen was smarter than that." Lizzie gazed at the white porcelain teapot, obviously reminiscing.

Kelly was just as fascinated by Lizzie's vibrant recollections of her high school years. Clearly, those were golden years in Lizzie's mind, enshrined forever. Kelly was struck once again that Helen held such an important place in the memories of both Stackhouse and Lizzie. Her aunt clearly carved out a niche for herself on her own terms.

"Was there any boy she paid particular attention to?"

"Well, she would walk to and from class with that handsome Curtis Stackhouse practically every day. You know, I believe I spied Curtis at the Wool Fair when we visited. And he's still a handsome man." Lizzie gave an appreciative nod, as if judging a fine wine.

Kelly grinned. "I saw him yesterday, and you're right. He's still a handsome man and a successful rancher now. He also remembered Helen." She left it at that.

Lizzie perked up. Her pink hair ribbon bouncing on her neat silver hairdo. "Well, I'm sure he did. That poor boy worshipped the ground Helen walked on. Wore his heart on his sleeve, too. That used to drive those other girls wild. One of them, Julie Fisher, had her cap set for Curtis, but he wouldn't give her the time of day." Lizzie giggled.

Surprised again at Lizzie's observations, Kelly decided to probe a little deeper. "So, Curtis Stackhouse was Helen's boyfriend, then. You said they walked to class every day, and he worshipped her."

"Oh, no, dear," Lizzie corrected, wagging her head. "I'm sure

Helen liked Curtis, but she didn't love him. He was simply a decoy, so no one would notice the boy she really loved."

Boy, Lizzie didn't miss a trick, Kelly thought in admiration. "Who was that? Do you know?"

Lizzie lifted her dimpled chin proudly. "I most certainly do. I saw them kissing behind the library. Lawrence Chambers stole Helen's heart. Poor girl. She knew he belonged to another."

Kelly stared in surprise. She wasn't expecting that answer. "*What?* Lawrence Chambers? Her lawyer?"

"One and the same."

Kelly wagged her head in amazement. "Brother, Lizzie, you missed a career in journalism. You should have been a reporter. I'm impressed."

Lizzie blushed in pleasure at Kelly's praise. "Thank you, dear, but Hilda and I were destined to be schoolteachers. Papa said so. And he was right. We were excellent teachers."

"Let's get back to Lawrence Chambers, okay?" Kelly picked up the thread. "What made you think he 'belonged' to another?"

"Well, it was common knowledge. Lawrence was from an old established and very wealthy Fort Connor family. He was already pledged to Charlene Thurmond. She was the daughter of his father's oldest friend and business associate, Henry Thurmond. I heard they'd been promised to each other as children." Lizzie shook her head sadly. "Poor Helen. She was just the daughter of sugar beet farmers, and not very successful ones at that. She never had a chance. But Lawrence loved her. There was no doubt about it. I could tell by the way he gazed at her in class. I'd catch him watching her in algebra."

Kelly sat quietly, sipping her coffee while her mind churned. Chambers. Lawrence Chambers. She'd never have guessed. Recalling the stark high school photo of an owlish, homely Chambers peering out from behind huge glasses, Kelly had to marvel. Judging from Lizzie's account, Helen could have had any boy she wanted. In fact, she had a heartbreakingly handsome young cowboy following her around like a puppy. Yet she spurned them all for the bookish and unattainable Chambers.

Helen had always referred to him as her oldest and closest friend,

Kelly remembered. Close was right. That explains the tremendous care and concern Chambers had always demonstrated toward Helen. *And it explained his intense grief at her death,* Kelly thought, recalling his emotional reaction in his office.

Or, did it? Kelly stared into her empty cup, as a niggling little thought wormed its way from the back of her mind. What if upstanding and trustworthy Lawrence Chambers was deliberately misleading her? Perhaps that emotional distress was cleverly designed to deflect further scrutiny? Clearly, Chambers had secrets to hide. Was he afraid his position in the community would be jeopardized if Helen's story got out? Helen would never reveal it, Kelly was certain.

Perhaps it's not about the story, the niggling thought whispered. Perhaps it's about money. Lots of money. Helen's property is worth a lot of money now. And Martha's, too. In fact, Martha's property could be worth a great deal if there's oil and gas beneath. And who was it that suggested the land be tested for minerals and other riches? Chambers.

Kelly recalled Martha's comments the day before she died. How Chambers was "taking care of everything." What if he had been surveying all of Martha's subterranean wealth and Helen found out? What if she felt betrayed and threatened to reveal his scheme? Had Chambers murdered Helen and Martha for their land? Did he try to run Kelly down on the trail to get her out of the picture or, at least, out of town?

Kelly set her cup back into its saucer, letting her thoughts settle as well. The image of frail-looking Chambers riding a bike at top speed would not come into focus. She was beginning to go in circles now, and all the theories were running into one another. She needed to sort through them all, to see which ones deserved further scrutiny and which ones made no sense.

"Do you have any more questions, dear?" Lizzie inquired. "If not, I need to check on Hilda's class. I'm in charge of copying patterns for everyone, and I think it's that time." She checked her watch.

"Oh, definitely. Thanks, Lizzie, you've been a great help," Kelly said, pulling some bills from her wallet and dropping them on the table. "I really appreciate your openness. And your memory is simply fantastic. I still think you'd have made a great reporter."

"Oh, hush, dear," Lizzie said with a giggle and a little wave as she walked toward the shop doorway.

Kelly gathered her things and headed back to the shop's main room. The library table was deserted, which suited her just fine. She needed time to think about Lawrence Chambers and all those theories that swirled inside her head. What better way than to use Mimi's method? She'd knit on it.

Pulling out her ever-expanding practice piece, Kelly picked up the stockinette where she left off. Knitting the remainder of that row, she purled the next, getting her rhythm back. In the adjoining room she heard the sounds of Hilda's class dismissing themselves and noticed several students wander into the room, checking pattern books and yarns. She was comfortably settled in and feeling positively meditative, until a loud voice shattered her peaceful state.

"Good heavens, girl! Are you planning to make a blanket of that thing?" Hilda boomed from across the room. Kelly jumped in her chair and dropped a stitch.

"Darn it, Hilda, don't scare me like that," she exclaimed, annoyed that her peaceful interlude had been interrupted. "You made me drop a stitch."

"Let it join the others. Surely you don't plan to use that piece," Hilda said as she came to stand beside Kelly's chair.

Kelly could feel Hilda's penetrating gaze and wondered how she could be considered such a good teacher. Did she intimidate her students into succeeding?

"Of course not," Kelly protested, not a little defensive. "I told you this is my practice piece. I'm practicing stockinette so I can—"

"Good Lord, girl, you've practiced enough," Hilda decreed, and reached over to yank the piece from Kelly's hands.

So shocked at Hilda's quickness, Kelly just stared at her for a few seconds. "Hilda!" she cried. "I was in the middle of a row!"

"Your stockinette looks fine," Hilda decreed, examining the stitches much as Lizzie had done. Then, to Kelly's amazement, Hilda whipped out a pair of small scissors and snipped the length of yarn that attached the piece to the remainder of its skein.

"*Hilda!*" Kelly protested, ignoring the students who were hiding their laughter behind pattern books. "Do you treat all your students this way?"

"My students don't need prodding. You do. It's time you started your sweater." She dropped the forlorn practice piece on the table.

"What?!" Kelly protested. "I can't do that sweater yet. It's too . . . too complicated. It has a pattern . . . and . . . and I've never followed a pattern before."

"You can read, can't you?" Hilda peered overtop her spectacles, her pale blue eyes hawklike.

Kelly couldn't believe it. She'd fallen into the clutches of the Nazi Knitter. Where had helpful Hilda gone? She managed to scowl back. "Patterns are different. They look strange. All those little lines and squiggles."

"That's only because you've never done one before. Everything new is strange at first. You simply need to choose a simple pattern. Come with me."

Hilda turned smartly on the heel of her industrial-strength nurses' shoes and headed toward the other room where all the new sweaters and tops were dangling from ceiling and cabinet doors and draped across shelves. Kelly gave in and followed after.

"Now, look at all you have to choose from," Hilda said, gesturing to the multitude of yarns spilling from crates and piled on shelves. "You need something to build your confidence, Kelly. I suggest you choose one of those bulky knit yarns you used so successfully with your scarf. We'll find a simple pattern, and you'll have a sweater before you know it. Then, you'll be ready to tackle that sweater you're pining for."

Kelly stared at Hilda, shocked at the clever suggestion as well as her uncanny read of what was causing the hesitation. The suggestion resonated within, but pride reasserted itself. Kelly wasn't going to capitulate that fast, so she forced a frown, even though her fingers were itching to dive into the crates and start touching.

"Wellllll . . ." she demurred.

"Stop stalling, girl, you know you want to do it."

Rats. Hilda was outsmarting her at every turn. Kelly wasn't used to that, but she gave respect where it was due—albeit grudging. "How long would it take to do a sweater with these yarns?"

"Not much longer than it took to knit your scarf. You remember how fast that went, don't you?"

Kelly nodded.

"And how proud you felt when you finished? And how—"

Kelly held up her hand. Only total capitulation would satisfy Hilda. "Okay, okay, you've convinced me, Hilda. I'll make the sweater. Brother, you're relentless, you know that?"

"I pride myself on it." Hilda said, and Kelly could swear she detected a twinkle in that stern gaze. "Now, look up there. See the sweaters with the larger pattern? They were knit with those yarns. Tell me which one strikes your fancy, and I'll find the pattern."

Kelly scanned all the sweaters that were displayed, searching for a simple design. She found it hanging in the corner. A sleeveless shell with wide neck. No scalloped edges to maneuver, no fancy edging. No frills, just row upon row of neat stockinette top to bottom. Plain and simple. "How about that one," she chose, pointing to the light pink creation.

"An excellent choice. Now, you choose a yarn you like while I find the pattern," Hilda ordered before she headed for the pattern books.

This time, Kelly eagerly complied with Hilda's instructions. She dove into the bins, squeezing and stroking yarns fat and thin. Obediently concentrating on the chunkier wools, Kelly found some of the variegated yarns she used for her scarf. But these were spring colors—pale azures, cool lavenders, and minty greens.

Eyeing the sweater once more, she noticed how even the stockinette looked and realized the chunky yarn that was so perfect in her scarf would not yield the same effect in the sweater. She needed an even thickness all over this time. She began to plunder other bins of solid colors—creamy oatmeal, lime sherbert, cherry parfait.

Caressing the pudgy bundles she noticed the different feel and checked the label. She was surprised to see that it was a blend of cotton and merino wool. Checking the tag that dangled from the sweater, Kelly saw that it was also a cotton blend. That settled it in her mind.

She grabbed four skeins when Burt approached. "Hey, Burt," she said, noticing his worried expression. *Not him, too,* she thought, bracing herself for another lecture.

"Do you have a minute, Kelly?" he asked, glancing over his shoulder. "I've got something to tell you."

Kelly sensed it had to do with Helen. "Certainly, Burt. Why don't we talk while you spin," she suggested, heading back to the main room. She dropped the roly-poly bundles of cherry parfait onto the library table while Burt settled at the spinning wheel in the corner. Kelly grabbed a pattern book and spread it out at the end of the table.

"You talk, and I'll listen," she suggested as she leaned over the book, pretending to read. "Hilda's about to descend on me with a pattern. So you better make it quick." She nodded toward Hilda, who was across the room busily flipping through pages.

Burt picked up his spinning where he'd left off, hands deftly working the roving as the wheel hummed. "I heard from my contact at the crime lab again. The DNA tests are final now, and the blood on the carpet and the remnant of burned purple wool are a match."

"Does it match the vagrant's DNA?" she ventured, already sure of the answer.

"Nope."

Kelly exulted inside, even though she couldn't reveal her reaction. "Told you," she whispered.

"Yeah, you did."

"What's Morrison going to do now? He has to let that guy go, doesn't he? He can't still cling to that worn-out intruder theory now, can he?"

No answer at first. Just the hum of the wheel. "Actually my former partner says Morrison is checking everything out, but the guy's staying in jail for the time being. A hearing's been set for next week, and he'd already been assigned a public defender. If there's not enough evidence, he'll be released."

"Sheeesh," Kelly complained scornfully. "Morrison cannot admit he's wrong, can he?"

"The intruder theory could still be the right one, Kelly," Burt pointed out. "Just a different intruder. It's clear someone else was in the house and left blood specks on the carpet. Who knows? Maybe that's why they took the purple wool. They were bleeding and they grabbed whatever was handy." The wheel picked up speed.

Kelly paged through the book, ostensibly reading. "I've thought the very same thing, Burt. And I think I know why there's blood on the carpet. Helen fought back. She stabbed her attacker. I'll bet that's why there was a broken needle on the floor. That's what she used to defend herself."

"Could be—"

"Finally!" Hilda boomed across the room, smothering Burt's voice. "I knew that pattern was here." She snatched the plastic page and strode toward the office.

"Isn't there any way we can light a fire under Morrison?" Kelly complained. "Every day he wastes makes it harder to find the real killer."

"Morrison's doing his job, Kelly. He's just thorough. Meanwhile, don't go poking around all by yourself anymore, okay?" Burt warned. "Otherwise Mimi will have heart failure. You really gave her a fright the other day. She won't admit it to you, but she was a basket case until Steve returned and reported you were safe and sound."

"I promise," Kelly said with a nod, spying Hilda headed her way. "We'll talk later."

"Here, you go," Hilda announced, presenting the pattern with a flourish. "And I see you've chosen a beautiful yarn. Well done, my girl."

Kelly didn't even hear Hilda's compliment. Her attention was focused on the well-tailored gentleman who now stood in the entrance to the main room. Kelly's gaze settled on the legal-sized leather portfolio in his hand, and her stomach tightened.

"Ms. Flynn, I have some wonderful news for you," Alan Gretsky announced, flashing his brilliant toothy grin.

"Why, hello, Mr. Gretsky," she replied. "How are you?"

Gretsky's grin got even wider if that were possible. "Fabulous, Ms. Flynn, especially now. My clients have made you a most generous offer. A most generous offer, indeed." He approached, leather portfolio in his outstretched hand.

Kelly stared at it, reluctant to accept the portfolio. She knew what was in there. A generous offer to buy Helen's cottage. Her cottage, now, but still—the cottage of memories.

Forcing herself to accept the portfolio, Kelly forced a lukewarm smile. "I bet I know what this is."

Gretsky chuckled. "Yes, I bet you do, Ms. Flynn. But I bet you'll still be surprised by the generosity of their offer. They were most sympathetic to your situation, what with the recent death of your aunt and all. So they were exceptionally generous with the purchase price. They wanted to make sure you did not share any unnecessary financial burden."

"I confess I haven't made up my mind yet," she said. "I've committed to staying here for three months. So, I'm not sure that will work with your clients' plans."

Gretsky dismissed her concerns with an expressive wave of his hand. "They're totally flexible, Ms. Flynn. Remember, they wouldn't be moving into the cottage. So, don't worry about it. You take the time you need to think it over. You'll notice the acceptance date is a month away. And if you haven't decided by then, why, I'm certain they'd be amenable to extending the date."

Brother, Kelly thought. *They want this land badly.* She turned the portfolio over in her hands. Gretsky had skillfully boxed her in. Now, she had no reason not to consider the offer. To refuse to even examine it would be financially irresponsible, her accounting voice piped up. She owed it to herself to see what kind of money Gretsky was so excited about.

"All right, Mr. Gretsky, I'll take a look," Kelly agreed. "But I can't promise you when I'll have an answer."

"That's to be expected, Ms. Flynn," he replied. "The clients are totally comfortable with that, as I said before." Glancing about, he added, "Please excuse the interruption, folks. I'll let you all get back to your business. You take care now, Ms. Flynn. Have a good day." He gave a friendly wave and left.

Kelly stared at the portfolio, then stared at the cherry parfait bundles on the table. She really wanted to sit down and start that new sweater, but she couldn't. She had to examine the contract offer. And that would take time.

She checked her watch. Brother, noon already. Even without the offer, she'd have to leave and get back to her corporate accounts this afternoon. Cherry parfait sweaters and following up Lizzie's tantalizing information about Chambers would have to wait. She glanced at Hilda, who was standing stoically, pattern in hand, and saw the sympathetic gaze meet hers.

"Well, Hilda, I guess that sweater will have to wait awhile, okay?"

"Don't you worry, Kelly," Hilda reassured. "I'll have everything in a bag in Mimi's office waiting for you. Whenever all of this business is finished."

"Thanks, Hilda," she said, scooping up her belongings. Glancing over her shoulder to Burt, she smiled. "Thanks, Burt. We'll talk again later. And don't worry, I'll be too busy for a while to get into trouble."

"I'll hold you to that, Kelly," Burt called as she left.

Seventeen

"So, the offer's legit?" Jennifer asked as she poured Eduardo's fragrant dark coffee into Kelly's stainless steel mug.

"Yep," Kelly replied, leaning against the side of the café's outside door. Pale, early-morning sunshine filtered through the wide windows in the corner where they stood. Daylight savings time said eight o'clock, but the late-April sun was still bashful. Another month would bring the brilliance and summerlike warmth. "I searched the company name listed as the buyer, and it's authentic. It's Big Box's property acquisition division," she said, savoring the delectable aroma right beneath her nostrils. She couldn't wait another moment and took a long drink.

Jennifer scanned the nearly empty café and asked, "How generous was the offer? Burt told us Gretsky raved about his client's generosity."

"He wasn't exaggerating," Kelly admitted. "They really did offer above market price. Way above, which would allow me to pay off that horrible mortgage plus penalties and fees for early sale and still walk away with money."

"Any contingencies?"

"None. They really want this property, Jen."

"Well, if you want me to take a look at the offer, let me know. Those clauses can hide tricky things."

"Thanks, Jennifer. I'd appreciate your help." She exhaled a deep sigh. "You know, I wasn't expecting to have to deal with something like this on top of everything else that's happened. I mean, I can't really think about the offer because these murders have totally claimed my attention. Even my work is taking a backseat. The only way I'm keeping up is to work way late at night." She took another deep satisfying drink.

"No wonder you need Eduardo's coffee," Jennifer commented with a wry smile. "I'd better get you one of our spare mugs to fill up as well. Where're you off to this morning?"

Kelly glanced around to make sure no one was close enough to hear their conversation. No worries. Eduardo was noisily preparing omelets at the grill, while Pete rang up receipts across the room. The other morning waitress was serving the only customer in the café.

"I'm going to see Lawrence Chambers, Helen's lawyer," she confided. "Lizzie was a gold mine of information. She wasn't allowed to date, so she kept meticulous notes on everyone else's social life, including Helen's. And she knew who the mystery boyfriend was."

"The hunky cowboy, I hope."

"Nope. He was just the decoy so no one would notice the boy she really loved."

"Well? I'm waiting. I may get a customer in my section any minute. Hurry up," Jennifer ordered.

"It was Lawrence Chambers."

"Really? Was he hunky back then?"

"Hardly. His school photo makes him look like an earnest owl," Kelly said, unable to hide her smile.

Jennifer sighed. "Well, if Helen chose him, he must have been special. Helen was a great gal. So, why're you going to see him?"

"I'm just fishing. See what I can pry out of him. If not, then I'll see if I can get him to take a stroll down memory lane. See what happens."

Jennifer wagged her head. "There you go, again. Stirring up trouble, poking around. Burt told us you promised to behave."

Kelly fixed Jennifer with a wicked grin. "*You're* telling *me* I should behave?"

Jennifer started laughing. "Okay, okay, you got me. I won't say another word. But I'm not gonna cover for you. You can go in there and tell everyone yourself what you're up to."

Suddenly Kelly remembered something. "Whoa, thanks for mentioning that. I've got to touch base with them. I may be a little late for practice tonight. Won't know until I log on to my office site." She headed toward the shop.

Lisa and Megan were still sitting at the library table, as were some other knitters. "Hi, folks," Kelly greeted them all as she settled into a chair. "Lisa, I may be a little late for practice tonight. I won't know how heavy my workload will be till I check with my office later, okay?"

Lisa glanced up. "Yeah, but if you make it a habit, we'll beat you."

"Severely," Megan added.

"I'll remember that." Kelly let herself relax as the soft laughter rippled around the table. But as Mimi entered and sank into a chair, one look at her expression swept all humor away. Her face was ashen.

"Mimi, what's wrong?" Lisa asked.

"I've just been notified by the new landlord that the shop's lease won't be renewed this September. The property's being sold," Mimi said solemnly.

Stitches and yarns were forgotten, dropped unnoticed to laps, as everyone stared at Mimi, clearly horrified at the announcement.

"But I thought your old landlord said that wouldn't happen," Megan protested, her pale face registering her shock at the news.

Mimi chewed her lip. "He said they 'probably' would extend the lease, but I could tell he didn't know for sure, even when he said it. That's why I've been so . . . so worried lately, wondering if this would happen."

Kelly leaned forward, wishing she had an answer. "Mimi, I'm so sorry. I know how much work you've put in here." She glanced around, feeling a little sick that strangers would soon own Helen and Jim's farmhouse. "I can't believe this is happening."

"Neither can I," one of the knitters spoke up.

"Is there any way around the lease?" the other asked.

Mimi shook her head. "No. All leases are renewed at the discretion of the landlord."

"Mimi, we'll help you look for another place, honest," Lisa offered. "And Jennifer will scour the multiple listings for you. She'll find something—"

"What will I find?" Jennifer inquired as she marched up to the table and deposited another full mug of coffee in front of Kelly.

"Thanks, Jen," Kelly said, glancing up. "Mimi's losing her lease in September. The farmhouse will be sold. You're gonna have to help her find another place."

"What!" Jennifer protested. "Who's the new landlord? How dare he throw you out. What's his name?"

"Some company called A&G Management. I've already checked the directory, and it's not listed. Who knows if they're local or out of town. Maybe they're from Denver." Mimi gave a dispirited shrug.

Jennifer frowned and stared out the wood-trimmed paneled windows. "A&G Management, A&G Management. I think I've heard that name somewhere. Let me look into it, Mimi. I'm curious." She slipped off her apron. "Listen, I'm leaving early. It's dead in there. I'm going to the office to start checking. I want to know who this A&G Management is." She turned to leave.

"Jennifer, I appreciate that, dear, but there's nothing that can change the lease. I don't want you wasting your time," Mimi said sadly.

"Don't worry, Mimi, I do this research all the time," Jennifer declared. "I'll get back to you later." With that, she was gone.

Kelly stared after her, then let her gaze drift slowly around the farmhouse that Mimi had transformed into a wonderland of color and texture. The thought of it being sold and possibly torn down made her sick to her stomach. She checked her watch and rose from the chair. If Chambers passed her scrutiny, maybe she'd ask him about Mimi's predicament. Maybe there was some legal loophole only lawyers knew.

She leaned over and patted Mimi's arm. "Mimi, I have to go ask Lawrence Chambers some questions. I'll see you later."

Kelly sped from the shop, eager to leave the pall that had settled over everyone inside.

Lawrence Chambers laced his fingers together and rested them against the polished walnut desk as he fixed Kelly with a sympathetic look. "I'm afraid Mrs. Shafer has no option but to leave at the end of August," he said. "I wish there was some legal loophole, Kelly, really, I do. I know how much that shop meant to Helen and to Mrs. Shafer."

Kelly let out a loud sigh, partly for effect. The lease discussion had established a friendly tone. Now, it was time for her to start probing. "Thank you, Mr. Chambers. I was afraid as much, but it never hurts to ask. Particularly since I have an offer to sell my property as well. I'm not sure yet what I'll do." She deliberately left it hanging.

Chambers' eyes popped wide. "Someone is offering on your house? Who is it? Do you know them, Kelly?"

"I researched the buyer name and it's the property acquisition division for Big Box." Another deep sigh. "I really don't know what to do. They've offered above-market value, which would allow me to pay off that awful loan plus penalties and fees. I confess, I'm tempted."

"Good heavens, Kelly!" Chambers leaned over his desk. "What are you hesitating for? Grab that offer and run all the way to the bank. It would provide a reasonable solution to that horrible loan problem."

Kelly surveyed Chambers. His expression radiated sincerity. Clearly, if he'd been trying to keep Helen's and Martha's land under his control, he would have registered some trace of dismay, even subtle, that the land was slipping from his control. But there was no hint of that anywhere in his expression.

"Well, I told the Realtor that I was pretty busy now, and he'd have to wait on a decision. It could be over a month, I don't know."

"Well, speaking as Helen's former adviser, I'd cast my vote to accept the offer. You've had your life disrupted far too long with this whole ordeal, Kelly. It's time you returned to pick up the pieces."

Kelly pondered his answer as well as his expression and concluded his sincerity was genuine. "I'm thinking about it," she admitted, then sipped her coffee as she tried to decide how she could possibly turn her questions toward the past and his shared history with Helen. How to broach such a delicate subject? "It's hard to concentrate on anything else, Mr. Chambers. I'm still so caught up with Aunt Helen's death."

Chambers settled back into his black leather armchair, his lined face gaining even more wrinkles now. "I understand, Kelly. It's the same for me," he admitted. "I still cannot believe Helen's gone."

Surprised by his sudden honesty, Kelly observed Chambers' somber mood. Her glance drifted to the vibrant quilted mountain scene that hung on the paneled wall beside them. An idea came suddenly, and Kelly gambled. "Was that the cabin you and Helen visited back in high school?" she asked in a quiet voice.

Chambers' face paled in an instant. His eyes grew huge. "Wha-what do you mean?"

Now he really did resemble a startled, blue-eyed owl, Kelly observed. "Martha told me that Helen and her boyfriend would escape to a mountain cabin up in the canyon all those years ago," she said, truthfully repeating Martha's piece of the puzzle. "Helen never revealed your identity, Mr. Chambers. Someone else did."

Gripping the arms of the black leather chair, Chambers stared at Kelly, rigid, clearly horrified by what he heard. "Wh-wh-who?"

"A high school classmate of Helen's who had a keen eye for people-watching. That person once saw you two together and remarked that you were obviously in love." She glanced to the quilt. "I'm guessing that's Helen's gift of shared memories and a remembrance of lost love."

Chamber's face regained some of its color, much to Kelly's relief. She didn't want to send the frail lawyer into cardiac arrest with her visit.

He gazed at the quilt, and his lower lip trembled. "She was the love of my life, my true love," he whispered. "But I was too scared of my father to stand up for her. God help me, I was such a coward. My family had my life all arranged, and my wishes meant nothing. I told Helen I'd confront my father and tell him I'd choose my own wife. Yet, every time I tried, I . . . I lost my nerve. That steely gaze of his would lock onto me and . . . and I would freeze."

His head sank to his chest. "I still remember Helen standing alone in the shadows behind the bleachers, watching my father and Charlene announce our engagement to all their friends. I'll never forget the stricken look on her face." A huge shudder shook his shoulders.

Riveted by his account of the story, Kelly now understood what had driven Helen into Curt Stackhouse's arms that night. "Was that graduation night by any chance?"

The question seemed to rouse him. "Yes, yes, it was. I remember now, we were wearing our caps and gowns."

Chambers' obvious remorse and regret tugged at Kelly. "Now I know why you took such good care of my aunt over the years," she ventured in a gentle voice. "And if it's any consolation, Mr. Chambers, Helen and Jim had a good marriage. I know because I was there growing up and visited regularly throughout my life."

He glanced down at his clasped hands. "Yes, thank God for that," he said with a sigh. "And I've tried to be a good husband to Charlene all these years. She's a good woman, and a wonderful mother. We have three grown daughters and eight grandchildren now."

That last image seemed to cheer him a bit, Kelly noticed. "Well, Mr. Chambers, you've been truly fortunate. You have a growing, healthy family. You should be thankful." Then added, pensively, "Helen and Jim weren't quite as lucky. They lost their only child when he was only five years old, and they couldn't have any more, Helen told me. They sort of adopted me as their daughter, especially after my own father died."

Chambers nodded. "I know how much Helen loved you, Kelly. Truly like her daughter."

Kelly felt another tug within. "Well, I felt the same way. She was the closest thing to a mother I ever knew. I don't know if Helen ever told you, but my mother walked out on my dad and me when I was a baby, so Helen was really important in my life."

"Yes, she told me."

Feeling old memories encroach, Kelly swiftly changed the subject. Now that Chambers was composed again, Kelly wanted to explore a theory that had recently surfaced in her mind. Deciding it might be easier if she wasn't looking directly at him, she glanced to the quilted mountain cabin and wondered how to probe yet another delicate subject. Once again, she jumped in.

"I'm sure Helen regretted giving up the baby years ago, especially since she and Uncle Jim couldn't have any more children. Helen had never hinted at the child's existence. As close as we were, she never let on. It was Martha who told me. Forgive me for stirring up these old memories, Mr. Chambers, but I thought you might have some information about the man. He's in his late forties now. And I've wondered if he was the reason Helen withdrew all that money."

She took a deep breath and continued, still focusing on the quilt. "Perhaps, he found out his real mother's identity. Adopted children do that, I've heard. And maybe he appeared suddenly and said something to frighten Helen. I don't know. Maybe she didn't want to have any contact with him. I do know she was worried those last few days, because she wasn't herself when I spoke—"

The rest of Kelly's explanation died on her lips at the sight of Chambers. This time he really looked like he might have a heart attack. His face was pasty white, nearly gray, and his hand clutched at his chest.

"Mr. Chambers, are you all right?" Kelly cried as she sprang from her chair. "Should I call a doctor? Is it your heart?"

Chambers stared ahead, eyes glazed, for an excruciating moment, before he whispered, "A child . . . she never told me . . . my God . . ."

Kelly sank back into her chair, amazed that Chambers didn't know and feeling guilty that she'd dropped the dramatic bombshell so abruptly. "I thought you knew," she ventured when she saw Chambers revive once again. "I mean, I assumed . . ." Her voice trailed off, realizing again how foolish assumptions could be. And how misleading.

"When . . . where . . ." he struggled.

"Helen's father sent her to Wyoming and Martha's family the summer after graduation. Martha said the baby was born in December. December eleventh, I believe."

Chambers stared, stricken, so Kelly continued. "Apparently Helen stayed throughout the holidays with Martha's family and the baby, then gave him up for adoption to the Sisters of Charity in Cheyenne. She came home to Fort Connor in early winter, I think." Seeing the guilt shimmer in Chambers' eyes, she drew another breath and reached for whatever reassurance she could find. "Helen met Jim that spring, and they were married the following fall. So, she started a new life, too, just like you, Mr. Chambers," she offered gently.

Tears welled in Chambers' eyes and splashed down his cheeks, as if a hidden dam deep inside had broken at last. "Oh, dear God, what did I do . . . ?" he cried, a sob catching in his throat. "Oh, Helen, Helen . . . forgive me . . ." He sank his head in his hands and wept. "I abandoned you and the child . . . forgive me . . . forgive me . . ."

Kelly sat, unable to move, wishing she had not been the one to cause such distress. Maybe her friends were right. She shouldn't be poking around in other people's lives.

Nothing, no amount of questions, could bring Helen back alive. Or Martha. She had mucked about for more than two weeks, intruding herself in other people's business and their personal lives, and she still wasn't any closer to discovering the killer's identity than she was when she started. Burt was right. Morrison would look into everything and find the truth. Surely, he would. She should stay out of it.

Chambers' sobs rose and fell now, the voice of lamentation. Kelly's heart squeezed. She had to leave. Chambers' grief was too raw and real to be witnessed. She quietly rose from her chair and slipped from the office. Once outside, Kelly took a small notepad from the secretary's desk and wrote her apology for causing him such pain. She folded the sheet and gave it to his puzzled secretary with instructions that Mr. Chambers was not to be disturbed.

Eighteen

Kelly dropped her tote bag on the floor of the middle room, then carefully set her empty coffee mug beside it on the polished wooden floor. She'd indulge in her morning ritual of Eduardo's coffee in a few moments. Right now, Kelly wanted to feel. Needed to feel. Touch. Sink her hands into the softness that spilled from every corner of the room.

She started with the round maple table in the center, its rich burnished wood peeking through the colorful bundles that covered the surface. Kelly sank both hands into a bin of silk and cotton yarns, luxuriating in the softness. Next, she fingered the gorgeous long-sleeved crimson sweater that appeared on display yesterday.

Silk and cotton or was it that special cotton she was hearing about? Whatever it was, it was beautiful, she thought, wondering if she'd ever get good enough to attempt sleeves like those. They were bordered at the wrist with a knitted ruffled effect. *How on earth did they do that?* she wondered.

One step at a time as Lisa would say, Kelly reminded herself, then let her hands disappear into a crate of boa yarns—frothy, softer-than-soft, and bold primary colors. They knitted up into flirty, sassy accent scarves she had seen flung over shoulders of old and young alike.

The coffee craving gene began to protest the delay of its morning caffeine rush. Kelly reluctantly left the tactile paradise and grabbed her things. She'd drop her stuff at the table, get a fill-up with Eduardo's blessing, then she'd be ready to apologize to her friends for all the worry her recent activities had caused them. *Mea culpa*s all around.

Last night's softball practice had helped release some of Kelly's frustration. With each throw, each swing of the bat, she let go. Afterward, she'd used work as an excuse to skip the get-together and gone home to a soak in the tub. Her corporate accounts had consumed the afternoon. Late night was hers.

She turned the corner into the main room and was surprised to see Jennifer talking excitedly to Mimi. Megan sat wide-eyed across the table, her knitting in her lap, which was a sure sign Megan was engrossed in the subject.

"Hey, guys, what's up?" Kelly asked, plopping her things on the library table.

Jennifer whipped around, amazing Kelly again how fast she could move if she wanted to. If only she could throw a ball. "Kelly, I discovered who A&G Management is," Jennifer announced. "You'll never guess."

"I'm sure I won't. Who is it?"

"None other than Alan Gretsky. He formed the company last year, and apparently that's when he began meeting with this Big Box associate. I heard from another agent in his office that Gretsky met this guy socially. Some connection with his wife's family in Denver or something. Anyway, he's been wining and dining this guy, hoping to work into a deal where he can score big. And this is it."

"Whoa . . ."

"Yeah, my thoughts exactly. Now you know why he wants the cottage. He needs both parcels to make this deal work. Big Box won't want one without the other."

"Mimi, when did A&G buy out your landlord?" Kelly probed. Mimi stood at the end of the table, her hands clasping a cone of novelty yarn. Her expression a mixture of uncertainty and confusion, with worry thrown in for good measure.

"I'm already ahead of you," Jennifer cut in, grabbing a legal-sized document from the table. "April fifteenth, just a week ago."

Kelly caught up with Jennifer. "So, no surprise that my offer appears this week. Once Gretsky had this parcel under control, Big Box could offer on the cottage."

"Exactly. He's probably already drawn up the contract to sell this parcel to Big Box, and he's just waiting for you."

Kelly frowned, picturing Gretsky and his big friendly grin. "Of course, he knew that I wouldn't want to stay once I learned the shop was leaving. He figures all he has to do is wait. Wait until I leave. Son of a . . . sailor."

Jennifer chortled. "What was that again?"

"One of my dad's sanitized navy curses." Kelly threw up both hands. "Coffee. I need coffee. Right now. Brain cells are shutting down, and I need to think about this."

Once again, Jennifer jumped into action. "Hold everything, I'll be right back." She snatched Kelly's mug and was gone in a flash.

Kelly stared after her, remarking, "Wow, look at that speed. If only we could teach her to throw. What do you think, Megan?"

Megan grinned, picking up her pink cotton blend again. "We could teach her to throw."

"And batting? You think?"

"Probably, but that's not the problem. It's the base running. Jen would never make it around because she'd stop to flirt at each base," Megan said with a wink.

At that moment, Jennifer slid into home, depositing Kelly's mug and her own on the table without spilling a drop.

"Impressive," Kelly observed. "We're thinking of offering you a spot on the team."

"Thanks, but no thanks. I don't like to stand in the sun and sweat."

Even Mimi smiled at that. Kelly picked up her mug, inhaled Eduardo's nectar, and drank deep. Once, twice, thrice, to the sound of soft laughter.

"Okaaaaay," Kelly said, sinking into a chair. "Alan Gretsky, A&G Management. Who does this guy think he is? Buying up land under one name, hiding identities—"

"It happens, Kelly," Jennifer declared. "Especially when there's a lot of money involved. And my friend from his office told me Gretsky's really hungry. Seems he's been trying to run with the top dogs and always falling behind. He's missed out on some important deals the past few years, consequently he's been particularly anxious to score big so he can get in the 'club,' so to speak."

"There's a club?" Megan jibed.

"Yeah, and a secret handshake, probably," Jennifer said with a laugh. Checking her watch, she added, "Listen, I have to get back to the café. We're swamped this morning. Feast or famine, you know. I'll try to stop by after work. See ya." She raced off.

Mimi sat on the edge of a chair, still clutching the fat colorful cone of novelty yarn. "Mr. Gretsky didn't do anything wrong, Kelly," she said in a quiet voice. "I know you want to help, dear, but there's really nothing you can do. A&G is a legitimate company, and it bought this property. It's all totally legal. Don't worry about me. I'll find another place."

Kelly scowled into her mug. That may be true, she mused, but that wasn't the point. Gretsky thought he could outsmart them. Kelly, however, prided herself on not being outsmarted. And thanks to her good instincts, she seldom was. This time would not be the exception, she vowed, as an idea swam through the caffeine to the surface.

"I know that, Mimi," she said. "But I don't like Gretsky trying to force us both out. He has control of your place, yes. But he doesn't have mine."

"Uh oh, I see that look on your face," Megan warned.

"Don't worry," Kelly warned. "I'm not going to do anything crazy. Or anything I'd need a Rottweiler for, either." She grinned. "I'm just going to see if I can shake up Gretsky."

"Oh, no . . ." Mimi whispered, clearly horrified.

"It's okay, Mimi, honest," Kelly explained, waving her hand. "I'm simply going to tell him that I've changed my mind, and I'm staying in Fort Connor for good. So, I won't be selling the cottage, after all." Kelly felt the idea resonate inside her with a surprising intensity.

"Why?" Megan queried.

"I'm hoping my announced change of plans will throw a wrench into Big Box's plan and they'll pull out of the deal. Then, if Gretsky's dreams of development riches go down the drain, maybe he'll change his mind about leasing."

"Boy, that's a stretch," Megan observed.

"Yeah, I know, but it's all I've got. So, I'm gonna run with it." With that, Kelly jumped out of her chair and grabbed her tote bag. "See you folks later," she called over her shoulder as she headed for the door, leaving Megan and Mimi staring after her.

"Caffeine rush," Megan decreed.

"Lord, I hope so," Mimi breathed.

METROPOLITAN REALTY proclaimed the large stainless steel letters on the wall behind the receptionist's desk. Kelly had already switched her demeanor when she pushed through the glass doors. She deliberately hesitated in front of the enclosed area, waiting for the receptionist to speak first.

"May I help you?" the attractive young blonde asked.

"Yes, please," Kelly answered in a breathy voice. "Is Mr. Gretsky here? I spoke with him last week about selling my house."

The young woman's face brightened. Sold houses meant paychecks. "Let me check with his assistant, Laura." She quickly dialed a number and waited. "Laura? One of Alan's clients is out front. Is Alan here? Ohhhh, all right." She hung up the phone. "Laura will be right with you if you care to wait." She indicated some plush leather armchairs and sofas in warm caramel and chocolate tones in the corner of the lobby.

"Thank you," Kelly replied politely, then spied a tall, thin woman hurrying down a corridor, headed her way.

"I'm Laura, Mr. Gretsky's assistant, may I help you?" she asked. Wisps of graying hair had escaped from the neat bun and feathered around her face, softening the lines and wrinkles.

"Well, I was hoping to speak with Mr. Gretsky," Kelly said, feigning a worried look. "I'm Kelly Flynn, and we spoke earlier this week about selling my home, and I—"

"Why don't we go to Alan's office, Kelly. It's more comfortable there," Laura suggested, gesturing to the corridor.

She ushered Kelly into a spacious office with huge windows overlooking tall cottonwoods bordering one of Fort Connor's waterways that crisscrossed the city. Called ditches by old-timers and canals by the newbies, they were a reminder of the city's early agricultural history.

"Please sit, Ms. Flynn, and I'll get your file." Laura settled across the room at an antique secretary's desk, which had obviously been restored with great care because the mahogany shone rich and golden.

Kelly settled into a rust-colored leather chair, relaxing into its comfortable embrace. Gretsky might not be running with the big dogs yet, but he knew which signals to send. Both his wardrobe and his office décor spoke volumes. Admiring his huge antique polished wood desk, she couldn't resist asking, "Mahogany? Walnut?" and glanced to Laura.

Laura smiled as she sorted through the files on her desk. "Walnut. Eighteen eighty, I believe."

"My compliments. It's beautiful."

"Here it is," Laura declared, opening a file folder. She scanned the contents for a moment. "Your property hasn't been listed for sale, has it, Ms. Flynn?"

"Uhhhh, no, not yet," Kelly demurred. "In fact, this is all so sudden, I . . . I really need to speak with Mr. Gretsky. You see, I told him I would need time to think, but then things have been happening, and . . . oh, gracious!" Kelly made an exasperated gesture. "Everything's changed suddenly. When's he coming back? I have to leave in a few—"

"He's out with clients right now, showing property. But he should return—" The ringing phone stopped her midsentence. She reached over, punched speakerphone, then went back to paging through the file. "Alan Gretsky's office. May I help you?"

"Yes, this is Main Street Frame Shop," a woman's high voice announced. "Is Mr. Gretsky there?"

"Not at the moment. I'm his assistant. May I take a message?"

"Yes, of course. Please tell him that the family quilt he brought in last month is all framed and ready for him to pick up. It'll be three hundred and forty-seven dollars. Tell him to ask for Sandy. I'm the one in charge of framing."

Laura started scribbling on a nearby notepad. Kelly, meanwhile, had perked up at the mention of the words "family quilt." Her buzzer went off inside.

"Sandy, I'll make sure to tell him. How late are you open?" Laura asked, continuing to scribble.

"Until five, oh and be sure to tell him it looks absolutely beautiful," Sandy's voice oozed pride. "We were very careful with the little fabric pieces that were sewn into the middle of all the squares, and the embroidery, too. Oh yes, and that tiny lock of baby hair. Simply precious. We were extremely careful. That's why it took so long to frame."

"I'll be sure to tell him," Laura promised. "Bye." She clicked off.

Kelly watched Laura examine the file's paperwork but didn't see her. All she could picture was Helen's quilt hanging on the cottage wall, each square filled with treasured pieces of Helen's early needlework, embroidery, crocheting, even tatting. And—in one square, a tiny lock of blond hair from their young son who died.

Her heart pounded so hard, Kelly was afraid Laura might hear it. That was Helen's quilt Gretsky took to the frame shop last month. And there was only one way he could have gotten it off her wall. He killed her. Gretsky was the murderer. He had to be.

Kelly fairly leaped from her chair. "Ohhh, my goodness, will you look at the time," she announced as she checked her watch. "I have got to get back to work. Consulting hours, you know. Have to be online when my boss is. Listen, you tell Mr. Gretsky I'll give him a call later and we can set a time to talk."

"I'm certain Alan will call any minute now, and I'll have him give you—"

Kelly waved no. "No, no, when I go online I don't even pick up my phone. I'll call him." Spying the open card holder, she snatched one of Gretsky's business cards. "I'll take his card to make sure I've got the number. Thanks so much. You have a good day, now," she said as she escaped through the doorway before Laura could say a word.

Speeding through the lobby and out the glass door, Kelly headed for her car—then on to Fort Connor's Old Town and the Main Street Frame Shop. With Gretsky's card in hand, she could pass herself off as his assistant, sent to pick up the family quilt for her boss. Having overheard the phone message, she already knew to ask for Sandy. Kelly would gladly pay $347 to have Helen's treasured heirloom quilt back in the cottage where it belonged. She would deal with Gretsky later.

Nineteen

Spying her friends' cars parked outside, Kelly raced up the brick walkway to the knitting shop's entrance. She patted the key in her pocket. Now that Helen's quilt was back on the wall safe and sound, Kelly wasn't taking any chances. She'd locked both front and back doors. Heart still racing, she fairly burst through the shop's doorway and rushed into the main room to find Jennifer, Megan, and Lisa knitting around the table. Burt looked up from his spinning in the corner.

"Kelly!" Lisa greeted her. "Jennifer told me about—"

Kelly silenced her with a finger to her lips, then announced in a hushed voice, "I'm glad you're all here. We've got to talk." She pulled out a chair closer to Burt and gestured for the others to move to that end of the table.

"Well?" Jennifer prodded when they settled. "We're waiting. Megan told us where you went. What'd Gretsky say?"

"He wasn't there. I spoke with his assistant instead."

"And?" Jennifer gestured. "C'mon, Kelly, keep talking. Do you want me to run back to the café and see if Eduardo saved some coffee?"

"No, I don't need any coffee. I'm wired enough as it is."

"Uh, oh, this is gonna be bad, I can tell." Megan screwed up her face.

"While I was in his office talking to his assistant, this call comes in. She puts it on speakerphone, and the message is from a frame shop in Old Town. The family quilt Gretsky brought in last month is ready, the woman says. The quilt with all the little needlework and embroidery pieces in the middle of the squares and the lock of baby hair." Kelly paused deliberately to let the message sink in.

Lisa and Jennifer stared intently as did Burt, but Megan drew back with a gasp. "Helen's quilt!" she cried. "How did he get it?"

Kelly leaned over the table and the others followed suit. Even

Burt's wheel stopped spinning. "The only way he could. Gretsky murdered Helen. He's the killer."

"What? That's crazy!" Megan cried. "You can't seriously believe he'd kill Helen for a quilt."

"No, of course not. I think he took the quilt after he killed her," Kelly explained. "I think—"

"Wait a minute, wait a minute," Lisa exclaimed. "Are you sure it's the same quilt?"

"Yes. I took one of Gretsky's cards and went to the shop. Passed myself off as his assistant picking up the quilt for my boss. It's Helen's all right, and it's hanging back on the cottage wall where it belongs."

"Clever girl," Burt observed. "But you're a long way from proving his guilt, you know that, don't you? Gretsky could always say Helen sold it to him before she died, and you couldn't prove differently."

"I know," she said, nodding. "But my gut tells me he's the killer. Now we have to prove it."

"Hold on," Jennifer interrupted this time. "Why do you think he killed Helen? What reason would he have?"

Kelly glanced toward the browsing customers. "I believe he's Helen's illegitimate son, the baby she gave up for adoption years ago. And I'll bet anything he discovered Helen was his birth mother and tried to force himself into her life. Especially after he discovered she owned a prized piece of real estate."

"Hmmmm," Jennifer mused aloud. "That makes sense. But it still doesn't explain why he'd kill her."

"I'll bet he tried to weasel the land out of Helen," Lisa jumped in. "And Helen didn't like it. In fact, I'll bet she didn't like him. Helen never did like pushy people."

"Yeah, you're right," Megan agreed. "But, still, that's not enough reason to kill."

"Look, I'm not sure what happened," Kelly continued. "Maybe Gretsky tried to intimidate Helen or threaten to expose her past or whatever. But something happened to worry Helen so much she deliberately took out a top-heavy mortgage in order to withdraw twenty thousand dollars. And I'll bet next month's salary that money was meant for Gretsky."

"For what?" Megan queried.

"To leave her alone," Jennifer supplied.

"And Gretsky wouldn't do it," Kelly picked up the thread. "Plus, I'll bet she also refused to sell her property. Chambers said Helen called before she died and told him she wanted to change her will. She wanted the land to be turned into gardens if I didn't want it."

"When did she call him?" Lisa asked.

"The day she was killed."

"Whoa."

"You know, you're right," Jennifer said with a nod. "That could have pushed Gretsky to the limit, especially if he'd made promises to Big Box."

"Absolutely," Kelly agreed. "I'll bet he'd been making plans the moment he discovered his birth mother's identity. And when she didn't cooperate, he killed her. Maybe in anger, who knows?"

"All of that is possible, Kelly, but you still have to prove it," Burt reminded. "How do you propose doing that?"

"We'll have to trap him," she said simply.

"Trap him!" Megan croaked. "Are you kidding? How do we do that?"

"With information, that's how," Kelly whispered. "First, we'll dig up everything we can on Gretsky. Then, we'll figure out how best to confront him with it."

"That'll be harder than you think, Kelly," Burt observed sagely. "I should know. I spent a lifetime doing it."

"I think you've been watching too many of those movies," Lisa said with a little smile. "But count me in. What do you want me to do?"

Kelly hunched closer. "I thought we'd each search something different. Megan, how about you doing a Web search on everything you can find on Gretsky. Google him, whatever."

"Will do," she said. "I've got even better sources than that."

"Megan 'Deep Throat' Smith," Jennifer joked. "Okay, I'll not be outdone by our resident geek. I'll turn over every real estate rock I can find and see if there's any dirt on him. Also, I'll check on his financial status. I've got friends who can help me there."

Burt leaned over. "And I'll ask my partner to run a discreet check on Gretsky."

"Boy, I wish we had a blood sample from Gretsky, then we could match it with the blood from the carpet—" Kelly said.

"Is it an unusual blood type?" Lisa interrupted. "If so, I have a friend who works at the hospital blood bank."

"Type O was found on the carpet and the wool. Same type as the suspect in jail," Burt offered.

"And nearly half the population," Lisa added with a shrug.

"But," Burt continued, "the crime lab also did DNA tests, and they show absolutely no match with the suspect."

"That's okay, Lisa," Kelly said. "You can check if he's a member of the health club or if he had a personal trainer. People gossip with trainers." She looked around at her friends. "Boy, I don't know what I'd do without you guys."

"We just don't want you working alone," Jennifer teased. "What are *you* checking?"

"I'm going to look into that Wyoming adoption agency, the Sisters of Charity. I'll also check if there're any state agencies that keep records on adoptees looking for birth parents." She looked at her watch. "It's almost evening now. Why don't we touch base tomorrow afternoon after lunch and see what we've turned up. Is that possible? Can we all meet here?"

They all nodded. Then Megan spoke up. "Who's gonna tell Mimi? Anyone brave enough?"

"I will," Burt volunteered.

"Bless you, Burt," Kelly said and kissed his cheek. "See you folks tomorrow."

Mimi was rearranging the antique trunks and wooden crates in the foyer when Kelly pushed open the shop's front door. She fairly pounced on Kelly when she entered.

"Kelly, what's this I hear about your trying to trap this vicious murderer?" she croaked in a whisper, so the customers browsing in the adjacent room wouldn't hear. Her gray eyes were as round as demitasse saucers.

"Shhhhh," Kelly reminded, finger to lips. She didn't have to wonder if Mimi was worried. She radiated anxiety, reeked with it. Kelly took a deep breath and endeavored to calm her. "Don't worry, Mimi.

We're all working on this together. I'm not going off alone to confront anyone. Even Burt's helping."

Mimi's attractive face puckered into a worried frown. "I know, he told me. But I still don't understand why you can't just let the police handle it. After all, you've found new evidence—"

"Which is entirely circumstantial, Mimi. Nothing I've uncovered proves anything. Gretsky's been too clever for that. We're hoping to confront him and maybe he'll slip and let out the truth."

Mimi stared horrified. "How?"

"We're still working on that," Kelly hedged as she headed for the main room. "But don't worry, Mimi. No one's doing anything crazy. I promise."

Everyone but Lisa was already seated around the library table as Kelly entered. Even Burt was in his corner, spinning, a large plastic bag at his feet overflowing with golden-blond wool. Kelly was reminded of the fairy tales from childhood. Damsels spilling golden hair from castle windows, witches casting spells on maidens, dwarves spinning straw into gold. She had to smile at the image of Burt beside a basket of straw.

"Hey, everyone," she greeted them, then let her things drop to the table and sat down. "When's Lisa coming? Anyone know?"

"Right now," Lisa's voice sounded as she sped into the room.

Jennifer looked up from her knitting and checked her watch. "Whoa, that's the fastest you've ever been able to get away from the health center. What'd you do? Put all your clients in the therapy pool and leave?"

Lisa grinned. "Naw, they'd turn into prunes before I got back. I merely switched some appointments with another therapist so I'd be freed up." She plopped into a chair.

Megan glanced up over her pink wool, which had grown considerably since yesterday. If Megan knitted when she was worried, she'd have that sweater finished tonight, Kelly figured. "Did you see Mimi pacing the foyer?"

"Ohhhh, yeah," Kelly said. "I tried to calm her down."

"Don't worry about it, Kelly. She's simply being a mom. You gals are family to her, you know," Burt said over the relaxing hum of the wheel as his fingers worked the roving.

"Okay, folks," Kelly said, retrieving a spiral notebook from her tote bag. "Now that we're all here, let's see what we've got." Glancing over her shoulders at the browsing customers wandering about, she added, "And remember to keep it down. We don't want to alarm the locals."

"I'll start," Burt said, letting the wheel slow to a stop. "The subject's record is clean. Only minor traffic offenses. Speeding. Parking fines. No scrapes with the law. No complaints from neighbors. Belongs to the country club, various professional organizations, community, philanthropic, etc., etc. The usual. Nothing suspicious whatsoever."

Kelly made notes as Burt spoke. "Okay, I might as well go next," she volunteered. "I turned up nothing useful. The Wyoming agency, Sisters of Charity, no longer handles adoptions, and the Church Diocese was absolutely no help. All they said was they 'think' the adoption records are still in sealed boxes in the Diocese basement, but they're not sure. And even if they were available, only the parties immediately involved would have access. Like the mother or the child. Also, my search for state agencies ran into a brick wall. Privacy rights and all that restrict access." She gave a sigh. "So, I turned up nothing."

"Well, I guess things really do come in three's, because I came up empty, too," Lisa remarked as she flipped open her water bottle and took a drink. "No record of Gre—" She caught herself. "Of the subject ever giving blood. At the hospital or at the Red Cross. So, nothing there. Also, he's not a member of the health club. I even asked some of the freelance trainers if they knew him, and no luck there, either."

"Well, I had *very* good luck," Megan crowed discreetly and leaned over the table. "I found biographical info from when he was a speaker at a real estate convention. He's married twenty-three years, has two teenagers, was born and raised in Cheyenne, Wyoming, and his birth date matches exactly. December 11, 1955. He went to the University of Wyoming and moved to Colorado twenty years ago. I even found an interview he gave to a business magazine where he mentions that he was *adopted*." Megan's eyes danced with obvious delight at her discoveries.

"Whoa, great job, Megan!" Kelly congratulated her and scribbled the information on her notebook.

"A-*hem*," Jennifer spoke up. "Megan's not the only one who hit pay dirt. I discovered that Gretsky's been trying to recover from some bad real estate deals that went sour during the last couple of years. He puts on a good show, but it's just that. Expensive tailoring, all flash and sizzle, but no steak. According to my source, who knows everything there is to know about every Realtor in this town, Gretsky is hanging on by his fingernails, hoping for a break. And he's depending on the Big Box deal to rescue him from financial disaster."

Kelly sat quietly, absorbing what Jennifer said. Reason enough to kill in her book. "Great job, Jennifer," she said. "That sounds like the key to Gretsky. Threat of financial collapse. I'd say that's motive enough for murder." She stared through the window outside. "We can use that to push him into confessing."

"Whoa, Kelly, hold the phone," Burt said, spinning wheel picking up speed. "Don't get ahead of yourself. Do you actually think a smooth operator like Gretsky is simply going to confess if you start asking him questions?"

"No, of course not," Kelly admitted, then leaned over the table even more. "I've been thinking about this since last night. And asking questions isn't going to get us anywhere. So I don't plan to ask." She gave an enigmatic smile.

"What are you going to do, then?" Lisa probed.

"I'll let him do his Realtor spiel, then I plan to go on the attack. Confront him. Shake him up. Accuse him. I want to wipe that phony smile off his face and make him mad."

"Are . . . are you sure that's a good idea?" Megan ventured.

Kelly nodded. "Remember, I'm not alone with him. You guys will be situated in adjoining rooms in case he threatens me."

"Except for me," Burt declared. "I'm staying in this corner."

Kelly shook her head. "Sorry, Burt. He'll clam up if he sees another man in the shop. I sense it. You can go into the spinning room right there," she pointed to the corner room, jutting off the main area. "You can even fix a mirror on the shelves so you can keep an eye on us if you want."

Burt scowled, clearly unhappy he wasn't closer, but acquiesced. "Okay, but only if I can rig up a mirror. I want to make sure this guy doesn't try something."

Megan's eyes grew huge. "Oh my gosh! Burt, do you think he'd try to hurt Kelly? I've got a bad feeling about this whole thing."

"I'd like to see him try," Kelly challenged.

"Don't worry, Megan, I'll come prepared," Burt reassured.

"Whoa, this is getting more serious than I thought," Lisa observed. "When are you planning on setting this up, Kelly?"

"I'm going to call Gretsky this afternoon and ask him to meet me here early tomorrow morning, say eight o'clock. That way, we'll avoid having customers in the shop."

"Hey, wait a minute," Jennifer spoke up. "We'll still have customers because the restaurant opens at six thirty a.m., so people will be here. How do you want to handle them?"

"I figured we could use those wooden screens Mimi uses to close off sections of the shop for classes. We could block off access going to the classroom area and the weaving room. So, your job, Jennifer, would be to make sure none of the café customers slips through into the shop, okay?"

"Gotcha. I can do that." Jennifer nodded.

"Megan and Lisa, why don't you two sit at the end of the classroom by the windows, so you can see but are too far away to hear our conversation." Kelly pointed, indicating the adjacent room. "Sit and knit and talk normally. I want Gretsky to feel totally comfortable. I'm going to be sitting at this end of the table alone when he arrives. He can join me here."

"Where are you going to put Mimi?" Megan asked.

"We'll make her stay in her office. And you and Lisa will have to make sure she doesn't peek out, okay?"

"Sounds like a plan," Lisa agreed. "What time do you want us here tomorrow?"

"Why don't we all get here a little after seven, okay?" Kelly glanced around and watched her friends nod in agreement. "I'm going to call Gretsky right now and tell him he has to come at eight o'clock tomorrow morning if he wants to talk to me about selling my property. He's got one chance."

"He'll be here," Jennifer concurred.

"And so will we," Burt added, gray eyebrows knotting.

Kelly caught Jennifer's eye and smiled. "Better tell Eduardo to make an extra pot of coffee tomorrow morning. We're going to need it."

Twenty

Kelly stroked the gathered bunches of mohair that draped along the wall beside the bookshelves of the main room. She tried not to pace, but it was impossible. So, she'd stop every few steps and squeeze a tempting yarn, caress a silky sweater, or fondle a frothy shawl.

Glancing over her shoulder, she observed Lisa and Megan doing the same. They were all too keyed up to sit down. Only Burt seemed calm, as the sound of his spinning wheel hummed steadily from the corner room. Craning her neck, Kelly spied the mirror Burt had discreetly wedged between the wools. Sure enough, she saw Burt spinning away, hands methodically working the roving into strands to feed the hungry wheel.

Jennifer's voice sounded behind her. "I think we have a visitor," she said, glancing toward the windows. "Here comes a black Lexus, and it's one minute to eight. He's right on time. Good luck." She sped through the middle room and was gone.

"Okay, folks, black Lexus at eight o'clock. It must be him," Kelly announced and headed for her spot at the end of the library table. The morning sun felt good as she picked up her practice piece and needles, pretending to knit.

The door jangled as it opened, and Gretsky's voice sounded, "Hello? Ms. Flynn, are you there?"

"In here, Mr. Gretsky," Kelly called out. "The main room with the fireplace, to your left." Her heart speeded up its already fast pace.

Gretsky appeared in the archway and gave Kelly a dazzling grin before he approached. It was all she could do not to gag. He was dressed as if he were about to be named Realtor of the year, she noticed, mentally adding the wardrobe's likely cost.

"Ah, Ms. Flynn, how good to see you again." He glanced about. "I didn't think the shop opened this early."

"It doesn't. We're here to help Mimi start sorting and packing. She has to leave this location. Apparently the new landlord doesn't want to rent. They want to sell." Kelly kept her attention on moving her needles through already-completed stitches, hoping Gretsky wouldn't notice that she was knitting nothing—thanks to Hilda.

"Oh, that's a shame," he replied in a sympathetic tone as he sat in the closest chair. "She's had this shop for several years, hasn't she?"

Smarmy bastard. We're going to nail you to the wall. She took a deep breath. "Yes, it's really sad."

"I gather you had time to examine the purchase offer, Ms. Flynn. May I call you Kelly? I like to be on first names with people."

Kelly gritted her teeth. "Please do."

He leaned back into the chair and withdrew a small notepad and fountain pen from his breast pocket. A Mont Blanc, no doubt. "I'm sure you had time to consider the generous nature of my clients' offer, Kelly. You can rid yourself of that high-rate mortgage with the proceeds and leave here with money to spare. I know you'll be glad to get on with your life."

Kelly couldn't listen to another word. She set her pretend knitting aside and fixed Gretsky with a glare. Using her coldest corporate voice, she asked, "Why didn't you just take the twenty thousand dollars and leave Helen alone? Why'd you kill her? Did she refuse to sell her property? Was that it? What drove you to murder your own mother?"

Gretsky went white in an instant. He opened his mouth but no words came out. He stared at Kelly with huge blue eyes. Helen's eyes, Kelly realized in that same instant. So that's why she'd liked him at first. He has Helen's eyes. Son of a . . . even her dad's full-blown navy curses wouldn't do justice now.

She leaned forward defiantly. "Did she threaten to tell her lawyer, Lawrence Chambers, about you? He told me she called him the day she died and said she was coming in to change her will. She wanted the property to become gardens for the city if I didn't want it. Helen did that because of you, didn't she, Gretsky? Because you were threatening her, pushing her—"

Gretsky sprang from his chair, face flushed with rage now. "What madness are you spouting, woman? Are you insane? Accusing me of . . . of *murder!* How dare you?"

Flushed with her own sense of righteous indignation, Kelly sprang from her chair and faced off with him, toe to toe.

"How are you going to explain having Helen's heirloom quilt in your possession when her will states it belongs to me?" Kelly pointed toward the cottage. "It's back on my wall where it belongs, Gretsky. But the woman in the frame shop will be glad to testify that you brought it in the day after Helen's murder. Your name's on the invoice. How are you going to explain that?"

Gretsky's lips twitched. "I . . . I bought it from her. When I went to see her about her property . . . several weeks ago. I admired it and she sold it to me." His features composed themselves once again as he glared at Kelly.

Kelly crossed her arms in front of her. "Sure you did. How much did you pay for it? Did you pay in cash? Did you write a check? If what you're saying is true, then there'll be proof. A paper trail, Gretsky. Even if you paid with a wad of cash you carry around in your pocket, Helen would have deposited any money given to her. I should know. I kept her accounts. And there would be a record of it."

His eyes darkened as they narrowed. "I don't know what you're talking about."

"Just like there'll be a record of the twenty thousand dollars you took from the house that night," she kept on pressing. "There's proof Helen had all twenty thousand in cash that night, yet not one bill was found. The vagrant in jail didn't have a dime on him when arrested. Police found nothing. That's because you had it. And unless you stuffed all twenty thousand in your mattress, there'll be a paper trail of that, too, Gretsky. Even if you tried to send it off-shore, we can find it."

"You are truly insane, Ms. Flynn, and I'm not continuing this conversation a moment longer." He turned on the heel of his expensive

Italian loafers, but Kelly's reflexes were quicker. She kicked over his chair, startling Gretsky long enough so she could run in front of him, blocking his escape.

"Do you know what I do for a living, Gretsky? I'm a corporate CPA. That means I know how to tie your finances into so many knots you won't be able to access your assets for years. Do you have enough cash reserve to support yourself and your family for two or three years until this case comes to trial? Of course you don't. I know how precarious your financial situation is right now. That's why you were so desperate to do this deal with Big Box. But Helen was in the way, wasn't she? That's why you killed her."

Gretsky's color began to fade again, and his mouth twitched. "I don't know what you're talking about. I'm going to talk to my lawyer right now and bring charges against you, Ms. Flynn. For defamation of character and slander. You should be committed."

Kelly didn't miss a beat. "While you're at it, ask him how much it costs to defend against a civil suit. Because that's what I'm going to ask Lawrence Chambers to bring. We may not have enough to force the police to bring a criminal case against you, Gretsky, but civil court is a whole different ballgame. All we need is a preponderance of evidence to prove wrongful death in Helen's case. That's easier for a jury to decide. A majority is all that's needed."

She watched fear flash across Gretsky's pale face, then was gone. He was on the brink. All she had to do was push him a little more. Kelly closed in on him, right up to his face, deliberately challenging. "What happened that night? You were already on the edge. What pushed you over?" she prodded.

An ugly sneer twisted Gretsky's mouth, and Kelly had no doubt she was the focus of his rage. "You conniving bitch," he hissed as he raised his hand to strike.

Kelly didn't flinch. "Careful, Gretsky, I don't go down as easily as Helen."

Different emotions played across his face now, Kelly noticed. The rage was gone, but fear had taken its place. Gretsky dropped his hand. "I'm getting out of here. I'm going to see my lawyer." He turned and headed for the foyer.

Kelly spotted Burt slipping through the weaving room, obviously heading for the foyer the back way. She had to stop Gretsky from leaving. Shake him up to slow him down. She'd used everything she had, and he still stonewalled. There was only one thing left, and it might not work. Kelly gambled and threw the dice anyway.

"Is that bandage on your hand from where Helen stabbed you? There was a broken knitting needle lying beside her body. She defended herself the only way she could. It must have been a deep wound, because it bled a lot."

Gretsky's step slowed, and he paused near the doorway.

"You tried to wipe up the blood with the purple wool, didn't you?" Kelly continued, slowly walking up behind him. "Blood specks were found on the carpet. Police did DNA tests and have the results now. They don't match Helen or the jailed suspect. That's because it's your blood, isn't it, Gretsky?"

This time Gretsky paused at the doorway, and his hand reached out to a nearby crate filled with canary-yellow yarn. He appeared to brace himself as his head bent forward. Kelly sensed he was balancing on the edge, but the ground was crumbling beneath his feet.

She gave the last nudge. "If you're innocent, you'll want to prove it, won't you? That's easy. Just give police a blood sample, and this will all be over."

Something inside collapsed, and Gretsky seemed to fold in on himself. He leaned against the doorway to the foyer. Burt appeared behind him and stepped forward, slipping his arm beneath Gretsky's, holding him up.

"Why don't you sit down and get this off your chest, Mr. Gretsky," Burt suggested gently, as he guided him back to the main room. "Tell us what happened. I'm sure you didn't mean to do it. What went wrong that night?"

Kelly picked up the fallen chair, and Burt guided Gretsky straight to it. He sank into the chair and leaned his head back, eyes closed. Kelly spied Megan and Lisa edge around the library table, and Jennifer peeked from the classroom.

Burt caught Lisa's attention and made a telephone sign with his hand. Lisa stealthily retreated to the classroom once more, calling the police, Kelly figured.

Gretsky heaved a huge sigh, more a shudder than a sigh. "It wasn't supposed to be like this . . ." he whispered at last. "She should have sold me the land. It was so easy . . . why didn't she? None of this would have happened. Oh, God . . ." He bent forward and sank his face into his hand.

Kelly waited for the sound of weeping, but it didn't come. Instead a bitter, rancorous voice emanated, full of rage and pain. "Why? Damn it, why? I've tried so hard. Done everything that they did. Wined and dined the same people, boozed and kissed ass, and still the deals didn't come. Why? I did everything they did. Looked the same, talked the same. Never good enough. Always falling short. Never quite measuring up. Smug bastards. Keeping me out."

Not sure who the "smug bastards" were, but Kelly guessed he meant the top dogs, the real estate elite. Burt sat in the chair beside him and leaned forward. "But you had a deal with Big Box, didn't you?" he ventured in a friendly tone. "That was worth something. I'll bet it made those smug bastards take notice, right?"

Gretsky's hands dropped from his face, and he stared at the floor. "Yeah, it did. They even let me into the club for a few days. But they were scheming behind my back to steal my client. I could tell. Thought they were better able to handle the deal," he sneered.

"But you showed them, didn't you? You found the perfect piece of land," Burt offered.

"Oh, yeah," Gretsky said, staring at the bookshelves now. "And just when I was about to lose the client." He nodded, obviously remembering. "This letter comes from the adoption researcher I'd hired the year before. And would you believe my very own mother lived in the same town? And even better, she sat on one of the choicest commercial parcels around."

"Wow, that was lucky," Burt said admiringly. Kelly watched his approach in fascination. Big, likeable, kind-faced Burt was a relentless interviewer. "So you got the landlord on this one to sell first, right?"

"Yeah, I needed that as the anchor. Once I got his commitment, I knew Big Box was in the bag." His face darkened. "But she refused to cooperate. After all those weeks of visits and phone calls and presents, she refused to sell. Even when I told her that I'd gone into debt to finance this deal with the developer. She still refused. I couldn't believe it. How could a mother refuse her only son?"

Kelly stared at Gretsky in growing disgust. It was obvious that he'd been so self-absorbed for so long he couldn't fathom any response other than his own.

"What'd you do then?" Burt prodded.

"I was desperate. I tried one last time. I came over late one night and told her she was ruining my career and my family's life. I mean, without that deal, I was going down the drain. The recession had wiped all my savings. I had nothing left and was in debt up to my ears trying to make this deal go through."

He stared at the windows for a long moment, saying nothing. Burt prodded once more. "Then what happened?"

Gretsky took a deep breath. "I'll never forget . . . she was sitting in that chair she liked, knitting. And she announces real calmlike that she was going to the lawyer and changing her will so the property would become gardens for the city if her niece didn't want it. She'd never sell it to me. Then, she pointed to an envelope on the desk and said there was twenty thousand dollars. That I should take it and leave. She never wanted to see me again. Claimed I didn't want a mother, just a meal ticket."

He closed his eyes, and his voice began to tremble. "Something inside snapped. Her rejection was one too many. My own mother . . ." His breath caught. "The next thing I knew, my hands were on her throat, choking her. I can't remember how long. I don't even remember her stabbing me. Just saw the blood on my hand . . ." His voice trailed off.

Kelly stared, appalled at the confession but feeling a huge weight lift off her shoulders in that same moment.

Burt leaned closer and whispered, "What about Martha, Helen's cousin in Landport? What happened there?"

Gretsky lifted his head slowly, as if it weighed a lot more than usual. "I was afraid Helen had talked to her about me. I couldn't take that chance . . ."

"How'd you find out about her? She kept to herself."

"I overheard them talking . . . I came to tell her about my clients." He pointed to Kelly.

Kelly's heart sank, as all those carefully hidden accusations and fears came creeping from the bushes where they'd been lying in wait. Ready to pounce. She knew it. She *was* responsible for Martha's death.

"And this big woman," Gretsky's hands jerked out in an attempt to gesture. "Was talking at the top of her voice. Hell, I didn't even have to eavesdrop. I could hear her all the way to the door . . . talking about Helen's cousin."

Kelly's breath caught. Hilda. It was Hilda talking that day in the shop. Gretsky'd overheard and was waiting in his car for Kelly that afternoon when she left. He talked about his clients' offer. Then he waited and followed her. Bastard.

"How'd you find her?" Burt probed softly.

He shrugged, shoulders drooping despite the expensive tailoring. "I kept an eye on her." Pointing to Kelly again, "Figured she'd pay a visit sometime."

"Smart."

"Yeah, I thought so." Then his toned, tanned face started to sag just like his shoulders, as if the realization of what he'd done was working its way through his body. He closed his eyes and whispered, "God help me . . ."

Burt slipped his arm under Gretsky's once again and helped him to his feet this time. "Let's get you downtown, Mr. Gretsky. You'll want to call your lawyer. A squad car is outside now."

Gretsky looked up, perplexed. "So soon?"

"Yes sir. Don't worry, I'll go with you," Burt promised and led him to the foyer and out the door.

Kelly stood watching, amazed at what they'd witnessed. Lisa and Megan and Jennifer gathered around. "That was unbelievable, wasn't it?" Kelly said.

"Thank God, it's over," breathed Megan. Jennifer and Lisa nodded, not saying a word.

Kelly stared out the windows. The morning sunlight shimmered on the dew-glistened greens. "I . . . I need some time to think. Let all of this sink in." Glancing toward the sunlight slicing through the skylights, she suddenly pictured Helen sitting on the patio, knitting. Sunshine. She wanted sunshine. Now. "I'm going to sit out on the patio for a while."

"We understand, Kelly," Lisa said and squeezed Kelly's arm. "We'll be inside."

Kelly turned to her friends. "Actually, I'd love to have you join me, if you want to."

"You bet we will," Jennifer said. "Let me go tell Pete."

"Don't forget Mimi," Kelly added with a grin. "She's still in her office waiting for the all-clear."

With that, Kelly headed outside into the Colorado sunshine, her friends following after.

Kelly's First Scarf

Use two skeins or balls of colorful chunky wool yarn (like Rowan Biggy Print, for example), which gives 5½ stitches to 10 cm/4 inches with US size 35 or 36 needles (19–20 mm).

Cast on 10 stitches and knit entire scarf in garter stitch using both balls of yarn. Bind off and tuck ends.

Lambspun's Whodunnit Shell

Very Easy Knit with Bulky Yarn

SIZES:	SMALL	MEDIUM	LARGE	XLARGE	XXLARGE
BUST:	40	44	46	50	52
LENGTH:	17	18	18.5	19	19.5

GAUGE: 2 sts/in

MATERIALS: US size 15 needles (or size to obtain gauge), 14-inch straight

Very bulky yarn with gauge of 2 sts per inch

INSTRUCTIONS:

BACK: With yarn required for gauge, CO 40, 44, 46, 50, 52 sts. Work in garter stitch, (knit every row) or if you like an edge that rolls, work in stockinette (knit one row, purl one row) throughout garment. Continue in garter or stockinette until piece measures 8, 8.5, 9, 9, 9 inches or desired length to armhole. At armhole edges BO 3 sts once, 2 sts once, 1 st once. Work on remaining 28, 32, 34, 38, 40 sts until piece measures 14.5, 15, 15.5, 16, 16.5 inches.

NECK SHAPING: Work 11, 12, 12, 14, 15 sts. Join second ball of yarn and bind off center 6, 8, 10, 10, 10 sts. Work remaining sts, turn. Working both sides at once, bind off 1 st from the neck edge 3 times. Continue working on reaming sts until piece measures 17, 18, 18.5, 19, 19.5 inches. Place remaining 8, 9, 9, 11, 12 sts on holders.

FRONT: CO 39, 43, 45, 49, 51 sts. Work in garter stitch, (knit every row) or if you like an edge that rolls, work in stockinette (knit one row, purl one row) throughout garment. Continue in garter or stockinette until piece measures 8, 8.5, 9, 9, 9 inches or desired length to armhole. At armhole edges BO 3 sts once, 2 sts once, 1 st once. Work on remaining 28, 32, 34, 38, 40 sts until piece measures 14.5, 15, 15.5, 16, 16.5 inches.

NECK SHAPING: Same as for back.

FINISHING: Join shoulders with three-needle bind off. Single crochet around every edge. Hand seam sides together.

Pattern courtesy of Lambspun of Colorado, Fort Collins, Colorado.

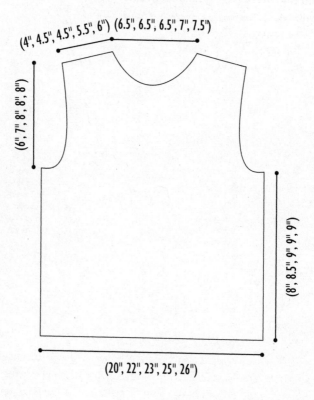

(4", 4.5", 4.5", 5.5", 6") (6.5", 6.5", 6.5", 7", 7.5")

(6", 7", 8", 8", 8")

(8", 8.5", 9", 9", 9")

(20", 22", 23", 25", 26")

Maggie's Cinnamon Rolls

DOUGH:

1 package active dry yeast

3½–4 cups of all-purpose flour

1 cup whole milk

⅓ cup butter

⅓ cup sugar

½ teaspoon salt

1 egg, beaten

FILLING:

2 tablespoons melted butter

1 cup packed dark brown sugar

3 teaspoons ground cinnamon

LEMON CREAM CHEESE FROSTING:

4 ounces cream cheese, softened

2 tablespoons butter, softened

1 tablespoon lemon juice

2 cups confectioners' sugar

OPTIONAL:

½ cup walnuts, pecans, or raisins

half-and-half

Stir together the yeast and 1½ cups of flour in large mixing bowl and set aside. In a saucepan over medium-low heat, combine milk, butter, and sugar. Add salt and beat till warm and butter is melted. Slowly add to flour mixture with beaten egg, stirring until well blended. Beat batter for 2 minutes, then stir in as much remaining flour as possible. Place dough on lightly floured surface and knead until smooth and elastic (5 minutes). Shape dough into a ball and place in a lightly greased bowl, turning once. Then cover and let rise in a warm place until doubled (about 1½ hours).

Make frosting. Combine softened cream cheese and butter. Stir until light and fluffy. Add lemon juice. Beat in confectioners' sugar gradually until well blended and smooth. If needed, add half-and-half until desired consistency. Set aside.

After dough has doubled, punch down the dough and turn onto a lightly floured surface. Cover and let rest 10 minutes. Grease a cookie sheet or large baking pan(s) and set aside. Roll dough into a 10 × 18 inch rectangle. Spread with melted butter. Stir together dark brown sugar and cinnamon and sprinkle over dough. Add nuts or raisins if desired. Tightly roll up dough from the long side. Pinch and seal ends. Cut dough into 1-inch sections and place on prepared baking sheet or pan. Cover and let rise until doubled (40–60 minutes). Brush rolls with melted butter. Bake in 350° oven for 25 to 30 minutes* until golden brown. Remove rolls to wire rack and frost while still warm. Makes approximately 12 rolls.

*Baking tip: For best results, please adjust baking time and temperature accordingly.

Needled to Death

Acknowledgments

My thanks to all the helpful alpaca breeders and ranchers in the Northern Colorado area who were kind enough to allow me a peek into their fascinating business. Most especially, I want to thank Marjean Bender of Kitchell Kriations Alpacas in Fort Collins, CO, who welcomed me to several alpaca shearings—as well as into her home. Over many cups of coffee and tea, she never ran out of patience with my endless questions about the alpaca ranching and the beautiful animals with the to-die-for soft wool.

One

Kelly Flynn grabbed her empty coffee mug as she opened the glass patio door leading to her cottage's small backyard. "Go for it, Carl. Another sunny day. Squirrels are waiting." She gave her rottweiler a parting pat as he raced outside, clearly eager to face the furry tormentors that kept him running.

Spying the deep rose circlet of yarn that rested on the dining room table, Kelly snatched her knitting bag with her latest project. The silk-and-cotton, raspberry sherbet yarn had tempted her for months in the knitting shop across from her home.

Kelly paused near her desk, nestled in a sunny corner of the cozy white stucco and red-tiled roof cottage. It was her cottage now. When Aunt Helen was killed, Kelly inherited everything, and her life turned upside down.

Glancing at her corporate client's folder beside the computer keyboard, she checked the clock. The analysis of the client's financial statements was going smoother than she'd anticipated. Some accounting issues were easier to solve than others. There was ample time for a knitting break.

The caffeine lobe deep in her brain sent out another insistent signal—coffee, now. Kelly headed for the front door. She could almost taste Eduardo's potent brew. The knitting shop had an attached café with the best regular coffee Kelly had ever tasted. Eduardo, the genial cook, always laughed when she asked about his secret for the coffee that kept her coming back for more.

July's intense heat radiated in the Colorado air even though it was only mid-morning. Afternoon would be brutal and in the high nineties, Kelly decided as she glanced at the shimmer coming off the adjacent golfing greens. That reminder caused her to turn and check on her dog's whereabouts.

Carl had developed an unfortunate habit these last three months she'd stayed in Fort Connor. Golf balls. They were an irresistible temptation to which Carl frequently succumbed. Kelly had tried several tactics to discourage him from climbing the fence and racing onto the greens to steal balls. Memories of angry golfer encounters were still fresh in Kelly's mind.

She spotted Carl standing, paws up on the chain-link fence. "Don't even think about it, Carl," she warned in her best attempt-to-control-dog voice. Carl looked over his shoulder in pleading mode. "Nope. You've gotten us in enough trouble already. Go play with your legal stash over there." Kelly pointed to a cluster of golf balls near several decorative pots filled with colorful shade plants.

Carl rolled his soft brown eyes in an obvious last effort to convince, then lay down in the grass and stared longingly at the greens.

"I know it's more fun to chase down stray balls, but you just can't. I don't want to have to bail you out of doggie jail," Kelly warned as she headed across the driveway toward Aunt Helen's former farmhouse, now turned knitting shop.

Passing by the oaken front door with its carved sign that read HOUSE OF LAMBSPUN, Kelly followed the flower-bordered pathway around the sprawling stucco and red-tile roof building to the café entrance. The enticing aroma of coffee greeted her as soon as she opened the door. She glanced around at the tables filled with customers lingering over late breakfast and brunch until she spotted a familiar face. One of her knitting friends, Jennifer, worked mornings at the café and afternoons as a real estate agent.

Kelly aimed straight for her. "Cof-fee, cof-fee," she demanded in a deep, raspy voice, mug in outstretched hand.

"Look, it's the return of the Coffee Zombie," Jennifer joked to the café owner. "Hide, Pete. She hasn't had her caffeine yet."

Pete's round face spread with a wide grin as he poured orange juice into a glass pitcher. "It'll only be a minute, Kelly. Eduardo's got some brewing. We had a business breakfast group in here this morning, and they drained the last drop."

Kelly's heart almost stopped. "Pete, don't even joke about something like that," she warned.

"It'll only be a moment. You can make it," Jennifer teased. "C'mon, have a doughnut." She gestured to the tempting pastries displayed in a nearby glass case.

Kelly tried to ignore them, but one lemon-glazed creation called her name. "Okay, but sugar's not gonna do it. I need coffee. I can only last so long on that supermarket brand I have at home. I've already spent most of the morning combing through one corporate account, and I've got several more waiting."

"Boy, you're surlier than usual this morning," Jennifer observed, handing her the napkin-covered doughnut. "Numbers not adding up? Clients getting unruly? I can help with that." She winked.

"Actually, everything's going smoothly. I just want to work ahead so I can take the whole day off tomorrow," Kelly said before she sank her teeth into the sugar.

"You guys have a game tomorrow?"

"Games all day. It's the Fantastic Fourth at the Fort tournament. Teams are coming from all over the state."

"I'd better tell Eduardo to put some more shoelaces in the coffee, then. You'll need it," Jennifer said with a laugh as she took Kelly's mug and headed for the kitchen.

Kelly brushed sugar flakes from her T-shirt and checked the barrette holding back her chin-length, dark brown hair. One of the best things about telecommuting to her office in Washington, D.C., was she could dress the way she liked. And in Colorado in the summertime, that meant a T-shirt and shorts.

Tomorrow would bring back a ton of memories, she was certain. She remembered playing in that same softball tournament years ago when she grew up here in Fort Connor. Lots of memories. In fact, that's all she had left from the past. The people were all gone—her dad, her aunt Helen, everyone.

"You're saved," Jennifer announced, coming toward her, mug in hand. "Coffee's ready, and you're all set. Go forth and knit." She handed the mug to Kelly. "I'll be over on break."

"Thanks," Kelly said and headed for the doorway that led into the knitting shop.

As always, her senses went on overload the moment she entered the shop. Room after room of the renovated farmhouse was filled with yarns of every hue and texture—frothy mohairs in ice cream colors, nubbly wools and luscious alpacas, seductively soft silk spun with cotton or wool or all alone. Kelly couldn't get through a room without stroking a fat skein or squeezing some enticing fiber. She'd become a "fiber fondler," as the shop's knitting regulars called themselves.

Rounding the corner into what was once the farmhouse living room, Kelly went straight to the long library table that now dominated the room. "Hey, there," she greeted two of her friends who sat around the table knitting.

"How's the sweater going?" Lisa asked, glancing up from the lacy ribbon vest she was creating.

"Well, okay, I guess. I'm still doing the ribbing along the edge," Kelly replied as she settled into a chair.

"Getting used to the circular needles?" Megan asked, pausing over the vivid purple froth that lay piled in her lap. Was that one of the new boa eyelash yarns that were so enticing?

"Yeah, gradually. It still looks strange, but I hope to finish the ribbing soon so I can start knitting the sweater. I mean, it doesn't feel like a sweater yet, just this circle of yarn." She held up the circle of rosy red yarn. The two slender wooden needles were connected end to end by a ribbon of thin plastic. Kelly scrutinized the rows of ribbing that covered the entire circumference and frowned. "You sure this is gonna work?"

Lisa grinned and brushed a lock of blonde hair from her forehead. "Ohhh, it'll work all right. Trust us."

"Wait'll you see those rows of stockinette stitch appear, then you'll be convinced," Megan added with her usual bright smile. With her fair, fair skin and almost black hair, Megan always looked delicate to Kelly—except, of course, when she was on the softball field. Underneath the porcelain, Megan was tough as nails.

"Okaaaay," Kelly said, still skeptical. "If you say so. I still don't understand how I'll get stockinette if all I do is the knit stitch. I mean, when I did my first easy sweater with the chunky yarn, I had to do it the regular way—one row of knitting, one row of purling. How do you get stockinette without doing that?"

"It just happens," Megan reassured.

Kelly pondered that and drank deeply from her mug, savoring the coffee's familiar harsh assault on her taste buds. "That's no answer. There has to be a reason why it works."

"Trust in the process," Lisa said with her enigmatic smile.

"That's what Jennifer always says, but that's hard for me," Kelly admitted, picking up the circular needles. "I mean, I spend most of my days examining the process with all my accounts. It's hard to switch off."

Mimi, the owner of the shop, leaned around the doorway. "It's magic," she said with a smile. "I couldn't help overhearing you, Kelly. Don't worry. It'll be fine."

"What'll be fine?" Jennifer queried as she approached the table, knitting bag over her arm.

"Oh, Kelly's worrying about knitting in the round," Mimi explained and went back to straightening the surrounding shelves of books and magazines.

"That's Kelly's standard operating procedure," Jennifer said, pulling a luscious, multicolored fringed yarn from her bag. "Whenever she starts a new project, she always worries that it won't turn out."

"Hey, not always," Kelly protested, compelled to defend herself even though she knew her friends were right.

"Yeah, you do."

"Always."

"I rest my case." Jennifer grinned. "You'll be fine. Just trust—"

"In the process, I know, I know." Kelly drank from her mug as she reached out one hand to fondle the glistening and vibrantly colored fibers that Jennifer was knitting into one of those new trendy scarves. Yummy soft. "I'm going to have to make one of those scarves. They are simply irresistible."

"Get a little further along on your sweater, first, before you leave it," Megan advised. "I know what it's like to be tempted away from a bigger project."

Kelly nodded and went back to creating the ribbing that would be the bottom of her new sweater. At first, it seemed strange to knit two stitches, then purl two stitches, but after a few rows, she actually saw the ribbed effect appear. Another few rows and she'd have created the inch required to form the sweater's edge.

Lisa broached another subject, one that had been niggling in the back of Kelly's mind. "How long do you think your boss will let you work away from the office? Did he give any clue when you went back to D.C. last month?"

"I don't know. He was doing his cool, aloof routine when I spoke with him. He does that whenever he wants to keep someone off balance." She frowned at the memory of sitting in her corporate CPA firm's offices, pleading her request for an extension of family leave.

With the death of both her aunt and her long-lost cousin, Martha, Kelly was suddenly the heir and beneficiary of a good deal of property. It would take several months to sort through both estates, even with trusted family lawyer Lawrence Chambers overseeing the process. Kelly didn't have a clue when she'd be able to return to Washington—or if she even wanted to.

"Well, you know how we all feel," Megan spoke up. "We want you to stay here with us."

Kelly felt her heart give a little squeeze. Deep inside, that's what she wanted, too.

"Any chance of that happening?" Jennifer probed. "You're managing those huge mortgage payments on the cottage, right? And you've got a renter for your town house back in Virginia. How's that working?"

"Oh, Chuck is great. He absolutely loves the place," Kelly replied. *All the more reason to let him have it,* the little voice inside whispered. If it were only that simple, Kelly thought. "But it's a delicate balance. The only way I can manage the cottage mortgage payments is with my CPA salary." She shook her head. "I can't quit my job."

"Well, we'll simply have to find a way for you to earn money here," Jennifer declared.

"Boy, that's not as easy as it sounds," Kelly said. "Consulting on my own simply wouldn't cut it. I've done some checking, with Megan's help."

"Something will come up. I can feel it," Jennifer said.

The front door's jingling bell sounded. More customers. Over the past three months that she'd been a regular, Kelly had noticed the ebb and flow of customers. Mid-morning to lunchtime was often hectic, with classes and customer questions. Then a brief pause often occurred before the afternoon press of customers and more classes began. Of course, weekends had no pause at all. It was nonstop shopping and classes the entire day. Kelly marveled at how Mimi managed to handle the constant flow of questions and instruction and helping customers find "just the right yarn" while staying so warm and reassuring. It must be her passion. It flowed over into everything she did and all she'd created. Kelly glanced to the billowy mohairs that draped against the walls and the stacked bins that bulged with summer-bright yarns. Mimi had truly created a wonderland here. No wonder knitters flocked to the shop.

"Well, hello, everybody," a woman's voice spoke from the doorway. "Looks like half the Tuesday group is here."

Kelly turned in her chair and recognized Vickie Claymore, another of the Tuesday group regulars. "Hey, Vickie. What brings you out of that beautiful canyon and into town?"

"Nothing much. Errands, that's all," Vickie said as she joined them at the table.

"When are you bringing some of your weavings?" Lisa asked. "I've got a friend who's been dying to buy one ever since she saw mine."

"That's great! Thanks, Lisa," Vickie said, her suntanned face breaking into a grin. "I hope to have some more ready by next week." She brushed her dark brown hair off her shoulder.

Vickie was one of the few fifty-plus women Kelly knew who could still wear her long hair hanging behind her back in a ponytail. Even mixed with gray, it still looked good on her. Kelly admired Vickie not only for her lively personality, but also for her artistic creativity and her shrewd business sense. Vickie was a successful alpaca breeder and rancher as well as a talented spinner and weaver. Instead of knitting on Tuesdays, Vickie would spin, sometimes on the drop spindle. Other times, she'd borrow a wheel from Mimi.

"Boy, if I lived in that gorgeous canyon, I wouldn't want to leave," Megan said.

"You would if you wanted to buy groceries and eat," Vickie said with a laugh. "Plus, it's good to get a break from the ranch. Makes me appreciate it more." She poured herself a cup of tea from the always-present teapot at the center of the table.

"Are all your baby alpacas born? Any more deliveries?" Kelly asked, remembering Vickie's concern for her herd.

"Yep," she replied, brushing dust from her jeans. Ninety degrees

or not, boots and jeans were necessary around the ranch. "All the
cria are safely delivered—thank goodness and natural alpaca mother
instinct."

Lisa looked up from the ribbon vest. "Cria?"

Vickie nodded. "That's the name for baby alpacas. We've got
twenty new ones."

"Wow. Is that a lot to care for?" Megan asked.

"Actually, the mothers do most of that. I just have to make sure
the moms are well-fed and cared for." She grinned, and her eyes lit
up. "Just like with humans, moms do most of the work."

"Doesn't your cousin, Jayleen, help out?" Mimi asked as she rearranged a bin of eyelash yarns. "You have nearly forty animals."

"Thirty-eight with the babies, and, yes, Jayleen comes every day."

"Oops, I almost forgot! I need to ask you a favor, Vickie," Mimi
said, abruptly turning from the bins. "There's a group of out-of-town
knitters from the Midwest who're visiting Fort Connor. They're a
touring group. Apparently they take yearly trips to different areas
of the country."

"Wow, touring knitters. Now that's something new," Jennifer
observed.

"Actually, there're several knitting groups that tour, I've heard,"
Mimi added. "This group is coming to see the shop after July
fourth, and they asked if I knew of any alpaca ranches they could
visit. I know this is short notice, Vickie, but would they be able to
tour your ranch Friday afternoon?"

Vickie leaned back in the chair and sipped her tea. "Friday. Yes, I
think that would be all right. What time would they come?"

"They're planning to have lunch at Pete's, so we can drive them
into the canyon afterward. Probably about two o'clock. Does that
work?"

"That'll work," Vickie agreed, smiling. "I take it they've never
seen an alpaca before, right?"

"Probably not."

"Okay, I'll give them the grand tour." Vickie drained her teacup
before she stood up.

"Vickie, you're a doll," Mimi said, her face losing its worried
expression. "Thank you so much. Now all I need are some volun-

teers to take them to the ranch." She surveyed the table. "Any of you girls want to take a drive into the canyon Friday? We'll need shepherds for this flock."

Kelly started to speak up, but Jennifer beat her to it. "I'll be glad to escort them, Mimi," she said. "I've been wanting to drive past some property in the canyon anyway."

Picturing herself driving through the shady, deep green canyon northwest of Fort Connor, Kelly chimed in, "Count me in, too, Mimi. I could use an afternoon in Bellvue Canyon."

Mimi beamed. "Thank you so much, girls. I'll take care of all the arrangements."

"I'll see you two on Friday, then," Vickie said as she headed toward the doorway. "If your flock behaves, I'll show them my looms. I'm weaving a new piece now with some of my herd fleeces. It's really striking, if I do say so myself."

"I'll bet it is," Kelly said. "I remember that beautiful rug you showed us last month. The patterns were gorgeous."

"You can see it when you come. It's on my floor now. Take care, folks." Vickie gave a wave as she left.

"Boy, Kelly, I didn't think you'd be up for supervising knitters after the last time," Megan teased.

Kelly remembered helping Megan last spring when they escorted a group of senior knitters to the regional Colorado wool festival. "Ohhhh, yeah," she grinned, recalling one mischievous knitter's antics. "Well, let's hope we don't have any 'Lizzies' in this flock."

Mimi threw up her hands in remembered horror as she scurried back to her office while Kelly and her friends laughed out loud.

Kelly sat down on one of her teammates' blankets that dotted the ridge above the city reservoir. She'd forgotten to bring a blanket of her own. Heck, it was all she could do to get to the field this morning.

After a long night spent poring over her client accounts, Kelly had overslept, awaking to the sound of an angry golfer's shout outside. "Damn dog! I knew he stole my ball," the man yelled.

Bolted awake, Kelly was about to go to Carl's rescue when she saw the time. It was past eight o'clock, and her softball team's first game was at nine. She vaulted out of the bed and into the shower, setting a new speed record even for her. She raced through the kitchen, poured a double ration into Carl's doggie dish, and shoved it under his nose. The golf ball scolding would have to wait. Carl, clearly ecstatic at the unexpected bowl of plenty, dug in.

Grabbing her first baseman's glove and her dad's USS *Kitty Hawk* baseball cap, Kelly raced out the door and into her car, hoping she had all her clothes on. There was no way she'd let her teammates down by not showing up on time. Thanks to uncommon good fortune with traffic lights and an unexpected parking spot, Kelly raced onto the field where her team gathered. Two minutes to spare.

"Boy, girl, you like to live on the edge, don't you?" Lisa joked.

"No, she just likes to give us all heart attacks," Megan said over her shoulder as they took the field. "I'm backup first base, and I'm lousy at it. So don't do that again."

Kelly swore alarm-clock vigilance and took her base, grateful for green lights.

Relaxing now under the blue velvet night sky, Kelly let out a sigh. So many stars. She was always surprised when she returned to Colorado and noticed the night sky. Not only was she a mile closer to the heavens, but there were more stars to see. Big-city light pollution kept her from stargazing back in the D.C. metro area. Occasionally, she'd driven out into the Virginia countryside to find a beautiful Blue Ridge mountain knoll just so she could see the heavens more clearly.

But it wasn't the same. The sky looked different here. And this ridge was right on the edge of town. She gazed up and tried to spot her favorite constellations, the ones her dad had taught her to see back in her childhood. She visually outlined the Big Dipper, then found the North Star and was looking for the Little Dipper when a familiar low voice sounded beside her.

"Want one? It's your favorite," Steve Townsend said as he sank to the blanket beside her.

"Thanks," Kelly said, accepting the bottle. "You read my mind."

Steve seemed to be doing a lot of that lately, Kelly noticed. Whether it was running interference for Carl with the angry golfers or taking time from his busy construction business to appear at her door with coffee when she needed a break from corporate accounts, Steve showed up. He was a nice guy. A really nice guy who had turned into a good friend—even if he was the star player for a rival team.

Kelly tipped the bottle with the colorful label and drank. Her hometown had developed into a center for special microbrewed boutique beers. The amber ale's cold, crisp tang fit perfectly with the summer night. The intense heat of the day had subsided now, and the air was gradually cooling, especially up on the ridge—one of the many benefits of mountain living.

"How's your knee?" Steve asked as he leaned back on his arm, stretching out his long legs, which were even longer than Kelly's.

Kelly checked her newly-scraped right knee. The sting of injury had lessened so much that Kelly had forgotten about it.

Her knees were always skinned when she was growing up. Softball, basketball, soccer—all took a toll. She was used to bandages. But living in the corporate world these last several years had taken her far away from simple pleasures like sliding into base, knees be damned. Suits and stress were the uniforms and routine of the day with no time allowed for standing outside in the sunshine. The clock inside Kelly's head ruled her schedule in six-minute intervals—billable hours. These last three months had given Kelly a taste of a different kind of life, delicious and tempting like a forbidden dessert. If only she could find a way to stay here and not starve.

"Oh, it's fine. I completely forgot about it. Actually, it feels kind of good to have skinned knees again."

Steve grinned. "How's that?"

Kelly let out a sigh and leaned back on her hands, staring out over the brightly lit city spread out in a carpet below. The fireworks display in City Park would be starting soon. "It reminds me of when I was growing up here and all the other places my dad and I lived. I was always playing ball and getting hurt. It's amazing I have any knees left." She laughed softly in the gathering darkness. The blue velvet sky had turned to black. "I didn't know how much I missed it until I came back and met Lisa and Megan and started playing again."

"Wasn't there a team in D.C. where you could play?"

"Oh, sure. Lots. But it was always a question of time. Never enough time. I worked late a lot at the office. Until my dad got cancer, that is. Then I made sure I visited him every night." Kelly felt an old familiar tug of remembrance as she pictured her father.

"That must have been tough."

"It was."

The aroma of hot dogs and hamburgers drifted by. "Last chance for hot dogs and burgers," Lisa called to the scattered players relaxing along the ridge. She wound a path through the blankets and chairs, a platter in each hand piled with cookout leftovers.

"Hey, I'll take another burger," a guy said as he slipped up behind Lisa and made off with his prize. "Who's got the beer?"

"Beside the grill, over there," someone else called out.

"I've got some chardonnay, if anyone wants it," Wendy, the team's catcher, said, waving from a nearby blanket.

"Boy, hot dogs and chardonnay," Steve joked. "That just doesn't work."

"Hey, I can't help it," Wendy explained with a laugh as she grabbed a glass from the guy beside her. "I don't like beer."

"And you call yourself a catcher."

Kelly let the sound of relaxed laughter float over her like the evening breezes that came over the mountains. It felt good here. Really good. Deep inside, she felt the warmth that always came whenever she considered staying in Colorado.

"Well, for what it's worth, you sure look a lot more relaxed and happy than when you first came into town back in April," Steve said.

"Yeah," Kelly admitted with a sigh. "That's because I am."

"Relaxed or happy?"

"Both."

Steve didn't reply. After a few minutes of comfortable silence, which Kelly spent tracing star patterns, he spoke up. "Well, maybe that means you should stay."

"If it were only that easy."

"You know, Kelly, there's a huge amount of business going on in this town. There're all sorts of ways to consult—"

A collective "Ahhhh!" spread along the ridge as the fireworks display blazed into the sky.

"Whoa," Kelly said. "I'd forgotten how pretty it is from up high.

Even prettier than being right beneath. That's where I usually was back in D.C. My dad and I would go find a spot near the Washington Monument."

"Sounds like fun."

"Yeah, it was. If you don't mind being crammed in with several thousand people. We could barely move."

"More than at City Park?" Steve teased.

Kelly sent him a look. "Ohhhh, yeah. Way more." She watched a spectacular flare of reds, blues, purples, and greens shoot through the black mountain sky. "It's nicer here," she said softly. "It's good to be back."

"Well, for the record, I'd be glad if you could stay, too." He gestured to Kelly's teammates, oohing and aahing at the colorful displays. "Even if you guys did beat us this afternoon."

Kelly grinned. "I'll take that as a compliment."

"Do that."

Two

Kelly eased the huge SUV around the curving canyon road more slowly than usual. These monster vehicles had a different feel to them, not at all like her sporty, super-responsive road car. She glanced into the rearview mirror. Jennifer was right behind her in Mimi's blue minivan, loaded like the SUV with touring knitters.

"How much farther is it? I thought you said it was 'just up the road,'" the knitter in the front seat asked for the third time in twenty minutes.

Kelly took a breath and searched for patience. This woman was something else. She'd done nothing but complain ever since she'd gotten into the automobile. It was too hot. The air-conditioning was too cold. She was tired. She was thirsty. Weren't there some alpacas they could visit in town? She didn't like curving roads.

Noticing the other women's rapt attention to the beautiful scenery outside the windows, Kelly tried to distract the woman, or at least her impatience. "This canyon is much greener and more deeply wooded than some of our others. That's because it's a north-facing canyon, and it holds the snow longer. That means there's more water available."

Fussy knitter piped up, pushing her glasses to the ridge of her nose. "Yes, and more snow to shovel, too, I'll bet."

"Absolutely," Kelly said with a laugh. "In fact, some of the upper roads don't get plowed by the county. The homeowners have to pay to have it done."

"Now, I wouldn't like that at all," Fussy declared, setting her mouth. Kelly noticed hard lines already etched in her face. Too much frowning, she figured.

"Well, the people who don't like it usually move back into the city after a couple of years, I'm told," Kelly observed. "You have to love being in the mountains to live comfortably here."

"Ohhhh, I'd love it," a woman's voice spoke up from the middle seat.

"Me, too," agreed another.

"Is that the place, over there?" Fussy asked, pointing to a farmhouse nestled between trees. Cows grazed in the pastures.

"No, but we're getting close," Kelly answered. "Just around this curve." She spotted Vickie's sprawling farmhouse in the distance and slowed as they approached the driveway.

"Well, finally!" Fussy declared.

Kelly kept her smile to herself as they bumped along the rutted driveway, listening to the stream of complaints coming from the next seat. The other women were laughing and chattering excitedly as they approached the farmhouse.

"Oh, look! Alpacas!" a woman proclaimed, pointing to the corral and pastures adjacent to the weather-beaten red barn.

"How do you know they're alpacas?" Fussy asked. "They look the same as llamas."

"Well, you're right. They are very much alike. But I've been to Vickie's ranch before. Otherwise, it's hard for most people to tell."

"What's the difference?" a woman asked.

"About a hundred pounds. Alpacas are smaller than llamas," Kelly replied as she pulled the SUV into a graveled area near the barn and parked beside Vickie's beat-up gray pickup truck. Exiting the auto, she motioned to a parking spot for Jennifer, who was coming up the driveway behind them.

"Okay, ladies," Kelly addressed the women who were unfolding themselves from the vehicle. "Let's get everybody together, then we can start our tour. Meanwhile, smell that mountain air." She took a deep breath. Out of the close confines of the car at last.

Jennifer parked the van, then hopped out and helped her charges alight, laughing and talking the whole time. Kelly wished she could be as entertaining as Jennifer, but she seemed to be missing that gene. Maybe she could foist Fussy off on her for the ride back into town.

"Wow, this is one beautiful place," Jennifer observed as she approached Kelly. "I haven't been here before, have you?"

"Yes. One time I came with Mimi when she was doing some weaving with Vickie. They were developing a workshop together." She glanced toward the farmhouse across the drive, wondering why Vickie hadn't come out to greet them. It certainly wasn't for lack of noise.

The gaggle of knitters had gathered around the fence, pointing and exclaiming at the alpacas scattered about the pastures. For their part, the alpacas simply gazed back with huge brown eyes and continued to graze peacefully. Kelly noticed one or two headed toward the fence, clearly as curious about the visitors as the visitors were about them.

Of course, their approach delighted the knitters no end, and cameras appeared from purses. Digital and film, the cameras snapped away as the women leaned over the fence. Thank goodness it was sunny, Kelly figured, or the flashes would have spooked the gentle beasts for sure. It did halt their approach, however, much to the ladies' disappointment.

"Will they let you pat them?" one woman asked.

"Some will. But we'll let Vickie be in charge of that," Kelly replied, wondering again why Vickie hadn't come out to greet them.

Checking her watch, she saw it was after two o'clock, so they were right on time. Maybe Vickie was in her sunny workroom in the back of the house, absorbed in her latest weaving project.

"She may have forgotten that we're coming," Jennifer offered, stretching, arms overhead. "Does she have a workroom or something?"

"Yeah, in the back. She may be working and waiting for us to ring the doorbell. I'll go check. You keep track of them," Kelly suggested and started across the gravel driveway.

She headed toward the front porch with its rough-cut pine beam posts and overhang that created an inviting, shady spot for the rocking chairs that were angled to enjoy the mountain view. A wide wooden deck also extended around the corner of the log home and along the side, creating a large, sunny patio.

As Kelly's foot touched the front step, she heard an altogether too familiar voice right behind her.

"Why isn't she out here to greet us?" Fussy demanded, catching up with Kelly. "Isn't that her truck in the driveway?"

"She's probably in her workroom in the back and couldn't hear us. Why don't you wait with the others while I go get her, okay?" Kelly suggested as she crossed the porch, hoping Fussy would take the hint.

She didn't. "I've already seen the animals. I want to see those weavings the shop owner was talking about."

Kelly reached for the doorbell, then stopped when she noticed the door was ajar. She rang the bell anyway and waited. And waited. Fussy wasn't good at waiting, she noticed, so Kelly rang again and waited some more while Fussy fidgeted.

"Well, where is she?" Fussy demanded. "Don't tell me we came all the way out here for nothing."

"Oh, she probably didn't hear it, that's all," Kelly reassured. She pushed open the heavy door, and they stepped into the entryway. "I'll go check her workroom. Why don't you stay here and admire the décor, okay?" This time Kelly let her voice assume a formal tone, and she gave Fussy an I-mean-business look for good measure. Fussy stayed put.

"Vickie? Hello?" Kelly called. "Jennifer and I are here with the tour group. Where are you?"

No answer. Kelly stood for another moment, letting her gaze sweep over the spacious log home. One whole side of the living room was floor-to-ceiling windows, affording a gorgeous view of the canyon and the mountain ranges in the distance. Vaulted ceilings and skylights allowed light to flood the room, highlighting the furnishings, some rustic, some modern.

Vickie had eclectic tastes as well as an excellent eye for art. Patterns and fabric and color were everywhere. A still life in the style of the old masters was separated from a colorful abstract by one of Vickie's striking weavings. Everywhere Kelly looked she saw art—painted, sculpted, woven, or carved. It was a visual feast.

Wishing she could simply stand and drink it in for several minutes like she did on her last visit, Kelly headed through the living room toward the back of the house. Once the touring group was enthralled in Vickie's demonstrations, she and Jennifer could enjoy their surroundings. Glancing over her shoulder, she noticed Fussy was edging out of the entryway.

"Wait right there," Kelly said, gesturing to the woman. "I'll be back in a minute."

When she skirted around the rust-colored leather sofa, however, Kelly came to an abrupt halt. Vickie lay on the floor, her dark hair spread out on the handwoven rug in stark contrast to her pale face. A pool of blood, blackish red, swirled across the intricate pattern woven into the gray and white wool.

Kelly's breath caught in her throat. What had happened? Why all this blood? Was Vickie still alive? Suddenly, she spotted an ugly red gash across Vickie's neck. Kelly swallowed down her revulsion. Vickie's throat had been cut.

She knelt beside her friend and gingerly placed her fingers on Vickie's wrist, hoping to feel a pulse. There was none. Vickie was dead. She'd bled to death. And hours ago, too, from the look of the blood. It was dried already in places where it had soaked into the fabric. The icy lump in Kelly's throat sank to her stomach. Was this a suicide? Or was it murder? Who would kill Vickie?

"Oh, my God!" cried Fussy, right behind Kelly's shoulder. "Would you look at that! There's blood everywhere!"

That did it. Kelly snapped into command mode. She jumped up and wheeled on Fussy, pointing straight at her. "*You!* Out! This minute. Go get Jennifer and tell her to bring her cell phone right away!"

"Well, I never—" Fussy huffed.

Kelly dropped her voice two octaves into the I'm-warning-you-Carl range. "Do it. *Now.* This is a crime scene, and the police need to be called. Go!"

Mention of the police clearly got Fussy's attention, because all color drained from her pinched face. She turned and ran from the house. Kelly took a deep breath and forced herself to look at her dead friend once more. How was this possible? Vickie was always so full of life and energy. Who would kill her? It had to be murder. Vickie had so many plans for the future. Kelly remembered her friend excitedly describing how her baby alpacas were already sold to other breeders. As soon as they were weaned from their mothers, she'd be "playing stork," as Vickie laughingly referred to her delivery trips. No. Vickie hadn't killed herself. Kelly was convinced.

She slowly walked around the great room, trying to absorb every detail she could in case she was asked later. She disturbed nothing but noted everything. There was no sign of a knife anywhere. Did the killer sneak up on Vickie? There was no way Vickie would stand still and let a crazed person slit her throat. So, what happened? Kelly wondered.

As she circled behind the sofa, Kelly spied a bronze bust lying on the floor beneath an end table. She remembered that piece because Vickie nearly knocked it over when she was hauling a huge weaving into the room to show them on their last visit. The Mozart bust. Kelly glanced to the cherry wood bookcase where she'd remembered it last. The space was empty.

Jennifer burst through the front door and raced into the room. "Kelly! Is it true? Did someone kill—?" She skidded to a stop when she saw Vickie. "Oh, my God," she breathed, hand to her throat. She went almost as white as Vickie.

"Jen! Jennifer, give me your cell," Kelly ordered in a sharp voice to snap her out of it.

Color started to rise in Jennifer's cheeks, and she shook her head as if to clear it. "Here." She offered the phone. "I'm not sure we'll have a signal, though. I lose it a lot in the mountains."

Kelly snapped open the cover, and, sure enough, there was no signal. One of the downsides of mountain living. "Damn," she said. "I didn't want to use the landline."

"Why?" Jennifer asked, turning away from the gruesome sight.

"There may be fingerprints. I don't want to smudge any before the police get here." She searched her pockets. "Do you have a tissue or something I can use?"

"Yeah, here." Jennifer dug in her back pocket and handed one over.

Kelly approached the kitchen, searching for a phone. Spying one on the wall, she carefully draped the tissue over the receiver and used her T-shirt to cover her dialing finger while she punched 9-1-1. She sincerely hoped she hadn't accidentally wiped off any other fingerprints in the process.

When the police operator came on the line, she calmly reported what she had found, where they were, and identified herself. The operator informed her that an investigative unit would be on the scene right away. Kelly gave the woman the description of Vickie's farmhouse as well as how far up the canyon it was located before she hung up.

Turning back to Jennifer, she saw her hovering at the edge of the sofa casting furtive peeks at Vickie. Death held an undeniable fascination for most people. Kelly remembered how her father looked when he died, but he was barely recognizable having wasted away with lung cancer. It wasn't the same. Vickie had been in the prime of her mature life, full of anticipation for the future and joyful, loving her work and her art. Kelly glanced at her dead friend. It wasn't the same. It wasn't the same at all.

"Do you really think someone killed her?" Jennifer asked softly, as if someone was listening.

"It has to be murder," Kelly declared, even more emphatically now. "Vickie wouldn't kill herself. But even if she planned to, she would have done it another way. If she'd wanted to bleed to death, she'd have done it in the bathroom or in the tub or something. Not on top of her gorgeous rug." Kelly shook her head.

Jennifer shuddered. "What a gruesome thought. I mean, I've been down sometimes, but never enough to do that." She grimaced again. "Who in the world would kill Vickie?"

"I don't know. I can't imagine—"

Suddenly, voices. Voices everywhere as the flock of touring

knitters swarmed into the house and scattered about the great room, tittering and squealing and shivering in turns as they pointed and peeked.

Kelly and Jennifer stood rooted in the kitchen, both clearly appalled at the sight. Vickie had been their friend, Kelly fumed within. Her death was not a stop on the tour schedule.

Fussy fluttered to the head of the flock and pointed to the victim. "There she is!" she proudly proclaimed. "I found her just like that!"

"That does it!" Kelly exploded as she strode over to the women. They were just like a bunch of magpies. She purposely stood between the flock and her fallen friend, then pointed to the door.

"Get out now!" she ordered. "Vickie was our friend and you have no right to invade her privacy like this. *Out!*"

"That's right, ladies," Jennifer spoke up. "This is a crime scene. You could get in trouble with the police for disturbing it. Now leave." She shooed them away.

Jennifer's stretching of the truth worked. The flock squawked and scattered out the door. Fussy, however, held her ground. She puffed out her chest in full huff. "What about you two? You have no right to be here, then."

Kelly was beyond the point of politeness. Manners be damned. She pointed right between Fussy's eyes. "You. Not another word. I mean it, or you'll walk back to Fort Connor." If Kelly's voice sank any lower, it would be in the river at the bottom of the canyon.

Fussy blanched, then turned and stalked out of the house, feathers dropping in her wake.

"Whoa, you go, girl," Jennifer teased. "I'd hate to see you really mad."

Kelly released a huge breath. "It's not a pretty sight, trust me."

Just then, the sound of a wailing siren pierced the air, farther away, then coming closer. The police. Thank God, Kelly sighed in relief.

"C'mon, let's get out of here," Jennifer prodded and motioned to Kelly.

Kelly took one last look at her murdered friend and followed Jennifer out the door.

Three

Kelly paced beside the pasture fence while she watched police detectives spread across Vickie's property—interviewing visiting knitters, searching the barn, and hurrying in and out of the sprawling log home. Since Bellvue Canyon was in the county, not the city of Fort Connor, this case belonged to the county police. It was their jurisdiction, and Kelly was relieved to see the number of squad cars lining the driveway.

The more cops, the sooner they'll find whoever did this, Kelly told herself as she paced. The horror had worn off, and the sense of outrage that someone could snuff out a life as vital and worthwhile as Vickie's took hold of Kelly now. Who could have done this awful thing?

Uniformed policemen were scattered from pasture to front porch, each with a pair of overwrought visitors. The women chattered, and the officers dutifully wrote everything down. Maybe one of them had seen something Kelly hadn't.

Another policeman strode by with a man carrying a large video camera setup, and they both entered the house. Kelly imagined them photographing every inch of the great room. Who knew where clues might be hidden? She only hoped the flock of magpies hadn't disturbed anything.

She glanced toward the pasture and observed the alpacas scattered about, grazing and studying all the human activity. Kelly searched for any sign of agitation but wasn't exactly sure what to look for. Her knowledge base about alpacas was pretty shallow. Vickie had been the one to educate most of them in the Tuesday evening group when she'd regale them with stories about the gentle beasts with the to-die-for soft wool.

Fleece, she corrected herself. Kelly had learned that much, at least. Just like sheep, alpacas were sheared of their heavy coats in late spring or early summer. Once the wool was cleaned of debris, it was carded, then spun into yarn. She'd seen an alpaca shearing only last month, when Vickie had invited the knitting group to her ranch.

Kelly'd been amazed how thick and heavy the fleece was, and how relieved the animals seemed to be when it was gone. Summer heat had already descended by early June. Kelly couldn't imagine wearing her winter coat outside in those temperatures. No wonder the animals were glad to be rid of it, noticing how they carefully sniffed and inspected each other as they returned to the common pen. Kelly still remembered the loud buzz of the huge razor and the methodical, efficient, almost rhythmic way the female shearer moved around each animal.

Jennifer's voice sounded behind her. "Well, I told them everything I saw, and I was finished in two minutes. Your favorite has been enthralling that guy for at least ten." She snickered and indicated Fussy across the driveway, still holding forth, gesturing animatedly to an attentive officer.

Kelly turned away with a shudder. "I can't look. Remember, you're taking her home."

"I know, I know. You can have one of mine."

"A quiet one, please."

Jennifer laughed softly. "Boy, an afternoon with you without caffeine can sure turn ugly."

"Don't even go there," Kelly warned.

"Too bad they won't let us use the kitchen. I'll bet Vickie has some coffee. Whoa, here comes another cop, heading for you, I'll bet," Jennifer observed. "I'll make myself scarce and see if I can hunt up a cola or something."

"Please," Kelly begged, watching a middle-aged, suit-clad policeman approach.

"Ms. Flynn, I'm Lieutenant Peterson, the detective in charge. Can you go over some things with me, please?" the man asked, his notepad already open and poised.

"Surely, detective, uh, Lieutenant Peterson. How can I help?"

He paged through the notepad. "You said you noticed a bronze statue or bust lying on the floor near the victim, is that correct?"

"Yes sir," Kelly replied. "I noticed it because I'd seen the bronze before on an earlier visit. It usually sat on the cherry wood bookcase against the wall."

He scribbled away dutifully, then looked Kelly straight in the eye. "Ms. Flynn, can you think of anyone who might have wanted Vickie Claymore dead?"

Kelly met his gaze. "No sir, I cannot. I never heard her say a bad word about anyone." Something in the back of Kelly's memory sent a niggling thought forward. Oh yes she did. There was one person Vickie had spoken of harshly.

The detective's gaze narrowed. "Are you sure?"

"Well," Kelly hesitated, not sure how much she should say. "She did say some strong things about her husband. Or, soon-to-be ex-husband, Bob Claymore."

"They were divorcing?" he asked as he wrote.

"Yes, they were, but it wasn't final yet."

"Was he still living here, do you know, or elsewhere?"

"Vickie said he was living in town. In Fort Connor. He's . . . uh . . . he's a professor at the university. That's all I know about him." That wasn't entirely truthful, but Kelly was already feeling uncomfortable talking about her friend's personal business.

"Was it amicable? The divorce, I mean?" The detective fixed her with his tell-the-truth look, which Kelly felt all the way down to her toes.

"Not exactly," she admitted. "I recall Vickie complaining to some of us at the knitting shop about Bob and, uh, the situation." Complaining put it mildly, Kelly recalled. Vickie had been in a white-hot fury when she discovered Bob was having an affair with a fellow weaver—a woman named Eva Bartok.

"Complaining about what?" he continued to grill, scribbling in the notebook.

Oh, brother, Kelly sighed within. Better tell him. "Vickie found out he was having an affair with a friend of hers. And . . . and she was pretty irate, to say the least."

"She was angry?"

"Oh, yeah. Furious is more like it. She filed for divorce the following week."

"Do you know the other woman's name?" he continued.

"Yes, Vickie said it was Eva Bartok. I don't know the woman personally and have never met her, so I'm afraid I can't help you there," Kelly answered, hoping the detective would let her go. He was like a pit bull.

"Was Ms. Stroud present when Ms. Claymore spoke of her husband and the divorce?"

Darn. Now Jennifer would be grilled, too. "Well, yes, she was, detective. You see, we're both part of the same knitting group that Vickie belonged to. We meet every Tuesday night at the shop in town—House of Lambspun."

The detective glanced around the grounds. Most of the visitors had finished their interviews, Kelly noticed, and she was grateful that Jennifer had corralled them together near the barn. All except Fussy, that is. She was still holding forth. Kelly closed her eyes. What was that woman saying?

"Are all these women in your knitting group?" he asked.

"Heck, no." Kelly caught herself before emitting her first response. "The rest of these folks are visiting from out of town and wanted to see a working alpaca ranch." She shook her head. "I guess they saw more than they wanted on this trip."

"Probably so, Ms. Flynn," he agreed and lowered his notebook. Kelly almost sighed in relief. "Thank you for your cooperation. You've been most helpful."

"I hope so, detective. I want whoever did this awful thing to Vickie to be caught and put in *jail*," Kelly declared.

"We'll do our best, Ms. Flynn, I promise," he assured her. "Can you think of anyone else that we should interview?"

Kelly paused for a moment but couldn't resist. "See that woman over there, gesturing?" She pointed toward Fussy. "I had the dubious pleasure of riding into the canyon with her. I'm sure she'll tell you exactly how to run your investigation, detective." She gave him a wry smile.

"I'll bear that in mind, Ms. Flynn. Thank you again," the detective replied, a twinkle in his eye.

Kelly watched him cross the driveway and head straight for Jennifer. She knew she should supervise the visitors while Jennifer was being grilled, but Kelly simply didn't think she could stand by calmly while they bombarded her with questions. Not now.

The sound of a truck engine approaching caught her attention, and Kelly watched as a mud-splattered navy blue pickup pulled to a jerking halt near one of the police cruisers. A slender woman with sandy blonde hair pulled back with a scarf jumped out of the truck and raced over to the closest police officer who was not engaged in interviewing.

Curious who the woman was, Kelly started walking toward them. As she drew closer, she noticed the woman appeared distraught and grasped at the officer's arm. Approaching close enough to overhear, Kelly paused.

"Officer, you've got to tell me what happened," the woman pleaded. "I'm Vickie's cousin. I'm the closest relative she has here. We work together every day. Please, please, tell me if Vickie's all right!"

The younger policeman hesitated for a moment before he answered. "No, ma'am, she isn't. I'm afraid she's dead."

The woman's mouth dropped open, and she gasped, "No . . . that can't be . . . how . . . ?"

"Let me get the detective in charge, Lieutenant Peterson. He'll want to speak with you. He'll explain everything. Stay right here, ma'am, okay?" the officer advised as he left.

The woman clasped both arms around herself and took a deep breath. Her head bent forward, and her shoulders began to shake. Kelly assumed she was crying and purposely glanced away for a few moments, not wanting to intrude on the woman's grief.

Kelly figured she must be Vickie's cousin who helped out at the ranch. Glancing back, Kelly saw the woman wipe her eyes with the back of her hand as she stared at the house. Kelly slowly approached, wanting to offer her condolences. "Excuse me, I don't mean to intrude, but I couldn't help overhearing your saying you were a relative of Vickie's."

The woman looked up, her eyes red, her face mottled from crying. "Yes, yes, I am. I'm her cousin, Jayleen," she said. "Can you tell me what happened here?"

Kelly shook her head. "I'm afraid not. We just arrived this

afternoon with a group of knitters who're visiting from out of town."
She gestured, indicating the crowded driveway and yard. "My friend
and I offered to show them around a working alpaca ranch. Vickie
was kind enough to volunteer." Kelly's voice softened. "When we
walked in, we found her lying on the floor. I'm afraid she was
already dead."

"My God . . . ," Jayleen whispered, closing her eyes.

"I just wanted to tell you how sorry I am about Vickie." Kelly
extended her hand. "I'm Kelly Flynn, one of Vickie's friends from
the knitting shop. She used to come and visit with us every Tuesday
night. She'd weave while we knit."

"Jayleen Swinson," the woman said, giving Kelly a firm handshake. "I remember her talking about that group."

"We all grew very fond of Vickie. She was so vibrant and full of
life. . . ." Kelly gestured as she lost the words.

"Excuse me, ladies," Lieutenant Peterson's voice interrupted as he
strode up. "You said you're a relative of the deceased, Vickie Claymore?" He directed the question at Jayleen.

Kelly took that as her hint to leave, and she quickly walked
toward the fence. She leaned over and pretended to watch the
alpacas while she strained to catch parts of the conversation. Maybe
cousin Jayleen had some idea who could kill Vickie. Why she was
deliberately eavesdropping, Kelly wasn't sure. Something inside her
was curious.

Peterson's questions were often lost, since his back was turned to
Kelly, but Jayleen's responses carried clearly on the slight mountain
breeze.

"I'm here every day, Lieutenant Peterson. I work with Vickie
and help with her business. I would know if she had any enemies.
We grew up together in Colorado Springs, Lieutenant. We're very,
very close. We do not keep secrets from each other. At least, we
didn't. . . ." Jayleen's voice faded.

Kelly heard a low mumble she took to be Peterson's question,
which brought an irate response from Jayleen.

"Absolutely not! Vickie would never commit suicide. Never. She
had too much going for her. Her . . . her business was successful, she
had plans, she . . ."

The rest was lost as the breeze shifted. So far, everything Kelly heard confirmed what she believed. Vickie didn't have enemies, and she wouldn't kill herself.

Another low mumble was followed by an angry explosion from Jayleen. "You bet she was divorcing Bob! Do you know what that—" She went on to describe in detail all of Bob Claymore's sins and transgressions, punctuated by colorful expletives.

Kelly smiled and imagined Lieutenant Peterson scribbling furiously in his little notebook. It was certainly an entertaining narrative, she had to admit. Even the alpacas had gathered closer to the fence, as if to listen. She held out her hand, palm up, and one came over to sniff.

"Sorry, no food," she apologized to the gentle creature as she reached to pat its graceful, long neck. Newly shorn, the animal felt nubbly and soft at the same time. Kelly noticed the tawny brown and white pattern covered the skin in the same pattern it appeared on the heavy coat when sheared.

Jayleen's responses continued to float over to Kelly as she patted the animals adventurous enough to approach. Meanwhile, she heard a litany of divorce demands and counterdemands. Vickie's business was more successful than Kelly knew, and apparently, her husband, Bob, wanted half of it.

"Can you imagine?" Jayleen demanded. "Bob Claymore didn't build that business! Vickie did, and it took her fifteen years. He has no right! That . . ."

More expletives drifted by, and Kelly noticed the alpacas seemed to pay attention. It made sense, she decided. After all, Jayleen helped Vickie on the ranch every day, so the alpacas knew her, were comfortable with her. If Jayleen was upset, the animals would probably notice. Carl always sensed her moods, Kelly reminded herself and wondered if alpacas did the same thing.

"Her estate? I don't know. I'm sure she'd be leaving it all to her daughter in Arizona."

This change of subject caught Kelly's attention. The divorce wasn't final, so legally, Vickie and Bob Claymore were still married at the time of her death, which meant . . .

"What!" Jayleen exclaimed. "You can't be serious. No way he gets half! That can't be right. They were divorcing!"

This time the string of curses must have startled not only the alpacas but Lieutenant Peterson as well, because Kelly heard him speak.

"Calm down, Ms. Swinson. I know you're upset, but—"

"Hey, look what I dug up from someone's backpack," Jennifer declared as she appeared at the fence beside Kelly. She dangled a can of soda. "It's not cold, but it's caffeine."

Kelly's caffeine lobe started vibrating. All attempts to eavesdrop were forgotten. Priorities beckoned, and right now she needed caffeine. Hot, cold, or lukewarm. "Wow, thanks, Jen," she said as she accepted the soda. Popping the top, Kelly took a huge gulp.

Jennifer grinned. "Maybe we'd better round up these ladies and head down the canyon. What do you think? It's nearly five o'clock now."

Kelly's stomach growled, reminding her of the time. She glanced toward the cluster of knitters, who were actually staying in one place this time. Police power, Kelly figured. She also noticed Fussy was among them, having obviously finished relating her story. Or, maybe the officer's ear had dropped off.

"Yeah, you're right. Last thing we want is to be stuck in a car filled with starving women. They could get surly. We'd better feed 'em."

"It's not them I'm worrying about—it's you," Jennifer teased. "I've seen you hungry, and it's scary."

"I wonder if the detective will let us leave," Kelly asked aloud. Watching Lieutenant Peterson close his notepad as he spoke with Jayleen, Kelly took that as a sign and approached them. "Excuse me, detective," she ventured. "Is it all right if my friend and I gather up these visitors and take them back to Fort Connor? We need to get them fed and to their hotel."

"Ah, yes, Ms. Flynn, that's fine," Lieutenant Peterson answered, his suntanned face cracking a smile. "They've had a busy day. Better take them home. If we need any more information, we'll be in touch with you."

"Thanks, Lieutenant Peterson, and I'll be glad to help any way I can," Kelly said.

"As will I . . . sir . . . uh . . . Lieutenant," Jayleen spoke up. "Do you want me to call Vickie's daughter, Debbie, in Arizona?"

"That's okay, Ms. Swinson. We'll be contacting the family. Is the daughter the only living relative other than yourself?" Peterson asked, opening his notebook once more. "Do you know her address and phone number?"

"Yes, she's the only other family Vickie has." Jayleen shoved her hands in the back pockets of her jeans. "I don't know the phone number off the top of my head, but I can get it for you real quick. Everything's right inside Vickie's office. I keep her books, so I'm in there every day. It'll only take me a sec."

She pointed toward the log home, which now had yellow police tape wrapped around the entire front porch and doorways. It looked to Kelly like a bizarre present, gift-wrapped in its mountain setting. Completely out of place.

"I'm sorry, but we can't allow anyone inside the house now. Our investigators have to complete their work. We're treating this as a crime scene. Do you have a record of the daughter's address and phone elsewhere? Does anyone else know her?"

"I may have her number at home in my office, somewhere. I'd have to look," Jayleen said. "My desk is a mess, but I should be able to find it—after I put the animals in the barn, that is. We can't leave them out overnight. I'll be able to do that, won't I? I mean, I'm here every morning helping Vickie around the ranch. It's one of my jobs."

Peterson pondered for a second. "I think the barn's been checked, so that should be all right. But you'll only have access to the barn and pastures. Don't touch anything else. The house will be locked up."

Jayleen's eyes got huge. "No sir. I wouldn't. Honest. Just the animals. That's all."

Kelly spoke up, "You know, if you can't find that number, Jayleen, I can ask Mimi Shafer, the owner of the knitting shop. Maybe she knows the daughter. Mimi and Vickie are, uh, were friends."

Lieutenant Peterson scribbled, then reached into his coat pocket. "Thank you, Ms. Flynn. Here's my card. Please tell Ms. Shafer to call if she has any information. Oh, and you can take your group and go now." He gestured toward the flock, clustered by the barn. "Good luck going home."

Taking that as her cue to go, Kelly sent him a warm smile. "Thanks, Lieutenant. We may need it."

Waving to Jennifer, she beckoned for the group to join her, then headed toward the SUV. With any luck, they could be out of the canyon and in Fort Connor by six o'clock. Kelly sincerely hoped the promise of a quick stop at a fast-food restaurant would be enough to keep the visitors docile on the trip back.

Carl nosed and sniffed the thick bushes lining the backyard fence, investigating every inch of the perimeter of his small kingdom. Kelly leaned back and sipped her coffee. She loved this time of the evening. The last light of summer sunset illuminated the treetops while the evening breeze seduced the leaves, whispering its night song.

Kelly relaxed into the shape-hugging chair. No matter how busy and stressful her workday turned out, it all disappeared during these hours. She gazed at the outline of the mountains, shadowed by impending twilight. The mountains nourished her. The breeze nourished her. Being outside nourished her. Heck, just being back in Colorado nourished her.

She took another sip of coffee, grateful for the umpteenth time that she was out of the close confines of the SUV and away from all those chattering women. The promise of food had worked, and the ladies kept their questions to a minimum, obviously content to entertain themselves on the return drive. Even so, Kelly had the beginnings of a headache, which started when she and Jennifer deposited their charges at the hotel and headed home themselves. Jennifer offered to call Mimi and tell her the sad news, and Kelly gratefully agreed. She didn't think she could answer another question.

Now, relaxed outside in the gathering dusk, Kelly felt all the accumulated tension from the disturbing day disappear. Only questions remained, darting in and out of her mind, as she watched night slowly capture the sky.

Who could have killed Vickie? Her husband, Bob? Remembering the angry accusations Jayleen had hurled this afternoon, Kelly had to admit he might have a motive. Apparently, Vickie wasn't about to divide up her successful alpaca business with him in a divorce settlement. But if she died before a settlement was reached and the divorce wasn't final, then Bob Claymore was still legally her husband. As such, he was entitled to a portion of her estate.

Kelly pondered the thought. Money could definitely be a motive for murder. People had killed each other over money since the beginning of time. But Bob Claymore was also the most obvious suspect. All of their friends knew he and Vickie were involved in a bitter divorce. Bob Claymore had the most to lose from the divorce and the most to gain from Vickie's death.

The last time Kelly had gotten close to a murder investigation, the obvious suspect turned out to be innocent. When her aunt Helen was killed, the police quickly arrested a suspect they believed responsible. But Kelly sensed the real killer was still out there and went on to prove it.

She took a deep, satisfying drink of coffee. A bird hidden in the treetop above warbled an evening song. Kelly listened to the lilting cadence, releasing all thoughts of motives and murder, and simply let herself drink in the delicious summer night.

Four

Megan looked up from the other side of the shop's long library table as Kelly dumped her knitting bag and sat down. "Kelly, how are you? I'm so sorry you were the one to find Vickie. That must have been awful!" she exclaimed, her naturally pale skin almost white with concern.

"It was," Kelly admitted as she set a mug of Eduardo's delectable nectar on the table. "I hope I never have to walk in on something that horrible again."

"Jennifer told us all about it this morning. Lisa was here for a while between therapy patients," Megan went on, picking up her needles again. The scarf of purple eyelash yarn was almost finished. "I had to go back for a conference call with my Boise client, but I promised Mimi I'd return after lunch. I was hoping you'd show up."

"How's Mimi taking it? Vickie seemed to be a very close friend."

"Oh, she was. Mimi said they'd known each other for over twenty years. Ever since Vickie moved here with her first husband. In fact, Mimi was the one who taught her how to weave."

Kelly sipped the flavorful brew. "They go back a long way, then. This must be hitting Mimi pretty hard."

The sound of Mimi's voice coming around the corner caught their attention. Mimi appeared, arms filled with pattern books, talking to Rosa, one of the shop assistants.

"I thought that lace pattern was in the latest issue of this knitting magazine. Maybe I'm wrong," Mimi said as she dumped the books on the far end of the table. Glancing up, she gave Kelly a wan smile before she went back to Rosa. "See if you can find it, would you, please? It's got the scalloped edges and roses."

Mimi walked toward their end of the table, straightening magazines and yarn bins along the way. Finally, she sank into a chair. She looked tired to Kelly. Grief was wearing on her. She'd lost a good friend with Helen's death a few months ago, and now another dear friend was gone.

"How're you doing, Mimi?" Kelly asked.

"I'm okay," she said quietly, staring into her lap. No knitting needles, Kelly noticed, to keep Mimi's restless hands occupied. "Still stunned, I guess. I mean, it's all so senseless. Who would kill Vickie Claymore? She was a warm, generous, caring person—a gifted craftsman and a successful businesswoman." Mimi wrapped her arms around herself and shook her head sadly. "I don't understand."

Kelly debated how to bring up the subject that had been playing through her mind last night, ever since hearing Jayleen's accusations. She'd have to work up to it. "Mimi, you know Vickie's cousin, Jayleen, don't you?"

"Yes, I've met her a few times over the years. I don't actually know her real well, but Vickie was always saying how much work she did around the ranch."

"She arrived at the ranch yesterday while the police were there," Kelly went on. "She was really upset, understandably."

"I imagine so," Mimi added. "Vickie has been like a big sister to her. Helped Jayleen straighten her life out after her last divorce. I think she even helped Jayleen get a job as a bookkeeper, too, if I recall."

Kelly sipped her coffee. "Well, that explains her forceful and rather colorful defense of Vickie's interests—in the divorce, I mean."

Mimi managed a small smile. "Yes, Jayleen can be colorful, all right. She's got quite a tongue on her."

"Ohhhh, yeah. She was describing all of Bob Claymore's transgressions to the police detective. And she was as furious as Vickie that Bob wanted half of the business. But then she really exploded when the detective told her he'd wind up with half the business now that Vickie's dead." Kelly gave a wry smile, remembering Jayleen's wrath. "The detective had to calm her down."

"Well, he's right. The divorce wasn't final, so Bob Claymore is still legally her husband," Mimi observed.

"That doesn't seem fair," Megan said, glancing up from her scarf.

"What isn't fair?" Lisa's voice spoke up as she appeared at the table and settled into a chair.

"Finished with therapy already?" Megan looked up in surprise.

"Yeah, two rescheduled, and I had some errands to run anyway," Lisa explained as she pulled the multicolored ribbon vest from her bag. "I take it you guys are talking about Vickie. That was horrible, just horrible." Lisa scowled. "What lowlife would sneak in and kill Vickie?"

"Maybe the killer didn't sneak in," Kelly suggested.

"You think she knew the killer?" Megan asked, her blue eyes growing as huge as demitasse saucers.

Kelly nodded. "I think it's a strong possibility. There's no way Vickie would let some deranged intruder cut her throat."

Lisa nodded. "You're right. Vickie would probably punch him out. And not just an intruder, either. Face it, Vickie wouldn't let anyone attack her. She was tough."

"What do you think happened?" Mimi asked, peering anxiously at Kelly.

Kelly glanced over both shoulders, checking for nearby customers, then said in a quiet voice, "I think she was killed by someone she knew. Someone she allowed into her home. Yesterday, I saw a bronze bust lying on the floor near Vickie. I think someone knocked Vickie unconscious, then killed her."

Mimi blanched, then shuddered. "Oh, that's so gruesome."

"Wouldn't she have regained consciousness before she died?" Megan whispered.

Lisa shook her head vehemently. "Not if her throat was cut right through the jugular vein. She'd bleed out quickly. Even if she awoke from the head trauma, she'd pass out from blood loss."

Both Mimi and Megan shuddered visibly this time. "How diabolically cruel," Mimi whispered.

"Yes, and only someone who knew Vickie would have been able to do it," Kelly added. "And that brings us back to Bob Claymore."

"Vickie's husband?" Lisa asked, clearly surprised. "I don't think so. I've worked with him on a community housing project. He's this laid-back literature professor. No way."

"Anyone can kill, Lisa," Megan said darkly, her fingers nimbly working the purple yarn.

"Boy, that sounds scary. Let me see if I can guess what you guys are talking about," Jennifer announced as she dumped her knitting bag on the table and pulled up a chair beside Kelly.

"Well, I'm not talking about this anymore," Mimi said forcefully as she rose. "I just can't. I still remember when we all came to Fort Connor and the university years ago. We were all happy. We raised our children, we went to parties, we built our businesses . . ." Mimi's voice trembled as she gazed outside. "And we didn't go around killing each other." She turned and rushed from the room.

"Poor Mimi," Megan ventured. "This is so hard on her."

"She was in tears on the phone last night when I called," Jennifer added. "I felt so bad."

"I sure hope the killer made lots of mistakes for the police to find, so they can catch him quickly," Kelly said.

"Do you really think her husband could have done it?" Megan probed.

Kelly released a sigh. "I don't know. But he sure sounds like suspect number one, judging by everything we've heard. He was the one with the most to gain from her death."

"Was that who Vickie's cousin was going off about yesterday?" Jennifer asked, taking the multicolored fringed yarn and needles from her bag. "Brother, I haven't heard that much swearing since my freshman year at an all-girls' college."

Lisa's knitting fell to her lap. Megan's jaw dropped. Kelly stared at Jennifer, incredulous. "You went to a girls' college?"

"Yeah. I promised my parents I'd try it for a year. Damn near killed me."

Kelly joined the laughter that rippled around the table as she reached into her knitting bag and withdrew her new sweater project. She examined the newest rows of stockinette stitching that she'd finished that morning while downloading files. Her friends were right. Knitting in the round produced stockinette. Kelly didn't care if it was magic or not. She was proud of herself. It looked good. The raspberry silk-and-cotton stitches were nice and even. She held up the rosy red circlet of yarn and noticed the twist that had appeared in the circle this morning.

How'd that happen? she wondered. It hadn't been there yesterday.

"Hey, look how much I've finished," Kelly announced, proudly holding up the circlet. "I had a ton of client files to download from my office this morning, so I got a lot done."

Lisa glanced up. "Looks like it's really coming along—" She stopped, peering at the circle. "Uh-oh."

That was enough to capture Megan's attention. She eyed the twisted circlet and asked, "What happened? It looked fine yesterday."

"Oooops," Jennifer observed and went back to her silky yarn.

Kelly sat perplexed, still holding the rosy red circle. She'd expected to hear a heartening string of "good job" and "looks good." Not this.

"What's with the 'oops' and the 'uh-oh'?" she demanded. "What's wrong?"

"How'd it get twisted?" Lisa asked.

Kelly shrugged. "I don't know. I must have shoved it into my knitting bag before I left for the canyon yesterday. It was twisted like this when I took it out this morning."

"Did you notice the twist?" Megan asked.

"Yeah," Kelly admitted. She didn't like the way this conversation was going.

"But you kept knitting," Lisa added, her needles working the ribbons in her lap.

"Yeah, I figured it would straighten out somehow."

"Like magic?"

"We gotta stop using the M-word with her. She's an accountant."

"Don't worry, Kelly, we've all done it," Megan reassured with an encouraging smile. "It happens easily when knitting in the round."

"*What* happened?" Kelly exclaimed, exasperated now. "What'd I do wrong?"

Jennifer turned to her and smiled. "Congratulations. You've created a Möbius strip. Start frogging."

Kelly stared at her. What? Möbius strip? Frogs? What did that have to do with yarn? "Möbius strip?" she asked, totally clueless as to what Jennifer was talking about. "You mean those twisty things that hang from the ceiling?"

"Yep. That's what the sweater turns into when the circle gets twisted."

"But won't the twist come out?" She placed the circle on the table and started working the yarn with her fingers around and around the circle.

"Let me know if it disappears," Jennifer said. "We'll call the knitting magazines. You'll make the front cover."

Kelly scowled at the uncooperative circle of yarn. Whenever she straightened the twist on one side, it corkscrewed on the other. Around and around, over and over. "Darn it," she fussed. "Now what?"

"Start frogging."

"Enough of this!" Kelly protested, disappointment mixing with annoyance now. "What do frogs have to do with anything?"

Megan giggled. "It's an expression we use for unraveling."

"You remember the sound frogs make. *Rip-pit! Rip-pit!*" Lisa joked.

Kelly stared at the circlet in disbelief. "Rip it out? All of it? But I've done so much, I—"

"Well, you can hang it from the ceiling as a decoration or rip it out and start over. Your choice," Jennifer added.

"I don't believe this." Kelly shook her head, still dumbfounded at her mistake. How could she do something like that? She thought she was doing so well. The stockinette looked so good. And all along, she was doing it wrong.

"Now, don't go beating up on yourself," Lisa advised. "We've all done it, Kelly. Knitting in the round is tricky until you get the knack of it. It's a common mistake."

"Yeah, yeah, yeah," Kelly grumbled.

"Uh-oh. Knitting angst is about to descend. I can feel it," Jennifer teased.

"You're right, it is," Kelly complained. "I thought I was doing so well. My stockinette really looked good."

"And it does look great," Lisa reassured. "Just think of this as extra practice."

Kelly released a dramatic sigh and listened to her friends chuckle. "Okay, what do I do to start unraveling, or frogging, or whatever it is?"

Jennifer reached over. "Here, let me get you started. First, we have to gently pull the yarn off the needles and plastic circle, like this." She started slowly working the slender wooden needles and attached plastic cord from the top row of stitches. "There, all out." She tossed the needle contraption on the table and handed the forlorn sweater attempt back to Kelly. "Now, just pull gently and it'll all start to unravel."

"Okaaaay," Kelly said dubiously, giving the yarn a tug. It cooperated, and the entire first row of stitches unraveled before her eyes.

"Here, wind the yarn around this," Lisa said, reaching into her bag and offering an empty paper towel roll. "You don't want to get knots in the yarn."

"Why not?" Kelly complained, indulging in a little self-pity. "I've managed to bungle everything else about this sweater."

"Oh, boy. The angst is getting deeper. She's about to go under. Look out," Jennifer teased.

"All right, all right," Kelly started to laugh, joining her friends. It was impossible to stay in a bad mood when she was around them.

The shop's doorbell jingled, followed by a familiar duet of voices. One high and girlish, the other low and deeply resonant, told Kelly the Von Steuben sisters had arrived. Both were elderly retired school teachers and two of the most accomplished knitters Kelly had seen yet.

"Hello, hello," Lizzie Von Steuben trilled as she fluttered into the main room, a vision of white and pink. "How wonderful to see all four of you this afternoon. What a treat!" She daintily set down her lacy knitting bag as she joined the others.

"Good afternoon, ladies," boomed Hilda Von Steuben as she strode through the room and settled at the end of the table.

The better to conduct class, Kelly thought and smiled to herself. Both spinster sisters were accomplished interrogators, Kelly
had learned. Only their styles differed. Lizzie would flit and flutter
around the subject, circling ever closer, while Hilda steamrollered
right to the point.

"Hilda, Lizzie, good to see you," Megan greeted.

Kelly joined in the ensuing small talk, waiting for Hilda to start
questioning. She could tell Lizzie was about to explode with curiosity.

"Kelly, I'm profoundly sorry you were the one to make the dreadful discovery yesterday," Hilda intoned.

"Ohhhh, yessss," Lizzie rushed in. "Such a horrible thing to see.
Are you all right, dear?"

"I'm doing fine, thank you, ladies," Kelly replied and launched
into a condensed version of yesterday's events in the canyon. Lizzie
and Hilda both sat rapt, not saying a word. While she talked, Kelly
watched Lisa check her watch and slip away from the table, as did
Jennifer. Kelly wound the sad tale to a close.

Lizzie bent her head over the misty gray shawl she was crocheting and didn't say a word, clearly affected by the death of one of
their own. Hilda seemed content to concentrate on the peach wool
that appeared to be forming into a baby blanket. Kelly glanced at
her watch, timing this welcome break from analyzing accounts.

"Has Vickie's daughter been notified yet?" Hilda asked after a
moment.

That comment caught Kelly's attention and reminded her she
told the detective she'd ask Mimi to search for the daughter's number. "Thanks, Hilda, that reminds me of something." She started
to push back her chair when Mimi appeared around the corner,
daytimer in hand. "Mimi, I just remembered. Do you know Vickie's
daughter's name and phone number? I think she lives in Arizona."

Mimi stopped where she was, clearly startled. "What? You mean
Debbie hasn't been notified yet? Good heavens!"

Kelly dug in her knitting bag and withdrew Lieutenant Peterson's
card. Handing it over to Mimi, she said, "I told the detective in
charge, Lieutenant Peterson, that you would call with the number.
Just in case Jayleen couldn't find it at her home. No one was allowed
in Vickie's office where all the phone logs would be, naturally."

Mimi took the card and headed toward the front of the shop. "I'll call right away."

"This will come as a terrible shock to the girl, I am sure," Hilda continued in a resonant contralto. "She's such a delicate little creature. I sincerely hope she's able to bear up under this tragedy."

"Oh, my, yes," Lizzie murmured, making soft little *tsk*ing sounds as more flower designs appeared in the smoky gray shawl.

The shawl looked scrumptious to Kelly, and she couldn't resist reaching over and squeezing the soft yarn. Lusciously soft. So soft it must be . . . "Alpaca?" she guessed.

Lizzie beamed, her round cheeks tinged pink. "Why, yes, it is. Good for you, Kelly. You're learning your fibers."

Kelly suppressed her smile and watched Megan do the same at the verbal pat on the head. "What sort of health problems does the daughter have?" she asked after a second.

"Debbie is afflicted with the most serious form of asthma. Truly life-threatening. That's why she lives in the drier climate in Arizona. She needs to be away from the irritants that could trigger an attack. She's been hospitalized countless times since she was a child, according to Vickie."

"That's awful," Megan exclaimed.

"And her mother was always such a picture of health," Lizzie commiserated, shaking her head. "I always thought it unfortunate that a woman as robust and strong as Vickie Claymore would have such a frail and fragile child as this Debbie appears to be."

"You've never met her?" Kelly asked, continuing her unraveling. It was actually a strangely soothing activity, she noticed, but not one she'd like to indulge in frequently. Kelly liked results, and the quicker she got results, the better.

"No, we haven't seen her since she was a young girl living with her family here in town," Lizzie answered. "Her asthma was serious but not as bad as it is now."

"It was the ranch that did it," Hilda decreed. "When Vickie divorced her first husband, she used the property settlement to buy an old ranch house up in Bellvue Canyon. She'd dreamed of raising and breeding alpacas. Unfortunately, it was that dream that spurred Debbie's disease to the next level."

Hilda's fingers worked the peach yarn, producing a spreading fan design in the blanket. The Von Steuben sisters' artistry always amazed Kelly. "What do you mean?" she continued to probe. "Was she allergic to the alpacas?"

"Oh, no," Lizzie spoke up. "It wasn't the alpacas."

"It was the ranch setting itself, apparently," Hilda picked up the thread. "The hay and dust in the stalls and pastures, the grasses the animals grazed, the surrounding trees and bushes. All of it triggered a dangerous attack when she was ready to go to college. Poor girl. She had a scholarship to Stanford, too."

"What happened?" Megan prodded, clearly as enthralled with this story as Kelly. "Did she drop out of college?"

"Unfortunately, yes," Hilda continued. "She was in and out of hospitals for over a year. That's when she had to move to Arizona to recuperate. She enrolled in the state school when she was stronger." She glanced up at Mimi, who was quietly rearranging yarn in the corner. "Exactly what did Debbie study, do you remember, Mimi?"

"Yes, it was biology. She's a researcher now, looking for a cure for these dreadful respiratory diseases." Mimi's voice had an edge to it.

"You sound like you spent a lot of time with Vickie," Megan addressed Hilda. "I'm sure this is hard for you."

Hilda set her needles down and was uncharacteristically pensive for a moment as she stared out the window. "Yes, it is. I'd grown quite fond of Vickie over the years. I taught her some of the advanced knitting techniques, and she tried to teach me to weave. I wasn't a very good student, I'm afraid."

"She was fond of you, too, Hilda," Mimi said in a small voice. "She said so many times. You reminded her of her mother."

That seemed to rouse Hilda, and she returned to the peach wool. "Poor misguided girl. An old fussbudget like me."

"Did you call the detective, Mimi?" Kelly asked, noticing her edge around the table.

"Yes, and he said he's already contacted Debbie. She told him she'd be coming to Fort Connor as quickly as she could." Mimi paused near the fireplace, decorated with hanging summer tops, and gazed out the window. "I feel sorry for Debbie. She was so close to her mother."

"I'm surprised she's able to come back here at all if her asthma is that serious," Megan commented as she rose to leave.

"Vickie said there're newer medicines now that allow Debbie to travel more. I believe she actually stayed with Vickie at the ranch last year for over a week."

Kelly checked her watch. Corporate accounts beckoned. "I'm afraid I have to get back to work, ladies. Maybe I'll see you tomorrow," she said as she carefully placed the circular needles and ball of unraveled yarn back into her bag and rose to leave.

"You'll see me tonight," Megan reminded her on the way to the door. "Practice, remember? Seven o'clock."

"Ohhhh, yeah," Kelly said, hitting her forehead. "Brother, I thought I put it on my calendar." Throwing a wave over her shoulder, she headed for the door. "See you, folks. Gotta run." She'd really have to push now to finish that client file before practice.

As she raced down the flagstone steps leading from the shop, Kelly heard her cell phone's insistent ring. Darn. She didn't need any interruptions right now. "Kelly Flynn here," she snapped into the receiver.

"Whoa, hello to you, too," Steve's voice sounded in her ear. She could hear the amusement.

"Sorry, Steve. I'm just hurrying back to my office to finish up some files before dinner. Totally spaced about tonight's practice. What's up?" she asked as she maneuvered the cottage door open and dumped her things on the sofa.

"We've got an invitation to dinner tomorrow night. From Curt Stackhouse and his wife, Ruth. I saw Curt at a builders' meeting this morning, and he reminded me we said we'd come over for dinner some night."

"We who?" Kelly played dumb, deliberately stalling. She'd been hoping Curt had forgotten his offer.

"You and me who." She could almost see Steve's smile.

"You and me, huh?"

This time she heard the chuckle. "Yeah, unless you want to bring Carl, too. We could let him run loose in the field. Or he can play with the sheep."

Kelly laughed, remembering the last time she'd been to Curt

Stackhouse's ranch. Carl spent the entire time galumphing through the tall field grass, chasing scents and scampering creatures. "Curt would not be amused," she said, settling at the computer. "Neither would the sheep."

"Okay, so it's back to us. You and me. For dinner. At Curt's. Think you can handle it?"

"Okay, okay," Kelly gave in with an exaggerated sigh. "What time are we talking about tomorrow night?"

"Seven o'clock. Does that work?"

"Yeah. Okay. Seven." She hesitated. "I'll meet you there."

Steve laughed out loud this time. "You want us to drive separate cars? Won't that look a little strange? What are we gonna do, meet in front of Curt's barn?"

He was right. It would look stupid. Rats. She hated it when he was right. She was being borderline ridiculous, but she couldn't help it. "Okay, I'll meet you at the Crossroads coffee shop. I've got some errands to run on that side of town anyway."

"You just don't want anyone at the shop seeing me pick you up, that's all."

Steve hit dead center on that one. Darn it, Kelly smarted. "No, that's not it—"

"Yeah, it is," he teased. "Listen, I've got a better idea. Why don't you pick me up? I'll be at my new site in Wellesley. Corner of New-port and Hampton streets. Six thirty, tomorrow. See you." And he clicked off before Kelly could say another word.

Five

"Thanks, Pete," Kelly said as she lifted her coffee mug and edged around the café tables, heading for the hallway that led to the shop. She'd been working at the computer ever since her morning run on the river trail. She deserved a fiber break, as she referred to her daily visits to knit and talk with friends.

Sometimes the workaholic inside her tried to make Kelly feel guilty for leaving her home office. Fortunately, it didn't last very long. She needed those breaks. She worked all alone now, not in the midst of an office filled with colleagues. Kelly missed the camaraderie. She didn't realize how much until she'd started telecommuting to her firm three months ago. Besides, she reminded herself, she got twice as much work done without all the interruptions for meetings that used to mark her daytimer. Now, she could actually leave her work without worry and was thankful she'd made so many good friends in the short time she'd been here.

Rounding the corner to the front room, Kelly stopped short. Once again, elves had come in and worked their magic overnight. Frothy new yarns were everywhere, spilling across the round maple table in the center of the room and tumbling from wooden crates that lined the walls. Steamer trunks that held scrunchy wools only months ago now brimmed with fat balls of new fibers that begged to be touched.

Kelly couldn't resist and set her knitting bag and mug on the floor, then sank her arms elbow deep into the chest of brilliant and bold boa yarns. Soft, soft, with little fibers that stuck out like eyelashes, and in every color imaginable. She squeezed strawberry scarlet and lime green, pineapple yellow and tangerine orange. Jelly bean colors. She'd been let loose in the candy shop and was playing in the candy bins. There was a big difference, though. These "candies" weren't fattening.

Moving to the bins along the wall, Kelly stroked longer-lashed yarns, some spiky in combination colors and others so silky soft they seduced her very fingers. Burnished copper and lemony yellow tempted next. She fingered a particularly seductive skein the color of good claret, then one of antique gold, another of moss green. Yummy, Kelly thought, picturing the gorgeous autumn scarves she could make from those colors.

That was it. She had to have one. Jennifer was knitting a similar long-fringed scarf, and Megan had finished the purple eyelash scarf and was working on a pink one now. Kelly wanted one, too. Now that she'd gotten her knitting-in-the-round back on track, she could take a break, couldn't she? Besides, everyone said these scarves knitted up quickly.

Now, which color to choose, she pondered, wandering back to the chest of boa eyelash yarns. Something other than red this time, noting that her very first chunky wool sweater was cherry red, and her latest project was a luscious raspberry silk and cotton. She wanted something different. Decisions, decisions.

Kelly was still immersed in color when she heard her name called. She turned to see Rosa in the doorway and another woman Kelly didn't recognize.

"Kelly, this lady wanted to talk to you," Rosa explained, then dropped her voice. "She's a friend of Vickie's and wanted to know what happened."

Scarves and jelly bean colors had to wait. Kelly scrambled from the floor. The woman stepped over to her, hand outstretched.

"Kelly, I'm Geri Norbert. Vickie was my closest friend. I live up in the canyon about two miles from her ranch. And I . . . I just wanted to ask some questions, if you don't mind."

Kelly shook her hand. It was warm and calloused. "Sure, I'll be glad to answer whatever I can, Ms. Norbert."

The woman's suntanned face creased with a grin. Kelly guessed her to be mid-fifties like Vickie. Her long, dark hair mixed with gray hung down her back in a fat braid. "Please call me Geri. Everyone does," she said.

Glancing over her shoulder at the knitting class taking place around the library table, Kelly gestured toward the café. "Why don't we have a cup of coffee at Pete's and talk, okay?" She reached to snag her knitting bag and mug before she headed back to the restaurant.

"Looks like you've already got yours," Geri said, following after Kelly.

"Yeah, I get a fill-up every morning. Helps me make it through all that computer work," Kelly replied as she aimed for a table in the back alcove. Noticing Jennifer wasn't working the morning shift, Kelly signaled another waitress, then added, "I can personally recommend their cinnamon rolls. They're wicked."

Geri pulled up a chair as Kelly sat down. "I shouldn't. My sweet tooth is too easily awakened. Better let it sleep."

"I'm not sure mine ever goes to sleep," Kelly joked as Geri ordered coffee. She purposely waited until the steaming cup arrived before she started relating the events of that day. Geri sat without saying a word, solemnly watching Kelly with wide gray eyes until the sad story was finished.

Kelly took a long drink of coffee and waited for Geri to speak. Remembering those events took a toll, she noticed. Each time she told the story, the emotions of fear and horror and anger returned to pull at her again. She shivered, despite the hot coffee.

"I still can't believe it," Geri said, stirring her coffee without looking up. "I'm sitting here listening to you, and it still doesn't seem real. I'm . . . I'm stunned. I still expect to see Vickie's truck pull up in my driveway." She swiped at her eyes in a brusque way, as if the tears had startled her.

"I know it must be hard," Kelly said quietly. "Especially if you and Vickie saw each other a lot."

"All the time. We helped each other out with the animals. I have twelve alpacas. I've also got a few sheep." Geri stared out into the café. "Vickie was going to get some lambs from me this spring and start a small flock of her own."

Kelly heard a slight tremor in Geri's voice and purposely stayed quiet while Geri stirred her coffee. It must be stone cold by now, Kelly observed. Geri had barely had a sip and yet stirred enough to dissolve a pound of sugar.

Geri cleared her throat. "Vickie's daughter, Debbie, called me last night. She was in tears. We both were by the time she hung up. She'll be coming in today. I told her I'd pick her up at the airport."

"That's wonderful, Geri," Kelly said, impressed at how quickly she'd stepped into a difficult situation and made herself useful. "I assumed her cousin, Jayleen, would handle things like that. After all, they're family."

"Jayleen's got too much on her plate right now. She's trying to take care of Vickie's animals and her own and handle all the book-keeping she does." Geri shrugged. "I offered to help with Vickie's alpacas, but Jayleen told me she could handle it."

Intrigued, Kelly followed up. "How many clients does she have? I'm a corporate accountant, so I know how consuming the work can be. And I don't have alpacas waiting to be fed, either."

Geri leaned back in her chair, and Kelly sensed she was relaxing a bit. "Well, I guess she's got about twenty alpaca breeder clients by now, plus any other stray clients she may have picked up. Enough to keep her busy." She swirled the cold coffee. "Vickie recommended Jayleen to other alpaca ranchers every chance she got."

"Did you use her services?"

"I do as much as I can myself, then I give it to Jayleen to put all the numbers together. That way, she charges me less. I've got a much smaller operation than a lot of the ranchers. Plus, I don't have a 'cash reserve,' either."

"Okay, you've got to explain that," Kelly said. "Now you've got me curious."

Geri grinned, highlighting the weathered lines around her eyes. Nice eyes, Kelly noticed. "That means I don't have a separate source of income coming in to run my ranch and pay the bills. A lot of people go into alpaca breeding when they retire from their regular jobs. That way there's steady money coming in. Me, I sink or swim based on how well my animals do."

"How many did you say you have?"

"I've got eleven females that are bred every year and one young herd sire that I use as stud. You've seen Vickie's prizewinner, Raja? Well, my Raleigh is Raja's son and has the same coloring. He's a gorgeous smoky gray like Raja. I'm expecting Raleigh to throw the same colors and females that Raja does."

Kelly held up her hands. "Wait a minute. What's this about throwing colors and females?"

"It's a term breeders use that means a stud whose particular color interacts with the females in such a way as to produce some beautifully colored offspring. Also, if he can produce more females than males, you make more money. The stud business is always a gamble, especially with a young male. Your income fluctuates, depending on the cria." Geri ran her finger around the rim of the cup. "But, I think my luck is about to change."

"What does luck have to do with it?" Kelly asked.

She looked up with a grin. "More than you think."

"Cria are the babies, right?"

"Right. And the female cria are your bread and butter, because they can produce a baby a year. That's why you can sell the females for more money. Lots more."

"Ballpark?" Kelly probed, her inner accountant thoroughly engaged now.

"Thousands or tens of thousands, depending on the bloodlines."

Kelly pondered. Brother, this alpaca business was much more complicated than she'd ever imagined. "Boy, I never knew it was so involved. I guess I assumed you just let them breed, then sold the babies."

Geri laughed. "Well, I guess that's what we are doing, but it's a helluva lot of work. We can't leave it up to the animals. The females are kept separated from the males until their babies are sold and they're ready to be bred again. That's why we don't need more than one herd sire until he's about to retire. Most of the time, we send our females out to be bred to other males."

"Around here or out of state?"

"Both. Those gals are on the road a lot."

"Do they come into season right after they wean the babies?"

"Actually, alpacas only ovulate when they mate," Geri continued. A musical jangle sounded then, and Geri slipped a cell phone from her back pocket as she rose from the table and stepped into a hallway.

Kelly did the same. Her inner clock was ticking away. Work was waiting, and she only had the afternoon left. Tonight was already scheduled. Dinner with the Stackhouses and Steve.

Geri snapped her phone shut. "Sorry, had to take that call." She extended her hand again and gave Kelly a warm smile. "I want to thank you so much for taking the time with me, Kelly. It's helped a lot."

"You're welcome, Geri. I enjoyed talking with you, too. And the alpaca lesson," Kelly said with a grin. She liked Geri. Maybe because Geri reminded her of Vickie Claymore—sharp, down-to-earth, with a good sense of humor.

"I wouldn't be surprised if Debbie comes to see you as well once she settles in," Geri added, heading toward the door.

Kelly followed after. "Please tell Debbie how sorry we all are for her loss. Our loss, too. If there's anything I can do to help, please let me know."

"Thanks, Kelly. I'll be sure to tell her," Geri said with a wave as she opened the door to a faded green pickup truck.

Kelly hurried across the gravel driveway to her cottage, dumped her knitting bag on the sofa, and headed for the sunny corner of the dining room that doubled as her office. She'd barely glanced at the client file when her cell phone gave its insistent ring.

"Darn it! Why does it always ring when I'm super busy?" she complained to the empty room as she flipped the phone open. "Hello, Steve, if this is you reminding me about tonight, don't bother. I haven't forgotten. Corner of Newport and Hampton in Wellesley, right?"

"Well, not really, Kelly," an elderly gentleman's voice answered. "I'm still here in Fort Connor. Where are you?"

Oooops, Kelly thought, suddenly embarrassed. "Ohhhh, Mr. Chambers, I'm so sorry. I thought you were a friend who was giving me a hard time."

Lawrence Chambers chuckled. "I'm glad you've met so many good friends here, Kelly. Helen would be pleased. And, as your *friendly* legal adviser, I have some good news. We've moved through the first legal hurdle in Wyoming in regard to your cousin Martha's property."

Kelly set her mug on the desk and leaned back into her chair, ready to absorb one of Lawrence Chambers's legal updates on her inheritance rights to Martha Schuster's Wyoming ranch. The fluttery sensation that always settled in her stomach whenever Chambers brought up the subject returned.

What on earth was she going to do with a ranch? With cattle, yet. Three hundred head, Chambers had estimated. It had been years since she was around livestock. She'd been a city girl for so long, the only thing she remembered was to watch where she stepped in a pasture. She'd be totally out of her element and totally useless. And Kelly hated feeling useless.

"Okay," Kelly said. "We've passed through the first phase. How many hurdles do we have left?"

"Well, we've still got several left to go. After all, the property is literally passing through Ralph Schuster's estate to his wife, Martha, then through her estate to your aunt Helen, then through Helen's estate to you." He laughed softly again. "It's certainly one of the most convoluted inheritances I've ever seen, to be truthful. But don't you worry, Kelly. All is going well and proceeding in perfect order. These things just take time, that's all."

The fluttery sensation lessened somewhat. "That's all right, Mr. Chambers. Take all the time you need. I'm not ready to even think about owning a ranch anyway," she admitted.

"Well, you might want to start thinking about it, Kelly," he suggested. "Why don't you go up there and take a look at the property? The ranch manager I hired says it's really nice."

"Ohhhh, I wouldn't want to interrupt him," Kelly demurred, not too crazy about the idea.

This time Chambers laughed out loud. "You won't be interrupting him, Kelly, I assure you. Besides, I hired him, and since I'm acting on your behalf as your attorney, technically, you're his boss."

Kelly understood that concept, but somehow she couldn't picture herself bossing cowboys around. Accountants, yes. Cowboys, no. "I dunno, Mr. Chambers. I'll think about it."

"You know, Kelly, you could always take some friends along when you go up there. Your knitting friends would particularly enjoy it, I think."

Kelly's antennae started to buzz. She'd heard the smile in Chambers's voice. "Why is that?"

"Ohhhh, didn't I tell you? There's approximately one hundred sheep on the ranch in addition to the cattle. So you'll be inheriting lots of wool along with the land. You take care, Kelly. Bye now."

"Sheep? I have sheep? What—?" Kelly exclaimed before she realized Chambers had already hung up. She could have sworn she heard him laugh.

Six

Kelly swirled the melting vanilla ice cream into a deep purple puddle of fresh blueberries, melt-in-your-mouth piecrust, and luscious blueberry sauce oozing into the cream. Homemade blueberry pie and ice cream. Yummmm. Kelly thought she'd slipped back in time to her childhood when Ruth Stackhouse placed the enormous, lattice-top dessert in the center of the table. Aunt Helen's blueberry pie was the best she'd ever tasted until tonight. Kelly had to admit, Ruth and Aunt Helen were tied for the honor.

She lifted another delectable spoonful to her mouth and savored it while the gentle hum of conversation surrounded her. Kelly was enjoying herself immensely. Curt and Ruth Stackhouse were wonderful hosts, warm and genial, and clearly loved entertaining guests. She had felt comfortable in their beautifully-appointed ranch home from the moment she entered.

Kelly stirred her coffee, which was surprisingly rich and strong, while she watched Ruth tease Curt about his refusal to wear a business suit. Curt responded in kind, and Kelly got the feeling that they'd been lovingly teasing each other for years. Something about watching Curt and Ruth together like this felt good inside. She didn't know why. It just felt good.

She leaned back in her chair and smiled, watching them enjoy each other, still teasing and joking together after nearly fifty years of marriage. Kelly toyed with the last piece of pie in her purple puddle.

She could tell both Curt and Ruth thought of Steve and her as a couple. It was understandable, she supposed. After all, Steve had been with her the first time they met, when Kelly was trying to unravel the cause of her aunt Helen's death three months ago. It was understandable, but it was wrong. Steve was just a friend. A softball friend. A provider of a steady supply of used golf balls for Carl. A good friend. But, still, just a friend. This "couple" thing was a place Kelly couldn't go. She'd been part of a couple once, years ago, and it ended painfully. Old memories still hurt. But she'd learned an important lesson: relationships were risky. And they often ended in loss.

After that, Kelly threw herself into her budding corporate career, taking time only for her dad and an occasional softball game—until her dad was diagnosed with cancer. Then, everything changed. Kelly's life narrowed its focus even more and revolved exclusively around her job, her dad, and hospitals. No time for softball, and certainly no social life. She even stopped seeing the few friends she'd made. After her dad died three years ago, Kelly felt numb for months—until her uncle Jim's heart attack. And the whole heart-breaking cycle of loss started all over again. By now, Kelly was an expert on loss.

Finishing the last spoonful of pie, Kelly closed her eyes in enjoyment. "Mmmm, Ruth, this is delicious," she said after swallowing the morsel.

"Why, thank you, Kelly," Ruth said, her lined face crinkling into a broad smile. "I love to cook for folks who enjoy eating."

"Well, you cooked for the right people, ma'am," Steve said. "That was a delicious dinner. And dessert. I hate to be disloyal to my own mom, but that's gotta be the best pie I've ever tasted, Ruth."

"Oh, go on," she shooed at him, a blush coloring her cheek.

"No exaggeration, Ruth," Kelly agreed. "I thought my aunt Helen's blueberry pie was the best, but yours beats all."

"See, I told you, Ruthie," Curt said, wagging his head. "You should enter your recipe in the county fair."

"Now, don't you start about that fair again." Ruth patted Curt on the arm as she rose from the table. "You know I don't like crowds." Grabbing the coffeepot, she offered it around. "Who'd like more coffee?"

Steve was right there, cup extended, and Kelly was next in line. She'd already downed the contents of her first cup and was ready for more.

"There's plenty more pie, Kelly," Curt teased. "I've been watching you keep an eye on it."

Kelly laughed as she settled back into the upholstered chair and relaxed. "I may need it, Curt. Especially after the news I've had today."

"Does your boss want you back in Washington?" Steve asked, his smile disappearing.

"No no, not that. I had a call from Lawrence Chambers. He's the lawyer who's trying to straighten out all this inheritance stuff. You know . . . Helen's estate and then Martha's. It seems I'm the only remaining heir to both." She shook her head. "Today he told me I've got sheep. Last time we talked, he told me I had cows. I swear, I'm afraid to talk to the man."

"Wait a minute, wait a minute," Steve said, holding up a hand. "That little place in Landport isn't big enough for livestock, is it?"

Kelly stared at Steve blankly.

"You told me you were inheriting Martha's property, right? Didn't she live in Landport?"

"No no," Kelly said, realizing the mix-up. She had deliberately left out some significant details when she'd told her friends about Cousin Martha's property. "She was renting that place. But she and her husband owned land up in Wyoming. That's where the sheep are. And the cows." She took another sip of Ruth's rich coffee and brushed invisible pie flakes off the tablecloth.

Steve leaned back in his chair and crossed his arms, a hint of a smile showing. "Okaaaay, so how many sheep do you have?"

Kelly swished the coffee in her cup, acutely aware that the others were focused on her intently. Both Curt and Ruth were leaning forward on the table, watching.

"About a hundred," she said, straightening her napkin.

Steve grinned. "And the cattle?"

Kelly glanced out into the kitchen, trying her best to look nonchalant. "Ohhhh, about three hundred. I think that's what Chambers said."

Steve turned to Curt, and they both started to laugh. Kelly heaved a dramatic sigh and tried to ignore them.

"Goodness, Kelly, that's a lot of livestock to take care of," Ruth commented.

"Oh, Mr. Chambers took care of that," Kelly said with a dismissing wave. "He's hired a ranch manager to handle everything."

"A ranch manager, huh?" Curt observed with a grin. "Tell me, Kelly, how much land are we talking about here?"

Nonchalant and offhand hadn't worked. And trying to ignore both Steve and Curt at the same time would take more energy than she had at the moment. So Kelly resorted to complete honesty. She looked Curt straight in the eye. "About seven thousand acres, I'm told. And damned if I know what I'm going to do with it."

Curt just laughed in reply. Steve raised his coffee cup to her, a wicked gleam in his eyes. "Congratulations, Kelly. You're a rancher, and you didn't even know it."

"That's not funny."

"Yeah, it is," he said, then burst out laughing.

"Don't start," she warned, trying to look severe, but that only made Steve laugh harder. He could be so annoying at times.

"That's a nice spread, Kelly. Have you gone to see it yet?" Curt asked.

She shook her head. "No. Chambers said I need to go take a look, but I don't really want to."

"Why?" Ruth asked.

Now that she'd gone the honesty route, she might as well go all the way. "Because the manager would probably ask me all sorts of questions, and I wouldn't know what he was talking about. I know nothing about running a ranch. The mere thought of all that land and livestock belonging to me is, well, it's scary. What am I supposed to do with it all? Martha mentioned she wanted the ranch to be turned into a nature preserve. How in the world am I supposed to do that? Do I sell all the cows? What about the house? And the equipment?" She gave an exasperated gesture.

Steve leaned over. "Hey, you're not alone, Kelly. We can help you. Both Curt and I can check out the land and the livestock. We can help you with all that. You don't have to do it by yourself."

"Damn right, Kelly," Curt said. "I'll be happy to help you. I do this all the time. And I know the people and places in Wyoming to contact for whatever we need."

Kelly felt the fluttery sensation in her stomach melt away, just like Ruth's delicious pie. She wouldn't have to do it alone. She'd have help. Suddenly the image of Martha's ranch didn't seem so foreboding.

"So, when would you like to go?" Steve asked.

"You mean up there?" Kelly pointed toward the kitchen.

Steve chuckled. "Yeah, up there, except Wyoming's north, so it's thataway." He pointed over his shoulder. "Where is it, exactly?"

"Wellll, I don't know exactly," Kelly hesitated. "All Martha said was it was west of Cheyenne."

To his credit, Steve did not burst out laughing at her comment, but Kelly could tell Curt was trying to hide his amusement and not doing a very good job.

"That leaves some pretty big territory, Kelly. We're gonna need some directions," Steve teased. "Or else we'll just head north till the wind starts to blow, then turn left."

Both Curt and Ruth laughed out loud at that, but Kelly bristled. She'd never liked being teased. What was it about her that made people tease her? Why was she so eminently teaseable? And, of course, whenever Steve succumbed to the urge, it annoyed Kelly all the more.

"I'm sure Chambers will give us all the directions we need," she said in her best attempt to appear haughty, which only succeeded in amusing Curt even more.

"Lord, Kelly, you've been out of the West too long," he said with a chuckle. "It's a good thing we've got you back. Don't you worry. We'll get you acclimated pretty damn quick. First, we'll get you something to wear that's better suited to tromping around pastures."

"We've got several pairs of extra boots you're welcome to use," Ruth suggested. "Boots and jeans will do a lot better."

Kelly was about to thank her, but Curt was clearly in a planning mode and already on a roll.

"Okay, then, what's your schedule like next week, Kelly? I'm booked all this week. Steve, how about you?"

"I'm afraid it'll have to be late next week or the week afterward for me, folks," Steve replied. "I don't want to leave the new site until the framers are in there. I've been putting out fires every day on this one. Can't risk being that far away yet."

"I know what you mean, son," Curt said, nodding in agreement. "Always a crisis or someone's screwing up. Well, the week after will work for me, too. How about you, Kelly."

Kelly ran through her mental daytimer. Since they were planning almost two weeks out, she'd have plenty of time to work ahead on her accounts. "No problem. I'll be able to work around it. But if you two are super busy, we can postpone the trip."

"Oh, no," Curt admonished, shaking his head. "You need to go up there and see what you'll be inheriting. We need to make plans. Besides," he added, "I'm really anxious to see this spread you've been teasing us with. You've got my nose for land itching. Now I've gotta go out and sniff." He grinned.

"Me, too," Steve agreed. "I'm curious. I want to check out the cattle. See what you've got. Who knows? Maybe Martha had some good bloodlines going."

Kelly shrugged. "Martha had been away from the ranch for over four years when she was killed. Helen took her in and kept her hidden in Landport after Martha ran away from her abusive husband. When they learned that he died in a car accident last year, Helen asked Lawrence Chambers to take care of Martha's inheritance."

The table fell quiet now, all laughter forgotten. "That's dreadful," Ruth said, her pale, thin face pinching with a frown.

"Was there a divorce? Are there any children?" Curt probed.

"None living. Their only son died in an auto accident and is buried on the property, Martha said. And her husband never filed for divorce, so they were still married."

"Sounds like a pretty complicated inheritance," Steve said after a moment. "All the more reason for you to go up and take stock of what's there, Kelly. You're the heir to all of it."

"Don't remind me," she said, grimacing. "I'm not sure I'm ready for all that extra responsibility. I mean, I'm still trying to figure out how to keep making those huge mortgage payments on the cottage."

Steve reached over and placed his hand on her shoulder. "Let's see what we can do to help you with that. This ranch could actually help you solve those problems."

"You bet, Kelly," Curt concurred. "Let's go up there and see if we can get some cash flow started. I imagine you could use that."

Cash flow? Now they were talking about something Kelly understood quite well. "Really? You think that's possible?"

Curt sent her a savvy smile. "Ohhhh, yeah. Think about it, Kelly-girl. You've got three hundred head of cattle. And sheep. You'll make something off their sale to start. Then, we'll go from there."

"And Kelly, if you've got sheep, then there're bound to be some fleeces to sell," Ruth added with the enthusiasm of the spinner and miller that she was. "What you and your friends don't want for yourselves, we can sell online. Spinners and weavers will snap them up if they're good quality. I'll be glad to help you with that. And what we don't sell as fleece, I'll mill and spin for you, and I guarantee you'll sell that. Mimi will probably buy them all to custom dye and sell in her shop."

Kelly stared at Ruth in surprise. Selling wool fleeces online to spinners and weavers. What a combination of Old World craft and New World high tech. "Wow, Ruth. That sounds great. You'd help me with that?"

"Of course, dear." Ruth gave her a motherly pat. "I'll be more than happy to help. I do this all the time."

Kelly felt the fluttery sensation take flight. At last. Muscles that had been tensed without her even knowing relaxed. This ranch business could work out. She didn't have to understand it all by herself. She had people to help her with each part of it. Like consultants. Now that made sense. And it made her feel a lot better. So much so, Kelly could feel the blueberry pie beckoning to her across the table.

She eyed the tempting dessert, blueberries and sauce oozing into the plate. The vanilla ice cream had softened during their discussion. Perfect. She could taste it already.

Curt chuckled. "I see you eyeing that pie again."

"You're right," Kelly admitted. "Thanks to you folks, I feel a lot better. And I hear that pie calling me."

"Ruth, go ahead and carve the girl a slice. And pile on the ice cream, too," Curt suggested.

"While you're at it, Ruth, leave a slice for me," Steve jumped in, plate in hand. "Can't let it go to waste."

"Don't mention 'waist,' " Kelly joked. "I may not have one after this slice. I'll have to run an extra mile tomorrow."

"Oh, for heaven's sake," Ruth fussed, placing a huge slice on Kelly's plate. "You're slender as can be." She plopped a large dollop of melted ice cream on top of the pie.

"Not after tonight," Kelly laughed and accepted the bowl that was filled to overflowing.

She'd barely gotten her spoon into the purple nectar when Steve spoke up. "Tell me, Kelly. Has Chambers mentioned anything about oil and gas deposits?"

"Yes, he said he was going to make some phone calls, but I haven't heard anything more," she said, then blissfully closed her eyes and savored the blueberry delight. When she opened her eyes again, she saw Steve and Curt grinning at each other, then her. "What? What's so funny?"

"Kelly, girl, if you're lucky, you may never have cash-flow problems again," Curt decreed as he leaned back in his chair.

Kelly pondered that for about two seconds, then succumbed to the sinfully rich summertime dessert.

"Good boy," Kelly said, rubbing Carl's shiny black head as she settled into her favorite patio chair. "Did you behave yourself while I was gone tonight?"

Carl placed his chin on her bare leg, all brown-eyed doggie innocence. Kelly laughed softly and continued patting her dog, letting the familiar night sounds close in around her. She'd just relaxed completely into the comfortable chair when her cell phone jangled, shattering the night sounds and probably scaring away the soft-voiced evening songbirds.

"Kelly here," she said into the phone, unable to disguise her reluctance to talk.

"Hey, Kelly, Burt here," a familiar deep voice sounded, catching her by surprise. "I can tell you're tired. Why don't I call back tomorrow?"

"No no, Burt, it's okay," Kelly replied, straightening in her chair. Retired police investigator Burt Parker never called unless he had something important to say. His calm advice and presence during Kelly's investigation into her aunt's death had been a godsend. "What's up?"

"Well, I thought you might be interested in what I've learned from my contacts back on the force—about Vickie Claymore's death, I mean. I know how hard that must have been for you to walk in on something like that, Kelly."

"Yeah, it was. How on earth did you handle that stuff, Burt? Did you ever get used to it?"

"Never."

Kelly could picture big old Burt, hovering like a protective bear, standing near the crime scene. "What did you find out? Did you guys find any fingerprints to trace?"

"Nope. None other than Vickie's. Everything was wiped clean. Doorknobs, tabletops, the phone, and most importantly, that bronze bust on the floor. I heard you saw it lying not far from the victim."

"Well, now, that's interesting, wouldn't you say?"

"Oh, yeah. It definitely looks to be a murder. And the killer had time to clean up afterward, too."

"Sounds like he wasn't afraid of being caught," Kelly added. "Which means it probably was someone she knew, right?"

Burt chuckled. "Go on."

Emboldened, Kelly pressed further. "Another reason I think it was someone Vickie knew is because she'd never turn her back on some crazed intruder so they could hit her on the head and kill her."

"Smart girl," Burt replied. "And you're right about her being knocked unconscious. The investigation shows she was hit on the head with that Mozart figure, then her throat was cut so she'd bleed to death before regaining consciousness. The weapon looks to be a small knife, like a pocketknife."

"Dammit! Who would be so cruel? The cops better find out who did it."

"Well, I'm certain they're doing their best, Kelly. Now, the other reason I'm calling is so we can have this conversation in private and not in the shop with listening ears. I want to know if there's anything else you noticed that was amiss? You've got a keen eye for detail, Kelly. What did you see?"

Kelly closed her eyes and pictured herself walking through Vickie Claymore's living room that awful day. "I saw Vickie lying on her beautiful handwoven rug. I checked her pulse when I saw the deep gash on her neck and all the blood. I also noticed the pool of blood had dried mostly and soaked into the fabric, which I figured meant she'd been killed hours earlier, right?"

"She was killed between nine p.m. and eleven p.m. the night before," Burt answered.

"All the more reason to believe it was someone Vickie knew. Who else would be visiting her that late at night?" Kelly probed. "I mean, we've eliminated the crazed intruder."

"Well, you've eliminated him. The police can't afford to eliminate anyone. So, tell me, did anything else strike you while you were there?"

Kelly searched her memory. "Nothing else was out of place other than the Mozart bust. Everything looked to be in the same place that I remembered seeing it two months ago."

Burt paused, and Kelly pictured him writing everything down in a little notebook similar to Lieutenant Peterson's. That brought a question to mind.

"Burt, I remember the county police were handling this case since Bellvue Canyon is in their territory, not the city's. You've got contacts with them, too?"

"Sure I do, Kelly. We've worked together on lots of things. Particularly something like a murder. Anything else you remember?"

"No, but I've got a question of my own."

"Shoot."

"Any suspects jumping out at your friends?"

"Well, it's a little early. No one is jumping out yet."

"Just fishing. I couldn't help but overhear Jayleen Swinson's tirade about Bob Claymore while I was standing around outside. And I remember Vickie talking about the divorce, too. It was bitter, Burt. Both of them seemed to be dug in and fighting each other. Sounded awful to me."

"Yeah," Burt sighed. "I've watched several friends go through that. Sounds like hell on earth. Listen, Kelly, I'll let you go. Take care of yourself, and I'll see you folks over at the shop when I next come in. Probably later this week."

Remembering something, Kelly tossed out a teaser. Burt was an excellent spinner and spun several of Mimi's fleeces for her. "When you're there, I'll tell you how I'm about to become the owner of several fleeces. At least, I think I am."

"Well, you've got me interested already, Kelly," Burt said with a laugh. "See you."

Kelly snapped her cell phone shut and went back to patting Carl while visions of woolly lambs carrying bags of fleeces danced through her head.

Seven

"**Looks** like you're making progress on the sweater," Megan observed, glancing up from the bubble-gum pink eyelash yarn in her lap.

Kelly held up the second version of her sweater in the round. "Yep, still straight, no twists, and I've got at least two inches of stockinette, too," she said proudly.

"Hey, look at that," Jennifer commented as she sat down to join them. "Good job." She leaned over and peered at the raspberry circle. "Stitches look good, too. See? It was worth all that frogging."

"Yeah, yeah," Kelly mumbled. "I just hope I never have to do that again."

"You won't. But there'll be other times you'll choose to unravel and start over," Megan added, fingers working at warp speed. "It's all a part of trying something new. If you don't like it, you frog it out, then try it again. Or something else."

Kelly looked up to see Connie, another of the shop's assistants, standing in the doorway. "Kelly, there's a woman out front to see you," she said, pointing toward the front room. "She said her name's Debbie Hurst, and she's Vickie's daughter."

Kelly dropped the knitted circlet and pushed away from the table. "Thanks, Connie. I'll go into the café. See you guys later," she said as she followed Connie to the front of the shop.

Standing beside the counter was a slightly-built young woman with short brown hair and a striking resemblance to her mother. The sight of those familiar features caused a tug at Kelly's heart. She approached the young woman, her hand extended.

"Debbie, I'm Kelly Flynn. Your mother was a dear friend of ours. We're all deeply sorry for your loss. It was our loss, too."

Debbie looked up at Kelly with clear green eyes and shook her hand. It felt cool to Kelly, even in the midst of summer. "Thank you, Kelly. That's very kind of you to say." Glancing around to

Connie, she added, "You're very kind. My mom talked about all of you a lot. You were very important to her."

"Geri Norbert told me she was picking you up at the airport yesterday. Are you staying here in town?"

"I stayed at the ranch last night," Debbie replied. "There's so much I have to do, so many details with her death and all, I barely know where to start."

Kelly had more questions but didn't want to stay in the midst of the shop. Plus, something told her Debbie might want to sit down. "Why don't we go into the café and sit down with some tea or coffee, okay?" she suggested.

"Oh, that sounds wonderful. I could use some tea," Debbie said with a smile.

Kelly guessed her hunch was right and led the way, choosing a quiet table in the back alcove. She pulled out Debbie's chair, then sat down herself and signaled the waitress. After she ordered, she looked at Debbie with concern.

"How are you feeling, Debbie? Mimi said you had to be careful coming back to the ranch environment."

Debbie nodded and leaned back into her chair, giving Kelly a chance to notice how thin she really was. Not much meat on those bones, Kelly thought, feeling positively pudgy beside Debbie, especially after all that blueberry pie last night.

"I'm doing okay," Debbie said after a deep breath. "There's a new medicine I'm on now which gives me more freedom than ever. Last year I actually stayed up there with Mom for over a week." She smiled, clearly proud of her accomplishment.

"Wonderful," Kelly enthused. "That will help a lot when you have to be up at the ranch. But you may want to stay in town at night while you're here. That way, you won't overtax your system." Kelly knew she sounded pushy, but there was something about Debbie that reached out—a fragility, vulnerability. Whatever it was, Kelly couldn't help responding.

"You know, Kelly, I was thinking the same thing. That way I'll only be around the grasses and other stuff when I absolutely have to."

Kelly leaned out of the way while the waitress set tea and coffee before them. She waited until Debbie had loaded her cup with sugar and cream before she broached the subject that had brought Debbie to the shop. "I have a feeling you want me to tell you about that day at the ranch. Am I right?"

Debbie set her cup in the saucer, then fixed a clear emerald gaze on Kelly. "Please. And don't leave anything out, no matter how awful it is."

Kelly took a deep breath and did as she was told, even though her insides still twisted with the telling of this terrible tale. She fervently hoped this was the last time she'd have to relate this story. Lowering her voice so no one else would hear, Kelly covered everything she and the others saw, said, and did that summer day.

While Kelly spoke, Debbie traced invisible patterns on the wooden tabletop, her face growing paler by the minute. Watching this, Kelly began to worry. Debbie'd looked pale and fragile when she entered the shop. Now, she looked like she might pass out. Kelly deliberately skipped her description of the detectives and their investigation and wound the tale to a close.

Debbie sipped her tea in silence, which Kelly didn't care to break. She'd talked enough. She also needed the quiet to dispel the ugly thoughts and feelings that the story always brought with it. Like a toxic residue, it clung to her whenever she touched it.

"Do you think the police are doing a good job of investigating this . . . this murder?" Debbie asked quietly.

"They certainly appear to be. I mean, they had scores of policemen up there as soon as I called, and they interviewed everyone thoroughly. Even those visiting knitters."

Debbie closed her eyes and took a shaky breath. "I still can't believe she's gone," she whispered. "Mom was so . . . so alive and . . . and healthy, and so . . . so joyous. She can't be gone." Her lower lip trembled, and Kelly spotted a tear sliding down Debbie's pale cheek.

Kelly felt her own heart ache. Debbie's grief so closely matched her own when she'd lost her dad and then Aunt Helen. A yawning emptiness had opened inside and threatened to swallow her whole. She reached out and placed her hand over Debbie's.

"I know what you mean," she said gently. "I lost my dad three years ago and my aunt Helen in April. She was like a mother to me. You can't believe they're gone at first. It hurts so much."

Her words turned the trickle into a flow, and Debbie placed her face in her hands and wept, her thin shoulders rising and falling beneath the blue cotton fabric of her dress. Kelly gave a reassuring wave to the concerned waitress and motioned for her to bring more tea, then reached over and placed her hand on Debbie's shoulder.

"That's okay, Debbie. No one's here. Just us. Go ahead and cry," she reassured.

Debbie's tears slowly subsided into wet snuffles. Grabbing the extra napkins the waitress had kindly supplied, she wiped her face and blew her nose. "I'm sorry," she said in a ragged voice. "I thought I had cried myself out."

That sounded familiar. "You know, my tears kept coming, too. All it took was for someone to say something kind, and"—Kelly gestured—"a deluge would start to flow."

"Thanks for saying that," Debbie said, wiping away. "And thanks for this." She lifted the extra cup of tea and drank it down.

Changing the subject, Kelly ventured, "Do you need any help arranging the funeral or anything? We'd be glad to help. Especially Mimi. She and Vickie were close friends."

"Thank you, Kelly, but Geri's already handling it for me. Thank goodness. I wouldn't know who to call or anything." She took another deep breath and sank back into her chair. "What I really need help with is sorting through all the records. I mean, there's so much there. I have to find insurance policies and contact them and notify her friends in Denver, and then I have to sort through all the business records." She gestured helplessly. "The lawyer says all the accounts have to be in order before he can start examining the estate. I'm a biologist. I don't know anything about financial records. My mom was good at it, but I'm lost." She shuddered in visible disgust.

Kelly recognized that shudder. She saw it a lot when she used to keep small business accounts, years ago. Numbers can confuse people. One of the things she remembered enjoying was helping people understand what was happening. Now she knew how she could help Debbie.

"Listen, Debbie, I'm a CPA, and I'd be happy to help sort through those records for you. Once I do, I'll be able to create whatever financial statements you'll need for the lawyers."

Debbie's green eyes turned puppy-dog grateful. "Ohhhh, Kelly, are you serious?" she breathed. "I mean . . . I would be so grateful if you could. And I'd pay you, of course."

Kelly waved the offer away. "No, that's okay. I'd do it for your mom."

Debbie sat up straight and lifted her chin. "My mom always paid her bills. I cannot accept your help unless you let me pay you. After all, anyone else I'd call in the community would charge a lot, and I'll bet most of them don't have your credentials."

Kelly opened her mouth, but she didn't have anything to say. Debbie had stated her terms clearly. It was up to Kelly to accept or decline.

"Okay. I accept your offer, but I'm clueless what to charge. So, I'll have to check into that."

"Good. Could you start tomorrow? That office is filled with stuff, and I don't know where to begin."

Kelly had to laugh at Debbie's eagerness. "Well, probably. It would be the afternoon before I could finish with my own office work. I'm telecommuting to my job back in D.C."

"That would be great," Debbie enthused, her relief obvious. "I promise I'll try to make some order of the papers on her desk. At least separate the bills from vendors and suppliers and all that. And I'll check the bank statements to see if they're accurate."

"Geri told me that Jayleen Swinson took care of your mom's accounts, so there should be a file somewhere of income statements at least," Kelly suggested. "I'll bet your mom also had a computer file."

"I'm sure she does. Mom was very thorough about her business."

Another thought intruded, and Kelly added, "Have you spoken with Jayleen? She'd know where everything is. Maybe she should do this for you. After all, she's been keeping the books. I don't want to step on anyone's toes here."

Debbie looked out into the café. "She left a message on my cell phone this morning, but I haven't talked with her yet. But, you know, I just don't think she's qualified to do this level of financial work. She's a bookkeeper. You're a CPA. I'd feel a lot better with you looking at Mom's accounts."

"Okay, then I'll be happy to help."

"You don't know how much I appreciate that, Kelly," Debbie said, her expression hardening. "The sooner I can get those records to the lawyer, the sooner I find out what that weasel is up to."

Kelly didn't have to ask who the "weasel" was. She had a pretty good idea Debbie was referring to Vickie's almost-but-not-quite-divorced husband, Bob Claymore.

Debbie eyed Kelly. "I take it you know all about the divorce proceedings? Mom said she told everyone."

"Aaah, yes. Vickie was quite forthcoming."

A smile flirted with Debbie's mouth before she bit it off. "Mom was furious. And so was I. The very idea that that weasel would try to steal half my mom's business. Dammit! It took her years to build it up. And he never contributed a thing! He was too busy screwing around at the university! Bastard. I never did like him."

Kelly had to lean away from the heat of fury that radiated from Debbie now. "It's certainly unfortunate the divorce was still unsettled when Vickie was killed."

Debbie snorted. "Unfortunate, yes. The timing is more than unfortunate for my mother. But not for him. It's all too convenient for Bob Claymore. A few more weeks and he would be out in the cold. Instead, he's salivating over my mother's business. Bastard."

Kelly watched the storm clouds contort Debbie's delicate features into an ugly mask. Her hatred of Bob Claymore was palpable. It was also evident that Debbie had already found the chief suspect in her mother's death.

"Listen, Debbie, do you have a cell phone?" Kelly ventured, hoping to change the subject. "I can call you when I'm on the way into the canyon tomorrow."

"Ohhhh, yes, of course," Debbie said and reached into her purse, withdrawing a business card. "But you'd better use the landline. You know how the canyon eats cell phone signals. Just come when you can. I'll be there, sorting papers."

"Will do. By the way, do you need a ride somewhere?"

"No, thanks, I've rented a car. I'm fine." She leaned on the table as she stood up, steadied herself, then caught her breath.

Kelly scrambled to her feet, reaching out. "Are you okay? You look like you're having trouble breathing."

Debbie waved away her concern as she headed for the doorway. "No, it's . . . it's just the altitude. It takes a while to acclimate."

Kelly wondered how much the intense emotion she'd just witnessed played a role in Debbie's sudden wooziness. "If you want to rest a little more, you're welcome to sit at our library table. We've always got a pot of tea there, too," she offered.

"Thanks, Kelly. I'll be fine. And thanks again for helping me with all this. I can't tell you how much it means to me."

Kelly was about to reply, but Debbie swiftly hurried out the door, as if she felt tears encroaching once more and wanted to leave quickly.

Feeling strangely unsettled, Kelly headed toward the main room. She needed some quiet time to think. There was so much going on inside Debbie—so many storms and different emotions. She seemed so vulnerable, and yet, Kelly sensed strong—almost violent—emotions erupting inside.

Megan was still across the table knitting as Kelly settled into a chair and picked up her circular sweater.

"Hey, how'd the visit go with Vickie's daughter?" Megan asked.

Kelly paused for a moment and simply knitted. "I think it was good for her. She got to cry some more. I sensed a lot of relief, too."

"Poor thing. I feel so sorry for her. I can't imagine losing my mom like that, can you?"

Her question caused an old wound to twinge way down deep. "Well, it was kind of like that for me when Aunt Helen was killed. She was the closest thing to a mother I ever knew. So, it was like losing my mom."

Megan peered over at Kelly. "You've never talked about your real mom, Kelly. Did she die when you were real young or something?"

"Nope. She walked out on my dad and me when I was just a baby," Kelly said, repeating the line she'd practiced since she was a child. Even so, it never lost its sting. "That's why my dad and I were so close."

"Oh . . . ," Megan said softly and ducked her head. "I'm sorry."

"Don't be. It's okay. My dad and I did great. We were a team." Deliberately changing the subject, she said, "Guess what? Debbie wants to hire me to help figure out Vickie's business accounts and draw up financial statements to take to the lawyers. I offered to do it for free, but she refused."

"Wow, good job," Megan said, her smile returning. "See how easy it is to find consulting? Sometimes it lands in your lap."

Kelly looked up from the neat rows of raspberry stockinette. Consulting? She hadn't really thought of it that way. "Well, I'm not sure you could call it consulting, but—"

"What else would it be?" Megan declared. "You're doing specialized work at her direction for payment. Sounds like consulting to me."

Kelly let that last thought play around in her head as the rows of stockinette slowly increased.

Eight

Kelly stared out the large window in Vickie's home office, which looked directly out onto the pastures and corrals. Several groups of alpacas were scattered about, grazing in separate pastures, their long, graceful necks bending to the ground as they searched for tasty grasses. She leaned back in her chair and took a drink from her ever-present coffee mug as she paged through the file folder of income statements.

Vickie's business was definitely profitable. Expenses and revenues both fluctuated month by month but were directly correlated with the business cycle of owning alpacas—breeding, shearing, babies, showing, breeding, over and over. Now that she had the accounts in front of her, Kelly could envision what Geri had tried to explain—the variability of income from stud fees and sales of alpaca offspring. What kept Vickie from "living on the edge" like Geri was that Vickie had a fair amount of cash reserves put away, either the result of thrifty saving or high demand for her alpaca services over the years.

Kelly picked up the folder containing the balance sheets for the business and paged back a few years, watching how carefully Vickie had built up her savings. Smart, very smart, Kelly thought, admiring Vickie's financial discipline. That was usually the Achilles' heel of most small businesses, she'd witnessed. Whether they tried to make a go without sufficient capital to begin with or they simply neglected to pay their required taxes, most small companies went belly up within five years. Kelly was always happy to find the ones that went on to succeed.

Noticing that the last balance sheet in the folder was dated three months ago, Kelly jotted a note on the pad beside her elbow. So far, so good. She was beginning to get a picture of what was there, what was missing, and what she needed to do.

"Aaaah! There it is," Debbie spoke up from across the office. She leaned over the papers spread out on a side table.

Kelly had set up a place for Debbie to sit and sort through documents while she used the desk and computer. "I thought you already found the insurance policy. What're you looking for now?"

"I was looking for the sheet with the funeral arrangements. I knew she had it here somewhere." Debbie looked over at Kelly and smiled. "Mom told me she had a file with everything in it. I thought she meant one folder. She meant the whole cabinet."

"Oh, boy." Kelly smiled ruefully. "What else do you need? I can stop this and help you get the policies."

"No, it's okay. I've already called the insurance person and gotten that started. Now, I can tell Geri—"

"Tell Geri what?" Geri asked, poking her head around the doorway. "I saw two cars parked outside, so I thought I'd drop by and see who was here. It's about time that yellow police tape was removed. I see you beat me to it."

"Hey, Geri, good to see you," Kelly greeted.

"Ohhhh, yes, Geri, come in, come in," Debbie beckoned. "We're trying to put all these papers in order, and thanks to Kelly, I think we can do it."

Geri pulled out a straight-back chair and straddled it backward. "Have you found those instructions yet?"

Debbie handed over the sheet. "Yes, here they are. It only took me two hours of searching." She shook her head.

Geri smiled. "No hurry. I'll handle everything. If I need your signature, I'll bring the papers to you."

"Geri, I don't know what I'd do without you," Debbie said, her gratitude obvious. "You've been a lifesaver ever since I arrived."

"It's the least I can do, Debbie. Your mom was my best friend. Is there anything else you need? Any help with the animals?"

"No, Jayleen must have been here early in the morning, because they were already out in the pastures. We keep playing phone tag. She left me another message saying she was taking care of them."

A loud slam of the front door sounded, and a voice called out, "Helloooo! Who's here?"

Kelly recognized Jayleen's voice, having listened to it at top volume when she vented her anger to the police detective.

"We're here in the office, Jayleen," Geri called out.

The sound of boots stomping across wooden floors got louder until Jayleen appeared in the doorway. Kelly noticed she looked surprised to see all of them there. "Hey, guys, what's up?" she asked, strolling into the office.

A slight look of displeasure seemed to pass over Debbie's face, then was gone, Kelly noticed. "We're trying to get all these papers in order, Jayleen. Insurance policies, bank accounts, things like that," Kelly explained in her best offhand manner.

"Hey, I can help with that," Jayleen offered. "I do the accounts. I know where everything is—"

Debbie held up her slender hand. "That's okay, Jayleen. We've got it covered. The lawyer needs financial reports, and Kelly's going to take care of everything since she's a CPA and knows how to do all that."

"Oh . . . oh, sure, I understand," Jayleen said, appearing slightly crestfallen. "Well, if there's anything I can do to help, you know, please let me know."

Feeling really uncomfortable now, Kelly jumped in. "I've got the file with all the income statements and balance sheets. You've done a great job, Jayleen. That makes it much easier when I do the financial reports."

Jayleen found a crooked smile. "Thanks. It's just good software, that's all."

Kelly grinned. "Don't give me that. I know the business. Software doesn't do it. You do. And you've done a good job."

"Thanks, Kelly."

Kelly nodded, then remembered something. "By the way, Jayleen, I noticed the last balance sheet was dated three months ago, yet the income statements are right up to date. Have you run an updated version yet?"

Jayleen shook her head. "Nope. I was waiting on the quarterly reports from Vickie's investment account. They should be in by now, but I wasn't able to get into the office to run them."

"No problem. I'll do it," Kelly offered.

"All the other statements are in the files." Jayleen jerked her thumb toward the cabinet.

"Thank you, Jayleen. You've been very helpful," Debbie said, the sound of dismissal in her tone all too evident.

Kelly flinched inwardly, feeling really embarrassed for Jayleen.

Jayleen responded by staring at her boots for a second before she turned toward the door. "You know, I noticed Raja wasn't acting like himself. I mean, he usually comes over whenever I come to the fence and whistle. The gals came, but Raja just stood out in the pasture and looked at me."

"He must be missing mom," Debbie said sadly.

"Maybe he picks up signals like our pets do," Kelly suggested. "My dog, Carl, always picks up on my moods, so maybe alpacas do, too."

"Maybe so," Jayleen said. "Well, it looks like you folks have everything in control here, so I'll just get along. You still want me to take care of the animals, don't you? I mean, they're used to me. I've been doing it for years now."

Debbie nodded, a flicker of gratitude appearing for a moment. "Yes, that'll be great, Jayleen. I simply cannot be carrying feed and letting them in and out. I'm afraid all that dust is already taking a toll." She took a deep breath.

Geri rose from her chair. "You okay?"

Debbie gave a little wave. "Yes, but I think I'd better go back into town soon."

Kelly noticed Debbie's pallor. "You know, I was about to head back into town, too. I can review these folders at home tonight. Why don't we both leave now? That way, I can follow after you."

"Oh, would you, Kelly? I'd be ever so grateful," Debbie said. "Let me get my things together."

Kelly did the same, gathering the files she needed to review and shoving everything into her briefcase.

"Well, see you later, folks," Jayleen said as she left.

Geri paused at the door. "Listen, Debbie, if you need anything at all, let me know. Meanwhile, I'll get on these arrangements. Talk to you tomorrow."

Kelly waved good-bye to both women, logged off the computer, and pushed back her chair to leave. She felt unsettled suddenly and didn't know why. There was a lot more bubbling under the surface of Vickie's family than she'd ever imagined.

Carl was at the fence yelping a greeting as Kelly headed toward the cottage's front door. "I'll feed you in a minute, Carl. Hold on—"

She broke off when she noticed a white paper attached to her outer screen door. Kelly snatched the typewritten note from the screen and read as she let herself into the house.

"What the . . . ," she said when she came to the second paragraph. "Carl!"

Dumping her things on the dining room table, Kelly yanked open the patio door to the yard. Carl was already jumping about, long pink tongue dangling, clearly anticipating dinner.

Kelly brandished the note and glared at her dog. "Carl, you've been stealing golf balls again, and I told you not to."

Carl's happy-dog expression disappeared, and his "Who, me?" face materialized.

"Don't give me that look," Kelly accused. "This is a warning from the greenskeeper. He says if you steal balls one more time, we'll have to go to court, and there will be a big fine."

Carl cocked his head and stared, obviously curious as to what had perturbed his owner. Kelly let out an exasperated sigh and glanced around the yard. Sure enough, there were several more golf balls than usual.

"Okay, that's it, big guy. You may not care if you get a police record, but I do. I do not want to pay to bail you out of doggie jail."

Kelly proceeded to walk around the yard, snatching up every

newer-looking ball she found. Steve had brought Carl old used-up balls, so it wasn't hard to tell the difference. Carl, of course, was right behind her, protesting ownership every step of the way. Once, he almost got to a ball before Kelly, but she snatched it first.

"Don't even think about it, Carl," she warned, with her sternest naughty-dog-scolding voice. "You can keep the old ones, not these."

Kelly then swung her legs over the fence, strode to the edge of the course, and threw all the balls as far as she could. Being a really good ballplayer, Kelly could throw pretty far. She returned to the yard to find Carl lying on the ground, head between his outstretched paws, sulking.

"Pout all you want," Kelly said. "You're coming inside with me after dinner. Furthermore, you'll have to stay inside while I work on the computer, and I promise it won't be any fun at all."

She wasn't sure, but Kelly thought she saw Carl screw up his face in displeasure.

Nine

Mimi was draping a turquoise sleeveless sweater over the antique dry sink in the knitting shop's center room when Kelly entered.

"Why, hello, Kelly. I haven't seen you over here early in the morning for a while," she said with a bright smile. "Has your work load lightened up a bit?"

"Actually, it's increased, Mimi," Kelly replied as she set her knitting bag on the library table. "I've agreed to help Debbie Hurst with her mother's business accounts and prepare financial statements for the lawyers. So I guess you'd say I'm consulting, in addition to my regular office work, of course."

Mimi positively beamed. "That's wonderful, Kelly! I knew you'd find some consulting sooner or later."

Noticing several bright eyelash yarn scarves dangling from a nearby cabinet door, Kelly fingered electric limeade and tangerine crush, envisioning one of her own. The last time she'd thought about making one of these scarves, she'd been interrupted. Maybe now was a good time.

"Go ahead and indulge yourself, Kelly," Mimi tempted. "I can tell you want to make one. Do it. It knits up so fast, you'll have it done in no time."

Kelly shook her head with a rueful smile. "I've heard that before. You folks always say that, because it doesn't take you guys any time at all. But me . . . ha!" She laughed. "Every time I start a new project, I find a way to screw it up."

"Not every time," Mimi protested, giving Kelly a maternal pat on the arm. "What about your chunky wool scarf? Your very first project. You didn't screw that up, did you?"

Kelly had to admit she hadn't. Hmmmm, she pondered. This would be a scarf. Maybe that's a good sign. Maybe she could knit this up as easily as she knit the woolen scarf. The bold colors beckoned to Kelly again. Touch, touch. She couldn't resist.

"Okay, okay, I'll give it a try," she said, sinking her hands into the chest filled with jelly bean colors. "Can you help me get started?"

"Absolutely. You pick a color while I get some size fifteen needles." Mimi headed for the front of the shop.

Kelly played in the overflowing chest, squeezing one yarn after another, even though they were equally soft. Which to choose? A brilliant turquoise blue and green combination, peacock bright, teased her, and Kelly held it up. Why not? She usually didn't choose those colors, but it was fun trying something different. Walking to a side room to check the mirror, she held the fuzzy ball of yarn under her chin. Not bad, she decided.

"Ohhhh, I love it," Mimi concurred enthusiastically, peeking around the corner, needles in hand. "It'll look great on you."

"I agree," Lisa said, leaning around Mimi. "I was coming in and saw you picking yarns. It's about time you made one of those scarves. You've been dying to try it."

Buoyed by the wave of enthusiasm from her friends, Kelly floated back toward the main room, convinced the scarf was hers to do. "Okay, here goes," she said, settling into a chair beside the long table. "Thanks for getting the needles, Mimi. Now, how many do I cast on?"

"For that kind of yarn and scarf, ten would be fine," Mimi replied. "That'll give you a scarf about this wide." She held her fingers approximately three inches across. "They're supposed to be long and narrow."

Kelly nodded as she poked into the soft ball to find a dangling end, and, finding it, she pulled enough to start knitting. "Okay, first I measure about three times the width to cast on, right?" she said, pulling the yarn between her fingers.

"Good for you. You're remembering," Lisa said, settling at the table. She withdrew a colorful ribbon shawl from her bag.

"I'm sure you won't need any reminders how to cast on, Kelly," Mimi said with a laugh as she headed toward her back office. "Not after starting your new sweater twice."

"Don't remind me," Kelly said with a groan, recalling all the casting on required for her sweater in the round. "That took forever, and I had to do it twice." She wrapped the peacock yarn around her thumb and forefinger and began the intriguing movements required to cast stitches onto the needle.

"Just think how good you are now, though," Lisa reminded.

"Yeah, yeah." Kelly counted the stitches appearing on her needle. Six more to go. This new yarn definitely felt different. Each strand was soft but also skinny, with little fronds or "eyelashes" of fibers sticking out at intervals.

"Hey, I didn't see old Carl barking around in the yard when I drove up. He usually bounds over and says hello when I come."

"Carl is staying inside the house all day. He's been a naughty dog."

"Uh-oh. Let me guess. Golf balls?"

"Yep. I found a note on my front door yesterday, warning me that he'd be arrested and thrown in the slammer if he stole again."

"C'mon, what'd it really say?"

"That there would be an official nuisance warning issued against Carl if he touched any more balls. And I'd have to go to court and pay a hefty fine."

"Ooooh, ugly."

"Definitely. I do not want to appear before some cranky judge and plead doggie mischief."

"Poor Carl. Stuck inside all day."

"Poor Carl, nothing. He brought this all on himself," Kelly declared righteously. "I told him not to chase any more balls."

"C'mon, he's a dog. He can't stop chasing balls any more than he can stop trying to catch the squirrels."

"I know," Kelly conceded, remembering a downcast Carl lying on the floor staring out the glass patio door, watching squirrels race across the fence unimpeded.

Without Carl on patrol, the squirrels would have a high old time—digging in the flowerpots, stealing apples from Aunt Helen's apple tree. Kelly envisioned scores of insolent squirrels dancing about on the patio, deliberately teasing Carl behind the glass. The squirrels in her backyard were a sassy bunch. She'd even witnessed a squirrel steal one of Carl's bones while he was stretched in the sun sound asleep. She found it in her gutter two weeks later.

"You could always buy a long chain. That way he could still be outside," Lisa suggested, her nimble fingers twisting ribbons around her needles.

"Hey, good idea," Kelly said, perking up at the thought. "Do we still have the big outdoors store north of town?"

"Yep. They probably have fifty-foot chains you could use. That way, Carl could still enjoy the yard but not get over the fence. And even if he did, he wouldn't get very far."

Kelly smoothed out the three rows of stitches she'd created with the new yarn. The larger needles gave the fluffy yarn its loose, open effect. It was pretty already. Peacock blue and green cried, "Wear me! Wear me!"

"I'll buy a chain today. I just hope Carl doesn't choke himself the first time he tries to chase a squirrel," she said, pushing her needle beneath a slender fiber. Sometimes the fibers were hard to pick up with the bigger needles, she noticed, and it took several tries to slide beneath each stitch.

"How's the consulting going?" Lisa asked. "Megan told me you're helping Debbie. That's great."

Kelly smiled. The knitting shop's grapevine was alive and well. News traveled faster here than in most offices she'd experienced. "She needed help with all the accounts. I haven't a clue what to charge, though."

"Megan will help you with that."

"Well, well, look how much you've done, Kelly," Mimi said as she drew up a spinning wheel at the end of the table. "I thought I'd join you gals while I finish up this fleece."

Kelly loved to watch Mimi spin, or Burt spin, or anyone else for that matter. She found the sound of the wheel soothing as it hummed its song. Mimi pulled the roving apart in her lap and started the wheel turning, her fingers working the fibers into strands, feeding the wheel. Yarn wound around the spindle, fatter and fatter.

"This is the last of Vickie's fleeces," Mimi said in a sad voice. "I'm going to mix this one with mohair and dye it shamrock green. That was Vickie's favorite color."

The jangle of Kelly's cell phone intruded. She slipped it from her purse and spoke softly, not wanting to shatter the quiet moment entirely. "This is Kelly."

"Kelly, I just wanted to tell you that I won't be going up into the canyon today," Debbie's voice came through. "I've lain awake nearly the whole night. I couldn't sleep, I was so angry. I'm going to the police today. Geri's taking me."

"The police?" Kelly replied, startled. "Why? What's the matter?"

"I took out the will from the file cabinet again, and you know how upset it made me when I first read it."

Kelly remembered all too well. Yesterday in Vickie's office, Kelly had worried Debbie's fury would trigger an asthma attack. "Yes, I remember." She noticed Mimi's wheel had stopped turning as she and Lisa listened intently.

"Well, I'm taking the will to the police detective today. I'm going to show it to this Lieutenant Peterson. It's so clear, a blind man could see it! Bob Claymore gets half of all my mother's property now that she's dead. Not just the house and the bank accounts but half of the business she spent years building. But she was divorcing him! He shouldn't get a thing. She was cutting him out!"

Kelly heard Debbie draw a ragged breath. "Debbie, are you all right? Please, don't get so upset. You have to be care—"

Debbie cut her off. "Dammit, Kelly, I don't care what happens to me. He's got to pay for what he did to Mom. I *know* he killed her! And the will helps prove it. Listen, I've got to go. We'll talk later. Bye."

Kelly bid her good-bye and flipped off her phone. Debbie's anger was so raw it was hard to listen without some of it rubbing off. "That was Debbie. She's taking the will to the police detective who interviewed us in the canyon to tell him her suspicions about Bob Claymore."

"Mimi, what's your feeling about Bob?" Lisa asked. "I worked with him on a community housing committee last year, and he seemed almost mousy to me."

Mimi's wheel picked up speed again. "Well, I don't know if I'd call him 'mousy.' But I also can't picture him hating Vickie enough to kill her."

"Maybe it wasn't hate, Mimi. Maybe it was simply greed. And maybe he'd fallen in love with that other woman," Kelly suggested. She noticed Rosa was nodding in agreement as she straightened the bookshelves behind Mimi.

"You mean Eva Bartok?" Mimi shook her head. "Bob would be crazy to choose Eva over Vickie. Eva's so . . . so . . ."

"Hateful," Rosa supplied. She brought a pile of magazines to the table and started sorting. "Eva tried teaching a weaving class at the community center once, and I swear, half the students left after two lessons. I was one of them."

"Oh, yes, I remember. I don't think Eva was ever asked to teach anywhere more than once," Mimi said with a rueful smile. "She's such a gifted artist, a truly exceptional weaver, but she lacks, I don't know, warmth, uh, people skills, whatever."

"You're being too nice, Mimi," Rosa said with uncharacteristic vehemence. "Eva was just plain mean. She was always making cutting remarks to students in her classes. I know some people who stopped weaving altogether because she'd said something cruel."

"Ooooh, really ugly. And sad," Lisa decreed.

"And she's also got a nasty temper, too. I heard she deliberately kept a weaver out of a competition because she was mad at her. Probably jealous. She was always bragging about her awards." Rosa's face betrayed signs of past slights.

"Bad karma," Lisa said sagely.

Rosa looked up from the magazines, and Kelly could tell she was debating whether to say something else. "You know, I accidentally walked in on Eva and Vickie having a big argument at the weaving conference last month. They were in the ladies' room, and ohhhh, boy, they sounded about ready to claw each other's eyes out."

"The Denver conference?" Mimi asked. "You're right, Rosa, I remember seeing both of them."

"Oh, they were there all right," Rosa nodded vigorously, her brown eyes wide with remembering. "They tried to shut up when I came into the restroom, but not before Vickie called Eva a . . . well, it was pretty ugly."

"I shudder to think what Eva said in reply," Mimi commented.

Rosa glanced toward the windows. "Actually, Eva didn't say anything. Vickie slammed out the door before she could. I just remember the expression on Eva's face." Rosa closed her eyes and shivered. "It was ugly. Really, really ugly. Worse than any name."

Kelly could almost feel the animosity coming off that scene Rosa described. She didn't know Eva Bartok, but she noticed the strong feelings she aroused in people who had crossed her path. Eva sounded like a woman who did not like being crossed. Did she harbor a grudge against Vickie? Had that grudge festered and brought forth enough hate to cause her to kill?

"How did Vickie and Eva get along before Bob's affair?" Kelly probed. "They were both weavers, so they must have interacted. Fort Connor isn't that big a place. Did they get along?"

Mimi seemed to ponder while her wheel spun. "Now that you mention it, I always got the feeling they didn't really care for each other. There was never anything said or anything overt, just something I felt." She gave a little shrug. "Whenever I was in the same room with them, it was like, well, like you could almost see the fur rise on their necks."

"Meow," Lisa said with a grin.

Kelly joined the soft laughter. "Well, that's interesting. Maybe Eva harbored animosity toward Vickie that spilled over after that confrontation in Denver."

"Look out, she's sleuthing again," Lisa teased.

"Ohhhh, Kelly, please, no," Mimi said. "I can't stand to think about it."

Kelly shifted her needle to start the next row of stitches. This scarf was easy. Just the knit stitch, exactly like her chunky wool scarf. She smoothed out the three inches she'd completed.

What the—? she thought, noticing the bulging curve along one side of the scarf. The bottom two inches of the scarf were nice and even, approximately three inches wide. But that was followed by another two inches of scarf that grew wider and wider with each additional row.

How'd that happen, she wondered? She counted the stitches in the even bottom rows. Ten stitches across. Then she counted the stitches in the row she'd just completed—while she was conjuring images of Eva Bartok as villain. Eighteen stitches.

"*Eighteen?*" Kelly complained out loud. "How'd I get eighteen? I cast on ten. What happened?"

Lisa glanced over and smiled. "Uh-oh. That can happen with those eyelash yarns."

"Please, not another 'uh-oh.' " Kelly slapped her hand to her forehead. "Why me? I'm doomed. Every time—"

"Angst alert. Dive, dive," Jennifer said as she dropped her knitting bag on the table.

"It's not funny. I've done it again. I've screwed something up. I tell you, I'm cursed," Kelly moaned.

"Quick, administer caffeine," Jennifer ordered. "Where's her mug?" Spying Kelly's mug, she shoved it near Kelly's nose. "Don't talk, just breathe deeply and take a drink. Better yet, drink deeply, then breathe."

Kelly deliberately suppressed the laughter inside, even though it bubbled around the table. "Coffee won't cure it," she said, but took a long, deep drink anyway. Then another. It might not cure it, but the caffeine rush sure helped.

"Cure what?" Mimi asked.

"Knitting incompetence," Kelly replied, sulking now. "Oh, it's so *easy!*" she mimicked, then gave a Bronx cheer. "Riiiight."

"Here, let me help you." Jennifer reached out for the misshapen scarf. "We can unravel these last few rows and get you back to where you went astray."

"Yeah, yeah, yeah."

"She's going down."

Kelly scowled at Lisa, who just laughed. "I know you get tired of hearing this, Kelly, but that happens to everyone. Those yarns are slippery little things."

"Then why do you all say 'it's so easy'?" Kelly demanded, pique at fever pitch. "It's . . . it's unfair advertising."

Everyone laughed at that. "Oh, Kelly, you are a delight," Mimi declared.

"Here we go," Jennifer said, showing her the much-shorter scarf again. "I unraveled the uneven rows, then threaded the needle through the loops, and you're ready to go." She handed it over. "My advice, count after every row to make sure you've still got ten. If eleven appear, then just knit two together to get back on track. Much easier to catch mistakes early."

"Thanks," Kelly grumbled, looking at the rows. "Okay, count after every row. Count after every row."

"And let's not discuss murder suspects anymore, okay? I'm sure that's where she got off," Mimi suggested.

At the sound of the doorbell jangling, Rosa looked up, and her expression changed. Kelly wasn't sure, but Rosa's face paled. "Mimi, uh, we have a visitor," Rosa said, pointing behind them.

Kelly turned to see a uniformed police officer approach from the front room—a county policeman, she noticed, when he drew close enough to see his shoulder patch.

"Excuse me, ladies," the officer began. "Is Mimi Shafer here? The shop owner?"

Now it was Mimi's turn to go pale, Kelly observed. "Y-yes, officer. I'm Mimi Shafer. What can I do for you?" She started to push away from the silent wheel.

"No need to get up, ma'am," he said and hastily approached. "I'm simply here to ask you if you could identify an item our investigators found at Vickie Claymore's home. We were informed you and the victim were close friends, correct?"

"Yes, sir, we were," Mimi said in a small voice.

The officer, who appeared to Kelly to be in his mid-thirties, withdrew a small plastic bag from his pocket. He held it out to Mimi. "We found this bracelet in the room where Ms. Claymore was murdered. We don't know if it belonged to her or to someone else. We've already asked Ms. Swinson if she recognized it, and she did not. We're hoping you might help us out."

Mimi took the package and scrutinized it. Kelly watched her expression carefully and saw the light of recognition go on in her eyes. "Yes, officer, I do recognize the bracelet."

The officer appeared relieved and withdrew a small notepad from his shirt pocket. "Excellent, Ms. Shafer. So you recognize it as belonging to Ms. Claymore?"

Mimi took a deep breath. "No, officer. It belongs to someone else. It's Eva Bartok's diamond tennis bracelet. I can tell because she had this little silver lamb especially made for it." Mimi fingered the tiny charm dangling at the end of the bracelet. "She wore it regularly. Eva claimed it was her good-luck charm."

Ten

Kelly ran up the steps to the century-old white frame church on a shady Old Town corner. She'd tried to keep track of the time but had gotten lost in a client's morass of numbers. The next time she glanced at her watch, another hour had magically evaporated. Suddenly, it was twenty minutes before Vickie Claymore's funeral, and Kelly hadn't changed clothes. She was still in shorts and a T-shirt.

Racing through her bedroom, she'd grabbed a sleeveless black dress, wiggled into it, and snagged some dressier shoes. Balancing on one foot, she struggled to finish dressing and caught site of Carl-in-Chains in the backyard.

Kelly had felt so guilty, leading Carl outside to race around, only to snap a fifty-foot chain to his collar. She'd bought a metal stake for the yard as well. Carl was pretty strong, and when he got excited, could exert a lot of rottie pulling power. A nearby water pipe looked too flimsy to Kelly. Besides, she didn't want to return to a flooded yard if the squirrels started tormenting Carl.

Pushing open the church's front door, Kelly stepped inside. Immediately, the hot, dry air of the old building enveloped her. Oh, boy. No air-conditioning, and it was ninety-five degrees already. Noticing the wooden pews were nearly full, Kelly searched for the familiar faces of her friends. She spied them near the front in a pew that looked tightly packed.

Kelly glanced about for a place to sit and heard a familiar soft voice speak up beside her. "Kelly, you can sit here. There's enough room." Kelly turned to see Rosa scoot over on the pew, leaving space.

"Thank you so much, Rosa," Kelly whispered as she gratefully settled into the spot. "I was working on the computer and lost track of time. Story of my life."

Rosa smiled. "Don't worry. I was late, too. I offered to stay at the shop until one of our student helpers could come."

Looking around at the full church, Kelly said, "This is quite a turnout and a tribute to Vickie that so many people have come."

"Yes, it is. Vickie was a good person, and she touched a lot of lives."

Kelly detected a slight rise in the subdued murmur of voices and noticed a slender and very stylish blonde about Vickie's age walk down the aisle.

"That's Eva Bartok," Rosa leaned over and whispered as the woman found a seat midfront.

Kelly had only caught a fleeting glimpse of her features, but she appeared very attractive. "Vickie's age?" she asked.

Rosa gestured. "Give or take a few years, I think."

Peering toward the front pews, Kelly scanned the heads. "Which one is Bob Claymore? I've never met him."

Rosa craned her neck, staring toward the front. "He's in the first pew, left-hand side. Starting to go bald on top."

Kelly spotted him. She also noticed there was no one else sitting beside him on that pew. Bob Claymore sat totally alone. Across the aisle on the other front pew, Debbie Hurst was surrounded by Geri on one side and Mimi on the other. Jayleen Swinson sat at the far end of the row, her curly blonde hair held back with a black ribbon.

"You know, I don't know anything about him, but I almost feel sorry for Bob Claymore," Kelly whispered as a black-robed minister approached the lectern. "No one will go near him."

Rosa nodded in agreement, and Kelly let her gaze finally settle on the long casket at the front of the church. She'd deliberately not focused on it before now. The sight of a casket made her uncomfortable, reminding her of all the loss in her life. Her father, Uncle Jim, Aunt Helen, Cousin Martha.

The minister's voice rose with practiced ease, his words floating out into the sultry summer air. Kelly prepared to zone out for the rest of the service. She'd heard all those words before. There were no words written that could truly console those left behind when cherished loved ones were stolen away.

"My gosh, I thought I was going to melt in there," Rosa exclaimed as she and Kelly finally broke free of the stifling church. "Fresh air, at last." She fanned herself.

Kelly shaded her eyes. The air might be fresh outside, but it was still hot, even in the shade. Softball practice would be brutal tonight. The sun would still be blazing at seven o'clock. She glanced around for Lisa or Megan but didn't see them. What she did see was Bob Claymore approaching Debbie Hurst, who was standing beside a black limousine and still flanked by Mimi and Geri.

"Look at that," she discreetly motioned to Rosa. "I wonder what Debbie will say."

Rosa shook her head, her long black braid slipping behind her back. "I don't want to know. She might take his head off."

Kelly watched Debbie's expression freeze despite the July heat. She drew closer to Geri, while Mimi looked dreadfully uncomfortable. Bob Claymore gestured as he spoke and appeared agitated. Then, a mask of disgust claimed Debbie's features, and she turned without a word and entered the limo, slamming the door behind her. Geri scurried around to the other side while Mimi took a moment to say a few words to Bob. His dejection obvious, he stared at the ground until the limousine drove away.

Kelly pulled her car to a stop in front of the cottage and jumped out, slamming the door. She had to get out of this dress before she died. After hours of a stifling, hot church service and a graveside burial in the blazing noontime sun, Kelly swore the fabric had been heat-sealed to her body. Racing inside her house, she peeled off her clothes and jumped into the shower. Afterward, she returned to her summer attire of choice—shorts and a T-shirt.

Grabbing a cold soda from the fridge, Kelly checked on Carl through the window. He was lying in the sun in the exact same position he'd been before she left. Kelly took a long drink, letting the cold soda chill her inside. She peered at Carl again. Was he all right? Had he been sleeping all that time in the hot sun? Why didn't he go under the tree in the shade?

Suddenly, the vision of Carl running to chase a squirrel and snapping his neck in the process appeared before her eyes. Horrified at the possibility, Kelly flung back the patio glass door and ran outside. "Carl!" she yelled. "Are you all right?"

Carl raised his head just enough to look over his shoulder at her, then flopped back down.

"Ohmygosh," Kelly cried, convinced that Carl had injured himself while she was gone. He'd been lying in pain for all these hours, baking, roasting in the hot summer sun, waiting for his neglectful owner to return and take him to the vet. Kelly sank to her knees next to her dog and ran her hands over his back and legs. "Carl, are you all right? What's the matter? Did you hurt yourself?"

Staring balefully at her, Carl lifted his head enough to lick her hand, then let it flop back to the ground. Tears sprang to Kelly's eyes. "Oh, no! You really did hurt yourself. We've got to get you to the vet."

At that, Carl lifted his head again. But this time he appeared to be tracking a squirrel's mad dash along the fence superhighway. The squirrel paused long enough to fuss at Carl in that chattering squirrely squeak. Clearly annoyed at the exchange, Carl suddenly scrambled to his feet and began to bark. Then, he took off for the fence, only to be yanked back rudely at the end of the chain. That did not stop the barking, however.

Kelly pulled herself from the ground. That old faker, she thought, smiling at her dog. He was trying to make her feel guilty. Watching Carl desperately try to reach the squirrel, barking ferociously, Kelly did feel guilty. The squirrel seemed to pause at intervals, as if he were teasing Carl to come and get him, knowing full well Carl could not. Finally, the squirrel leaped to a nearby cottonwood, gave Carl a rodent version of a Bronx cheer, then scampered into the leafy branches above.

"I'm sorry, big guy," Kelly apologized as she patted Carl's head. "I don't know what else to do."

Instead of enjoying the pat, however, Carl immediately started barking again, staring toward the driveway beside the cottage. Kelly turned to see a man tentatively approach the fence, then draw back at Carl's ferocious barking. Something about the man looked familiar.

"Can I help you?" Kelly said as she approached the fence.

The man hesitated and looked over her shoulder. "Is he okay?" he asked, clearly concerned. "I don't want to make him mad."

"No no, it's all right," Kelly reassured. "Did you wish to speak to me?"

"Yes, yes I did," he answered, looking her full in the face.

Kelly remembered where she had seen him—that morning at the funeral. "You're Bob Claymore?" she inquired, offering her hand across the fence. "I'm Kelly Flynn. I believe I saw you at Vickie's funeral this morning."

Claymore almost looked grateful as he shook her hand. "Thank you. I was hoping you might do me a favor, Ms. Flynn. Mimi Shafer told me you were assisting Debbie with Vickie's business accounts, I believe."

"Yes, that's correct," she replied, adopting a businesslike tone. She had no idea where this conversation was going. "What sort of favor are you talking about, Mr. Claymore."

"I simply wanted you to ask Debbie if she would please meet with me, if only for a few minutes. She's refused to talk with me since her mother died. I can understand her anger and grief, but . . . but now she's making wild accusations to the police."

Claymore's face took on the desperate look Kelly had seen that morning when he'd obviously tried to plead his case to Debbie. "I'll certainly mention it to her, Mr. Claymore, but I'm not sure my saying anything will make a difference."

Claymore's whole body seemed to sag with that. He ran his hand through his thinning gray hair. "I've asked everyone, Ms. Flynn.

Mimi Shafer, Geri Norbert, Jayleen. I . . . I don't know anyone else who might get through to her. I know how much she loved her mother, but to think that I could kill Vickie, why, it's . . . it's unthinkable. I loved Vickie. I couldn't hurt her." He stared off toward the golf course. "And now she's gone to the police with all these awful accusations. It's . . . it's unbelievable! They came to my office at the university, for God's sake. And they interviewed me there. I was so ashamed. I couldn't even look at my colleagues afterward. What must they think of me? Do they believe me to be capable of murder?"

Kelly watched the anguish play across his face and decided that Bob Claymore would have to be an excellent actor to feign all that emotion. Her earlier feelings surfaced, and she softened her tone. "Mr. Claymore, I promise I will try to convince Debbie to see you. All this animosity isn't good for either of you. And it certainly doesn't serve Vickie's memory."

Claymore glanced back to Kelly, gratitude evident in his eyes. "Thank you, Ms. Flynn. I . . . I appreciate that more than you know."

"She may bring others along with her. I'm sure you'd understand if she did."

Claymore nodded. "Of course. She's free to bring anyone she wants. I just want to have an opportunity to clear myself in her eyes."

"I understand, Mr. Claymore. I'll do what I can."

Carl started barking again, and Claymore gave Kelly a wan smile as he backed away. "Thank you," he repeated as he walked away.

Kelly watched him all the way to his car, wishing she didn't feel so unsettled.

"See you tonight at practice," Megan called over her shoulder as she sped through the knitting shop door.

"Don't forget your sunscreen," Kelly teased with a wave as she headed toward the main room.

Burt sat in his favorite sunny corner, spinning a smoky gray fleece. Kelly settled into a nearby chair and pulled the peacock blue and green scarf from her bag.

"How are you, Burt?" she said, picking up the scarf where she left off. It was really looking good now, and she was almost finished. The pudgy ball of boa eyelash yarn had dwindled to the size of a walnut. "You heard about the visit we had from the police, didn't you?"

Burt smiled, feet moving back and forth, setting the wheel's rhythm. "Yes, Mimi told me about the bracelet and the visit."

"I imagine Eva Bartok was questioned. I mean, after all, she's the woman who'd been screwing around with Vickie's husband."

"She was questioned yesterday as a matter of fact," Burt replied.

Kelly waited, anxious to hear what had transpired, or whatever Burt could reveal. "Well, what came out of it?" she demanded after Burt sat silent for over a minute.

Burt glanced toward the adjoining rooms. They were alone at the library table. "She has an alibi," he said in a hushed voice. "She was with a book discussion group at the university the night Vickie was killed."

The hum of the wheel filled the room as Kelly sat quietly knitting while Burt spun. Try as she might, she simply could not come up with a suspect other than Bob Claymore. Problem was, now that she'd met him, seen the anguish in his eyes, and heard the despair in his voice, Kelly felt sorry for him. And that made it harder for her to picture him as a killer.

Was all of that a ruse? Kelly wondered. All of that anguish and despair looked real. Was it possible Bob Claymore really was the killer?

She paused to count stitches again. That was the only way she'd been able to control the yarn's tendency to multiply. Whenever she found an extra stitch, Kelly would simply knit two stitches together.

"Burt, is he the only suspect the police have so far?" she probed again.

Burt gave her a smile. "Well, let's just say he's the best suspect the detectives have at the moment."

"Because of the divorce and the terms of the will, I'll bet."

"Well, that, and the fact that he doesn't have an alibi. He says he was home reading. All alone."

Kelly sighed out loud. "Oh, brother. That doesn't look good."

"Now that they've questioned Eva Bartok, he may get another visit from the detectives."

"Why's that?" Kelly asked, noticing two customers chatting in the adjoining room.

Burt leaned closer. "Eva claims she lost the bracelet two weeks ago, right after she'd spent the weekend with Bob Claymore."

Kelly stared at Burt. "Sounds like Eva thinks Claymore is trying to frame her. What do you think?"

Burt shrugged. "It depends on whether you believe her story. The detectives said she only mentioned Claymore after they told her where they'd found the bracelet. Apparently she got pretty mad after that."

"And Eva has an alibi, right? So it can't be her," Kelly mused in a low voice. "So, she couldn't have dropped the bracelet at the scene. And that leads us right back to Claymore. Assuming, of course, that he's the one who stole it."

"Or that it was stolen at all," Burt reminded her with a smile. "Who knows, maybe it dropped off her arm when she was visiting Vickie one day."

Kelly shook her head. "From what I've heard, Vickie and Eva were not on visiting terms. In fact, I heard they had a really bad argument at the Denver weaving conference the week before Vickie died."

Burt sat back. "We'd picked up lots of gossip about the bad blood between those two women, but our network missed that. Where'd you hear it, Kelly?"

"From the Lambspun network, Burt," she said with a grin. "Our grapevine beats them all."

Eleven

"Fill 'er up, Pete," Kelly requested, leaning over the café counter with her outstretched mug.

Pete grinned. "You really know how to start the day, Kelly," he said, filling her stainless-steel mug with the dark brew.

Kelly's cell phone rang, and she struggled to grab her mug and knitting bag and answer her phone, all at the same time. "This is Kelly," she managed as she wound her way through the knitting shop.

"Kelly, I'm going up into the canyon in a little while to finish up the insurance claims," Debbie's voice came over the phone. "Will you be coming up today?"

"I'll be up this afternoon, Debbie," Kelly promised. "I have to get to a certain point with my office accounts, then I can head out. Probably after lunch." She dumped her knitting bag and mug on the library table, then waved hello to Jennifer and Megan, who were already knitting.

"Oh, good." Debbie sounded relieved. "I was hoping you would come. Tell me, have you made much progress with the financial reports?"

"I've reviewed all the income statements. Now I have to access the remaining records on the computer and update those. Once I finish that, then I can start to draw up the reports. Oh, that reminds me." Kelly dug into her bag and withdrew the completed blue and green scarf. "You'll need to call the investment bank and ask them to fax a statement showing all activity from the first of July. We've got last quarter's statement, but we need to see if Vickie made any withdrawals or deposits during those first few days. The statements are in a folder on the desk."

"I'll call as soon as I get to the ranch," Debbie promised. "Oops, got another call."

"See you this afternoon," Kelly said, then flipped off her phone. She picked up the peacock scarf and dangled it in front of her friends. "Ta-dah!" she announced.

"Whoa! Look at that," Megan said. "Good job, Kelly."

"See, we knew you could do it," Jennifer added, her needles busily working another long-fringed scarf. This one was tangerine and coral.

Kelly reached over and fingered the luscious summer colors. "I haven't seen these colors before. Did we get a new shipment?"

Jennifer nodded and pointed to the room behind her. "Check out the wooden crates in the corner. New yarns came in."

Kelly jumped up from her chair and headed for the yarns,

nearly running into Steve, who had rounded the corner at the same moment.

"Whoa," he said, stepping out of the way. "You folks need traffic signals on this corner."

"How about truck mirrors?" Jennifer suggested. "They could stick way out so we'd see who's coming."

"Sorry," Kelly apologized. "You caught me in the midst of fiber fever. New yarns." She pointed to the corner.

"Do you have a minute?" Steve asked. "I'm on the way back to the site, but I wanted to check something with you." He pulled out a chair and straddled it backward, clearly not staying long.

"What's up, Steve?" Megan teased. "You trying to recruit Kelly for your team?"

Steve grinned. "I would if I thought I had a chance."

"Dream on," Kelly taunted as she settled back into her chair.

"No, I'm here to check out the itinerary for tomorrow." He pulled a notepad from his pocket.

"Tomorrow?" Kelly stared blankly for a moment before she remembered. She slapped her hand to her forehead. "Oh, yeah, our Wyoming trip."

"Yeah, our Wyoming trip. Tomorrow. Early. So set your alarm. We're leaving at seven a.m."

Kelly's eyes popped wide. "Whoa. Guess I'll have to run at daybreak. Okay, who's driving? Do you need me?"

"Nah, we're covered. Curt's taking his truck, and I'm driving mine. We figured some of you might be up for a road trip."

"You know, Kelly, I could come along and take a look at your cousin's house," Jennifer offered. "Give you an estimate of market value. Let me check the Wyoming multilist this afternoon and see what the comparables are. Do you have a description of size, rooms, and all that?"

"No, but I'm sure the lawyer does. I could ask Chambers to fax me something," she replied. "Thanks for offering, Jen. That'll help a lot."

"Hey, I'd like to go, too," Megan piped up across the table. "I need a break after the project I finished yesterday. Brother. I'm exhausted."

"Sure," Steve invited. "We have plenty of room. Both trucks can take three up front."

"Chambers said he coordinated everything with Curt. Are we meeting with the ranch manager?"

Steve flipped open his notepad. "Yes. Chet Brewster. He'll be there to take us around and answer any questions. Then he'll take us on a tour around the entire ranch. We'll need to see which areas would work for a natural area and which areas wouldn't."

Suddenly the enormity of the endeavor settled in on Kelly again. "Wow, I don't know what I'd do without you guys," she said, nodding to Steve and Jennifer. "And Curt. I'd be clueless. Totally clueless."

"That's what friends are for, Kelly," Steve said, and gave her shoulder a squeeze.

Her cell phone jangled, and Kelly stepped away from the table to answer. Lawyer Chambers came on the phone. "Kelly, I thought I'd fax you a description of Martha's house and contents from my files. I figured you'd need it for your trip tomorrow."

"Mr. Chambers, you're a mind reader. I was just about to call you. Thanks so much."

"It's no bother, Kelly. One more thing. I've learned there are some alpacas on the ranch as well as sheep and cattle."

"Alpacas?" Kelly exclaimed, causing everyone at the table to turn and stare. "What am I going to do with alpacas?"

"The same thing you do with sheep and cattle, Kelly," Chambers said with a chuckle. "You count them, then decide to sell them or keep them. Take care and call me afterward. I'll look forward to hearing from you."

Once again, the wily old lawyer hung up before Kelly could register any more complaints. She swore she heard him laughing.

"You've got alpacas, too?" Megan asked. "Wow."

"Yummy," Jennifer decreed. "Think of all the wool."

"Oh, brother, now I've got alpacas," Kelly said to the heavens. "What next? Pigs and chickens?"

Megan giggled, but Steve patted Kelly on the shoulder as he turned to leave. "I think we've just filled that last seat in the truck. You're going to need someone to advise you on the alpacas."

"Can't you and Curt do that?" she asked.

He shook his head. "Nope. Curt and I are cattle and sheep guys. You need someone who can check out the herd, then look at the alpaca registry papers and estimate what they're worth. I'm sure there's paperwork there." He grinned as he walked away. "See you bright and early tomorrow."

Kelly stared after him. Today had just started, and it was already jam-packed. There weren't enough hours to get everything done. Vickie's accounts would take quite a chunk of time. Kelly shoved her scarf back into the bag and grabbed her mug. "It looks like my day just exploded," she said with a good-bye wave. "I'll see you two tomorrow morning. Jen, I'll fax that house detail to your office as soon as I get it." Without waiting for a reply, Kelly was out the door.

The printer hummed, and Kelly reached both arms high over her head to stretch. Leaning back into Vickie's comfy desk chair, Kelly watched the pages of neat columns and figures drop into the printer tray.

It was dusk already, she noticed through the window, and she'd only finished half of what she'd planned to accomplish this afternoon. Of course, all the extra errands in town had slowed her down. Kelly rubbed her eyes. It had taken twice as long to enter all of the expenses since Vickie's death. Darn it. She'd hoped to get this part finished before she took off for Wyoming tomorrow. She checked her watch. Maybe if she worked a couple of hours more.

"What is this?" Debbie said from her cluttered table across the room. "This can't be right. Mom always paid her bills on time. She was scrupulous about that."

Kelly groaned inwardly. Every time she thought she had all the expenses, either she or Debbie found more. They really needed Jayleen's help, but when Kelly suggested it, Debbie shook her head no.

"Oh, great, there go the totals again," Kelly said, deliberately heaving a dramatic sigh. "How much is it?"

"Over five thousand dollars," Debbie exclaimed. "That can't be right."

"Boy, that's a lot of alpaca feed. Who's the vendor?"

"It's not a vendor. It's some organization of alpaca breeders, I think. All it says is 'Advance Registration Fees.'"

Kelly reached across the desk for the folder of assorted invoices and statements already paid. She thought she remembered one unpaid invoice in the pile. "Here's the bill," she announced, holding up the invoice. "And it's dated June first. Everything else is paid. Wonder why this one isn't."

"That is so unlike Mom. I can't understand it."

Kelly saw an opportunity and decided to reopen a closed subject. "I bet Jayleen knows what's up with this bill." She glanced out the window toward the empty pastures. "Darn. We missed her. She's already put the animals in and left. I wish we'd found it earlier. Why don't I call her?"

Debbie's mouth pinched in an expression Kelly was growing used to. "Yes, I suppose you'll have to."

"We could really use her help, Debbie," Kelly tried again. "It's taking us a lot longer to finish these accounts, because we're having to find everything first."

Debbie shook her head again. "No, we're doing fine. I'd rather pay you and make sure everything's done as it should be."

Kelly sighed out loud and debated asking the one question that kept playing through her mind. Then she decided, *what the hey,* and jumped in. "Debbie, why don't you like Jayleen? I mean, she's a cousin. Everyone said she and your mom were very close. What's up?"

Debbie fidgeted with the invoice for a moment. "I just don't like her. She's . . . she's so rough and crude." Debbie wrinkled up her face in displeasure.

"You mean the swearing and all that," Kelly said, remembering Jayleen's loud and liberal use of profanity when Lieutenant Peterson interviewed them.

Debbie rolled her eyes. "Yes, that, too, but she's just so loud and stomps around. Like a bull in a china shop."

"Well, she's certainly not a shrinking violet, that's for sure," Kelly joked.

"I also think she took advantage of my mother over the years. She was always borrowing money from Mom."

"Really? Did she borrow a lot?" Kelly's curiosity piqued.

"Ohhhh, I don't know how much over the years, but my mom kept track of it." Her mouth pinched again. "Jayleen always had problems with money, and my mom always bailed her out. I used to tell her not to be so accommodating, but Mom would laugh and say Jayleen had had a rough life." She gave a disgusted snort.

"Did Jayleen pay Vickie back?"

"Yes, she always repaid the loans," Debbie admitted, begrudgingly, it seemed to Kelly. "And she hasn't borrowed any money for a couple of years, my mom said."

"Well, that's good. Probably a sign that Jayleen's business is doing better," Kelly ventured, compelled to say something in Jayleen's favor.

"Humph. My mom's the one who built Jayleen's business. She recommended her to every one of her friends. Jayleen wouldn't have anything without Mom's help."

Clearly there was more here, so Kelly gambled and probed deeper. "Debbie, I sense there's something else about Jayleen that bothers you. Not just the money. What is it?"

Debbie laid the invoice in her lap and stared out into the rapidly darkening sky. "She's a drunk. Or she used to be. And she was so awful. My mom always tried to help her out. Rescuing her, bringing her home, trying to sober her up." Debbie shivered. "I still remember seeing her one night, when I was in high school. Her husband left her and took the kids. And Jayleen went on a binge. She was staggering around the kitchen, screaming and crying, and threatening to kill herself. It was so awful . . . and so ugly." Debbie's voice dropped lower.

Kelly began to understand. Debbie's world was curtailed and circumscribed. Carefully controlled, antiseptic almost. No overexertion, no excess, no throwing caution to the wind. Debbie's life literally depended on restraint.

"That must have been scary to watch," she ventured.

Debbie nodded. "It was. I always ran upstairs to my room whenever she came."

"She's sober now, right?" Kelly pried. "I mean, I don't see how she could manage all she does and go out on binges."

Debbie stared into her lap. "Mom said she's been sober for ten years. Let's hope she stays that way."

"Okay, I'll give her a quick call tonight and see if she knows about that bill," Kelly said, changing the subject. "Meanwhile, I'll keep that invoice with the other."

"I should go now," Debbie said, gathering the papers on the table as she rose. She dropped the invoice on the desk. "I hate driving down the canyon when it's dark."

"I'd leave now, too, but I want to get a little further on these entries," Kelly said, noticing Debbie's pallor. "You know, maybe you shouldn't come up into the canyon tomorrow. You're looking really tired."

"I wish I didn't have to. But there's still so much I have to sort through. At least I finished with the insurance today," she said, hesitating at the door. "Thanks so much for all your hard work, Kelly. I can't tell you how much I appreciate it."

Kelly gave her a warm smile. Debbie looked as if she needed it. "You're welcome, Debbie. Now, you take care of yourself, okay? Drive carefully down the canyon."

Debbie nodded and gave a parting wave over her shoulder. Kelly found herself staring after her and not knowing why.

The jangle of her cell phone startled Kelly so much she jumped. The quiet of Vickie's office had settled over her like a blanket as she stared at the computer.

"This is Kelly."

"Hey, Kelly, Jayleen here. I got your message. Which bill are you asking about?"

Kelly reached for the file folder. "It's from some alpaca organization for registration fees. But it's a hefty sum. Over five thousand dollars." She sorted through the papers. "Here it is. Five thousand two hundred seventy."

There was a pause on the other end. "That's the bill for the local chapter's fees for next year's exhibition. You mean it's not paid yet?"

"Nope. This is stamped SECOND NOTICE, and it's unpaid. My concern is, do we have any more bills like this floating around? I'm really trying to get some totals so I can do the reports."

"No no, I get everything paid the very day Vickie asks me to. I don't understand. She told me she was paying that bill the first week of July. It was already a month overdue. I thought that was strange, because Vickie is almost fanatic about paying her bills on time. Are you sure there's no entry in the checking account?"

"Nothing. I checked the bank, too."

"That makes no sense. Listen, do you want me to come over and help you look? I'd be glad to. I've got some time tomorrow."

Kelly debated, then decided against it. She didn't want to upset Debbie. "That's okay. Besides, I won't be here tomorrow. Say, that reminds me," she said, suddenly remembering. "I could really use your help another way, Jayleen. I'm afraid it would take most of tomorrow, though."

"I'd be glad to help you, Kelly. Any way I can. What do you need?" Jayleen replied, her voice revealing that Kelly's attempts at kindness had not gone unnoticed.

"Well, I have to go to Wyoming with some friends tomorrow and check out my cousin's ranch. She died and left a lot of cattle and sheep. And I learned today there's a bunch of alpacas there, too. Now, I've got cow and sheep people, but I need an alpaca expert."

Jayleen chuckled. "Well, I don't know if I'm an expert, but I think I can help you out, Kelly. Cow and sheep people, huh?" She laughed a husky, low laugh.

"Boy, Jayleen, you're a lifesaver," Kelly enthused over the phone, deliberately not revealing she'd asked Geri first. Geri had pleaded too much business in town. "Listen, here comes the bad part. We're leaving from my house near the Lambspun shop at seven a.m. We can swing by your place in Landport about seven thirty. How's that?"

"Why don't I meet you at Harvey's Restaurant at the crossroads? I like to have breakfast there. Besides, it's on the way out of town."

"That's great. Thanks again, Jayleen. See you tomorrow." Kelly snapped her phone off, relieved that the last lingering problem of the day had been solved.

Surveying the littered desk, Kelly decided, *enough*. It was nearly nine o'clock, and she was starving. Brewing some of Vickie's coffee had helped, but that had worn off long ago. She needed to go home. Besides, poor Carl was probably starving.

The image of Carl-in-Chains, starving no less, spurred her on. She closed out the computer accounts and straightened all the folders that lay open on the desk. Gathering what she needed into her briefcase, she snapped off the desk lamp and left the office.

Thank goodness she'd remembered to turn on the lights in the great room. The idea of being alone in a pitch-black house where her friend had been murdered wasn't a pleasant thought. Kelly felt a chill pass over her as she hurried toward the front door, deliberately not looking toward the spot where Vickie was slain.

She pulled open the front door and fumbled for the keys as she stood on the doorstep. "Darn it!" Kelly exclaimed in exasperation as she searched in her briefcase.

Just then she heard a loud slamming sound near the barn, and Kelly jumped around to peer through the night. The moon was shrouded, so she couldn't see distinctly, but she thought she saw the door to the alpaca barn open.

That's funny, she thought, as she stepped off the wide porch. Jayleen always closed the doors and dropped the metal hook through the lock every night. Kelly hesitated in the yard, debating whether to approach the darkened barn. She shouldn't leave it open. Predators lived in the canyon—mountain lions and coyotes. Alpacas were gentle prey, like sheep.

She swallowed down her uneasiness and walked to the open barn door, even though part of her wanted to run to her car as fast as she could. Kelly took a deep breath and entered, reaching around the corner for a light switch. The smell of hay and feed floated out to her in the darkened doorway, and she thought she heard the animals rustle.

Her fingers found the switch, and the barn flooded with light, causing her to squint. She stepped inside, quickly surveying the open stalls and holding pens. Several of the alpacas blinked back at her, then went back to sniffing the smoky gray alpaca in their midst. Kelly recognized Raja, surrounded by the others. Her stomach unclenched. Her imagination was running wild, that's all. Dark house. Murdered friend. She shook all the images away.

"Hey, guys. Have a good night," she said as she retreated through the doorway. Reaching for the door so she could close it, Kelly noticed the metal hook lying on the ground near her feet. She picked it up, flicked off the lights, and closed the door, shoving the hook through the slot. It must have blown off with the wind, she told herself as she walked toward her car.

But there was no wind tonight, not even a breeze, a little voice in the back of her mind said.

That thought caused a ripple to run up Kelly's spine. Had someone been sneaking around the property? She quickened her pace to her car. Whether her imagination was getting the best of her or whether someone had actually been poking around the property uninvited, it didn't matter. She was definitely not going to work alone at night in that house again.

Suddenly the deep rumble of a truck engine sounded in the distance. Kelly paused at her car door and peered down the driveway. The throaty rumble revved, rising then falling, like a truck was shifting gears and pulling away.

This time the ripple turned into real fear. Had someone parked down the road and then crept around the ranch at night? And she was sitting all alone in an empty house, scene of a grisly murder.

Kelly yanked open the car door, swiftly checked the backseat, and jumped inside. Revving the engine loudly, she locked the doors and zoomed down the driveway, spitting gravel in her wake. Dark canyon roads be damned. She planned to beat all speed records back into Fort Connor.

Twelve

"**Whoa,** hold on, it's going to get rough," Steve said as he maneuvered his truck.

Kelly stared out the window at the deep ruts carved into the long road leading to Martha Schuster's ranch. "These aren't ruts, they're canyons," she observed as they bounced along, her head barely missing the truck ceiling.

"Is this the scenic part?" Jennifer asked, bracing herself against the dashboard and the door.

"You may want to put some gravel on this road before winter," Steve suggested, steering around a crevice.

"Is that expensive?" Kelly asked. She hadn't even seen the ranch yet, and she was already spending money.

"Well, it's a long road, so it won't be cheap. But I'll give you names of the contractors I use, so they'll give you a fair price."

"Are we there yet?" Jennifer asked in a plaintive voice as she braced herself against the ceiling. "I need three hands."

"Almost there," Steve announced. "See, there's the house and the barn coming into view now."

Kelly spotted the two-story, white frame house up ahead. It was bigger than she'd envisioned. The road curved, and she spied a huge red barn. Then a garage. Was that a triple car garage? A gray pickup, which she took to be the ranch manager's, was parked in front. Fences were everywhere. From the paved county road all the way up the dirt road leading to the ranch, Kelly saw fences. They seemed to stretch for a mile before they reached the ranch house.

"Whoa, that's a good-sized house, Kelly," Jennifer observed. "And a barn, a big barn, too."

"It's even bigger than it looks," Steve added. "Wait'll you get up close."

Oh, great, Kelly thought. The ranch kept getting bigger and bigger, and she felt smaller and smaller.

"Triple car garage, nice," Jennifer continued, pointing. "And look, there's another outbuilding. Looks like storage."

"Or an office," Steve said, as they drove into the barnyard area.

"All this and seven thousand acres. Hmmmm . . ." Jennifer observed.

Kelly could almost see the calculator inside real estate agent Jennifer's head, tallying market values as she surveyed Martha's property.

Her property, soon, Kelly reminded herself and felt a flutter inside her gut. All of this belonged to her, or it would as soon as the lawyers finished passing paperwork back and forth. That old feeling of being overwhelmed settled over her again. "Wow, this is even bigger than I thought it would be," she said, her voice coming out softer than usual.

Steve pulled the truck to a stop beside the triple garage, then turned to Kelly with a smile. "C'mon, Kelly, let's go take a look at what you've got." He grabbed a cowboy hat from behind the seat, pushed open his door, and stepped to the ground. "Hold on Jennifer, I'll help you out," he said, then grinned up at Kelly. "I'd offer to help you, too, but you'd just scowl."

Kelly made a face and waved him away as she jumped to the ground. "Go help Jennifer."

"Oh, yes, Mistah Steve. I'd just love your help," Jennifer gushed in a perfect imitation of a magnolia-drenched drawl. "This big old door is so heavy."

Steve lifted Jennifer to the ground, then tipped his hat. "Glad to be of service, Miss Jennifer, ma'am."

"Hey, I'm not old enough to be a ma'am," Jennifer teased, then pointed to Steve's Stetson. "Nice hat."

"I didn't know you owned one," Kelly said. Not every man could wear a Stetson. Some men wore the hat. Some, the hat wore them. Steve looked natural. "Colorado cowboy, huh?"

Steve laughed. "Part-time. The rest of the time, overworked builder."

Kelly walked over to the fence and stared down the road. She spotted Curt Stackhouse's black truck in the distance, spitting dirt and gravel as it drove. Letting her gaze roam over the pastures that surrounded the ranch compound, Kelly turned slowly in a circle, surveying her soon-to-be domain.

Ye Gods! Look at all that land. Those pastures stretched for miles—all the way to the mountains, surely. She visually outlined the low-lying, gentle ridges in the distance. Were those cows out there? Good grief. They looked like cows. Lots of cows. What was she going to do with cows? She'd never really felt comfortable around cows when she was a child. Whenever she'd visited a friend's farm outside town, she'd stayed clear of the big, clumsy creatures. Sheep were different. Aunt Helen and Uncle Jim had sheep when she was a child. She had a little bit of "sheep memory." But no memory for cows.

She scuffed her borrowed cowboy boots in the dirt, causing little clouds of dust as she rejoined Steve and Jennifer. "Cows. Lots of cows."

"Cattle," Steve teased. "Don't worry. That's what Curt and I are here for."

"Think of them as steak, barbecue, and roast beef," Jennifer suggested. "Can we cook one up for lunch?"

"I don't think it's that easy," Kelly said, laughing at last as she watched Curt pull his big black truck right beside Steve's big red truck. "Serious Trucks," her dad used to call these monsters of the road.

Curt Stackhouse stepped down to the ground. If ever there was a man who looked like he'd been born to wear a Stetson, Curt was it. A true cowboy, cattle and sheep rancher, and sometime land developer, Curt still reminded Kelly of that brash young cowboy in Aunt Helen's high school yearbook photo—the photo signed, "Yours, always. Curt." Kelly had to smile. She bet young cowboy Curt had been a heartbreaker back then.

Curt strode around the truck, clearly aiming to help Megan and Jayleen alight. No need, Kelly observed with a grin. Jayleen had already jumped down and was helping Megan make it to the ground. Jayleen, like Curt and Steve, wore her Stetson, and it fit her as naturally as her leather gloves. Colorado cowgirl, without a doubt.

Kelly glanced up at the sun. It was still early morning and not too hot. The wind hadn't kicked up yet, but it would. Wind was Wyoming's trademark. She adjusted her trusty USS *Kitty Hawk* baseball cap—her kind of hat.

Megan peered out at the landscape from under her floppy white sun hat, her face smeared with SPF 300+ sunscreen. "Wow, Kelly, look at all of this," she exclaimed.

Jayleen strolled over, hands shoved in her back pockets. "This is some spread you've got here, Kelly," she observed with a smile.

Curt walked up beside them, Steve and Jennifer close behind. He stared toward the mountains in the distance for a minute.

"Kelly-girl, you've got yourself a nice piece of property," he said, then clapped her on the shoulder. "Congratulations, you're now a rancher."

Kelly visibly flinched in reply, which made everyone laugh out loud. "It's so *big*. And it's got cows. *Lots* of cows."

"Cattle," Curt echoed Steve.

"Cows, cattle, whatever," Kelly said, rolling her eyes. "All I know is there're a lot of them. Over there." She pointed toward the mountains. "I swear, this place goes to the mountains."

"It's big, but it's not that big, Kelly. Those mountains are farther away than you think," Steve reminded.

"You've been out of the West too long, girl. Been working in those city canyons. Looking city pale, too. You've got that computer-green color around the edges," Curt observed with a sage nod.

"Hey, I'm working on it," Kelly protested with a laugh, holding up her arm. "I can't help it if my job makes me sit in front of a computer all day."

"I know what that's like," Jayleen chimed in, even though her ruddy complexion belied her fifty-some years. Even her sandy blonde hair revealed only a few strands of gray. "But I don't get on the computer till nighttime."

"Well, Steve, you ready to check out some cattle?" Curt asked.

"Yes, sir," Steve replied, squinting toward the mountains. "Wonder if that manager has some extra horses we could borrow. It'd be a lot easier on horseback."

"Sure would. Let's ask him." Curt said. "By the way, that's a fine-looking hat, son."

"Thank you. Had to replace my old one. It blew into the middle of a pigpen when I was helping some guy over in Greeley."

"Now that's a picture," Jayleen said, chuckling. "Sorry, couldn't help it."

"Please tell me we don't have pigs," Kelly begged.

Both Curt and Steve shook their heads. "You would have smelled them," Steve replied.

Kelly sniffed. "I smell something, and it's ripe."

Steve grinned. "That's the cattle."

"Oh, brother."

"Pigs are worse," Curt said.

"Much worse," Jayleen concurred, clearly enjoying Kelly's consternation.

A screen door slammed, and Kelly turned to the ranch house. A tall, lean young man bounded down the front steps.

"Whoa," Jennifer murmured beside her ear as the ranch manager drew nearer. "I pictured this manager guy being old and gray. Things are looking up."

"Hey, you're here to help me with the house, remember?" Kelly teased.

"Morning, folks. I'm Chet Brewster," the young man announced as he strode into their midst. "Mr. Chambers said you'd be driving up today."

Tall, lean, and ruggedly handsome, Brewster looked like he stepped right out of the cowboy storybooks—or at least, Cheyenne Frontier Days.

Curt stepped up, hand outstretched. "Chet, I'm Curt Stackhouse." He gestured to Kelly. "We're all friends of Kelly's, and we're here to help her take a look at this spread."

Kelly took that as her cue and reached for Brewster's hand. "I'm Kelly Flynn, Mr. Brewster. Pleased to meet you," she said with her brightest meet-the-client smile.

Chet chuckled. "Call me Chet, ma'am. My father's Mr. Brewster. And I'll be glad to show you folks around."

Ma'am? Kelly thought in surprise. Did she look old enough to be a ma'am?

Steve stepped up and introduced himself as well as the others, then added, "Do you have any horses we could use, Chet? It would be much faster to check out this herd on horseback."

"Oh, yes, sir. We sure do," Chet replied. "I kinda figured you might want that, so I've got three already saddled. Do you want to check out the sheep, too? They're over in the back pasture." He pointed behind him.

"We'll check those, too. How many have we got?" Curt asked.

"Over a hundred now, with the new lambs." He glanced to Kelly. "Are you riding with us, ma'am? I can saddle another."

"No, I don't think so, Chet," Kelly said. She hadn't ridden since she was a child and was sure she'd forgotten everything she ever knew. She'd probably fall off into a big, fresh cowpie. "That's why these guys are here."

Gesturing toward the house and barn, Chet said, "You and your friends are free to look at anything you want. House, barns, storage, pastures. I've got some coffee and doughnuts in the kitchen, too."

Kelly grinned. She liked this guy already. "Chet, you're a lifesaver."

Chet looked embarrassed. "It's nothing, ma'am. Make yourself at home. We won't be gone too long."

Jayleen stepped up. "I'm here to take a look at the alpacas, Chet. I can see where you've got the pastures separated, but I only see two animals. You got any more?"

"Yes, ma'am. We've got three more with one on the way," he said proudly, then pointed toward the garage. "The garage was turned into an alpaca barn. They go between the corral and pastures and the barn."

Jayleen turned to Kelly. "Not bad. You've got the start of a nice little herd. I'll know more when I see the paperwork on them. Registry papers and all that."

"Do you know where the owner kept his records, Chet?" Kelly asked. "Is there an office in the house where we can look for documents?"

"Sure is, ma'am," Chet said with a respectful nod. "Right off the front hallway on the right."

Kelly didn't know how much longer she could take the "ma'am" moniker. "We'll be looking at more than animals today. My friend, Jennifer, is a real estate agent, and she's come to do a market analysis of the property while we're here."

"Charmed, Mr. Brewster. Absolutely charmed," Jennifer said in a sultry voice as she offered her hand.

This time, Jayleen wasn't the only one staring at her boots to keep from laughing, Kelly noticed. She watched Cowboy Chet fall beneath Jennifer's spell. "Ummmm, glad to meet you, too, miss."

"Where're those horses, son?" Curt cut to the chase.

"Right this way, sir," Chet recovered quickly, pointing at the stable. "You ladies take care now," he added and tipped his hat as he followed after Curt and Steve.

"How come I'm a ma'am and you're a miss?" Kelly asked dramatically.

"You're his boss. You have to be a ma'am," Jennifer replied.

"That cowboy doesn't know what hit him," Megan predicted, then giggled.

Jayleen gave a loud laugh. "Damn, you girls are a hoot."

"Okay," Kelly said. "What do we tackle first?"

"We're closest to the alpaca barn, so why don't we start there?" Jayleen suggested as she headed toward the converted garage.

Kelly quickened her pace to keep up with Jayleen, who was already pushing the door open. A familiar smell of hay and feed greeted Kelly when she entered the barn. It was a little cooler, too, she noticed and wondered if the animals sought shelter from the brutal summer sun the same way humans did.

"There you are, little mom," Jayleen crooned to an ebony black alpaca in the large corner stall. Two alpacas stood beside her, one a creamy caramel color and another, milky white.

"Wow, they're pretty," Kelly remarked as she approached the stall. Jayleen was rubbing the pregnant female's nose, so Kelly extended her open hand, palm up, in case the alpaca wanted a sniff. The female took a tentative step forward and reached her long, graceful neck to sniff the tips of Kelly's fingers. It tickled, Kelly noticed.

"Good girl, make friends with your new owner. C'mon, you two," Jayleen continued in the same low, musical cadence as she beckoned the others over. "She's a beauty, Kelly. I can't wait to see who she's been bred to." Pointing to the others, she added, "And so are these two. Boy, I hope the owner has some pictures of them with their full coats before they were shorn."

"Do they bite?" Jennifer asked as she and Megan neared the stall.

Jayleen laughed. "They won't bite you. Go on, rub their noses." Both Megan and Jennifer extended their fingers to be sniffed.

"So, these alpacas look pretty good to you?" Kelly asked.

"Damn right, girl," Jayleen said. "But I want to see who they've been bred to and what the babies looked like." She bent down belly level with the animals. "Yep, I'm right. I thought these two are females. Good. They're worth a helluva lot more."

"Geri explained a little bit about how this business works," Kelly said, remembering. "You want female babies because they'll sell for more, and the better the sire, the better the colors of the babies' coats. Right?"

Jayleen grinned. "That's about it in a nutshell. That's why I'm hoping the owner kept pictures along with the records. Then, I can give you a much better idea of what this herd is worth."

Kelly glanced toward a second open door leading to a separate corral and watched the remaining two alpacas slowly approach. "Looks like we've got a gray and a dark brown."

"Smoky gray and chestnut. Good colors. Hey, I'm excited, almost like this is mine," Jayleen said, her tanned face creasing into a grin as she leaned over the other stall fence. "C'mon, you two, say hello. Bet you guys are the little boys, right?" she said as she bent to check. "Yep. You got yourself two young males, Kelly. Not old enough to breed yet, but they will be. They sure are pretty, too. Wonder what colors they'll throw."

Kelly rubbed the smoky gray nose of the closest male. To her surprise, he pushed his face toward hers. She jumped back.

"Don't be scared. He just wants a kiss, don't you, little boy." She shoved her face next to his, making kissing sounds. The smoky gray obliged. "Teenagers," Jayleen said with a laugh.

Kelly carefully leaned forward so the smoky gray could give her a half sniff, half kiss. "Tickles," she said.

"Boy, I really wish there were some fleeces left. I'm dying to know what these animals produce."

"Well, I think you've got your wish, Jayleen," Megan called from across the barn. She stood in the doorway of an adjoining room. "I see several bags of fleeces in here."

Jayleen let out a whoop and raced over, Kelly and Jennifer in her wake. "Doesn't take much to get her excited, does it?" Jennifer observed.

White plastic trash bags lined the floor, fleeces spilling over the sides. Caramel, charcoal, beige, and white, creamy white, and ebony. "Wow," Kelly said in admiration. "Look at that. Burt will be spinning into next year with all these bags."

Jayleen was already examining and fingering a charcoal gray fleece. She gently lifted it from the plastic bag. "Hey, help me with

this one. I think it's the entire blanket. We can unroll it over here."
She bent to one knee as the others did the same, and they slowly
unrolled the thick coat.

"Whoa, this is even thicker than I imagined," Megan said. "And
longer, too."

"That's why it's called a blanket," Jayleen explained. "It's shorn
in one piece from the shoulder to the flank. That way it looks better
for alpaca shows." She stroked the luscious wool. "This is a beauty.
Someone must have planned to enter it."

Kelly let her fingers indulge themselves in the lusciously soft
coat. The fibers were over six inches long and silky. "This really
looks good enough to show?"

"Damn right. You've got some excellent quality, Kelly. In fact,
you might think about entering next year's wool market." Jayleen
glanced to the other bags. "Let's see what else we've got here." She
started rolling up the charcoal blanket once more and slid it into
the plastic bag.

Kelly noticed the other side of the storage room was filled with
even more bags. Bags stacked on top of bags. Five alpacas couldn't
have produced all this, she thought. "Has he been storing these
fleeces for some reason? Why are there so many?"

"That's a good question," Jayleen said as she lifted two bags from
the stack and checked inside. One fleece looked palomino gold. The
other was long, white, and curly. "Well, of course," Jayleen said,
chuckling as she fingered the fleeces in both bags. "These are sheep
fleeces. We forgot about the sheep. Your luck is holding, Kelly.
These look real good, too."

In the fascination with the five-alpaca herd, Kelly had completely
forgotten over a hundred sheep. Yikes! Were there a hundred fleeces
in here? Burt would be spinning the rest of his life. She'd have to
put him on retainer.

Megan and Jennifer were already checking out the bags,
exclaiming over the softness. Kelly chose a bag filled with creamy
oatmeal-colored fleece and sank her hands down to her forearms in
the soft wool. Surprisingly soft. She fingered the fibers, then chose
another fleece, and another. Black, milky white, palomino gold. Each
time enjoying the rich lanolin that coated her hands afterward.

Jayleen pulled out a notepad and pen from her pocket and began scribbling away, counting and checking bags, peering into containers. Kelly felt slightly guilty for playing in the fleeces while Jayleen was actually doing something useful. Then she reminded herself she hadn't found a way to be useful on this ranch yet. In time, Kelly hoped she could learn what she needed. Meanwhile, she was grateful she'd brought experts who knew what they were doing.

"Do you have any idea what all this is worth?" Kelly asked Jayleen.

"A general idea, but I need to see the paperwork. See what the bloodlines are, check some invoices, all that stuff." Jayleen shoved the pad and pen into her back pocket.

"I think it's time we checked out the house and found that office Chet mentioned," Kelly said, rubbing the lanolin into her skin.

"Good idea," Jennifer said. "I need to take a look at the house. I printed out the public records info from the state website, so I can start with that. Plus, I've got recent sales data for this area of Wyoming. Land sizes, property descriptions."

"Did you bring a camera?" Kelly asked, snapping off the light as they left the storage room.

"Digital, plus extra memory card. I'm ready."

"Bye-bye, guys," Jayleen called to the alpacas watching them from the stall. The teenagers had returned to frolicking with each other outside.

The sun's bright glare hit Kelly as soon as they emerged from the barn. She pulled her hat down and squinted into the distance. She wasn't sure, but she thought she saw three men on horseback in the far pasture.

Jayleen shaded her eyes. "We'll let the guys count the sheep and cattle. We'll take care of the tricky stuff, right?"

"I'd be glad to help," Megan offered as they walked toward the ranch house. "I may not know anything about alpacas or real estate, but I can certainly sort through papers."

Kelly paused for a minute at the front steps of the large, two-story, white frame ranch house. A weather-beaten front porch stretched the width of the house. Two rockers and a glider sat invitingly, beckoning her out of the sun. She could picture herself sitting there drinking a lemonade like she did years ago as a child on Aunt Helen's shady patio.

Brother, where did that memory come from, she wondered? She shook it away. This property was going to be sold. She could not afford to become attached to it.

"Okay, team, here we go," she joked. "Jennifer, real estate. Jayleen, registrations of all four-legged residents on this ranch. Megan, you can help me with everything else."

Suddenly, a horrifying thought struck. Kelly cast her face to the heavens. "Please let there be a file cabinet and not cardboard boxes." With that, she ran up the steps, her friends following behind.

Thirteen

"**Found** another one," Megan announced, paging through the stack of papers on the floor. "This one says Ryeland. Do we have that breed yet?"

Kelly ran down the list she'd made of the various breeds of sheep. "Yeah, we've got that one. Put it in the pile to be copied. I'm going to have to make a binder with all these certificates and pictures. Otherwise I won't be able to remember which one is which."

She took a drink of the last of Chet's coffee. Not bad. Not great, either, but right now she couldn't be choosy. It was nearly noon, and she was hungry. She hoped the guys didn't return from their cattle tour with big appetites, because the doughnuts and coffee were long gone. She and the others had convinced themselves that sorting through disorganized files had a much higher stress level than riding the range looking at cows. Therefore, they deserved the doughnuts. But she didn't look forward to explaining her line of reasoning to the guys.

Kelly leaned back in the cushioned armchair. Sunlight poured through the windows of the cozy ranch house office. She glanced around the cluttered desk, file folders stacked on top of each other and on the floor. Both Jayleen and Megan sat in opposite corners, each surrounded by piles of paper. It had taken three hours for them to get this far, and Kelly estimated they'd only checked a third of the files in the cabinet.

Then, there was the desk itself. Kelly didn't want to think about that. She'd opened all four drawers earlier and found stacks of developed photographs, all wrapped in rubber bands with sticky notes attached. All those memories shoved in a drawer, she thought sadly.

She reached her arms over her head and stretched. "I'm hungry. How about you two?"

Megan nodded over her pile. "Oh, yeah."

"Maybe Chet has sandwich stuff in the fridge?" Jayleen suggested.

"He doesn't. I saw some eggs and things, that's all," Jennifer said, appearing in the doorway. She collapsed in a nearby chair. "Wonder if they deliver pizza out here."

"Dream on," Kelly said.

Megan looked up. "Well, if he's got eggs, I can take a break from sorting and make something for us. Let me take a look." She scrambled from the floor.

"Bless you," Kelly said. "We can't finish this office today anyway. There's simply too much. I'll have to spend a whole weekend here." She grimaced.

"Okay, let me see what I can find in the kitchen," Megan said as she left.

"At least we got all the alpaca certificates and most of the sheep and cattle info," Jayleen said as she set her stack of papers on a nearby table. "It's a good start, Kelly. Now we can come up with a rough idea of what these animals are worth."

"I can't tell you how much I appreciate your help, Jayleen. I'd be lost trying to figure out all this animal registry business." Glancing to Jennifer, Kelly asked, "How's your real estate survey going?"

"Except for a couple of shots of the pastures and views, I've got everything I need. I'll put it all together in the office and come up with a market analysis." She leaned forward. "Kelly, have you taken a good look at some of these furnishings? I think there're some antiques here. I'm not an expert, but I have a hunch. C'mon, let me show you."

"Go on, Kelly," Jayleen said, shooing her from the office. "I'm going to get these registry papers in some kind of order."

Kelly followed Jennifer into the living room, which was darkened by heavy green drapes drawn across the windows. She stood for a moment, letting her gaze drift across everything—glass china closets, overstuffed sofas, portraits and paintings with ornate frames hanging on the walls, end tables, tea tables covered with lace cloths and crocheted doilies, curio cabinets filled with porcelain and glass figurines.

Memories were everywhere. Kelly could feel them all around her. Here were Martha's memories, she thought, remembering Martha's spare and empty house in Landport. All of her memories had been left here. It looked to Kelly as if Martha's husband had kept the room exactly the way it was when Martha ran away four years ago. Kelly could smell the dust.

"Boy, I don't think he ever cleaned in here," she said. "The dust must be inches thick."

"Hey, it protects the furniture," Jennifer joked. "Take a look at this end table." She pulled back the white lace cloth that draped across the top. "Looks like mahogany. And it looks old. Just like that one over there." She pointed to a round table at the end of the sofa.

"I don't have a clue about antiques," Kelly admitted. "We'd have to have an appraiser give us an idea."

"Don't worry. The auction people have appraisers they work with. Believe me, they know antiques when they see them. I bet this place is filled with them."

"Auction? I thought you said I'd list it with a real estate agency."

"You'll list the *empty* house. That means you'll need to sell off everything inside. And from what I've seen today, these furnishings will bring in a fair amount of money." Jennifer gave a firm nod. "Those antique dealers are all over estate auctions like fleas on a dog."

Kelly pictured strangers pawing through Martha's treasured belongings. That didn't feel right somehow. Martha wouldn't like that. "I don't think I want people poking around Martha's house."

"They won't. Everything's moved outside. No one goes into the house except you and the auction people. I've been to several over the years. Believe me, they're well organized."

"I don't know," Kelly hesitated, glancing around at the lifetime of Martha's family memories. Even though they weren't her memories, Kelly still felt protective. "I'm going to have to think about this whole idea. Something about selling all of Martha's memories at auction . . . well, it doesn't seem right."

"You could always put them in storage, I suppose," Jennifer suggested. "Until you get a bigger place."

Kelly shook her head. "This is getting way too complicated. Sheep and alpacas are easier than this stuff. I'll think about it later."

"There's no rush, Kelly. Take all the time you need," Jennifer said. "I'll be outside finishing the pictures."

As Kelly headed away from the world of antiques and back to the stacks of paper, she noticed an enticing aroma wafting from the kitchen. Was that bacon? Kelly homed in on the delectable scent.

There was Megan, mixing bowl in one arm, vigorously stirring something. "Wow, you really are fixing breakfast," Kelly said in admiration.

"Well, I found a lot more than eggs in the fridge. Then I saw all the flour and baking stuff in the cabinet and decided I might as well make a big meal. We'll be driving around the ranch this afternoon, and we're all hungry."

Kelly grinned. "You are something else, Megan. I didn't know you could cook."

Megan looked up, a smudge of flour on her nose. "Oh, this isn't really cooking, it's just breakfast."

"Whatever you call it, it smells delicious, and you're a lifesaver." Sniffing the air again, she detected a tantalizing scent beneath the bacon. "Do I smell coffee?" she asked, salivating already.

"I made a fresh pot. I've seen you without caffeine, and it's seriously scary."

"I am forever in your debt." Kelly made a deep bow, then poured herself a cup before she headed to the sunlit office.

Jayleen was rearranging piles on the floor. "I finished sorting the alpaca certificates by date, and I've updated your sheep list with what we've got so far." She set the clipboard on the desk, then pulled up a straight chair and straddled it backward.

Kelly glanced at the list as she settled into the armchair. "This is great, Jayleen. It'll make the rest of my search so much easier."

"I actually enjoyed seeing what you've got," Jayleen said. "There're some good bloodlines here. If you decide to keep those two males, I'd like to see what they can produce. If it's half as pretty as those fleeces in storage, I may use 'em as studs. You set your price."

"For you, Jayleen, no charge."

Jayleen closed her eyes and shook her head. "Absolutely not. This is a business. You never let friendship or relationships interfere in business. I learned that from Vickie."

"She was a tough businesswoman, huh?" Kelly asked, curious.

"The toughest," Jayleen said as she looked out the window. "I remember when I was building my herd and didn't have money for prizewinning studs. I asked Vickie if her stud, Raja, could mate with my best female. Just once. I was hoping I'd get some of those gorgeous colors and another female to sell." A crooked smile twisted her mouth. "Vickie didn't even take a minute to think about it. She refused flat out. She'd put too much time and energy into building Raja's reputation to give away his services free."

"That must have been hard to take, considering you two are family and you're very close." Kelly could almost feel the rejection coming across.

Jayleen shrugged. "I understood. Vickie worked damn hard to build that herd. Besides, she helped me in other ways. She helped me build my bookkeeping business by loaning me money to buy all the computer equipment I needed to start up. I always paid her back, though, with interest."

"She charged you interest?"

"Sure did. Market rate, too. That's okay. It's business." Jayleen gave a firm nod in emphasis.

"Boy, she didn't cut you any slack, did she?" Kelly said, trying to square this version of Vickie with Debbie's account.

"Hey, nobody else would lend me money," Jayleen said. "I'd just come out of a rough patch in my life. Real rough. My credit was shot to hell, my job history was spotty. I had a chance to turn it around, and Vickie helped me do it."

"Is that when you came to Fort Connor?"

She nodded. "Yep. I sold my house and took every dime I could to buy the place in Landport and start my herd. I bought two females from Vickie and saved up money for stud fees."

Fascinated by her story, Kelly probed, "Is that when you started the bookkeeping business."

"Yeah. I was working two jobs in town and barely getting any sleep. Vickie suggested I could replace the income from the second job with my own business. She loaned me the money to start. It was rough the first year, but it's getting better every year." Jayleen smiled. "I'm actually earning money now."

"I'll bet Vickie helped you build your client base," Kelly said, already knowing the answer but curious what Jayleen would say.

"Absolutely. I couldn't have built it without her. Thanks to her, I've got enough clients so I don't have to work in town anymore." Jayleen gave another one of her decisive nods. "It's been worth every penny of commission."

The accounting lobe of Kelly's brain perked up. "Commission? Who're you paying commission to?"

"To Vickie, of course. She gets a cut of every client's total business. Plus I do her books for free."

Kelly stared wide-eyed at Jayleen. Whoa. She hadn't expected to hear something like that.

"Vickie told her friends about her arrangement with you, right?" she probed, watching Jayleen's face.

Surprise registered. "I guess so. I mean, she told me it was done all the time and not to worry about it." Jayleen's blue eyes became huge. "I didn't do anything wrong, did I?"

"No, Jayleen, you didn't do anything wrong," Kelly said with a reassuring smile. "But Vickie may have. She encouraged all her friends to use your services. And if she didn't tell them about the commissions she received from you, then she was effectively getting money under the table off their business. Without their knowledge."

"I never thought about that," Jayleen said, staring out the window. "Well, I guess it doesn't matter now. Vickie's dead."

Kelly stared out at the Medicine Bow range as it sliced rough and barren across the landscape. Treeless ridges, not like Colorado. She also noticed three horsemen near the barn. The guys had returned from their mini—cattle drive.

"Hey, look who's back," she said, pointing out the window. "Shall we go out and greet them? I've about had it with this paperwork."

"Sounds good to me," Jayleen said, swinging herself out of the chair in one movement. "Say, do I smell bacon?"

"Megan's making a big breakfast, bless her. I wasn't looking forward to explaining why the doughnuts were gone," Kelly said as they headed for the front door.

Jennifer was standing at the foot of the steps, camera in one hand, shading her eyes with the other. "Well, ah declare, the menfolk have arrived at last," she said, drawl dripping off her tongue.

Jayleen hooted. "Jennifer, you are something else."

"Well, thank you kindly, Miz Jayleen. I'm just hopin' that young handsome cowboy isn't too tuckered out by the ride. I'd like to visit with him," Jennifer drawled as she sashayed toward the barnyard.

Kelly and Jayleen followed after, not bothering to hide their laughter. "Which handsome young cowboy you talkin' about, Miz Jennifer? I see two of 'em," Jayleen teased.

"Why, that sweet little ol' Chet, of course. He's the only one not taken."

Kelly jumped on that comment like a grounder to infield. "Hey, Steve's not taken. He's free as a bird," she insisted. Jennifer ignored her, the menfolk clearly in her sights by now.

Kelly motioned to Jayleen. "Let's stand here and watch. Jennifer in full flirt is an experience to behold."

Jayleen chuckled. "Damn, that girl reminds me of me when I was younger. Lord, the trouble I used to get into." She shook her head. "And the bad habits I picked up along the way. Along with the men. Picked up a lot of those along the way, too."

Surprised how forthcoming Jayleen was about her past, Kelly decided to ask the same question she'd asked Debbie. "Is that what

I feel coming from Debbie? I sense she's uncomfortable around you, Jayleen. That surprised me, since you're all family."

Jayleen stared toward the mountains. "No surprise, Kelly. She remembers me from those bad times, when I was drinking." She let out a sigh. "I was an alcoholic back then. An ugly drunk. Vickie was the only one who cared enough to help me. She'd come get me and sober me up, let me stay with her. And, of course, Debbie saw all that. I guess she's never forgiven me." Her voice drifted off.

Kelly reached out and put her hand on Jayleen's arm. "Sounds like you've put all that behind you, Jayleen, and built a whole new life. You're to be congratulated—at least in my book."

Jayleen gave her a shy grin. "Thanks, Kelly. I've been sober ten years. You're right, it's a whole new life. Tough sometimes, but I wouldn't trade it for those highs and lows like before."

Jennifer and the "menfolk" approached, and Kelly noticed that Chet was already ensnared in Jennifer's spell. He strolled beside her, grinning boyishly, while Jennifer talked. Curt and Steve, however, looked like they were trying their best not to laugh out loud.

"Back from the range, huh?" Kelly greeted them. "Those cows stand still long enough for you to count them?"

"Nah, we brought 'em back here for you." Steve said. "They're your cattle. You can count 'em."

Sure enough, Kelly spotted black shapes coming across the pasture. Cow shapes, headed her way. "You did that on purpose, didn't you?"

Steve grinned slyly. "Curt and I thought you needed to spend some quality time with your cattle."

"Riiiight. Like I'm going to climb over the fence and start petting them. I'd just step in a fresh cowpie and mess up Ruth's boots."

"You got nothing to fear, ma'am," Chet offered earnestly. "Cattle are pretty docile unless you rile 'em up."

"Where's the bull?" Jayleen asked, surveying the pastures.

"Old Cujo is out there, ma'am. He'll be in when he wants to. Now, he has a pretty bad temper, but I don't reckon you'll be patting him." Chet grinned.

"Why didn't you bring in the sheep?" Kelly asked, peering into the far meadow. She could see the sheep grazing. "Sheep don't scare me. I'll pat them."

"We'll see all the sheep you want, Kelly, right after we've had something to eat," Curt said as he took Kelly by the elbow and led her toward the house. "Right now, we're going to find those pizzas Chet's got in the freezer. We've worked up quite an appetite out there."

"Any chance there's a doughnut left?" Steve asked.

"Nary a one, Mistah Steve," Jennifer said. "Kelly ate them all."

"Did not. Scarlett finished off her share."

"Lies, all lies." Jennifer fanned herself with the property description.

"Sorting through those files really wore you out, huh?" Steve said.

"Don't start," Kelly warned as they approached the front steps. "Nothing was in order. It was a big mess—"

"Hey, everybody," Megan called from the doorway. She'd found an apron from somewhere and looked positively adorable, standing there like she stepped right out of a magazine ad from yesteryear. "Breakfast is almost ready. Bacon's done and the biscuits are baking. But I could use some help setting the table while I scramble the eggs." Without waiting for a reply, Megan disappeared inside once again. The screen door slammed shut.

"Did she say biscuits?" Chet asked.

"She sure did, son."

"Oh, lord."

Kelly watched all three men race up the front steps, jostling each other as they crowded through the doorway, clearly eager to be the first one to offer his assistance to the cute cook. Imagine that, Kelly mused. Biscuits can beat out sex.

"Well, I nevah." Jennifer frowned, hand on hip. "I guess the way to a man's heart is truly through his stomach."

Jayleen laughed. "Gals, we'd better get in there now before the menfolk eat it all."

You know, after that breakfast, we should be running around this ranch, rather than driving," Kelly said, as Steve's truck bounced over the pasture.

"I don't think I'd get very far," Steve said. "Not after all those biscuits."

Kelly laughed. "Yeah, I noticed you had your share plus half of mine."

"Hey, you finished the doughnuts, remember?" Steve countered.

Jayleen chuckled. "You two are something else."

Kelly heard a certain tone in Jayleen's voice but kept her mouth shut. What was it about people that made them want to pair others up? Like they were filling some modern-day Noah's ark. Kelly wasn't having any of it.

"Have to admit I never did quite get the hang of biscuits," Jayleen said. "I can grill up a steak and fix a mean chili, but biscuits? Never got the knack."

"You don't need a knack," Kelly teased. "You go to the refrigerator case in the store and buy them. They're in little cans that you whack against the counter. They practically jump right into the pan, ready to bake."

After she stopped laughing, Jayleen added, "Kelly, you'd be running all day to see this place. Seven thousand acres stretches quite a ways. We've been driving for an hour, and we're still on your land."

Kelly stared out the window, amazed again at the amount of property that would soon be hers. She looked to the west. The Medicine Bow Mountains cut across the horizon, rough and rugged. The Sierra Madres and Continental Divide loomed behind, aching for winter's touch.

Martha was right. This land would make a beautiful natural area with its abundance of antelope and jackrabbits, coyotes and prairie dogs, songbirds and hawks, and all the myriad smaller wildlife that scurried and hunted in the day and in the dark. It would be perfect. But what would she do about the house? Would she section off the house and barns and sell them? Would she keep everything else as the natural area? Could she accomplish both? And what if they found oil and gas? What would she do then?

She couldn't think about all that now. She had her hands full wondering what to do with all the cattle, sheep, and alpacas. Should she sell some? If so, how many? Cattle, sheep, or both? Kelly had already started thinking about keeping the alpacas after Jayleen's enthusiastic description of their bloodlines. Plus, Kelly had to admit she loved those fleeces.

Oh, brother. She forgot the fleeces. She'd have to hire Ruth to clean and mill and spin some of them. She'd give Mimi first choice of which ones she'd like to buy. Then she'd give a bag to Lisa and Megan and Jennifer and two bags to Burt. Oh, and a bag each to Lizzie and Hilda.

Remembering the old nursery rhyme from childhood, she almost laughed. *Baa, baa, black sheep, have you any wool? Yes sir, yes sir, three bags full.* Kelly had much more than three bags, for sure, and recalled Ruth's comment about selling them online.

"You know, Curt's wife, Ruth, said I could sell fleeces online to spinners. Do you think that's a good idea?"

"You bet you can," Jayleen replied. "You should save any you want for next spring's wool market, then offer the rest to spinners and weavers. Same goes for the alpaca fleeces. And I can help clean and spin some if you're in a bind."

Watching Chet's gray pickup turn to the right up ahead, Kelly figured they were coming up beside the sheep pasture again, which meant they'd circled the ranch as well as crisscrossed it twice. Spotting sheep in the distance, Kelly asked, "What do you think, Steve? How many of these cows and sheep do we sell?"

"Curt and I are still thinking about that," he said, steering around a low bush. "There's some good quality here, so you'd get a decent price. Curt's going to draw up a spreadsheet, then we'll have a better idea."

Kelly stared at him like he'd sprouted horns. "*Spreadsheet?* You've got to be kidding. For cows and sheep?"

Steve grinned at her. "Modern-day ranching, Kelly. Get used to it."

She rolled her eyes. "Oh, great. More office work. That's all I need. I already spend most of my life on the computer."

"You can always hire it out," Jayleen suggested.

"Great idea," Kelly enthused. "I can pay you to do it."

Jayleen shook her head. "I don't do cattle operations, Kelly. I don't know enough about it."

"And I do?" Kelly exclaimed. "I don't even know enough to call them by their right names. Cows. Cattle. Whatever."

"Don't even worry about it, Kelly," Steve said. "You told me Lawrence Chambers already has an accounting firm doing the financial work now. You can keep using them until you've decided what you want to do with the ranch. Keep it, sell it, donate it, or a combination of all three."

That got her interest. "I could do all three?"

"Sure you can. But don't even start thinking about that yet, because everything could change if there's oil and gas on the property."

Kelly had momentarily forgotten about that scenario. She'd been focusing on what she could see on top of the land—the sheep and cattle—totally ignoring what might lie beneath.

"Whoa, oil and gas," Jayleen said, then whistled. "You're right. That would change everything."

"You mean I couldn't donate it?"

"Sure you could," Steve said. "You only lease the mineral rights below the ground. You still own the land. You could still designate land as a protected area if you want. Who knows? You might even want to keep some of those sheep and cattle. Jayleen said you've got some real good breeds. Curt's eyes lit up when she mentioned a couple." He laughed.

"He can have any sheep he wants," Kelly declared.

"He probably doesn't want to buy any, Kelly," Jayleen spoke up. "Most likely he wants to use your rams' services."

Kelly still hadn't integrated the concept of earning money when certain animals mated. Not only would she have to keep track of their food and shelter, but she'd also have to monitor what they did in their spare time.

"I notice you didn't mention selling off the alpacas," Steve said with a smile. "Thinking about keeping them?"

She nodded. "I'm thinking about it. Those fleeces are beautiful."

"I told you," Jayleen teased. "It's contagious."

Kelly watched Chet holding the long metal gate open for them to exit the pasture and head back to the barnyard. Tour was over. She glanced at her watch. After three o'clock. If they left for Fort Connor now, she and Megan could still make ball practice tonight. Dinner would have to be a drive-through on the road. Unfortunately, she didn't remember seeing much in the way of food along the road.

Steve pulled his truck to a stop and opened his door. "Okay, quick stop before we head back to town. I've got practice tonight. How about you, Kelly?"

"Yep. Megan and I have to be at the ball field by six," she said, sliding out of the truck and into a gust of wind. She grabbed her *Kitty Hawk* cap before it blew into the nearby corral. The corral was now filled with cattle. Where there were cows, there were cowpies.

"You two are gonna play ball tonight?" Jayleen asked, stretching. "Boy, you make me feel my age. I've gotta go home and take care of my animals and Vickie's, then do my accounts. I plan to fall on the sofa after that."

Remembering an earlier comment, Kelly asked, "Is Raja acting okay? You said he was acting funny for a while."

Jayleen stared toward the back pasture where Curt's truck could be seen in the distance. "You know, he is, and he isn't. He's acting fine for a couple days, then I swear, he starts acting skittish again. I can't figure it out. And truth be told, I just haven't had the time to spend with the animals like I used to. Not right now. I've gotten a new bookkeeping client, and I'm staying up till two a.m. to set up his accounts."

"That sounds familiar," Kelley commiserated.

"Did you like what you saw, ma'am?" Chet asked as he joined them. "I've been trying real hard to take good care of it. It sure is a nice spread."

"I want to thank you again for the fine job you've done, Chet," she reassured, giving him her brightest smile. "I also appreciate your explaining things to me so I didn't feel stupid."

"Thank you kindly, ma'am," Chet said with a blush. "Do you, uh, have you decided yet what you're going to do? Are you going to sell it, you think?"

Kelly shook her head. "No, I haven't, and I probably won't decide for a while, Chet, so I hope you can continue on here as manager."

Chet beamed. "It would be a pleasure, ma'am."

Curt pulled his truck alongside them and jumped to the ground. Kelly noticed Chet was right at the door to assist Jennifer and Megan.

"The bull looks pretty good," Curt gestured to the corral as he approached. "Good bloodlines from what Jayleen told me."

Kelly stared toward the corral, peering at the cattle, trying to figure out which one was . . . whoa. That had to be him. Her gaze settled on a huge black steer with horns jutting out as thick as a man's arm. Almost as if he knew she was observing him, the bull turned toward Kelly and stared. Scowled would be more like it. He certainly didn't look friendly. The bull snorted and swiped his paw on the ground once, as if announcing who was the one in charge.

"Cujo, is that his name?" Kelly asked. "Surely he's got another name. Those alpacas and sheep have fancy names, and they're not even half his size."

"He's got a name almost as long as he is," Jayleen said. "Can't remember what it is, but I saw it on the certificate."

"That reminds me. I want to take a quick look at those registry records again," Curt said, settling his hat tighter on his head. "Is that okay with you folks? I know you and Megan have to get back into town for ball practice."

"Go ahead, Curt. Check all the papers you need. We'll wait for you here," Kelly said.

"Jayleen, I'm going to need your help. You still got that list?"

Jayleen slipped the notepad from her pocket. "Sure do."

Glancing over his shoulder at the threesome near the truck, Curt called out, "C'mon, son. I need to take another look at those sheep after I check the records." He headed toward the house with Jayleen right behind him, while Chet gave Megan a big smile before he followed after.

"Looks like I have time to make a few calls," Steve said, flipping a cell phone from his pocket. "Provided I find a signal." He walked toward the barn.

"Let me know if you find one," Jennifer called as she and Megan joined Kelly at the corral fence. "I've got to check in with my office. My cell's coming up blank."

Kelly wasn't sure, but she thought Megan looked a little flushed under her floppy sun hat. "Don't worry, Megan. We can make it back in time for practice," she said, hoping to distract an attack of Megan's super shyness. A gust of wind pulled at her hat, and she gave it another tug.

"Curt's really impressed with the ranch, Kelly," Megan said.

"I mean, he was telling us all about different breeds of cattle and sheep. He knows all about them. Boy, he's a walking dictionary. It was fascinating, right, Jennifer?"

"He lost me after he explained how you cross one sheep with another."

"Actually, it was—" Megan cut her sentence short when another wind gust lifted her floppy sun hat and sent it sailing right into the corral. It landed right beside a large squishy cowpie.

"Oooops," Jennifer said, laughter escaping.

"Whoa! I just bought that yesterday!" Megan protested, clearly irate that her hat was about to become a cow doormat.

Kelly was about to say something reassuring when Megan spun about and climbed up and over the fence in seconds. Horrified, Kelly called out, "Megan, don't!"

It was too late. Megan had already jumped to the ground and raced across the corral to fetch her hat. Unfortunately, Cujo had also noticed the sun hat and the girl racing to get it. The huge bull snorted, pawing the ground.

Kelly didn't think twice. She scaled the fence and called out, "Megan, stop. Don't move," she ordered as she swung her leg over and dropped to the ground. Cujo lowered his big head and fixed Kelly with an angry glare.

Megan stood, seemingly immobilized at the sight of the bull across the corral, her face as white as the hat dangling from her hand.

Kelly slowly inched toward her, hoping to catch her attention as well as distract Cujo's. "Megan, back away and head for the fence," she warned. "Back away, now. . . ."

Suddenly another shape appeared at the corner of her eye. Steve dropped to the ground and let out a loud whoop, waving his hat in the air. Cujo spotted the moving Stetson and snorted in Steve's direction.

Megan snapped out of her trance just as Kelly grabbed her arm, and they both took off for the fence. Megan scrambled over and threw herself onto the ground. Kelly grabbed the top of the fence just as Cujo let out a ferocious bellow. She swiveled around to check on Steve and nearly lost her grip. Steve let out one last whoop and tossed his hat right in front of the angry bull, then took off for the fence. Cujo charged the hat with a vengeance.

Kelly swung her leg over and climbed down. Steve was already helping a shaken Megan to her feet. The slam of a screen door brought Curt, Jayleen, and Chet running from the house.

"What in Sam Hill happened? I heard that bull roar," Curt demanded as he strode up, looking all the world like an irate father about to break up a rowdy teenage slumber party.

The three participants stood silent while Jennifer spoke up. "The wind blew off Megan's hat into the corral, and she climbed over the fence to get it—"

Chet's eyes nearly popped out. "Megan, you climbed in with that bull!"

"I didn't see him," she squeaked, clearly too scared to be embarrassed.

"And then Kelly climbed in to rescue Megan. Then Steve climbed in to rescue both of them. He distracted the bull long enough for Kelly and Megan to escape. But he sacrificed his new hat to do it."

Curt peered at both Kelly and Megan for a few seconds, and Kelly could tell he was dying to deliver a scolding lecture on using common sense. Instead, Curt took a deep breath and stared at the corral and Cujo and the flattened Stetson that lay at the bull's feet. Stomped flat. "That's a shame, son. It was a fine hat."

"Yes sir, it was," Steve agreed, staring into the corral.

Kelly saw Jayleen turn her head to keep from laughing. Chet, however, still looked appalled at what they'd done. "I'll get your hat, sir. Just let me move these steers along." He hurried over to the corral and started that same waving motion Steve had used.

Megan grabbed Steve's arm, the reality of what happened clearly settling in. "Oh, Steve, thank you, thank you, thank you! We would have been killed if you hadn't jumped in and caught that bull's attention."

"Thanks doesn't do it, Steve," Kelly said when she caught his eye. "Cujo would have stomped us instead of the hat. One of us for sure."

Megan shuddered. "Oh, my gosh. I can't believe I did something that stupid. We could have all been hurt!"

"Well, I, for one, think both of you owe Mistah Steve a new hat, don't you folks?" Jennifer said with a wicked smile. "Mercy, Mistah Steve, you managed to save two damsels in one fell swoop."

Steve laughed. "Actually, Kelly distracted Cujo long enough for Megan to escape. I jumped in to make sure Kelly didn't try to argue with him instead of running like hell."

This time, everyone laughed out loud, and Kelly didn't mind a bit being the subject. She felt the accumulated tension from the entire day release. "I was about to thank you again until you said that," she teased.

"I sure am sorry, sir," Chet said as he walked up, a crushed Stetson in his outstretched hand. "He stomped it pretty good."

Steve took the remains of his hat and popped the brim out. Casualty of the range. A bent and broken reflection of its former self. He exhaled a dramatic sigh. "It sure has been a bad month for hats."

Fourteen

Kelly stood in the middle of the asphalt parking lot and stared up at the pink stucco building's bright neon sign. "You sure this place has carryout? It looks like a casino." She reached her arms high overhead in a long stretch. It felt like she'd spent the whole day in a truck.

"It is a casino, but it also has a restaurant and hotel," Jayleen said. "I stopped here one night with a bunch of local breeders when a storm blew in. You know how this road gets in the winter."

"Well, at least it's more interesting than fast food," Kelly said, watching Curt and the others walk up. "Is it like Blackhawk and Central City?"

Jayleen shook her head. "No, not even close. It has slots and poker games, but that's all. Nothing fancy like those places."

"Casino, huh?" Jennifer said, as they approached. "Too bad I'm strapped for cash right now."

"You're always strapped for cash," Megan joked. "And you work two jobs. How do you manage that?"

"It takes concentration and consistent, steady spending," Jennifer replied.

"Hate to disappoint any of you who're gamblers, but we don't have time to play. We're gonna have to grab the food and go," Curt said, running a hand through his pewter gray hair.

"Accountants make lousy gamblers anyway," Kelly confessed as they headed for the casino entrance.

"I've gambled enough on my business," Jayleen said, grinning.

Steve slipped his cell phone back into his pocket as he stepped forward and opened the door for everyone. "Same here, Jayleen."

The sight of the phone jiggled Kelly's memory. She needed to call Debbie and check if those faxes had come in from the investment account. Debbie had called yesterday, so they should be there. With luck, she might be able to finish Vickie's accounts by this weekend. This double workload was beginning to pinch, and Kelly was feeling the pressure build. The sooner she could finish the work for Debbie, the better.

"I'll join you in a minute," she said and flipped open her phone. No signal. "Steve, can I use your cell phone, please? Mine's out of range."

"Sure thing," he said, handing it over. "Want us to order you something?"

"Thanks. Get me a cheeseburger, fries, and a diet soda, please. I'll be right in."

Kelly headed back into the casino parking lot, which was crowded already. The late afternoon sun was as brutal as midday in July, so Kelly searched for a bit of shade in the wide open. The casino had been planted right on the prairie land, only a stone's throw from the main highway into Fort Connor. Not a tree for miles. She found a sliver of shade beside Steve's truck and leaned against it while she dialed Debbie's number.

The phone rang several times, then finally switched to voice mail. She left a brief message, asking about the faxes and reminding Debbie that she'd meet her at the ranch tomorrow.

Kelly flipped the cell closed and was about to head back into the casino when she spotted Geri Norbert, exiting the casino from a side door. She started to call out a greeting until she spotted the expression on Geri's face as she strode to her truck.

Anger? Fear? A mixture of both? Whatever it was, it held Kelly in place. Instead of calling out, she stared as Geri slammed her truck door, gunned the engine, and roared out of the parking lot. Her truck turned south, Kelly noticed, back toward Fort Connor.

What on earth was wrong? Kelly wondered. Geri seemed to ooze calm and control, a cool self-assurance. Whatever had happened to upset her so?

Kelly entered the casino and glanced about for her friends. An expansive lobby opened in two directions—hotel, one way, casino and restaurant, the other. Kelly saw Jayleen hovering on the edge of the casino, while Megan and Jennifer strolled through the slot-filled aisles.

The brightly lit, mirrored room was nearly filled. Every machine had a person seated in front. Continuous, artificial machine-music filled the air, tinkling and jingling, punctuated by other game noises, honks, bongs, and bells. As Kelly drew beside Jayleen, she also detected the distinct sound that was so dear to every gambler's heart: *Ka-ching, ka-ching.*

"The guys are in the café." Jayleen gestured toward the casino room. "They always put the restaurant on the other side so you have to walk through to eat."

"Not much of a gambler, huh?" Kelly asked, noticing her hovering on the edge of the room. "Neither am I. I take a certain amount, use it, then leave. I'm not much fun."

"It's not the gambling that keeps me out," Jayleen said. "It's the liquor. The bar's in there, and of course, they bring drinks right to the machines for you. I can't be around that."

"Even after ten years?"

Jayleen nodded. "You never stop being an alcoholic, Kelly. That's why I still go to my meetings."

"You know, I just saw Geri Norbert outside when I was making my phone call," Kelly said, changing the subject. "She didn't see me, though. I was going to say hello, but she looked mad or something. She looked strange. Is she all right?"

Jayleen stared at Kelly solemnly for a moment, then glanced at her boots. "You sure it was her?"

"Positive. It was her truck, too."

"That is too damn bad, then," Jayleen said, shaking her head.

Something in the sound of Jayleen's voice set Kelly's instincts humming. "What's the matter? Is she a closet gambler or something?"

"Yeah, I guess you could call it that, although I don't think any addiction can be kept in the closet. Sooner or later, it's gonna come out and bite you in the butt."

"Brother, that's a surprise," Kelly said, sorting through all the images she had of Geri and trying to make these new pieces fit in the puzzle. "She always looked and acted so controlled and all."

Jayleen gave her a rueful smile. "The key word is 'acted,' Kelly. We learn to conceal what we're doing and what it's doing to us." She wagged her head sadly. "I thought she'd stopped. Vickie told me that Geri had sworn to her she stopped. And that was two years ago."

"Did Vickie try to help her like she helped you?" Kelly probed.

"She sure did. She loaned Geri money to make her mortgage payments when she was behind. Geri would have lost her house and land if Vickie hadn't done that."

"Same loan arrangements you had, right," Kelly continued, curious if Vickie showed favoritism between friends and family.

"Not quite. Geri didn't have another income like I did, so Vickie loaned her the money and had it secured by a lien against Geri's property. Kind of like a second mortgage. Geri made monthly payments, market rate, of course. I know because I deposit all the checks."

"Did she pay on time?"

Jayleen nodded. "Last year, she did. But she's been late several times this year. I remember Vickie being upset about that, too. She didn't like waiting for her money. That's why I always paid on time every month."

"Boy, if she'd nearly lost her property once, why would she risk gambling again? You'd think it would have scared her away," Kelly mused out loud, watching Jennifer walk toward them.

"Being scared doesn't even faze you, Kelly," Jayleen explained. "When you have an addiction, nothing else matters. It's a compulsion. And you've gotta admit you've got it before you can cure it. I offered to take Geri to the weekly meetings they have in town for gamblers. But she almost bit my head off for suggesting it. Boy, I wish I'd tried again."

"Hey, what are you two so serious about?" Jennifer asked as she strolled up.

"Nothing much," Jayleen said and walked toward the ladies' room.

"Something I said?" Jennifer asked, pointing.

"No, I just saw a friend come out of the casino, and Jayleen told me she's a compulsive gambler who'd promised to stop. Now I'm worried about her," Kelly explained without saying too much.

Something in the back of her mind niggled at her. What was it? Something Geri had said when they were talking once. What was it? She'd remembered it for some reason. The day Geri came to the shop and introduced herself, wanting to hear all the details about Vickie's death. She recalled Geri saying, "My luck is about to change." When Kelly asked what luck had to do with the alpaca business, Geri had given her a sly grin and replied, "More than you think." There was something behind that grin that had bothered Kelly. Now, she wondered if Geri was talking about gambling and dreaming of "a big win."

"I've heard that's a hard habit to break," Jennifer said with a sympathetic nod. "I'm sorry for your friend."

Kelly stared out into the casino. She liked Geri a lot, and she didn't like the thoughts going through her mind right now. Maybe she was jumping to conclusions. Maybe there was another reason Geri was here this afternoon. Kelly wished there was some way she could know for sure. Perhaps she could ask someone here at the casino. Surely they would remember regular players.

She turned to Jennifer, an idea forming. "You know, I don't want to jump to conclusions about my friend. I want to find out. But I'm going to need your help."

"Sure. What do you want me to do?"

"They must have a bartender here, I bet. Why don't you go and chat him up and ask him about my friend. Tall older woman with dark hair in a braid down her back. She just left. She was wearing a red top with jeans. Find out if she comes here often. Say you were surprised she came here, blah, blah, maybe you two can share a ride next time, you know, whatever works."

"Don't worry. I know how to handle it, but I'm curious. Why don't you go ask him?"

Kelly grinned. "Because you're ever so much better at getting guys to talk to you than I am. You're a master."

"So let me get this straight. You're ordering me to flirt? On command?"

"If you would, please. Pretty please."

Jennifer gave a dramatic sigh. "Well, if you insist. See you later. Don't let anyone eat my chili burger." She headed for the far side of the room where Kelly glimpsed the bar.

"Where's she off to?" Jayleen asked when she returned.

"I sent her on a mission to pump the bartender. I figured he might know if Geri was a regular customer," Kelly explained. "I wanted to make sure we weren't making assumptions."

"That was smart," Jayleen said. "I remember lots of gamblers at the bar with me in the old days. They'd drink after they won, and they'd drink after they lost. Usually, they drank a lot after they lost."

"I like Geri a lot, Jayleen, and I don't want to jump to conclusions. Maybe she was here for some other reason."

"Boy, I hope we're wrong, but after your seeing her here today, I've got this bad feeling I can't shake."

"Me, too," Kelly confessed. "That's why I sent Jennifer in there to flirt and find out."

"Flirt and find out?" Jayleen said, smile winning out.

"Yes, I ordered her to go—"

"Hey, Kelly, go help Steve, will you?" Megan said as she approached them, hands filled with carryout bags. "He's got most of the orders. We're still waiting on a couple."

The unmistakable aroma of french fries permeated through the bags and straight to Kelly's nose. Her stomach growled on cue. "C'mon," she beckoned Jayleen. "We don't want the guys lifting all those heavy burger bags all by themselves."

"Curt gave me his key, so I'm putting these bags in the truck. Soon as we've got everything, we can leave," Megan called over her shoulder as she headed for the door.

"Why don't you help Megan. I'll help the guys," Kelly suggested to Jayleen as she turned toward the restaurant.

She found Steve and Curt leaning against the takeout counter, waiting for the last of the orders. Kelly wasn't the least upset at the delay. After all, even a consummate flirt like Jennifer needed a little time to extract information. Waiting patiently, however, was not one of Curt's strengths, so she tried to distract him with the continuing saga of Carl and the golf balls. Curt seemed mildly amused, but nothing really worked until the orders arrived. Then Curt was all smiles and heading for the door.

Kelly deliberately lagged behind her hungry friends, hoping to spot Jennifer, when she scurried up from the side and fell into step.

"Here, let me help you carry these. That way I can steal some fries," Jennifer said as she reached for a bag. "Flirting for hire has its costs."

"Did you find out anything?" Kelly probed. "Did he remember her?"

Jennifer nodded, as she popped fries into her mouth. "Oh, yeah," she said when she could. "She comes regularly. Usually comes at night, though. He was surprised to see her this afternoon."

Kelly pushed through the entrance doors, her worries about Geri solidifying. "Darn, I was hoping it wasn't true," she said sadly as they crossed the hot asphalt. Heat shimmered off the surface at this hour.

"I know, Kelly. And I can tell you want to help her, but you can't. She has to do it."

Everything Jennifer said was true. Kelly knew it. But she didn't have to like it.

Kelly wiped sweat from her forehead and adjusted her *Kitty Hawk* cap. This was getting painful. The Greeley team's best batter was at the plate again. He'd probably hit another homer and bring in the runners on second and third, just like he did last time, she thought dismally.

She couldn't believe how badly her team was playing. Lisa couldn't throw a strike, the catcher dropped crucial throws, the infield bobbled balls, and the basemen dropped them. Everybody stunk tonight. Kelly couldn't understand it. When she and Megan starting dropping balls, she chalked it up to their road trip to Wyoming.

Hours in a truck must have dulled their edge. But then everyone on the team started messing up, as if it were contagious or something.

Crack. The batter popped the ball high and took off for first. Kelly's foot instinctively touched the base as she watched the ball land foul. Maybe their luck would change. Maybe the other team's bats would go cold. Maybe she could get a hit this time rather than strike out. Maybe—

The batter connected on Lisa's next pitch, and Kelly squinted her eyes into the setting sun as she watched the ball sail up, up, up as if it were headed for the foothills. She exhaled an exhausted sigh. And then again, maybe not.

"I still can't believe how badly we played," Sherrie said, staring morosely at her beer.

"We stunk pretty bad," Kelly commiserated before she took a sip of her favorite ale, Fort Connor's pride and joy. The prizewinning ale slid down her throat, bringing its familiar and welcome tang. Even better, it was icy cold. "Whatever it was tonight, we were all off," she added.

Kelly leaned back in the outdoor café's metal chair and let the summer night settle over her. Glancing around the plaza of Fort Connor's quaint Old Town, she saw other groups like hers—friends out together on a summer night, sharing stories, celebrating victories and consoling defeats, enjoying each other. Enjoying the sweet summer languor that drifted by in the night breeze like the delicate white gauze from the cottonwood trees.

She liked it best like this, before the nightlife arrived in full force, ready to dance till dawn . . . or as long as the management would allow. Kelly didn't know how Jennifer did it. There was no way Kelly could keep numbers straight if she'd spent the whole night partying. She'd never been much of a partier, even in college. Wild binges and overdrinking never had appealed to Kelly. She liked being able to remember what she did the night before and not be embarrassed. That type of partying had never looked like fun to her.

Face it, maybe you're just boring, that insidious little voice in the back of her mind whispered. Kelly pondered that. Maybe she was. She'd always noticed the "wild and crazy" guys steered a wide path around her, even in college. Of course, that drop-dead-you-moron look she cast their way probably had something to do with it. It was fine with Kelly if they stayed away. Those guys seemed so childish. She always felt more grown-up than a lot of her peers. Maybe that was it. She was older. She was surely getting older. The Big 3-0 loomed this fall. Ye Gods!

Megan's voice caught her attention. "Personally, I think it was the bull's fault. My whole timing was off after that."

Kelly joined her teammates and their shared laughter around the table.

Steve came up to their table and leaned over Megan. "Well, I'm glad you guys have something to celebrate. We were whipped bad tonight," he complained.

"Us, too. We're just celebrating the bull," Megan joked. "Hey, let's toast Steve. He saved Kelly and me today."

Mugs and glasses were raised all around amid cheers and more laughter. "You're a good man, Steve," Kelly said, raising her glass before she drained it.

"Thanks, thanks, but I was just trying to get a workout after chowing down on Megan's biscuits. Those are lethal. Hey, maybe that's why we all lost tonight," he said with a wicked grin.

"Megan, don't you dare bake again," Kelly teased as she pushed back her chair and rose to leave. "See you guys later."

Waving good-bye to Megan and her teammates, Kelly started off through the plaza. Steve fell in beside her, she noticed.

"Hey, I've been thinking about old Carl's predicament, and I've got an idea that might get my buddy out of bondage," he said.

"Tell me, because Captive Carl is really laying on the guilt. I know he's running around when I'm not there, but whenever he sees me, he falls on the ground and lies there. Mister Morose."

Steve laughed. "What you need is something that will keep him from climbing over the fence, that's all. So you could either use a hot wire, you know, electrify the fence—"

"He'd get fried!" Kelly exclaimed as they walked through the adjoining streets lined with boutique shops of every description.

"All it takes is a couple of zaps, and dogs get the message. After a month or so, you could probably turn it off."

Kelly pictured Carl getting zapped and didn't like it. Plus, the image of a month's worth of fried squirrels piling up on her lawn wasn't appealing. Even Carl would get tired of squirrel.

"Ooooh, I don't know about zapping." She shuddered.

"Then you could have angle arms installed and string fence wire around the top. That always works with climbing dogs. The arms angle in and keep the dog from reaching the top. They try, but they always fall off."

That idea sounded better. "They don't hurt themselves falling off?"

Steve shook his head. "Nah, they don't get that far up. It's the angled wire that keeps them in."

"That sounds promising," she said. "Is it expensive?"

"Not that bad, and cheaper than repeated court fines," he said with a grin. "I can give you the name of one of my contractors who does fencing. He'll give you an estimate. He's good, and he's fair."

"Boy, you have a contractor for everything," Kelly teased as they rounded a corner. "My car's parked down here. Where are you parked?"

"One street over," he said, pointing behind him, but staring at the building across the street from them.

"Something wrong?" she asked, watching him stare for a full minute.

"Nope, just dreaming," he said. "I've always thought about what I'd like to do with this building."

Kelly scrutinized the dilapidated old warehouse that occupied half of the small block. "Is it for sale?"

Steve shook his head. "No, a packing company is using it to assemble their shipments. But some of the other Old Town warehouses have already been renovated. Like that one over there, on the corner." He pointed. "That used to be a dairy, and now it's shops below and lofts above."

Kelly surveyed the stylish lines of the building. The architect had captured some of the same design elements as the vintage buildings in Old Town. Yet, there was an updated, modern flair to the building as well.

"Retail and residences, huh?"

Steve grinned. "Yeah. Something like that. That's why this warehouse appeals to me. It's got potential. And that always fascinates me."

"I'm glad you can see it. It looks pretty sad to me," Kelly observed.

"Hey, that's the challenge," Steve said. "That's what makes it interesting. You understand that, Kelly. You can't resist a challenge, either." Steve winked at her before he turned to walk away.

Fifteen

"**Okay,** Eduardo, fill 'er up," Kelly said, grinning at the café's grill cook as she set her mug on the counter.

"Hey, don't you mess with Eduardo. He's fixing my order," Jennifer intervened, grabbing Kelly's mug. "I'll get your coffee."

Kelly surveyed the café. Every table was filled. "Looks like you're pretty busy this morning."

"We're busy every morning, which sure helps my budget." Jennifer pointed to the outdoor deck. "See those guys with Pete? They're builders. He's thinking about adding on. Isn't that great?"

"Wow," Kelly said in admiration. "Pete has to be doing well to consider remodeling. That's a big investment."

Jennifer leaned against the counter. "Remember a few months ago, when we were all afraid Mimi would lose the shop and Pete would lose the restaurant? Boy, what a difference a few months can make."

"You're right," Kelly agreed, remembering the role she'd played in that situation. "I'm so glad Lawrence Chambers was able to convince the owners to keep the property."

"Gotta take care of my customers," Jennifer said, pushing away from the counter. "See you later. Your scarf looks great, by the way."

"Thanks," Kelly said, touching the peacock blue scarf for the fifth time since she'd draped it around her neck that morning.

It did look great, Kelly had to admit, catching sight of herself in a wall mirror as she headed into the shop. This scarf was different from everything else she had in her closet, but she didn't care. It was bold and bright, and it made her happy.

"Kelly, how are you?" Mimi greeted as Kelly turned a corner into the main room. "Isn't that your new scarf? See, I told you it would look fantastic. Now you should make another with a different kind of yarn."

"Let me bask in the pleasure of finishing this one first," Kelly said, admiring the new yarns Mimi was arranging for display. The round maple table was the focal point of the room, and it never failed to capture Kelly's attention, especially since Mimi and her staff kept the displays changing frequently. She fingered the ribbony yarns spilling from the top of a glass vase. Shiny rainbow colors, muted earth tones, an entire spectrum of light captured in each skein. "Wow, these are great. Would they work as a scarf?"

"Sure. Or, even better, an open lacy vest like the one Lisa made." Mimi pointed in the corner where a vest of ribbon yarns dangled. "It's simply the knit stitch with larger needles, of course."

Kelly stroked the ribbony yarn, now entwined in neat, open rows. Every time she saw a new yarn, her to-do knitting list got longer. The mention of to-do lists prodded her again.

"Oh, that reminds me, Mimi. We brought back some of the fleeces from the ranch. Mr. Chambers said it was all right. I want to give you first pick."

"Oh, Kelly, you're so sweet," Mimi said as she rearranged a bin of fringed yarns. "You don't have to do that."

Kelly waved away her objection. "Nope. Not a word. They're my fleeces, so I decide what to do with them. Besides, once this process is completed, I'll have so many I won't know what to do with them all. I'll have to put Burt on retainer to spin for me. And I'll have to find another miller, because Ruth will be too busy to process all of these."

Mimi's smile disappeared. "I'm not sure Ruth will be able to take on any more, Kelly. She came in yesterday with some of my fleeces, and she didn't look good at all. She was so drawn and pale, I made her sit and drink a cup of tea with me before she left. I tell you, I'm worried about her. Maybe this work is too much for her. You know, lifting the bags, all that."

Bags of fleece don't weigh much, Kelly mused. Something else was wrong. "Does Ruth have any health problems you know of? She looked fine to me a couple of weeks ago when Steve and I went to their house for dinner. Then again, I'd never met her before, so I couldn't tell if she was always that pale or not."

"No problems that I know of," Mimi said, shaking her head. "And she's always so cheerful. Maybe I'm just worrying for nothing."

"You know, Mimi, when this ranch thing goes through, I'm going to really need your help," Kelly said, deliberately changing the subject. "Both Ruth and Jayleen suggested I sell all those extra fleeces that are in storage to spinners and weavers online. I'm sure you do that already, so I'd appreciate any guidance."

"Of course, Kelly. I'll walk you right through it." Mimi patted her arm.

The timer went off inside Kelly's head, and she turned toward the door. "I'll talk to you later, Mimi. I really should get more of my office work done this morning before I head into the canyon to help Debbie."

"How's that coming, Kelly?" Mimi asked. I imagine Debbie is anxious to finish up so she can leave. She's been here much longer than usual. I'm starting to worry about her. The last thing she needs is a bad asthma attack."

"I'd hoped to finish today or tomorrow," Kelly said, pausing at the door. "But I had a voice message on my cell from Debbie yesterday. She said some investment statements came in by fax, and she has questions. So, it may take a little longer." Smiling at worrywart Mimi, she added, "Don't worry. I'll finish as fast as I can so Debbie can leave."

Kelly reached for the door, but it opened on its own. Megan and Lisa stepped inside.

"Hey, perfect timing," Lisa said, heading toward the main room. "I want to hear all about yesterday. Megan already told me the scary part."

"You'll have to fill her in on everything else, Kelly. After the bull, the rest is a blur," Megan said, dropping her knitting bag on the library table.

Kelly hesitated in the doorway, debating whether or not to stick to her regimented routine and go back to pore over client files, or . . . sit and knit with friends for a while. Friends won out. After all, she'd be spending the entire afternoon poring over Debbie's accounts.

"Go ahead, Kelly. I can tell you want to," Mimi said with a knowing smile. "Those files of yours aren't going anywhere."

"Don't start reading my mind, Mimi," Kelly warned with a grin. "My head can be a scary place sometimes. All those numbers and stuff."

She started toward the main room and her friends until she caught sight of a skein of the long-fringed fibers that had captivated her last week. Silky soft, wine-colored strands, rich purples from merlot to Beaujolais and rosé, spilling over into golds, the color of aged cognac and brash chardonnay. Kelly could almost taste the oak.

Mimi's soft laughter sounded behind her. "I'm not reading your mind this time, Kelly. All I have to do is look. Go ahead and start a new scarf. I've seen you lusting after that yarn for over a week. Do it."

"But I don't have my needles with me," she said. "I can run back and get them. Size fifteen, right?"

"You take the yarn, and I'll get you some more needles," Mimi said, walking toward the front room. "If you go back home, you'll feel guilty and sit down at the computer and work instead of knitting with your friends like you want to."

Kelly watched Mimi speed toward the front room and the knitting supplies. Brother, she really hoped other people couldn't read her mind as easily as Mimi. How did she do that, anyway? Kelly selected a luscious skein and joined her friends.

"Megan says you've got fleeces to spare," Lisa said, her needles working another loose-weave vest. This fiber was different, not ribbons or fringe. It looked like feathery string.

"Yes, and you'll each get your own bag," Kelly said, setting her mug on the library table as she pulled out a chair.

"Wow, our own fleeces," Megan said. A soft gray mohair was forming into a shawl in her lap. "I may have to take Burt's spinning class again."

"Here you go, Kelly," Mimi said, bustling into the room. "Use these for now, then you can transfer it to yours later. Or keep these. You can never have too many needles, you know."

"If you say so. Besides, it sounds tricky transferring onto other needles." Kelly slipped the silky fibers from their wrapper.

"Nope. It's easy."

"I remember what happened the last time you said that," Kelly reminded, winding a length of the wine-colored fibers around her hand in casting-on fashion. "Ohhhh, it's *so* easy!" she taunted in a high-pitched voice.

"Cast on ten, like your other scarf," Mimi advised before she left the room.

"Megan said the ranch is huge. Cows, sheep, even alpacas. Sounds fantastic, Kelly. I can't wait to see it."

"Well, I'll be going back up there on a weekend to sort through files. Help me sort, and I'll buy dinner."

Lisa's reply was drowned out by a booming contralto voice in the doorway behind them. "Returned from the wilds of Wyoming, have you?" Hilda exclaimed as she strode to the head of the table and sat down. "Jennifer told us all about your adventures. Thank heavens you're safe and sound." Lizzie fluttered in behind her sister and perched on the chair beside Kelly. "Goodness, dear. You had quite an experience up there, didn't you? It was a very brave thing you did. But much too dangerous. Promise us you'll be more careful next time."

"Yes, indeed," Hilda said, peering over her glasses at Kelly. A frothy white shawl lay in her lap. "You're too brave for your own good, Kelly. You don't want to be foolhardy."

Kelly nodded dutifully as she cast on stitches. "I promise, ladies. I will never jump into a bull pen again. Megan will have to fend for herself next time."

"Megan, dear, you look in one piece. But I'm sure the experience was frightening," Lizzie said in a hushed voice, her eyes wide.

Lizzie's nimble fingers were already working a salmon pink wool. Was that another baby sweater?

Megan nodded obediently. "Oh, yes. I definitely plan to stay out of Wyoming, in case that bull has a memory."

"I have a sun hat for you, Megan," Hilda added. "It ties under the chin. I suggest you use that when you're out and about in the countryside."

"Why, thank you, Hilda, but I plan to stay in the city for quite a while."

"If it has a floppy brim, we can give it to Scarlett," Kelly joked. "I'm sure she'll use it."

"I heard that," Jennifer said, pulling up a chair at the table. "And don't make fun of Scarlett. She has great taste in hats."

"Beg pardon," Hilda inquired. "Who is Scarlett?"

"She's one of the many personalities that Jennifer entertains us with periodically," Kelly said, pushing the needle beneath a soft strand. The big needles and the silky-soft fiber made for slower going, she noticed. Like the boa eyelash yarns, it would be easy for extra stitches to "accidentally" creep onto the needle. Kelly vowed vigilance and counted the row.

"There was a dear Southern lady in our altar guild several years ago," Lizzie mused aloud. "Charlotte Something-or-another. Such a lovely, melodious accent, too. I loved listening to her speak."

"Why don't you channel Scarlett for a couple of minutes?" Megan teased. "Lizzie would enjoy it."

Jennifer gave an airy wave of her hand. "I'm afraid Scarlett is busy right now and does not want to be disturbed. She's sharing a julep with a handsome riverboat gambler. I'm sure you understand."

Lizzie giggled. "Oh, my, that does remind me. All the gentlemen used to flock around Charlotte, like flies to honey. Southern charm, I suppose."

"Nonsense, Lizzie. Her first husband left her a sizable estate, if I remember correctly," Hilda remarked. "Money sets them buzzing."

"Well, there's something else that sets men buzzing," Jennifer said, a new sweater taking shape on her needles. "I learned that much in Wyoming."

Lizzie's bright blue eyes lit up. "Really, dear. Do tell."

"Honestly, Lizzie. You're incorrigible," Hilda said, wagging her head in older sister fashion.

"It's biscuits," Jennifer said solemnly.

"Biscuits?" Lisa laughed. "What do you know about biscuits? You don't cook."

"That's precisely my point." Jennifer heaved an exaggerated sigh. "I learned there's a definite limit to sex appeal. Biscuits win out in the end."

Kelly noticed a flush creep up Megan's pretty face as she concentrated on her knitting.

"Okay, what's with the biscuits?" Lisa demanded. "Megan didn't say a thing."

"Megan made this fantastic breakfast for everybody at the ranch," Kelly explained.

"It wasn't fantastic," Megan demurred.

"Was, too."

"The guys were all out roaming the range," Kelly explained. "Jennifer, Jayleen, and I were working on ranch records, and we were all starving. So Megan goes into the kitchen and whips up this feast with bacon and eggs and homemade biscuits. She saved us all from starvation."

"Wow, homemade biscuits," Lisa said. "I'm impressed."

"It was nothing," Megan replied, cheeks tinged pink.

"It was wonderful," Kelly continued. "You should have seen her standing in the doorway calling us in to eat. She looked absolutely adorable in this cute apron—"

"Oh, stop."

"Definitely adorable."

"—with flour on her nose," Kelly continued with a grin.

"Did not!"

"Did, too."

"That's all very charming, dear, but what does that have to do with sex?"

"Lizzie! I don't know what I'm going to do with you."

"I'll tell you, Lizzie." Jennifer turned to her with a wicked smile.

"Scarlett was making progress with this handsome young cowboy named Chet. He's the ranch manager. Anyway, things were coming along marvelously until Betty Crocker steps out on the porch and announces breakfast. With homemade biscuits, yet. Chet ran up those steps and into the house faster than you can say 'Tara.' He was gone with the wind."

"Enough," Megan begged with a laugh.

"Scarlett's not exaggerating," Kelly added. "Those three guys nearly killed each other trying to be the first one in the door. It was all we could do to find a seat at the table."

"I declare, it was so demoralizing," Jennifer said, hand to breast. "I may be forced to take cooking lessons."

"That'll be the day," Lisa retorted.

"Well, it all goes to prove what my mother said many a year ago," Hilda intoned, fingers nimbly working the milky white froth foaming into a shawl in her lap.

"Which saying was that, dear?"

Hilda stared off into the yarn bins. "You can catch a man with cookies and cake, but you'll hold him with good biscuits."

"Amen," Jennifer said with a righteous nod.

Kelly snickered. "Well, it's a good thing I'm not trying to hold on to anybody, because the biscuits I make come from a can."

"I didn't want to hold on to Chet, just play with him for a little while."

"Jennifer!" Megan fussed, flushing brighter, as everyone else laughed.

"I predict little ol' Chet will be heading down to Fort Connor some weekend. Mind my words," Jennifer said.

"Well, he's coming to see you, then," Megan declared, picking up the knitting that had fallen in her lap.

"Not on a bet," Jennifer continued with a devilish smile. "He'll be coming to see you. I may have nice buns, but he's much more interested in your biscuits."

Kelly joined the laughter that rocked the table while Jennifer dodged every ball of yarn that Megan threw at her.

Sixteen

The curving road wound through the rugged, craggy ravine. Kelly steered easily around the curves as the road climbed up, up, up into Bellvue canyon. Thick pines clustered on both sides of the road, separated by boulders that looked like the slightest nudge would send them crashing down.

She never minded this drive. Even though consulting for Debbie had doubled her workload, Kelly still looked forward to driving to the ranch. It was peaceful and relaxing. Of course, she'd never had to drive this road in the winter with snow and ice. Remembering some people's stories, Kelly decided she definitely wouldn't want to slide all the way to the bottom of this canyon.

The road opened to patches of pine forests dotted with homes and fences. Modest bungalows perched beside a creek that cut through the canyon. Log homes, sturdy, two-story framed houses, and more elaborate construction appeared one after another along the road. Some sat side by side, others were separated by acres of pastures.

Now that she'd climbed higher, Kelly could glimpse the vistas through the opening in the pines. It would be nice to have a mountain home here, a stray thought teased. Kelly pondered the idea for several minutes as she guided her car around the familiar bends and twists.

That could only happen if she quit her Washington, D.C., job and stayed here permanently. But she couldn't afford to quit. She'd been over this again and again in her mind and always came back to the same place. Still, the question danced through her mind like a feather on the wind, darting about when she least expected it.

Another thought teased. What would happen if the Wyoming ranch turned out to be an income producer? Would she be able to quit the D.C. job and stay here? She'd already been away from the corporate accounting atmosphere for so long, Kelly wondered if she'd ever be able to "suit up" again and live in such a regimented fashion as before. These few months here in Fort Connor had given her a taste of something she'd forgotten, something she didn't even know she lacked: freedom. Kelly had never thought of her former life as lacking freedom, until she came here. Until she came back home.

What *would* she do, Kelly mused, if she had the choice? That thought played in her mind while she drove through the alpine scenery of the upper canyon. The images her imagination created were intriguing enough to hold her attention until she turned a bend in the road and approached Vickie's ranch. Then, the unwelcome sight of police cars in the driveway scared every pleasant thought away.

Kelly drove down the driveway, her heart pounding. What happened? Had a burglar broken in at night? Where was Debbie? She screeched her car to a halt and jumped out, slamming the door. Debbie was nowhere in sight. Kelly surveyed the pastures. Vickie's alpacas were grazing normally. They didn't look perturbed at all, Kelly noticed. Maybe Debbie had heard a prowler.

She spotted a uniformed officer heading her way, and Kelly sped toward him. "Officer, what's happened here?"

"Ma'am, we're going to have to ask you to leave," the young man said. "When we have more information, we'll answer questions, but not right now."

Kelly's breath caught in her throat. "Officer, I work with the owner of this property. My name is Kelly Flynn, and I've been working with the ranch owner, Debbie Hurst." Kelly caught sight of Lieutenant Peterson standing on the front porch. "There's Lieutenant Peterson," she said, pointing. "He knows me. Could I speak with him a moment, please?"

"Lieutenant Peterson is very busy right now," the officer replied in a perfunctory tone. "When we have—"

"Officer, I was the one who found Vickie Claymore's body two weeks ago," Kelly interrupted. "I believe Lieutenant Peterson will give me a couple of minutes. Please."

The young man's expression changed instantly. "I'll be right back, ma'am," he said and scurried off.

Kelly watched him speak with Peterson and saw the detective turn her way. To her relief, Peterson walked toward her. "Lieutenant Peterson, you remember me, don't you?" she asked as he drew near.

"Yes, I do, Ms. Flynn. What brings you out to this ranch today? You've got incredible timing," he said.

"I've been helping Debbie Hurst sort through her mother's business records and create financial statements so the estate can be settled. Usually, I meet Debbie here in the office in the back." Kelly pointed toward the other side of the house, even though she had a sinking feeling Lieutenant Peterson already knew where it was.

"Ms. Flynn, when was the last time you spoke with Debbie Hurst?" he asked, slipping a familiar notepad from his pocket.

The cold feeling that had been creeping into her gut claimed Kelly now. "Where's Debbie, Lieutenant? Is she all right?"

Peterson caught Kelly's frightened gaze and held it. She could feel his probing. "No, Ms. Flynn, she's not. I'm afraid she's dead."

Kelly froze for a second. She was sure her breath was frosted. "How . . . what . . . what happened?"

"That's what we're trying to discover, Ms. Flynn. Ms. Hurst was found on the floor of the office last night. She was not breathing. Apparently, she suffered a severe respiratory attack, so we're trying to determine the exact cause of death. Now, back to my question. When did you speak with her last?"

The ice in her brain started melting. "Yesterday, I had a message from her on my cell phone. I was in Wyoming with some friends all day yesterday, then I was playing softball last night, so I didn't speak with her personally. It was the day before when I spoke with her. We were here working in the office together."

"Did she seem upset? Or did she look as if she were having trouble breathing?"

"Well, she always has difficulty breathing up here at the ranch, because of the grasses and all. That's why she uses an inhaler. But she was acting normally. I mean, she's been very anxious to get these records finished so she could leave for her home in Arizona. This whole trip has been stressful for her, and all of her friends have been worried."

"Was she disturbed about anything? Anything recent?" Peterson asked, scribbling in his notepad.

"No," Kelly answered, surprised at the question. Then she remembered Debbie's voice message. "The only thing I recall was

the voice message she left yesterday. She said the faxed bank statements had some discrepancies, and she wanted to go over them with
me. That's why I'm here," Kelly added in a plaintive voice.

"What time was that call? Can you check your phone?"

Kelly obediently flipped open her cell even though she knew she
wouldn't have a signal. "I'm afraid I don't have a signal, Lieutenant.
I can call you when I get back into range. My call log will have a
record of the time."

"Thank you, Ms. Flynn, I'd appreciate that." He reached into
his pocket and handed her a card. "Here's another, Ms. Flynn. I'm
assuming you no longer have the first one I gave you." A small smile
appeared for a second.

"Thanks, Lieutenant. I'll call as soon as I leave the canyon," Kelly
said. "Can I ask a question, sir?"

"You can ask, Ms. Flynn, but I make no promises to answer."
This time Peterson gave her a real smile.

"Who found Debbie? Was it Jayleen Swinson? She takes care of
the alpacas. As soon as we got back into town last night, she headed
up here."

Peterson started scribbling again, which wasn't a good sign. "No,
Ms. Flynn, it wasn't Ms. Swinson who discovered the body, and I'm
not at liberty to say who it was. We'll make it a point to speak with
Ms. Swinson, though. You take care now, and drive safely out of the
canyon."

With that, Peterson turned around and headed back to a small
group of investigators assembled on the porch. Kelly watched a uniformed officer start to wind yellow tape around the sprawling log
home. Again. She stared almost in disbelief that death could strike
twice in this peaceful mountain setting. Part of her still couldn't
believe it.

Kelly headed for her car. Jumping in, she sped away from the
ranch as fast as she could. This time, she didn't even pay attention
to the beautiful mountain scenery as she tore out of the canyon. The
awful memories from Vickie's death were tugging at her, and this
time they'd brought a new friend. Guilt.

This would never have happened if she'd been there yesterday.
If she hadn't gone to Wyoming, then she would have been there

to help Debbie when she had her attack. Surely that's what it was. A sudden asthma attack. Hadn't Mimi told her how worried she was about Debbie? This very morning Mimi was worried about an asthma attack. And it happened. And Kelly wasn't there to stop it.

The sporty car shot forward, picking up speed, responding to the increased pressure of Kelly's foot. It was all her fault. She knew Debbie was getting tired. She'd seen how pale Debbie looked these last few days. Why had she gone to count cows when Debbie needed her? Debbie probably spent the whole day up here working while Kelly was gone.

She wheeled around a curve, feeling the centripetal force tug at the car, pulling it over the line. It was all her fault. If she'd been there, Debbie wouldn't have overworked. She wouldn't have died.

Kelly rounded another curve just as a red SUV swerved into view. Thanks to razor-sharp reflexes, Kelly was able to hug the inside of the curve just in time. She braked immediately, slowing to a safer speed.

Idiot! What are you doing? You know better than that. Slow down and stop this drivel about your being responsible for Debbie's death. Kelly recognized the voice of her guardian angel. Nary a fluffy feather on this angel. Kelly's angel specialized in kicking butt.

Kelly realized the truth. She was not responsible for Debbie's death. Debbie could have died just as easily in the motel room all alone.

Checking the scenery, Kelly noticed she was almost out of the canyon. She flipped open her cell phone and tossed it on the seat, waiting for it to wake up with a beep. Meanwhile, Kelly tried to figure out who had found Debbie and called the police.

She'd been sure it was Jayleen until Peterson said it wasn't. After all, Jayleen headed over here last night about six o'clock. That means Debbie hadn't been discovered yet, or there would have been police cars all over. Jayleen would have called. So, it had to be later in the evening. Who would come that late? Who would even know Debbie was here?

Geri. It had to be Geri. She's the only one who kept in regular contact with Debbie like Kelly did. Jayleen said she tried to stay out of Debbie's way, because she didn't want to upset her.

Kelly glanced accusingly at the little phone, willing it to resur-
rect. It lay silent on the seat as she wound toward the mouth of the
canyon. Finally, as she reached the edge of Landport, the phone
beeped into life. Pulling over to the shoulder, Kelly punched in
Peterson's number and left a voice message. Time of Debbie's call
was eleven twenty yesterday morning. She searched the directory
as she headed back into traffic, then dialed Geri's number. Geri
answered on the third ring.

"Geri, it's me," Kelly exclaimed, breathless. "I went up to the
ranch to finish the accounts, and the police were there. They told
me Debbie died yesterday! An asthma attack. It's horrible. I cannot
believe this happened."

Geri's voice sounded strained and raspy, as if she'd been crying.
"I know, I know. The police told me this morning. I drove by and
saw the cars. . . ." Her voice faded away.

"You didn't find her?" Kelly asked in surprise. "But, but I thought
it surely was you who called them."

"No no, it wasn't me," Geri said. "I saw her yesterday afternoon,
but then I ran some errands and went back to the ranch."

Kelly remembered Geri's late-afternoon trip to the casino. Lots
of errands, indeed. "Who in the world found her, then?" she wondered out loud.

"Wasn't it Jayleen? I assumed it was her. I haven't called or
anything."

"No, I asked the detective in charge if it was Jayleen, and he said
it wasn't," Kelly replied.

"Who could it have been? Oh, God . . . I can't believe this,"
Geri's voice quavered. "Poor Debbie, dying all alone like that."

That image bothered Kelly, too. "I know, that haunts me as
well."

"I . . . I've got to hang up, Kelly. I'll talk to you tomorrow." Her
phone clicked off.

Kelly flipped off the phone, puzzling over who would come to
the ranch in the evening. As she passed by a stretch of properties,
Kelly recognized Jayleen's truck pulling into a driveway. Without
hesitation, Kelly wheeled in behind her, following Jayleen all the
way to the barn area. A modest house and barn occupied the edge

of what Kelly guessed to be about five acres. Not much, but enough to raise a small herd, she thought as she exited her car.

"Thought that was you behind me," Jayleen said as she strolled up, hands in hip pockets in her trademark fashion. "What's up? You look like hell."

"Debbie's dead," Kelly blurted. "I went up there to meet her in the office, and police are crawling all over the ranch again. Just like when Vickie died."

Jayleen's mouth dropped open, and her eyes popped wide. "What! That can't be! Wh-what happened?"

"They said it looked like an asthma attack."

Tears sprang to Jayleen's eyes, and she ran her hand through her tousled hair. "Not Debbie, too. No! This can't be happening." She turned from Kelly and walked several paces away, her head hanging.

Kelly stayed silent, watching a hawk sail from the pasture into the foothills, hunting. After a minute, Jayleen rejoined her, wiping the back of her hand across her face.

"I'm so sorry, Jayleen. It hurts to lose family. I know."

"When did it happen? Yesterday, when we were gone?"

Kelly nodded, somber. "Yeah, and you can imagine how I feel because I was up in Wyoming and not here with Debbie." Guilt twisted its knife once more.

"There's plenty of room in that guilty tree, Kelly," Jayleen said. "I went out there last night and raced through the chores. Got those animals in the barn in two shakes flat. I saw Debbie's car in the driveway, but did I go in and check on her? Noooo. And this morning, too. I was in such a hurry to get back to my own business."

Kelly watched the emotions play across Jayleen's face and offered the same advice to her she'd given to herself. "Jayleen, don't do that to yourself," she said softly, her hand reaching out. "I blamed myself all the way out of the canyon and nearly ran into some guy on the curve. I'm not to blame for Debbie's death and neither are you. You didn't check in on Debbie because you knew it would bother her. You told me so before. And she could just as easily have had the attack at night in her hotel."

Jayleen snuffled and swiped at her eyes. "I guess you're right, but I feel so bad! Her dying alone and all, right after her mother. Who . . . who found her? Geri?"

Kelly shook her head. "No. I talked with Geri on the way here. She said she last saw Debbie in the afternoon, but not after that. She also mentioned she ran some errands yesterday. I guess those errands included a trip to the casino."

Jayleen stared off. "Well, who in hell found her then? Nobody else knew she was working at the ranch except us."

"That's what I've been trying to figure out," Kelly said, catching sight of a police cruiser coming down the county road.

It slowed as it approached Jayleen's driveway and turned. Uh-oh, Kelly thought. Time for her to leave. She didn't want to test Lieutenant Peterson's patience.

"Sorry, Jayleen," Kelly apologized. "I should have mentioned this earlier. Lieutenant Peterson told me he was coming to interview you."

Jayleen gave Kelly a wan smile. "That's okay, Kelly. I'll try to behave myself better this time. I think he got upset with me last time we met."

Kelly smiled and waved good-bye as she headed for her car while the police cruiser pulled up in the graveled driveway.

"This is horrible, just horrible," Mimi said, a tear trickling down her cheek.

Kelly reached across the secluded café table and squeezed Mimi's arm. "I know, Mimi. It's tragic to lose both of them."

Mimi leaned her face in her hands and wept quietly. Kelly gently patted her arm, not knowing what else to do. It was impossible to console another's grief. Not really. It was best to let them mourn. Tears had helped her, Kelly recalled.

"I'm losing too many friends, Kelly," Mimi said. "This is heart-breaking."

"I understand, Mimi, I truly do," Kelly soothed as best she could. Pete peered around the corner then and looked at Kelly with concern. She lifted Mimi's cup so he would bring some more tea. "Mimi, why don't you go home and take some private time to your-self. Everybody understands. We're all concerned about you. You've known Vickie and Debbie the longest, so this hurts you the most."

Mimi sniffled into a tissue. "I don't know. . . ."

"This has been a terrible shock. You need to go home and rest. Take care of yourself, otherwise we'll be hovering around you."

Mimi stared at the new cup of tea that miraculously appeared. "Thanks, Pete," she whispered. "Maybe I will go home. Tell Rosa to—"

"I'm right here, Mimi," Rosa said, slipping into the chair beside her. She patted Mimi's other arm. "Don't you worry about a thing. Jennifer will take you home. You drink your tea. Everything will be fine here."

"And don't come in tomorrow morning, either, or we'll send you back home. Right, Rosa?" Kelly warned as she rose to leave.

"You got it," Rosa said, nodding her head.

"I'll call you tomorrow, and you'd better be at home," Kelly said as she headed to the shop entryway. Mimi was in Rosa's capable hands now.

Kelly stopped by the library table long enough to grab her things. She needed to return to her own office now, where she imagined client files were stacking up in her computer mail in-box. Thankfully, there was no practice tonight, so she could catch up on her office workload. Another night spent in front of the computer.

All of the work she'd done for Debbie was in limbo. The ranch office and all its files were off-limits for now. Kelly had no idea when she'd be able to finish. And who would be in charge when she did finish? The lawyer handling the estate? Maybe she should call the lawyer. Debbie had been in regular contact with him over the will and its provisions. Kelly needed to introduce herself and tell him the financial reports were nearly finished. After all, the estate couldn't be processed without them.

As Kelly approached the foyer, Burt entered the shop. "Kelly, I just heard," he said. "Jennifer is outside waiting to take Mimi home, and she told me. How's Mimi doing?" His gaze was warm and compassionate.

"Heartbroken, as you can imagine," Kelly answered truthfully. "We told her to go home and stay there for a couple of days. She needs to take care of herself."

Burt nodded, staring off toward Mimi's office. "You're right. Is there anything I can do? I'm teaching a spinning class tomorrow, but I'll be glad to do whatever you folks need."

Thoughts began pulling at Kelly, demanding her attention. She'd been chewing on some of them all the way from Landport. "Actually, Burt, there is something you can do." She gestured toward the main room once again and chose a spot at the end of the library table for them both. "There are several things about Debbie's death that are puzzling me, and I was hoping you could find the answer," she said as she sat down.

Burt smiled as he settled his large frame in the small chair. "Tell me what's puzzling you, Kelly, and I'll try to find the answers, if I can."

Kelly pondered for a moment. "First, I'd like to know who found Debbie. I asked Geri Norbert, but she said it wasn't her. Lieutenant Peterson told me Jayleen didn't find her, either. Then he added he 'wasn't at liberty to say' who it was. But Geri, Jayleen, Mimi, and I were the only ones who knew Debbie was working up at the ranch."

"More people than that knew Debbie was there," Burt countered. "Think about it, Kelly. She'd been here for over two weeks and had been contacting lawyers and banks and all sorts of people, including police."

"Okay, you're right," Kelly conceded. "But I want to know who found her and why Peterson is being so secretive about it."

This time Burt grinned. "Secretive? Sure you're not exaggerating, Kelly?"

"Not at all, Burt." Kelly leaned forward over the table even though they were the only ones in the room. "When I drove up to the ranch yesterday to meet Debbie, Peterson and his guys were crawling around there just like they did when Vickie died. They were putting police tape over the place like before. Something told me they wouldn't do that if it was a natural death."

"Well, she didn't die a natural death," he said. "Apparently it was an attack of this asthma or whatever. Peterson was just following procedures, Kelly."

"I don't think so, Burt. My instinct tells me something else is going on. Peterson came out and started asking me questions just like he did when Vickie died. Writing down everything in his little notepad."

"What kind of questions?"

"When did I last speak with Debbie? Did she seem upset or disturbed about anything? Anything recent?"

The expression on Burt's face changed. Imperceptible, but Kelly saw it. "Anything else?"

"No, he said he'd talk to Jayleen after I reminded him she was there the night before with the animals."

"Did she talk to Debbie while she was there?"

Kelly shook her head. "Debbie doesn't like Jayleen because she . . . well, she had an alcohol problem years ago, and Debbie still has a lot of bad memories of her mom trying to help Jayleen. I could feel it when Debbie talked to me about it in the office one night. So Jayleen tries to keep her distance."

"So, Jayleen was there last night to care for the animals, and Debbie's body was found later, right?" Burt asked.

The change in Burt's tone was slight, but Kelly detected that as well. He was suspicious. "What are you thinking, Burt? That Jayleen might have done this? That's crazy."

"Nothing's too crazy to be ruled out in murder," he said. "Tell me, does Jayleen go to the farm in the morning to care for the animals?"

"Yes, and she told me she'd been in a terrible hurry, that's why she didn't check on Debbie. She feels terrible that she didn't, just like I felt awful for being away in Wyoming."

"Did Jayleen mention there were police cars at the ranch?"

Kelly shook her head. "No, there couldn't have been, or she would have called me. In fact, she would have gone to talk to them herself. I know Jayleen."

"Do you? How long have you known her?"

"Well, not very long, actually," she admitted. Now, Burt's suspicions had magically transferred to her mind. How well did she really know Jayleen? Sure, she liked Jayleen as a person. Really liked her. But maybe there was a side of Jayleen she hadn't seen. A side she kept hidden.

"What time did you folks return to town?"

"About six o'clock. Megan and I rushed to ball practice, and Jayleen took off for the canyon. She was way behind with her chores and all her work. She has a bookkeeping business on the side, too, you see." Kelly added the last part in an effort to explain Jayleen's hurried state. Surely Burt couldn't be serious. Jayleen couldn't kill Debbie. Could she?

"Sounds pretty busy to me. Is money a problem for Jayleen?" he asked.

"Yeah, like it is for all of us, I guess," she answered lamely. Burt's interrogation was making her very uncomfortable. Kelly didn't like the thoughts that roamed around her head now. In one last effort to deflect Burt's attention from her friend, Kelly offered, "Hey, maybe Peterson was asking all those questions because they saw signs of a prowler. You know, a break-in, or something."

"Maybe," was all Burt said, but it was the way he said it that convinced Kelly her questions had brought more suspicions than answers. And in the process, had put her friend, Jayleen, right in the middle of the police radar screen.

Seventeen

"Okay, Carl, that's enough," Kelly called out. "The guy will be finished in a moment. Don't scare the man to death, or he'll never come back."

Carl looked over his shoulder at her, as if he was considering what she said, then launched into another ferocious series of barks at the Intruder Who Dared.

Kelly watched the fencing contractor measure and scribble, scribble and measure around the fence and yard. She hoped the estimate wouldn't be too high, but she'd already convinced herself that angled fencing was the only remedy she could live with. Something had to be done to release Captive Carl.

She clicked the mouse, and her printer hummed, client account pages obediently drifting into the tray. Kelly leaned back in her desk chair and drained the last of Eduardo's coffee—early morning version. It was now mid-morning, and she needed a refill.

Her cell phone jangled, and Kelly flipped it open. Maybe it was the estate lawyer returning her call.

"Kelly Flynn."

"Ms. Flynn, Gerald Huff here. I got your message. Yes, please finish up the financial statements as soon as you can. We're adrift in the water without them, you know."

"Yes, I know, Mr. Huff, and I promise I will get to them the moment police allow me onto the property," she said.

He paused. "This is all so unfortunate. I must confess I've never had an estate quite like this one."

"It's more than unfortunate. Several of us were friends with both women." Kelly couldn't resist adding, "I suppose this makes it much easier for Mr. Claymore, right?"

"Yes, it does. He's the sole heir now." Huff's sympathetic tone changed back to business. "Please drop the statements by my office when you're finished, Ms. Flynn. And be sure to include a bill for your services. When the estate is finally settled, you'll receive payment. I wish I could pay you now, but alas, the only ones with access to Vickie Claymore's bank accounts are now dead."

"That's all right, Mr. Huff. I don't mind waiting." Finishing the call, Kelly tried to shove the phone in her pocket and realized she was still wearing her spandex running shorts from this morning's workout.

Rounding the corner into her sunny bedroom, Kelly quickly changed clothes. Carl was barking at the fence guy again.

Brother, what would she do when the fence was being built? Carl would have to be inside all day, giving him even more reason to be morose. Kelly didn't think she could stand those guilty stares much longer.

"Okay, let's go outside for a pit stop," she called out to Carl, who was still standing sentry at the patio door. Kelly scooped up her phone and Carl's leash, hanging beside the kitchen cabinet. At the sound of the magic jingle, Carl raced over to the front door, jumping in place. It took three tries to snap the leash.

"Calm down, Carl. We're not going out to bark at the fence guy.

He's scared of you enough as it is," Kelly explained as she tried to hold back her enthusiastic dog. She knew she should have taken him to obedience classes when he was a puppy. "C'mon, let's go find a bush or something."

Unfortunately, the bushes Carl was attracted to were across the driveway in the knitting shop's gardens. Kelly jerked Carl away and searched the driveway area for a less offensive place. Spying a telephone pole hiding inside some scraggly pine trees, Kelly made a beeline for it. Carl needed no prodding.

Her cell phone jangled again, and Kelly flipped it open while Carl proceeded to sniff every neighboring bush. "Kelly Flynn here."

"Kelly, this is Jayleen."

Kelly felt the uncomfortable thoughts from last evening return. She'd managed to push them away with account files and workload this morning. Now, they were back. "Hey, Jayleen, how're you doing?"

"Okay, runnin' ragged, as usual. I just wanted to let you know that I survived the police questions yesterday."

"Oh, good, good. What'd he ask, anyway?"

"Just what time I came to check on the animals that evening. Then he asked me why I didn't go in to see Debbie. I didn't really want to get into all that stuff from the past, so I just told him that I was runnin' behind. Same thing yesterday morning."

"Did he have a problem with that, you think?" Kelly probed.

Jayleen paused. "He did look at me kinda funny after that."

"Well, he probably looks at everybody that way," Kelly said. "After all, he's a detective."

"Yeah, I guess," Jayleen replied. "You know, he did say something that made me think."

"What was that?"

"He asked me if I saw the police notice on the front door yesterday morning. I told him I didn't because I was in such a hurry, I didn't even look. Now, I'm wondering. Why didn't they put that yellow tape around the place right away, rather than waiting until yesterday afternoon?"

Good question, Kelly thought. She'd been wondering the same

thing. Did the police assume it was an accidental death at first, then find something to change their minds?

"I don't know, Jayleen. Maybe because they had a bunch of investigators with them yesterday afternoon. Maybe they're the ones with the yellow tape," she joked in a really feeble attempt at humor.

Jayleen chuckled anyway. "Maybe so. Listen, girl, I've gotta run and take care of business. Talk to you later." She clicked off.

Kelly stared out at the golfers wandering the greens while she let all of Burt's suspicions about Jayleen dart about in her head. Burt was a skilled investigator. If he was suspicious about Jayleen, she should be too. Why, then, was it so hard to picture Jayleen as a killer? Was it because she'd gotten to know her and liked her? That had to be it. Even so, wouldn't Jayleen have said something that tipped her off? Kelly prided herself on her good instincts. Surely she would have picked up some signal, some feeling about Jayleen. If Jayleen was guilty, then she was one heckuva good actress.

A memory triggered. Something Jayleen had said to her in the casino. Kelly had mentioned that Geri always "acted" in control. Jayleen pointed out the key word was "acted."

"We learn to conceal what we're doing . . . ," she'd said.

That made Kelly feel even worse as she pictured Jayleen playacting for everyone's benefit, pretending to be a helpful friend. If that was true, Kelly had never been so wrong about someone in her entire life.

She guided Carl back to her cottage doorstep and ushered him into the house before she closed the door. "Stay here for a minute, boy. I've got to talk to the fence guy."

At the mention of the Intruder Who Dared, Carl's ears perked up, and he raced to the patio door, on patrol. Kelly rounded the corner to the yard as the fence man approached. She saw him anxiously peer around her, clearly worried that Carl was hiding, ready to jump out.

"Don't worry, he's inside," she reassured.

"Good, good," the man said, visibly relaxing. "Sorry, but big dogs scare me. I've been bitten one time too many."

"Ohhh, Carl would never bite anyone," she declared with a wave of her hand. "He's really a big sweetie."

The man stared at her like she was totally crazy, but he was too polite to point it out.

"He is a good watchdog, though. He keeps prowlers away," she went on. "He probably thought you were a prowler."

"Whatever you say, ma'am," he replied, scribbling on a clipboard. "I've come up with an estimate. We can use the fence you have already and add the extra height we need. And the angle arms, of course." He handed her a sheet of paper.

Kelly read the notations. It wasn't cheap, but she could live with it. "That sounds good. When can you start?"

"I can have a crew here tomorrow morning. It'll take no more than one day, if we get an early start." The man jerked his thumb toward the house. "Can he stay in the house again? My guys can work a lot faster if they're not looking over their shoulders." He gave Kelly a small smile.

"Absolutely. I'll keep Carl inside with me while I work. No problem."

"Okay, ma'am, we'll be here at seven in the morning," he said as he strode to his truck. "See you then."

Kelly waved good-bye and felt one of the burdens on her shoulders slide off. Now, if she could return to Vickie's ranch and finish those reports, she'd really feel better.

Time for a mid-morning coffee fix, she decided, then headed toward Pete's café. As she walked through the garden patio, she heard a familiar voice call her name.

"Kelly, I was looking for you inside," Geri called from the parking lot.

"Hey, Geri, how're you doing?" Kelly asked. "I was about to have some coffee. Join me."

Geri tossed her long, dark braid over her shoulder as she approached. "Sure. Why don't we stay outside?" She pulled out a chair at a nearby umbrella table.

Kelly signaled the waitress as she sat down, then waited for her to scurry away with their orders before she spoke. "How are you doing, Geri? You sounded pretty upset on the phone."

Geri stared at her jeans. "Better. It was just too much at one time. Vickie, then Debbie, and then all the extra work with my business. I mean, I've had two different females arrive for breeding this week. On top of all this horrible . . ." Her voice drifted off.

"Your business sounds like it's doing well," Kelly said, making room for the huge pottery cup filled with black nectar. She took a deep drink and savored it.

"It's getting better," Geri said, staring off into the backyard of the café as she sipped her coffee. "I mean, there's always risk in this business. You don't know if the breeding will take and then what type of babies come out. That's the crucial part. Reputation can make you or break you as a breeder."

Kelly watched Geri worry as she stared, lines creasing her face. She even looked older than she did the last time Kelly saw her. Worrying over a business can do that to a person, Kelly mused. Then another thought intruded. Maybe the worry was caused by something else entirely. Maybe it was the gambling. Maybe Geri has lost more money than she could afford. Kelly remembered Geri's stormy expression from the day at the casino.

"Is everything all right, Geri?" she probed gently. "You look really worried."

Geri turned to her with a startled expression. "Me? Oh, no, I'm okay. Just super busy, that's all." Then, she abruptly drained her cup, pushed back her chair, and stood. "Listen, Kelly, I've got to run now. I have a whole list of errands today. But promise me you'll call if there's anything you need for Debbie. Do you have someone to handle the funeral arrangements like I did for Vickie?"

"Mimi's handling it. She wants to, and it's helping her, you know, deal with the deaths."

"I understand," Geri said as she turned away. "Let me know if there's anything else, okay?"

"I promise," Kelly said with a good-bye wave and watched Geri climb into her truck and drive off, wondering if those errands included a run to the border casino.

Kelly finished her coffee alone, then returned to her cottage. Securing Carl on his backyard chain, she ignored the resentful pout as she settled back at her computer. If she worked straight through without stopping for lunch, she could catch up with her clients. Then, maybe, she could escape to the shop for a late-afternoon knitting break. Maybe.

"Everybody left?" Rosa asked as she hurried through the knitting shop's main room.

"Yeah. I'm leaving in a few minutes, too. Practice tonight after dinner," Kelly said, slipping the needle beneath a silky strand.

"That scarf's looking good," Rosa said.

Kelly stroked the lusciously soft fiber. "Thanks. I think so, too. It'll be great for fall."

"Well, don't wait till then to wear it," Rosa teased as she turned a corner.

Not a chance, Kelly thought, as she admired the scarf. Halfway done, she couldn't wait to show it off.

"All alone, Kelly?" Burt's voice sounded behind her.

All warm and fuzzy thoughts fled. She watched him pull up a chair beside her, which was a sure sign he planned to talk. The last time they spoke, she'd asked a lot of questions. Maybe Burt had some answers.

"Hey, Burt, how are you? Did you have a chance to talk with your contact?"

Burt leaned one arm on the table and hunched forward. "Yes, I did, and I learned a lot."

Kelly couldn't resist looking up with a grin. "Good."

Burt smiled. "I figured you'd like that."

"Okay, tell me, was I off base thinking Peterson was sniffing around for more?"

Burt nodded. "You were right. They first treated Debbie's death as 'illness-related' because of her asthma history—until the medical examiner had a chance to check her. He found bruising on her neck. Not really obvious, unless you looked closely."

Kelly stared, wide-eyed. "Was she choked to death?"

"I'd say it sounds more like someone 'helped' an asthma attack kill her. And with someone as frail as Debbie appeared to be, it wouldn't take much to do that. A steady grip on her throat would keep her from drawing a breath. Then maybe the asthma kicked in and did the rest. Who knows exactly how it happened."

The awful suspicion that had lurked in the shadows of Kelly's mind slid through her now, cold as a snake. "Murder," she whispered.

"That's how they're handling it and have been since yesterday. You happened to go up to the ranch at the same time Peterson and his boys were searching for evidence."

"I knew he was up to something." Kelly said, nodding. "And that explains the tape."

"What do you mean?"

"Oh, Jayleen brought up something this morning that I found odd, too. We had wondered why the police didn't put any tape around the house until yesterday."

Burt nodded. "That's because it was considered death due to illness until the ME gave his report. Tell me, what else did Jayleen say?"

"Peterson asked her why she didn't check on Vickie, and she told me she pleaded too busy, rather than go through all that old baggage."

"Old baggage can hide some interesting things."

Kelly decided to veer the subject away from Jayleen if she could. "Who found Debbie?"

Burt glanced over his shoulder, even though they were alone in the room. "Bob Claymore," he whispered.

That surprised Kelly. "What? Why would he go up there? Debbie hated the very sight of him."

"Well, they were jointly inheriting the property. Maybe he went to the ranch to discuss it with her."

Kelly shook her head vehemently. "That wouldn't happen, Burt. Every time Claymore suggested talking with her, she refused. I know, because I asked her to meet with him, too. He begged me at the funeral to intercede for him. He looked so wretched that I agreed and asked her. Debbie flat out refused. She was convinced he killed Vickie. She didn't want Claymore near her. You can understand that."

"Claymore approached you at the funeral?" Burt asked, peering at her.

She nodded. "He looked awful. I tell you, Burt, if he was acting then, he should go pro. He was drawn and haggard and kept talking about these accusations Debbie was making to the police and all. And how ashamed he was when the police came to his office at the university." Kelly stared at the scarf lying quietly in her lap. "I confess, that got to me."

Burt took out a small notepad and pen and started making notes. "Why'd he ask you?"

"He said he'd asked everyone else, and she'd refused to see him. He'd heard I was working with her up at the ranch. I guess he thought he'd give it another try."

"So, he knew she was up at the ranch regularly, right?"

Kelly nodded. She could see those wheels spinning in Burt's head. "When did Debbie die, Burt?"

He flipped through his notepad. "Time of death was approximately twelve noon to two o'clock."

The same time she and her friends were sitting down to a rowdy and hearty breakfast in Wyoming, courtesy of Megan. Back in the canyon, Debbie was dying.

"When did he go up there? When did he find her?"

Burt paged through his pad again. "Not until that evening. The call came in to 911 about seven thirty. Ambulance and cruiser were dispatched. Apparently, the dispatcher said he sounded distraught."

"That's understandable. I can attest to what it feels like to walk in on a dead body," Kelly said, then grimaced. She watched Burt continue to jot down notes. "Once an investigator, always an investigator, right, Burt?"

"Yeah, I guess so," he agreed, then slipped the pad into his shirt pocket.

"This makes Bob Claymore look even worse, doesn't it?"

"It sure doesn't help. He was pretty high up the list of potential suspects in Vickie's death, and now he's the one who finds Debbie dead." Burt shrugged. "Either he's incredibly stupid, or incredibly smart."

"Smart? How do you figure that?"

"If he's really devious, he could be purposely acting the distraught, disorganized professor, stumbling onto a murder scene. After all, there's no proof to link him to either murder."

"Did they find any fingerprints on her neck? Or something like that?" Kelly asked.

Burt shook his head. "Nope. No prints."

Kelly pondered. "I guess the main thing against him is motive. Without a divorce, he inherited half the estate. Now that Debbie's gone, Bob gets it all." That thought brought a taste of indignation with it. "Son of a . . . sailor."

Burt chuckled. "That's a new one."

"One of my dad's sanitized navy curses. Burt, do you think Claymore is really that conniving?"

"Kelly, I've seen a lot of criminals over the years, and anything is possible. The human heart is capable of harboring all sorts of emotions, good and bad, no matter what the situation. Mix money into the stew, and it gets more complicated." He glanced at his watch. "I've got to go. I promised Mimi I'd take her spinning class tonight."

Kelly carefully folded her silky scarf and placed it in her knitting bag. She'd learned to be more careful with these delicate fibers. Pushing back her chair, she joined Burt as he walked to the door. "You know, Burt, part of me suspected Debbie was murdered, but I didn't want to see it. I mean, losing Vickie that way was bad enough. Now, this killer has taken both of them." She shook her head.

"Well, it might not be the same person, Kelly. We don't know that," he said as he pushed the door open. "I'll talk to my friend tomorrow. Meanwhile, take care of yourself." He gave a wave as he walked to his car.

Kelly pondered the possibility of two separate killers as she headed toward her cottage. She did not like the thoughts that invaded her mind. One killer was bad enough, but two?

Her cell phone jangled, and she slipped it from her pocket as she opened the cottage door.

"Kelly, this is Jayleen again. I was just up at the ranch putting the animals in, and the cops are removing the tape. Thought you'd like to know."

"Really? That's great," Kelly said as she dumped her bag on the sofa. "Maybe I'll be able to go back to the ranch tomorrow. Thanks for telling me, Jayleen."

"It's nothing. I knew you'd be pretty anxious to finish. Gotta go. Bye now."

Kelly scooped dog food into Carl's supper dish while she checked her cell phone directory. Punching in Lieutenant Peterson's number, she left a brief message asking permission to return to finish her murdered friend's accounts. She was hoping the sympathetic look she'd spotted in Peterson's eyes was genuine. Kelly needed to bring closure to this business. Peterson was doing it his way, and she was doing it hers.

Eighteen

Kelly stared at the papers and folders littering Vickie's desk. She'd looked through every folder, sorted through every stack of papers, even searched the desk drawers, and still there was no sign of those faxed statements. Kelly knew she hadn't imagined Debbie's message on the phone to her. It was Debbie's last message, so it radiated in Kelly's mind.

Debbie had received the faxes from the investment bank and noticed several "discrepancies," as she put it. She had questions. Kelly was determined to examine those statements thoroughly as soon as she arrived at the ranch this morning. She owed both Debbie and Vickie her very best effort, nothing less.

There was only one problem. The statements were nowhere to be found. Kelly had been looking for over an hour and getting more aggravated by the minute. "Darn it! Where are they?" she exclaimed to the empty office.

A long black nose pushed against the window screen. Carl. He'd heard her voice. "Hey, boy. How're you doing?"

Carl replied with a whine.

"Sorry, Carl. I can't let you run free. You'd spook the alpacas," she said as she sank into the desk chair.

Carl barked this time, then looked over his shoulder at the alpacas that were placidly grazing in the pasture. Kelly did notice they'd moved farther from the house than usual.

"I know, it's boring, but it's still better than being locked in the house all morning."

She leaned back and took a deep drink of coffee as she surveyed the office for the third time. This made no sense. Why weren't those statements here? Debbie wouldn't have thrown them away, and neither would the police. Debbie wouldn't have hidden them, either. She kept all Vickie's documents in three folders, which were stacked neatly on the desk. Kelly had gone through each folder twice.

She released a frustrated sigh. All her plans for finishing up this assignment were "blown out of the water," as her dad used to say. She couldn't finish the accounts without them. And she was so close, too. Kelly swished the remaining coffee in her mug. Thank goodness she'd brought a refill.

There was nothing left to do but call the investment bank and ask them to refax the statements. Maybe she'd get lucky, and they'd fax them today. If not, she'd simply have to return tomorrow. Meanwhile, she'd finish everything else this morning.

"Okay, then," Kelly said out loud, causing Carl to poke his face in the window once more. "Let's find that phone number and get this moving."

Kelly shuffled through the folders until she found the one labeled "Banks." Paging through, she located the investment bank's quarterly statement ending June 30. Punching in the phone number, she worked her way through two menus until she found a real person who could facilitate her request.

"Account and PIN number, please," the young woman demanded.

Kelly rattled off the account number on the statement, then searched for the requested PIN code. "Hold for a moment while I get it," she said and reached into the stack of folders. She'd remembered seeing a list that had account numbers on the inside of one of the folders. Finding the folder, Kelly ran her finger down the long list of numbers and repeated the necessary PIN number.

"Thank you. You should receive the faxes by tomorrow," the woman said.

Kelly hung up the phone and stared at the open folder in her lap. Vickie had written bank account numbers, PIN numbers, credit card numbers, even e-mail IDs and passwords all inside the front of the folder. Not a good idea under most circumstances, Kelly knew, but she figured it made sense in Vickie's business. After all, Jayleen did the bookkeeping. She had to have access to all the account information.

"Okay, back to work," Kelly muttered as she sorted through the folders on the cluttered desk.

At least one big job would be finished today, even though it wasn't hers. Carl would have a safe and secure backyard playground. No more Mister Morose. Look out, squirrels. Carl would be on patrol once again. Good thing, too. Those squirrels were getting too brazen for words. Kelly was sure she'd spotted a fluffy-tailed chorus line dancing across the patio this morning.

"I told you to lie down, Carl," Kelly called to her dog as she turned another corner of the curving canyon road. "All we've got is curves and more curves. Give up and lie down."

Carl ignored her, continuing to stick his head out the window, ears flapping in the wind, as Kelly sped up the canyon road.

She wound around another curve, and Carl hit the seat once again. Doggie wipeout. Clearly undaunted, he scrambled to his feet and shoved his head out the window. Flying, no doubt, Kelly thought.

"Not much farther, Carl," Kelly said. Since she was leaving earlier than planned, she'd decided to stop by and check on Geri. She'd remembered how worried Geri looked yesterday. Maybe there was some way Kelly could help.

She rounded the last curve leading to Geri's place. Geri's herd of alpacas was grazing in the pasture, but Kelly barely glanced at them as she turned into the driveway. Her attention was completely drawn to the man standing beside the fence with surveying equipment. Measuring instruments and clipboard in hand, he was obviously surveying Geri's property.

Was Geri refinancing or something? Kelly wondered. Another thought intruded. Geri had gambled with her house once before, according to Jayleen. Had she been foolish enough to jeopardize her property again?

Her curiosity really pushing now, Kelly pulled her car onto the side of the driveway and got out. She deliberately parked away from the surveyor so Carl would not go into a frenzy of barking.

"Hi, there," she called to the man as she approached. "You're surveying, right?"

The older man glanced up at Kelly. "That's right. Are you Ms. Geraldine Norbert?" He glanced at his clipboard.

"No no, I'm a friend of hers," Kelly said. "I was wondering why the property was being surveyed, that's all." She gave the man her brightest smile.

"I just work for the county, ma'am. I survey what they tell me to," he replied, bending over his instrument once more.

Kelly was about to pry again when a truck engine sounded down the driveway, coming closer. Geri roared up and jerked the truck to a screeching halt, kicking up dust clouds.

Geri leaned out the window. "Listen, don't do another thing. This is all a mistake," she said to the surveyor, her face ashen. "I've paid the mortgage, I swear!"

"Ma'am, I'm sorry, I just survey the properties the county tells me to," he explained.

"Look, I'm going to the courthouse. I'll get a receipt! Whatever it takes. Just take my name off that list, please!" Geri begged.

"Ma'am, I don't make the list, I just follow my instructions."

Kelly stepped forward. "Geri, is there anything I can do?" she offered. The fear on Geri's face was heart-wrenching.

Geri stared at Kelly, as if seeing her for the first time. "No, no . . . I just need to get to the courthouse . . . This is all a mistake . . . a mistake. . . ." She jerked the wheel and gunned the engine. The battered green truck lurched out of idle and roared down the dirt driveway to the canyon road.

Kelly watched the truck disappear around the curve. The surveyor continued to measure and jot information on his clipboard. "Look, mister, I know it's none of my business, but I'm really worried about my friend," she said. "What list is she talking about? Is the county taking her land for taxes or something?"

The man looked up from his clipboard. "No, ma'am. The list I work from shows properties coming up on foreclosure." He shook his head. "This is the part of the job I hate," he said, returning to his instruments.

Kelly walked back to her car, a sinking feeling in her gut. Geri had looked so scared—and with good reason. She was about to lose her house and land. That meant she'd lose her business, too. If only there was a way to help. Should Kelly even try? Vickie had tried helping Geri before. Why had she slipped back into those old habits? Why?

Carl woofed as she approached. Kelly leaned against her car and patted Carl's smooth black head while she gazed out at the mountains. Geri had a beautiful view—rolling ridges with high peaks behind. In September, those high peaks would be snowcapped. Glancing around, Kelly noted the small farmhouse, barn, and a couple of outbuildings. It wasn't as big as Vickie's, but the setting more than made up for that.

A creamy white alpaca wandered into her line of vision as it grazed in the adjacent pasture. Ample pastures, too, Kelly noticed. Another alpaca caught her eye then—a smoke gray, almost bluish color. Kelly blinked. That looked like Raja. Or his twin. That had to be Geri's young herd sire, Raleigh. She'd said he was sired by Vickie's prizewinning male.

Carl whined. "Okay, we're going," Kelly said, settling into her car. "You've got a big surprise waiting for you when we get home." Waving at the surveyor as she drove past, Kelly flipped on her phone and was surprised when she had a signal. She called Jayleen, who answered on the second ring.

"Jayleen, this is Kelly. I've just been to Geri's, and there's a surveyor there measuring her property. He said it was on the foreclosure list."

"Oh, no!" Jayleen cried. "I can't believe Geri'd do that again."

"Well, there's a chance it's a mistake," Kelly went on as she rounded a curve. "She came tearing down the driveway and told him she'd be back with a receipt. She claims she made the payments, so maybe there's a mix-up. I sure hope so."

Jayleen sighed. "I hope so, too, Kelly. Dammit! How could she do that to herself all over again? And Vickie's not here to bail her out this time."

"Part of me feels sorry for her, and part of me doesn't," Kelly admitted.

"I know what you mean, Kelly," she said with a sigh. "I'd like to kick her butt around the block. Damn fool! Risking her business she'd worked on for years. Every year her herd's been growing, and now she's risked it all."

"You know, I saw some of her herd a few minutes ago, and that male of hers is Raja's twin for sure. She ought to get some beautiful babies out of any breeding with that bloodline."

"Well, sometimes it doesn't work that way, Kelly. You can have a great sire and expect the offspring to be the same, and they can turn out to be a bust. I'm afraid that's what happened with Geri's male, Raleigh."

"What do you mean? Doesn't he produce the same colors as Raja?"

"Not yet, he hasn't. But on top of that, he seems to be a dud at breeding. He'll mate, but it doesn't seem to take. When the females are checked in a month, the ultrasound shows no baby. Not good."

Brother, this breeding business was definitely trickier than she thought. "Wow, maybe that's why Geri got into trouble with the gambling," Kelly speculated. "Maybe she was trying to make up for losses in the breeding business. Maybe—"

"Kelly, don't get ahead of yourself. We don't know what happened to put Geri back on that path."

"You're right. I just wish there was some way to help," Kelly said, hugging the curve as she slid around it.

"So do I, Kelly. But this is something Geri's going to have to take care of herself this time. Gotta go now. Bye."

Kelly closed her little phone and tossed it on the seat while she tried to stop worrying and enjoy the luscious alpine scenery surrounding her.

"Go get 'em, Carl," Kelly said as she opened the gate to the newly finished backyard. Carl took off, racing around the perimeter, nose to the ground, sniffing every footprint. He'd be occupied for hours. Kelly fingered the sturdy addition of extra chain link topped off with twelve inches of metal and strung wire angling inside. There was no way Carl would be able to climb out of there. It was like a penitentiary. Thank goodness, she thought with relief. No more shouts of angry golfers on a Saturday morning or threatening notices posted to her front door.

"Hey, the fence looks great," Steve called out as he crossed the parking lot. "I was passing by and thought I'd cheer up Captive Carl. Looks like he's got his freedom back."

"Yeah, he's no longer Captive Carl. I guess he's Convict Carl, now," she joked. "This is a penitentiary. He'll never get out."

Steve chuckled. "Yeah, it does look formidable. But that's the only way you'll keep him inside." He pointed. "Look, there he goes now, checking it out."

Kelly watched Carl stand on his hind legs, front paws on the chain link, staring at the metal above his head. "Golf ball party is over, big guy," she said with a laugh.

Carl turned, took one look at Steve, and forgot about the penitentiary. He bounded over to the gate, barking a friendly greeting.

"Hey, how's my golf ball buddy," Steve said, laughing as he let himself in the gate. He grabbed Carl about the neck and they both fell on the ground in a rottweiler version of Wrestlemania. Kelly wagged her head, watching the two of them do the slobber-and-roll. It's gotta be a guy thing, she decided. Rolling in a yard with dog poop. Not her idea of fun.

"Thanks again for suggesting that guy Manny," she said when Steve had extricated himself from Carl's embrace. "He certainly does good work."

"Yeah, Manny always does a first-class job. That's why I use him." Steve escaped through the gate with a final pat.

"He was afraid of Carl, though, so I took the big guy with me up to the ranch today to work."

"How's that going, by the way?" Steve asked as he strolled toward his truck. He'd obviously come straight from the building site, dirt on his jeans and denim shirt, mud on his boots. You could mistake him for one of his workmen. Kelly had the feeling Steve liked it that way.

Kelly exhaled an exasperated breath. "Brother, it's the job that doesn't end. Every time I think I can finish and close up the accounts, something new appears."

"Think of it as your first consulting job, so you're working out the kinks," he suggested with a smile.

"I guess," she said, peering toward the sun angling over the mountains. "Well, I'd better go in and do some of my work before I run off to practice."

"Me, too. I think we play you guys next week." Steve stopped beside his truck and leaned against it. "By the way, pick a night when you're free next week. I want to take you out to dinner. There's this great little bistro in Old Town. Good food. Good jazz."

Kelly didn't see that coming, so she didn't have a quick response ready. Instead, she just stared back at him.

Steve grinned slyly. "Caught you by surprise, didn't I? Come on. You have to eat dinner, don't you? So do I. What about it?"

"Uhhhh, ummmm," she hesitated while she thought of a viable excuse. Steve's suggestion was unsettling, and she didn't know why exactly. She had an idea, but she didn't want to go there. Not yet.

"C'mon. I think you'll really love this place."

"Yeah, well . . . why don't we just go somewhere after practice next week?"

"Because you'll invite the whole team. I want to go to this place with you."

He was teasing her, and Kelly knew it, but she wasn't ready to give in. Not yet. "Alone, huh?" she said archly.

Steve laughed. "Not exactly. There'll be a bunch of people in the restaurant with us."

"Well . . . ," she hedged.

"C'mon, Kelly. We've already gone to dinner together at Curt and Ruth's house. This is exactly the same, just without Curt and Ruth." His grin turned wicked.

Rats. He was outflanking her. Kelly didn't like being outflanked. But she also didn't want to act like an idiot, either. Steve was right. They had already been to dinner together.

"Okaaaay," she agreed in a bargaining tone. "Only if we meet at the restaurant after work."

"Separate cars again, huh?" Steve chuckled. "You really are afraid someone at the shop will see us going out."

"No, I'm just afraid you'll roll around with slobbery Carl before we go, that's all," Kelly teased as she headed for her front door.

Steve laughed. "Okay. Friday night, next week. Six o'clock."

Kelly gave him a thumbs-up sign and waved good-bye as she escaped into the cottage. As long as they were joking and teasing, it was fine. Anything other than that was . . . well, was something else. And she just wasn't ready for something else. At least, not yet.

Nineteen

Kelly rounded the corner from the café into the knitting shop and nearly ran right into Mimi. "Whoa, I'm sorry, Mimi. I've gotta slow down on those corners," Kelly apologized, stepping back.

"That's okay, Kelly. I was lost in thought and not paying attention," Mimi said.

Mimi still looked pale, instead of her usual radiant self. "How're you doing, Mimi?" she asked gently, unable to conceal her worry. "You still look tired. Maybe you should go back home."

"No no," Mimi refused, shaking her head. "I'm rattling about like a bean in a can back at home. This is where I want to be. The shop is home to me, Kelly. You know that. Besides, I'm much happier when I'm busy."

Kelly understood. Nothing drove her crazier than being idle. Her engine didn't idle well. It choked and stalled. "You know best, Mimi," she said with a smile. "It's great having you back."

Mimi beamed her warm smile as she turned toward her office. "Thanks, Kelly. You just missed Lisa. She had to leave for a morning appointment," she said as she left the room.

Kelly set her mug and knitting bag on the library table as she pulled out a chair. She didn't mind knitting alone for a few minutes. Her scarf was nearly finished anyway. A few more rows and she could bind off the silky creation before she headed into the canyon to Vickie's ranch.

She slid the needle beneath a colorful strand and started another row, letting the quiet of the sunny morning settle over her. That relaxed feeling settled in as well, Kelly noticed. Almost meditative. She knitted several rows, savoring the tranquility until a familiar voice sounded beside her.

"I'm glad I found you here, Kelly," Burt said, drawing up a chair beside her.

Meditation over. Kelly let the scarf and needles drop to her lap. The expression on Burt's face commanded her attention. "You've heard something, haven't you?" she said.

Burt nodded. "I spoke to my friend yesterday and asked how the investigation was going. He told me Bob Claymore was called into the department for questioning again. This time, he brought his attorney with him."

Kelly's eyes widened. "That means Bob Claymore really is the chief suspect, right?"

Burt shrugged in the way he did when he didn't want to say yes, she noticed. "Let's just say he's aroused considerable suspicion. My friend also said that Claymore swore Debbie called him at his office asking him to come to the ranch that night."

"Riiiight," Kelly said skeptically.

"Well, Claymore maintains she called and left him a message. Apparently, she talked with his secretary at the university."

"There's no way. Debbie hated his guts, remember?"

Burt nodded. "I know what you said, but my friend says they checked it out. The secretary confirms she received a call from a woman named Debbie that afternoon."

That took Kelly completely by surprise. "What!"

"I was surprised to hear that, too, considering what you'd told me about Debbie's feelings toward Claymore. But he's telling the truth, and the secretary backs him up."

Kelly pondered the surprising bit of information. "What in the world was so important that Debbie would ask him up to the ranch?"

"Maybe she'd decided to drop her grudge and settle the estate reasonably," Burt suggested. "People do change their minds, Kelly."

"Well, whatever it was, it got her killed," Kelly said in a bitter tone. "What do you think happened? Did they start to argue? Did Debbie accuse him of killing her mother to his face? Whatever it was, it drove him to murder!"

Burt held up both hands. "Whoa, Kelly. You're jumping to conclusions here. There is absolutely no proof that Bob Claymore killed Debbie. He may have had incredibly bad luck to show up there and find her dead, that's all."

Kelly gave a disdainful snort. "But there's no one else who could have done it, Burt. Debbie didn't have any enemies. Neither did Vickie."

"Each one of us has done or said things in our past that have hurt others," Burt said sagely. "Sometimes those things come back to haunt us. Maybe there's someone else out there who harbored ill will toward these women."

That thought wormed its way into Kelly's mind, wiggling stray thoughts loose. Disturbing thoughts about other people. Burt was right. Bob Claymore was the obvious choice of killer. But what if he wasn't? That meant the real killer had cleverly concealed his or her identity.

"You're right, Burt," she admitted with a sigh. "I guess Bob Claymore is the easy choice."

"That's why investigation is tricky, Kelly," Burt said as he rose from the chair. "We have to look at the obvious as well as the hidden." He pointed toward the front. "You take care now. I promised Mimi I'd help with the spinning. See you later."

Kelly waved as he walked away, then checked her watch. Once again, her scarf would have to wait. Time for her to head back to the ranch. With luck, those faxes would be waiting for her, and she could finally finish the job that refused to end.

Leaning back into Vickie's desk chair, Kelly flipped through the folder in her lap until she found last month's bank statement. She sipped her coffee as she ran her finger down the entries at the end of the month. Then, she picked up the two faxed pages from the investment bank. Sure enough, there were several entries during the first week of July. It was a good thing she'd waited. The financial reports would be totally skewed without this information.

She flipped on the computer, relieved to be in the homestretch at last. All she had to do was enter these transactions into the accounts and run new balances. Then she could create the necessary reports and be finished. Finally.

Kelly would have cheered out loud, but it might have startled the alpacas. Without Carl's presence, Vickie's large herd was grazing closer to the house today.

The computer screen beeped into life, and icons popped into view. Kelly was about to click on the accounting software program when she noticed a flashing symbol at the bottom of the screen. The tiny envelope flashed brightly, indicating e-mail. Probably the last of Debbie's correspondence, Kelly thought. Since she couldn't finish the accounts yesterday, Kelly never turned the computer on.

She clicked the flashing mail icon, feeling uncomfortable reading Debbie's mail. There might be a business letter here as well, she told herself, as the in-box appeared on the screen.

The name highlighted on the message caused Kelly to catch her breath. Bob Claymore. Her mouse hovered over the message while Kelly debated whether or not to continue. Curiosity overcame privacy, and she clicked.

"I can't thank you enough for calling, Debbie. I'll be there at seven. Bob," the message read. It was simple, yet that wasn't what riveted Kelly's attention. It was the second message printed below Claymore's. A message from Debbie.

"If you want to speak with me, then come to the ranch after dinner. I'll be in the office. Don't call. My cell isn't working."

An alarm went off inside Kelly's head. That message wasn't from Debbie. It didn't even sound like her. And Debbie's cell phone was working fine that day. She'd called Kelly earlier that morning. Who sent this e-mail?

Kelly stared at the computer screen, her mind buzzing. Maybe Bob Claymore really wasn't the killer. This message surely came from the ranch office computer. Here was the proof. The message was sent—Kelly stared at the date and time—at one fifteen in the afternoon. Burt said Debbie was killed between noon and two p.m. that day.

A chilling thought snaked its way through the others. The killer sent this message. Whoever murdered Debbie deliberately invited Claymore to the ranch to discover the body, knowing that Claymore would be the primary suspect.

Kelly leaned back into the chair and tried to order her thoughts. She needed to let the police know. Grabbing the phone, Kelly searched her briefcase for Lieutenant Peterson's card and dialed the number. Once she'd worked through two different levels of police department personnel, she finally reached the detective.

"Ms. Flynn, the desk officer says you have something of importance." Kelly could picture the middle-aged detective peering at her.

"Yes, sir. I'm at the Claymore ranch right now finishing the financial reports, and I've discovered an interesting e-mail that was addressed to Debbie Hurst. I can forward it to you right now, if you'd like."

Peterson paused. "Who is the e-mail from?"

"The e-mail itself is from Bob Claymore, but I think you'll see the message preceding that one is of the most interest. It's supposedly sent from Debbie, but I noticed the time on the message was one fifteen p.m. of the day she was killed."

Another pause, then Peterson replied with his e-mail address and a curt "thank you."

Kelly dutifully entered the detective's address and forwarded the suspicious messages. Unfortunately, the unsettled feeling didn't leave.

Closing the e-mail program, Kelly clicked open the accounting records. Only one thing would distract her from the disturbing thoughts racing through her head. Numbers. Lots of numbers. She reached for the faxed statements and clicked into the expenses screen.

Kelly methodically entered the cash withdrawals into the records. She understood why Debbie had questions. The transactions were larger amounts than usual. Two thousand dollars. Three thousand dollars. Five thousand. Forty-five hundred. Thirty-five hundred.

Picking up the quarterly statement again, Kelly scanned for withdrawals. Much smaller amounts. She looked at the faxes. Brother, Vickie must have had some hefty expenses come due at the first of the month to be taking out several thousand dollars.

A remembered conversation flashed into Kelly's mind. She recalled Jayleen saying that an alpaca exhibition bill still wasn't paid. That must have been it. Vickie withdrew the money to pay for that. Kelly sorted through the bank statement folder for the checking account and scanned that statement. No deposits matched those amounts, either.

That didn't make sense, Kelly thought, as she sipped her coffee. Vickie wouldn't pay a bill that large in cash, would she? Surely Jayleen would know. Kelly reached for her phone again, then something stopped her. Something about those withdrawals, what was it? She studied the statement again, the amounts, the dates . . . the dates.

The last entry jumped out at her. She'd been so focused on the actual numbers, she'd scanned right past the last entry. "Withdrawal Transaction Denied." Then the date was listed. The day Debbie was killed.

Kelly carefully set her mug on the desk before she dropped it. She studied the list of withdrawals again, paying careful attention to the dates of each of the transactions that had gone through successfully. Her heart started beating faster. Two thousand dollars were withdrawn the day Vickie died. Three thousand dollars, the following day. Five thousand dollars, one week later. And so on.

Debbie didn't make these withdrawals. Kelly knew it. Debbie was scrupulously coordinating every check she wrote and every bill she paid with Kelly. Plus, Debbie was using her mother's business account exclusively. Never the investment accounts. And Vickie certainly couldn't have withdrawn the money. The transactions didn't start until the day Vickie died.

Kelly's heart skipped a beat this time as the implication of these transactions crystallized. The killer had gained access to Vickie's accounts and was stealing money. Had Debbie discovered something that led to her death? She must have. Kelly recalled Debbie's last message. She found "discrepancies" in the statements. Indeed, there were. Had Debbie noticed the suspicious dates first? Something caused the killer to strike again.

This time the disturbing thoughts weren't content to race through Kelly's mind. They went into hyperdrive. Surely Vickie wasn't killed for a few thousand dollars, was she? Who needed money so badly they'd kill for it?

Kelly flipped open another folder on the desk, the folder with all of Vickie's account numbers and PIN codes written on the inside cover. Anyone who had access to this office could have found the folder, copied the numbers and withdrawn the money.

Jayleen's face popped to mind first. Kelly wanted to kick herself, but she had to consider it. Jayleen kept Vickie's books. It would be easy for her to steal. Had she? Did Vickie find out and threaten to turn her in to the police? Kelly tried picturing that, but it wouldn't come into focus. Besides, Jayleen had been in Wyoming when Debbie was killed, so she couldn't be guilty. Could she? Were there two killers?

That question was too confusing to even think about.

Another face appeared. Geri Norbert. Geri seemed to have fallen into serious money problems. Kelly hated herself for considering it. Geri's panicked, fear-pinched face still radiated in her mind from yesterday when the surveyor appeared on her property. Had Geri needed money so badly she'd killed for it?

Enough, Kelly thought to herself as she sprang from the desk chair and headed for the kitchen and her coffee refill. She couldn't think about this anymore. Her head was spinning. Right now, she needed to concentrate on finishing the financial reports so she could deliver them to the estate attorney.

Then, she'd pay a visit to the bank and see if she could pry some information loose. Kelly wanted to see the time of those withdrawals. Who knows? Maybe the ATM had a camera.

Kelly tapped her pen against the files in her lap while she waited for the bank account manager to return. It had taken over half an hour plus a call to the estate attorney's office to convince the bank personnel that they could answer one simple question: What time of day was each withdrawal transaction processed?

Recrossing her legs again, Kelly shifted in her chair. She'd given up trying to relax. It was impossible to relax. She was sitting next to the window and was roasting in the July sun. The bank's air-conditioning seemed to be nonexistent, and the music was starting to get on her nerves.

Mercifully, the manager's assistant scurried in Kelly's direction, a sheet of paper in her hand. At last.

"Sorry to keep you waiting, Ms. Flynn, but it took me awhile to find all the transactions," the woman explained as she sat down. Spreading the computer printout on her desk, she pointed to several lines of text that were highlighted. "Here's each one, with date and exact time of day and the amount."

Kelly quickly scanned the lines. The first transaction occurred on the afternoon of Vickie's death, approximately the same time Kelly had brought the visiting knitters to the ranch. Then she read the last entry for the denied withdrawal. Five thirty-eight in the afternoon on the day Debbie was killed.

Recalling that day, Kelly remembered checking her watch when they drove into the casino parking lot. It was almost four thirty in the afternoon. Minutes later, she watched Geri drive off toward Fort Connor, which was less than an hour away. Geri would have had enough time to return to town and drive to the bank. If she had lost more than she bargained for at the casino, Geri may very well have risked another withdrawal.

"May I keep this copy, please?" Kelly asked, reaching for the sheet.

"Of course, ma'am, I printed it for you," the woman replied. "I hope we've been able to help."

"You definitely have. Thank you again," Kelly said as she dropped the paper in her portfolio and rose to leave. As she started to walk away, Kelly remembered something. "By the way, do your ATM machines have cameras?" she asked the assistant.

"No, ma'am, they don't. We hope to install them next year."

"Several of the other banks in town have them, don't they?" Kelly probed.

"Yes, I believe so. Our branch has been a little slower to adopt, but we're catching up." She gave Kelly a beginner-salesman's smile.

Darn it, Kelly thought, as she headed for the parking lot. A picture would solve this entire puzzle. They'd see who withdrew the money. Her cell phone jangled, and she flipped it open as she slid into her car.

"Kelly, Jayleen here. I've just found out why Raja has been acting funny lately. Last night, I finally had some breathing room, and I took some time with Vickie's herd like I used to. Raja was acting skittish again, so I checked him out, and, well, I started getting suspicious."

"Suspicious?" Kelly asked, merging into Fort Connor's version of rush hour traffic.

"I began to notice little things, like his teeth and other stuff. Enough to make me check his ID tag."

"I don't remember seeing tags on the animals. Are they in their ears, like cows?"

"No no, we don't do that with alpacas. We insert a tiny metal ID under the skin behind their left ear. The number is recorded on their registration certificate. That way, we can ship these guys and gals all over the country and make sure we get them back. The right ones, I mean," Jayleen explained.

"Hey, that's slick," Kelly said. "But if it's inserted under the skin, how do you check it?"

"With a handheld scanner unit. It reads the code on the metal ID, and the number flashes on the screen. Anyway, I scanned him, and it's another number entirely. It's not Raja."

"Ohhhh, brother," Kelly said. She didn't have to think very long for someone's face to come to mind. "Are you thinking what I'm thinking?"

"I'm afraid I am," Jayleen said with an aggravated sigh. "Geri Norbert's Raleigh is a mirror image of Raja. I'm thinking she switched them so she could use Raja to breed those two females that arrived last week. Damnation! Why would she do something like that? It's gotta be the gambling."

Jayleen bit off a few choice expletives while Kelly pondered the new information. Had Geri stolen Vickie's prize male as well as Vickie's money? Kelly had no proof of the withdrawls, but maybe they could prove Geri had switched the alpacas. First, they needed to scan the male in Geri's pasture.

"Jayleen, are you at your ranch? I need to talk to you right now," Kelly said, switching into a westbound turn lane.

"I'm here. What're you thinking? I can hear something in your voice, girl."

"I'll tell you when I'm there. It's all speculation right now. But first, we need to check out Geri's male. See if it's really Raja. Could you use your scanner for that?"

"Sure, but I'd have to sneak into Geri's barn at night to do it."

"Is there any way you can track the number on the look-alike in Vickie's pasture?"

Jayleen paused. "Yeah, I can check with the vet. Geri uses the same one that Vickie and I do. The vet will be able to check the records. I'll call her first thing in the morning."

"Are you okay with all this, Jayleen? I don't want you to do anything that makes you uncomfortable," Kelly added.

"I'm fine, Kelly. In fact, I'm startin' to get mad now. If Geri took Raja to breed those females, that's the same as stealing in my book. And she's got to answer for it. I'll be glad to help any way I can."

"I've got an idea, Jayleen. But I'm going to need your help. See you in a few minutes." Kelly tossed her phone to the seat. If she was right, then Geri Norbert had even more to answer for than switching alpacas in a pasture.

Jayleen leaned forward in the ladder-back chair, her hands clasped between her knees. She stared at Kelly, her blue eyes wide. Even Jayleen's normally ruddy complexion had paled as Kelly repeated her suspicions about Geri. "Good Lord A-mighty," Jayleen said softly. "That's more than I want to think about. I mean, stealing Raja and Vickie's money is bad enough, but . . . but killing . . ."

Kelly swirled the coffee in her cup before she drank. Thank goodness Jayleen had a pot on the stove when Kelly arrived. She didn't think she could tell this story without sustenance of some kind.

Lacking food, she'd take caffeine. Kelly shifted position and sank deeper into the upholstered chair. Most of the furniture in Jayleen's small, but cozy, living room showed years of wear. Comfortable and broken in, Kelly's dad would call it.

"I know, Jayleen. I don't like to think Geri could do it, either. But those withdrawals are simply too damning to ignore," Kelly said. "Only someone who was close to Vickie would have access to her office so they could see the folder with account numbers. And unless you know of someone else, that leaves Geri, you, and me."

Jayleen screwed up her face. "What about Bob Claymore? That bastard had the most to gain from all of this. Maybe he took the money."

"Why would he?" Kelly countered. "He was about to inherit half the estate."

"You've let him off the hook, haven't you?"

Kelly shrugged. "Well, it's pretty clear he's telling the truth about Debbie. That e-mail message came from the ranch office, no question. Plus, he didn't show up until evening. Debbie was killed earlier in the afternoon, the police say."

Jayleen shook her head. "I just hate letting that bastard off. He's . . . he's . . ."

"So easy to suspect," Kelly finished the sentence. "I know. I felt the same way. But that e-mail shows the killer was trying to frame Claymore by luring him up to the ranch."

"You think Geri schemed all of this?"

"I don't know, Jayleen, but all these circumstances keep adding up. Geri needed money badly. Whether her business was going bad or whether she gambled too much, her house was going up for foreclosure. The surveyor said so. I called Jennifer on the way over here and asked her how foreclosure works, and Jennifer said there's all sorts of time built into the process so the home owner can save their property. I mean, they just don't sweep in and grab your house if you miss a couple of payments. It has to be more than that, and the person is given every chance to pay up before the county steps in. So that means that Geri had been missing payments for several months before it got to this point."

Jayleen leaned back in her chair and crossed her ankle over her knee. "Well, she'd been making her loan payments to Vickie every month. Maybe she was skipping her mortgage to do it, hoping she could catch up later."

"Maybe she was hoping she'd win big and be able to pay everything off," Kelly suggested. "Who knows what the final straw was. Maybe the county contacted her about the looming foreclosure. Something happened to drive her to desperation."

Jayleen stared off into the room for a full minute before speaking. "Or maybe she had a blowup with Vickie."

The tone in Jayleen's voice captured Kelly's attention. "What do you mean? Was there a problem between the two?"

Jayleen exhaled a long sigh. "Whenever Geri was late with her loan payments, Vickie would lay into her. She could be pretty harsh at times. I was there when it happened a couple of months ago, and, well, there was this look that flashed on Geri's face . . . just for a moment." Jayleen stared at her boots. "Well, it was ugly, that's the best I can describe it."

"Had they argued about the loan before?"

"Not in front of me, but I could tell Geri chafed about the lien Vickie put on her house. But she was careful to keep that below the surface."

Below the surface, simmering, Kelly thought. "If Geri was skipping her mortgage payments to pay Vickie and then lost more money at the casino, that could drive her to do something desperate. Or at least ask Vickie for an extension on her loan or maybe forgiving a payment."

Jayleen shook her head vehemently. "Vickie would never agree to that. Friends, family, it didn't matter. She was hard-nosed about money and never budged an inch. Plus, she'd be suspicious if Geri even asked. Vickie would know right away that Geri'd been gambling. She'd smell it out. Then, she'd hit the ceiling." She flicked some caked mud off her boot. "Damn, now I wish I'd lied when she asked about those commissions."

"You mean that percentage you gave to Vickie for every client?"

Jayleen nodded. "Last month, Geri was in the office when I was doing the books, and she overheard a message on Vickie's answering machine when I talked about the commission on my new client. Geri asked me straight out if I'd paid money to Vickie for everyone's business, including hers." Jayleen shut her eyes, as if the memory bothered her. "She caught me off guard, and I couldn't lie. Not with her staring daggers at me like that."

"Was Geri mad?"

"Furious. That ugly look flashed over her face for a second."

Kelly thought about that for a moment. "Maybe that's what happened. Maybe Vickie refused to help her, and Geri got mad and accused Vickie of using her friends for her own financial gain."

"Oh, no. I could have stopped it. Why didn't I lie?"

"Jayleen, none of us can stop what's going on inside someone else's head. You know that," Kelly countered. "Geri may have killed Vickie in rage. We don't know what happened between those two."

"But why kill Debbie?" Jayleen asked. "What threat was she?"

"I think Debbie discovered those suspicious withdrawals first. She left me a message on my cell when we were in Wyoming. Maybe she spoke to Geri, and Geri got scared. Who knows?"

Jayleen stared at Kelly. "You know, all we've got is a bunch of suspicions, Kelly. No proof at all. How're we gonna go to the police with that?"

Kelly swished her coffee again. It was cold, but she drained it anyway. "I've been thinking about that. And the only thing we can do is confront Geri and try to make her confess."

Jayleen's eyes nearly popped out. "What! Confess to two murders? Are you kidding? She'd never do that. Why would she? She probably thinks she's in the clear. Everybody thinks Bob Claymore killed both of them."

"That's why you and I will have to put pressure on her. Tell her we know about the gambling and the alpaca switch. Make her think we know even more. Push her hard and see if she cracks."

Jayleen whistled between her teeth. "Boy, that's a big gamble, Kelly-girl."

"It's the only thing I can think of, Jayleen." Kelly glanced out the window. Nearly dark. They'd talked for over two hours. She pulled herself from the comfy chair. "Listen, call me as soon as you find out if that's Raja in Geri's barn, okay? Do you recognize his ID?"

"Sure do, but it'll be after midnight, probably. I figure the wee hours would be better for sneaking around," she said with a wry smile as she rose from her chair.

"I'm willing to bet next month's salary that Geri has switched alpacas. She's got Raja, and Raleigh's in Vickie's barn. And if you confirm it, then I'll call Geri early in the morning and ask her to meet me at the ranch office. I'll tell her that I've found something in the records concerning her loan, and I need her help to explain it. I'll make it sound urgent."

"Boy, Kelly, I hope you have a backup plan if this doesn't work," Jayleen said as she walked Kelly to the door.

"One crazy plan at a time, Jayleen," Kelly said as she left, the sound of Jayleen's laughter drifting after her.

Twenty

"You're up to something, Kelly, I can tell," Jennifer said, as she refilled Kelly's mug in the corner of the café. "All these questions about foreclosure. And you're more antsy than usual, even for you." She held the mug out of reach. "Go on, spill it, or no Eduardo coffee." She sniffed the steamy brew. "Aaaah, smell that."

"You are cruel, you know that?" Kelly said, then laughed as she glanced over her shoulders at the filled tables. "I can only give you a hint right now, but I promise I'll come over late this afternoon and explain the whole thing. Right now, I don't know if I'm being overly suspicious or if I'm on to something."

"My money's on overly suspicious. You're an accountant. It's what you do."

Kelly grinned as she headed toward the knitting shop. "Well, there is that. I promise I'll tell you later. Until then, I'm just trying to do my civic duty as a good citizen."

Jennifer eyed her skeptically. "Somehow, I don't think you mean picking up trash along the highway."

Kelly waved and scooted out of voice range. She was hoping to find Burt before he started his early morning spinning class. She needed a favor.

It was after one a.m. when Jayleen had called to tell Kelly the alpaca in Geri's barn was indeed Raja. Not only did he nuzzle her like usual, the ID tag number matched when she scanned him. That was all Kelly needed to hear. She called Geri first thing in the morning.

Geri had hesitated a moment when Kelly asked for her help, but when Kelly prodded once more, Geri agreed. She'd meet Kelly at the ranch office after one o'clock. Kelly and Jayleen planned to be there waiting for her.

Kelly's cell phone rang, and she slipped it from her pocket as she huddled beside several bins of yarn. "Jayleen?" she said, recognizing the number.

"It's me. We were right. The vet confirmed the alpaca in Vickie's pasture is Geri's herd sire, Raleigh."

Kelly felt another piece of the puzzle fall into place in her mind. "Okay. My salary's safe then. I'll see you around ten thirty." She flipped off the phone as voices came around the corner. One of the voices was Burt's.

"I can move that wheel for you, if you'd like," Burt said, as he and Mimi walked into the room.

"Oh, would you? That would be wonderful," Mimi said, then glanced up. "Hi, Kelly. You missed Megan and Lisa, but they'll be back this afternoon."

"That's okay. I'm only here to ask Burt a question."

"Well, drop by later, why don't you?" Mimi suggested as she headed toward the front of the shop. "I've missed talking with you."

"What's up, Kelly?" Burt asked, peering at her almost the same way Peterson did. "You've got that look."

Brother, she couldn't hide anything. Jennifer could read her, and so could Burt. Kelly gestured Burt toward the empty library table and pulled out her phone. "Burt, what's your cell number?"

Burt recited the number, then added, "There's something else on your mind, Kelly. What is it?"

Kelly grinned. "Everybody's reading my mind today. Boy, I'm going to have to work on that. What an invasion of privacy."

Burt didn't reply. He folded his arms across his chest and waited.

"Burt, I need a favor."

"What kind of favor?"

"If I called you this afternoon, would you be able to get in touch with your friend in Peterson's office quickly?"

Burt's eyes narrowed. "What're you up to, Kelly?"

"I'm going up to Vickie's ranch to meet with Geri Norbert. Ask her some questions. And if the answers are what I think they'll be, I'll need you to send Peterson's boys up there."

Burt reached out and took Kelly by the shoulders. "Kelly, don't you go getting into something you shouldn't. You could get into trouble. What do you know about this Geri?"

"I've uncovered enough to suspect her of Vickie's murder, and Debbie's, too."

Burt drew back in shock. "Exactly what have you uncovered, may I ask?"

"Jayleen and I have proof that Geri stole Vickie's prizewinning alpaca stud. He's in her pasture right now. And we think she's been stealing money, too. These withdrawals were made after Vickie's death." Kelly reached into her bag and handed Burt a copy of the bank printout. "The last entry was made while we were coming back from Wyoming, right after we spotted Geri driving away from a gambling casino. Geri was also about to lose her house in foreclosure. You may want to give this bank statement to your friend in the department."

Burt took the printout and scanned it. "Kelly, this is all just—"

"Circumstantial, I know," Kelly agreed, feeling Burt's wave of skepticism wash over her. "That's why Jayleen and I are going to confront Geri and see if she'll confess." Somehow, saying it out loud to Burt made the plan sound even crazier than it did last night at Jayleen's.

Burt stared at her in disbelief, then rolled his eyes. "Kelly, Kelly, don't be naïve. You have absolutely nothing on this woman."

"I know. But Bob Claymore has been interviewed twice based on circumstantial evidence," Kelly countered. "Admit it. There's no proof he killed either woman."

Burt frowned at her. "What if this Geri gets violent? Have you thought about that?"

Kelly shrugged good-naturedly. "Hey, there's two of us. Jayleen looks pretty sturdy. We can take her." Deciding retreat would be a good idea, Kelly backed away. "Keep your phone turned on, okay?" she said, giving him a bright smile.

"Depend on it. You be careful, and don't press your luck."

Kelly gave another wave and escaped out the door. Burt didn't understand. Luck was all she had to press.

Kelly rearranged the folders on Vickie's desk, carefully concealing the small tape recorder she'd brought along.

"Hey, don't cover that, or it won't pick up anything," Jayleen warned from her spot beside the window, which looked out toward the driveway. Alpacas were scattered about the pastures, grazing peacefully.

"Maybe beside the in-box," Kelly said, moving the recorder. "There it's partially hidden by the clock, now."

"Whoa, here she comes. Better make that call, Kelly."

Kelly flipped on the recorder as she grabbed her phone. Burt picked up on the first ring. "It's me, Burt. Could you make that call, please? She's driving up now."

Burt sighed loudly. "Okay, Kelly. But if you're wrong, you're gonna do more than piss off a friend. You're going to piss off the county police, and that's never a good idea." He hung up before Kelly could reply.

"Okay, let's get to work over these papers and look busy," Kelly suggested, waiting for Geri. A moment later, she heard the sound of boots walking across Vickie's hardwood floors. Kelly took a deep breath and bent over the folder on the desk.

"Hey there, Kelly," Geri said as she entered. Glancing over at Jayleen, she added, "Hi, Jayleen. Are you helping Kelly?"

"Yeah, we're both trying to get these records done so that damn lawyer will get off our backs," Jayleen said as she looked up from the stack of bills she'd strewn across the desk. Debbie would have been appalled at the mess.

"Thanks for coming, Geri," Kelly said, leaning back in the chair. "Why don't you sit down. I've got a few questions that I'm hoping you can help me with."

Geri tossed her dark braid over her shoulder and pulled up a chair on the other side of the desk. "Sure. Be glad to. You said you saw something with my loan. What exactly did you find?"

"First of all, I was surprised to see that the loan was secured by a lien on your property. Was that your idea or Vickie's?"

"It was Vickie's. She, uh, she was kind of a fanatic about money, you know," Geri said with a shrug. "She wanted to have extra security, I guess."

"But why your loan? Vickie had loaned money to Jayleen before and never asked for a lien. Why you?" Kelly probed.

Geri glanced back at Kelly, then Jayleen, then examined her jeans. "I don't know. Vickie could be funny sometimes."

Kelly let the warm tone disappear from her voice. "Was it because of your gambling? Vickie had loaned you money once before when you were about to lose your house, right?"

A flush crept up Geri's neck, spreading to her cheeks. "That's past history," she retorted. "I stopped all that. I'm paying back every damn dime!"

"But history has a way of repeating itself, doesn't it, Geri?" Kelly continued. "You broke your promise to Vickie. You're gambling again. I saw you leaving the casino last week when we were driving back from Wyoming. The bartender says you're a regular. How much have you lost? Is that where your mortgage payments went? Into the slots?"

Geri's cheeks flamed. "Are you spying on me?"

"You gambled away the mortgage money, didn't you, Geri?" Kelly pressed. "You paid Vickie's loan so she wouldn't get suspicious. Were you planning to make a big score and pay everything back? Instead, you lost even more, didn't you? That's why your house is on the foreclosure list, isn't it?"

"Not anymore it isn't!" she declared hotly. "I paid up everything I owed. And I've got the receipt to prove it."

"Where did you find the money to make all those back payments?"

Geri glared at her. "My business is growing. I . . . I've had two new breeding females arrive. I've got the breeding fees and . . ."

"And you've got Vickie's Raja as the stud, right? What better way to build your reputation than to use a prizewinning stud, rather than your own. Clever, Geri. Except Jayleen and I found out."

"Wh-what are you talking about?" Geri's face started losing color.

"I heard you sneaking into the barn last week. You left the barn door open, and I heard your truck drive off," Kelly said. "Plus, Raja was acting different. That's because you were sneaking him over to your place every time you had a new female to breed, weren't you? You switched Raja for Raleigh, hoping we wouldn't notice."

"You—you're crazy, I never—"

"We scanned them, Geri," Jayleen spoke up, walking across the room to the file cabinet beside the door—blocking any sudden escape, Kelly thought. "I found Raja in your barn last night. And Raleigh's in our pasture right now. If you don't believe me, we can go out and scan him again. I verified the ID number with the vet. It's Raleigh." She leaned against the file cabinet and fixed a hard gaze on Geri.

"Is that how it started? Stealing Raja?" Kelly went on. "But you needed more, didn't you? That's when you went to Vickie, right? Did you ask her for more money, and she turned you down? Did she find out what you were doing with Raja? Did she threaten to turn you in to the police?"

Geri leaped out of her chair, her fury evident. "I am not going to sit and listen while you two trash me! To hell with both of you!"

Jayleen stepped forward. "Sit down, Geri. You're not going anywhere until you answer our questions," she said in a low voice.

Geri pulled herself up, clearly indignant. "Who are you to ask me questions?"

"You and Vickie had a fight, didn't you?" Kelly continued, as if Geri hadn't said a thing. "When she refused to give you money, you accused her of stealing from her friends by taking commissions from Jayleen. Am I right?"

Geri glared at Kelly, then Jayleen, then sank back into the chair. "You bet I was mad about those commissions. That's illegal, and she knew it. Dammit! She knew how hard it was for me to make everything work, and she was stealing from me all that time. And she had the nerve to refuse me when I asked for an extension on my loan payment. That's all. Just one extension, so I could catch up. She went on and on about bills to pay and exhibition fees and how she was depending on that money and how I was causing her trouble. Hell, she had plenty of money in the bank. I knew it."

Geri stared toward the window for a moment. Kelly deliberately didn't interrupt, watching different emotions flash across Geri's face instead.

"That's when she started her sermon," Geri continued with a sneer in her voice. "On and on. I couldn't listen to that crap again. So I snapped back at her. That's when she really went off on me. Accused me of gambling. I don't know how she guessed, but she ranted and raved. How could I do that after she'd bailed me out years ago? Didn't I learn my lesson? Over and over, like she was some kind of preacher. Finally, I just had it, and I yelled at her to shut up."

Geri's face darkened. "Well, that did it. She told me she was finished with me. Told me to get out of her sight. Never wanted to see me again. She was through helping me, because I didn't appreciate it. Told me to get out." Geri gave a derisive snort. "She was supposed to be my best friend, and she treated me like dirt. I couldn't believe it. And then, she had the nerve to warn me that I'd better never be late with my loan payment again. 'Remember, I've got a lien on your ranch,' she said."

Kelly watched the storm clouds rage across Geri's face, and gambled. "Is that when you picked up the bust and hit her?"

Geri gave Kelly a look that chilled her all the way to her toes. "I don't know what you're talking about. Bob Claymore killed Vickie so he could get her money."

"No, he didn't, Geri." Kelly dropped her voice to the floor. "You killed Vickie in a rage. Then you stole her money. You found the account numbers in this folder, didn't you?"

Geri's gaze darted to the desk, then back to Kelly. "You're crazy if you think you can pin this on me," she said, then sprang out of the chair again. "I'm getting out of here right now!"

This time, Jayleen stepped right in front of Geri, hands on hips, as if she dared Geri to get around her. "Geri, you're makin' me mad. You'd better start tellin' the truth about what happened that night, or I swear I'm gonna break your arm."

"Back off, Jayleen. You don't scare me," Geri said scornfully as she pushed against her. Jayleen grabbed Geri's arm in one smooth movement and twisted it behind her back. "Stop, you're hurting me!" Geri cried out.

Jayleen let go and shoved Geri back into the chair. "Start tellin' the truth, Geri, or I'll really get mad," she warned.

"I *am* telling the truth," Geri whined, rubbing her shoulder. She shot a belligerent look at Jayleen.

Kelly had only one thing left to gamble with, and it was a bluff. She took a deep breath and deliberately changed her harsh tone to one of sympathy. "You and Vickie had an argument that got out of hand, didn't you? You killed Vickie in a rage. Then you stole thousands of dollars from her investment account. That's how you paid up your mortgage, isn't it, Geri?"

"I told you! I got that money from breeders."

"We went to the bank, Geri. They have pictures of you at the ATM. And we know you lost money gambling. We've been to the casino to ask about you."

Geri paled in an instant. Kelly watched fear dart across her face briefly, then it was gone, replaced by a hate-filled glare. Her eyes narrowed. "You have no right to pry into my private life. You don't know what I've been through."

"We know you were struggling. You were about to lose your house and ranch and everything you'd worked for. That's why you went to Vickie for help. You were desperate. And when she refused you and threw the gambling in your face, you snapped. That's what happened, isn't it?"

Geri's mouth flattened into a thin, angry line as she stared out the window for a long minute. Even from the side, Kelly could see different emotions raging across her face.

"She told me I didn't belong in the business since I was so careless with money. She said I deserved to lose my ranch," Geri continued in another voice—a voice Kelly hadn't heard before. This voice seethed with animosity. "Vickie had everything, everything. And she still wanted more. Stealing from her friends. From *me*. And I was the one she called on whenever she needed help. *Always.* Never once did she pay me. *Never.* She didn't even give me a break on stud fees, either. Even when she knew I was scraping by, trying to build my herd. *Selfish bitch.* She had it all and wanted to take mine, too. I knew what she was thinking. She was planning to grab my herd. *Steal them.* That's why she didn't lend me the money. She wanted my animals. Well, I wasn't going to let her steal everything I'd worked for. Took years to build. No way. I stopped her. She'll never get her hands on my ranch. *Never.*"

Kelly sat mesmerized. A bone-deep resentment oozed out of Geri, pooling at her feet in a rancid puddle. Kelly could almost smell the stench.

Geri turned another face to Kelly, and Kelly caught her breath. There was someone or something looking out from Geri's eyes. "Yes, I hit her," Geri continued in that strange, calm voice. "I only wanted to hurt her, but once I saw her lying on the floor, then I knew I needed to finish it. That's when I pulled out my knife and slit her throat. Then I watched her bleed to death on that new rug of hers." Geri's mouth twisted into a chilling smile. "Served her right. She was too arrogant. It was time to settle accounts."

Kelly watched the strange light dance in Geri's eyes as she recalled killing her best friend. "Did you leave that bracelet there?"

"Yes. Eva dropped it in Denver, practically under my nose. I was going to sell it to a guy at the casino. Then I had a better idea. I knew the cops would trace it to Eva, and she would point right back to Bob." She sneered. "Those two deserve each other."

After a moment, Kelly asked softly, "And, Debbie? Why kill her? She was harmless."

"No she wasn't. She had a mean streak like her mother. When she saw those statements, she started asking questions. Too many questions. So . . . I shut her up." Geri smirked. "It didn't take much. She started to have one of those attacks, and I just helped it along. Then I destroyed those statements so you wouldn't find them."

Chilled by what she'd just heard, Kelly stared back at Geri, or whatever Geri had become. A slight movement from Jayleen caught Kelly's attention. Jayleen gestured out the window and nodded. The police.

In an attempt to appeal to what was left of Geri's sanity, Kelly spoke up. "You're going to want to get this off your chest, Geri. You can't live with something like this."

Geri snickered. "Don't be ridiculous. There's no proof that I had anything to do with Vickie's death. Or Debbie's. You have nothing."

"We have those photos at the bank," Jayleen spoke up, picking up Kelly's ruse where it left off.

"That proves nothing. I'll simply say Vickie gave me permission to withdraw the money to pay my mortgage. You can't prove otherwise." Geri rose from the chair and shoved her hands in her jeans pocket. She smirked at both Kelly and Jayleen. "Now, if you'll excuse me, I've got a ranch to attend to."

Kelly rose from her chair and leaned across the desk. "I think you'll be staying awhile longer, Geri. The police will want to talk to you."

"Give it up, Kelly," Geri said disdainfully. "You've got nothing on me. It's just your word against mine."

"Look outside. They're here now," Kelly said.

Geri stared at her, incredulous for a split second, then went to the window. "Son of a . . ." Geri let loose a stream of expletives that made even Jayleen stand up straighter.

"You better start practicing those lies, Geri. It's easy for the police to trip you up. You may forget and slip and make a mistake," Jayleen warned.

Geri flashed both of them an incendiary glare. "You two are

desperate, aren't you? Well, it won't work. I told you, you've got nothing on me. Nothing! It's just your word against mine."

Kelly reached over the desk and picked up the small tape recorder, tape still running. She held it up for Geri to see. "I think we've got all the words we need."

Geri's jaw dropped as she stared at the recorder. Her look of shock changed to rage in an instant. "Damn you!" she swore and lunged forward.

Jayleen stepped in front of the desk, as if to block her, until voices called out from the living room.

"Ms. Flynn? Lieutenant Peterson, here. Where are you?"

Jayleen stepped away and drew back. "I think I'll let the police handle it from here," she said.

"I'm in the back, Lieutenant," Kelly called out. "In the office."

Geri stared from one woman to the next, panic darting across her features as she backed into the corner. There, another transformation occurred. Kelly watched the malevolent Geri disappear like smoke and leave a terrified Geri crumbled in a heap, collapsed in the chair.

"Don't let them touch me, don't let them touch me," she whimpered. "Please! Please, I didn't mean to do it, please."

Lieutenant Peterson appeared in the doorway, and the sight of him elicited a wail from the corner. Peterson peered at Kelly. "Ms. Flynn, exactly what is going on here?"

"I think you'll want to hear this, Lieutenant Peterson," she said, holding out the recorder as she approached. "Then you may have some questions for Ms. Norbert."

"Ms. Norbert is going to need a lawyer, Lieutenant Peterson. She's not in real good shape right now," Jayleen said, gesturing to Geri, who was hunched over and weeping softly in the corner.

Peterson accepted the recorder, then glanced from Kelly to Jayleen to Geri, then Kelly again. "Ms. Flynn, why don't you and I go into the living room and have a little talk? We'll start from there."

The silky fibers caressed her skin as Kelly wrapped the finished scarf around her neck. "How's it look?" she asked her friends seated at the knitting shop's library table.

"Fabulous," Lisa commented, glancing up from the fringed string she was turning into a vest.

"Told you it was easy," Jennifer teased, relaxing with a mug of coffee. "It looks great."

"See, you are getting better. Lots better. I can't wait to see your sweater when you're finished," Megan said, another bright boa eyelash yarn in her lap.

"Where is that sweater, Kelly?" Mimi asked, holding a china cup and saucer—her afternoon appointment with Earl Grey.

"Well, it's back at home, spread out on the table, waiting for my love affair with the scarves to stop, I guess." She fingered the luxuriously soft yarn. The love affair may never end, she thought.

"That'll never happen," Jennifer joked. "There are too many luscious yarns that keep coming into the shop."

"It's all Mimi's fault," Kelly said with a laugh. "She keeps buying yummy yarns. I could spend my whole salary here, if I let myself go."

She turned to Burt, who was sitting in his favorite spinning spot at the end of the table. "Burt, stop spinning. No more mohair and silk or other gorgeous yarns. Mimi's going on a yarn diet."

"Never!" Mimi protested with a laugh as the others joined her.

"I think we should start Kelly spinning. Then maybe she'd get hooked on that rather than running around solving crimes and getting into trouble and worrying all the rest of us in the process," Burt said, hands methodically working the roving as it fed onto the wheel. He glanced up at Kelly and gave her a wink.

"Knitting's complicated enough for me, Burt," Kelly said, stroking the silky fibers again.

"That's one incredible story," Jennifer said, staring out into the room. "Who would have thought that nice Geri Norbert had all that hate inside her."

Lisa and Megan nodded silently as they bent over their busy needles. Mimi set her teacup on the table and leaned back into her rocker as she continued a light blue sweater, the color of Colorado skies.

Her soft voice spoke up. "Well, I'm glad it's over and justice has been done. Thanks to our Kelly."

Kelly smiled. "I was just trying to help, that's all. So was Jayleen. I couldn't have done it without her. Or, her muscle."

Jennifer chuckled. "That Jayleen is something else, isn't she? We'll have to see more of her."

"Maybe she'd like to teach a class," Mimi said. "I could ask her."

Kelly was about to encourage that suggestion when Rosa appeared around the corner, her face white with concern. "Mimi, someone just called and said Ruth Stackhouse is in the hospital. She's had a heart attack. A real bad one."

Mimi's needles dropped to her lap. All color drained from her face. "Ohhhh no!" she whispered. "I knew something was wrong. I just knew it! When did it happen? Who was it that called?"

"I don't know who it was, Mimi. She said she was calling all Ruth's friends. Apparently it happened yesterday. She's in Front Range Hospital Cardiac Unit."

Mimi gathered up the yarn in her lap. "I'm going there right now," she announced.

Burt appeared by her side. "I'll drive you over there, Mimi. I don't want you on the road worrying like you are now. You could have an accident."

Kelly unwrapped her scarf and shoved it gently into her bag as she stood up. "I'm going, too. We can all go together."

"Don't worry, Mimi, I'll close up like usual. Everything will be fine," Rosa promised. "You go see Ruth. I'll say a prayer for her."

"I'm so sorry, Mimi," Megan spoke up. "I didn't know Ruth, but I heard wonderful things about her."

Jennifer looked up at Kelly. "I'll say a prayer, too. I remember a few from all those years ago."

Kelly glanced around the table at the concerned faces of her friends. She was lucky to have such good friends. And she kept making more friends. Expanding the circle. Friends who cared about her, and she cared about them. The longer Kelly stayed here, the harder it was to leave. She didn't want to leave these friends.

She gave Jennifer a pat on the shoulder. "That's sweet, Jen. Prayers are good."

Burt and Mimi hurried to the door, Kelly following behind. She paused in the doorway and glanced back to her friends. "I'll be there tonight for practice."

"Promise?" Lisa called after her.

"Promise," she yelled over her shoulder before she stepped outside into the late-July sunshine. Kelly always kept her promises.

Tropical Shell in 4 sts/in

This sleeveless shell is great for summer or to wear as a vest or under a jacket or cardigan in colder weather. It's made in the round up to the armholes and the shoulders are knitted together.

FINISHED MEASUREMENTS IN INCHES:

SIZES:	XS	S	M	L	XL
BUST (at underarm)	31	33	37	39	45
ARMHOLE DEPTH	6	7	8	9	11
LENGTH*	16	17	18	19	21

Length is easily adjusted between the bottom edge of the sweater and the armhole.

MATERIALS: Heavy worsted weight yarn or any combination of yarns to obtain gauge.

SIZES:	XS	S	M	L	XL
YARDAGE	400	425	450	500	600

NEEDLES: US size 7—24- or 32-inch circular needle (for ribbing). US size 9—24- or 32-inch circular needle (or size necessary to obtain gauge).

ADDITIONAL SUPPLIES: Stitch holders, tapestry needle, size G or H crochet hook.

GAUGE: 4 sts and 5.25 rows = 1"

SEED STITCH PATTERN: Row 1: *k1, p1*. Repeat from * to * to the end of row. Row 2: Purl the knit stitches and knit the purl stitches.

INSTRUCTIONS:

BODY: With smaller circular needle, CO 120 (132, 148, 156, 180) sts. Join in a round being careful not to twist stitches. Place a marker at the beginning of the round. Work in k2, p2 ribbing for 1" from the beginning. Change to larger needle, and st st. Work until piece measures 9" from the beginning. Change to Seed Stitch Pattern, and continue working in the round, until piece measures 10½" or desired length from the beginning.

SPLIT THE WORK AS FOLLOWS: Work 60 (66, 74, 78, 90) sts in seed stitch. Place the remaining stitches on a stitch holder. Work back and forth in seed stitch for the remainder of the pattern.

BACK:

SHAPE ARMHOLES: BO 3 sts at each side, once. BO 2 sts at each side, once. BO 1 st at each side, once. [48 (54, 62, 66, 78) sts remain.] Continue working remaining sts until piece measures 14 (14½, 15, 15½, 16) inches from the beginning. End on a WS row.

SHAPE NECK: RS Row: Work 12 (14, 16, 18, 20) sts, BO center 24 (26, 30, 30, 38) sts, and work to the end of the row. Turn and work back across shoulder. Join a second ball of yarn for the other shoulder and work to the end of the row. Work both sides simultaneously using both balls of yarn. Decrease 1 st at each neck edge 5 times. Continue working remaining sts until back measures 16 (17, 18, 19, 21) inches from the beginning. Place shoulder stitches on holders.

FRONT: Work the same as for the back.

FINISHING: Join shoulders with the three-needle bind off. Work a border of single crochet around the neck and armhole edges. Sew in all loose ends.

Pattern courtesy of Lambspun of Colorado, Fort Collins, Colorado.

Kelly's Eyelash Yarn Scarf

Usually one ball of eyelash or similar fringed yarn will produce a scarf approximately three inches wide when worked on US size 15 needles (10 mm). This size needle gives a lacy appearance to the finished scarf.

Cast on ten stitches and knit entire scarf in garter stitch, finishing ball of yarn. Bind off and tuck ends.

If a tighter or looser stitch is desired, then adjust needle size accordingly.

Ruth's Blueberry Pie

BUTTER CRUST PASTRY
   3 level cups all-purpose flour
   2–3 teaspoons salt (as desired)
   1 cup (2 sticks) regular butter, cold
   7–9 tablespoons cold water

Measure 3 level cups flour into a large mixing bowl and stir in salt. Mix well. Cut in cold butter with pastry blender or two knives. Add salt, if desired. Mixture should be coarse and crumbly. Sprinkle in tablespoons of cold water gradually, mixing well with fork, until all dry ingredients are moistened. Form pastry into two equal balls. Lightly flour rolling surface (pastry cloth, wax paper, or other) and rolling pin. Roll one ball into pastry for lower crust wider than glass pie plate, so there is at least a 1–2" overhang of crust. Fit crust into pie plate, leaving overhang on lower crust for completion of lattice top.

This recipe allows for an ample amount of pastry. Do not be concerned if pastry tears when trying to remove from rolling surface. Butter crust is light and delicate and tears easily, but is also easily repaired. Fit crust into pie plate and "seam" together the torn edges by dipping a finger in cold water and lightly brushing across the edges. Edges disappear when baked, and that same delicate, fragile quality of the pastry when handling is responsible for the melt-in-your-mouth flakiness of the butter crust.

Roll second ball of pastry into a circle for the lattice top (should be larger than pie plate). Cut pastry into strips approximately one-half inch wide, ready for completed pie filling.

BLUEBERRY PIE FILLING
   ⅓ cup all-purpose flour
   ½ cup regular white sugar
   dash cinnamon
   1 teaspoon freshly-grated lemon rind
   1 tablespoon freshly-squeezed lemon juice

4 cups fresh blueberries
2–3 tablespoons butter

Heat oven to 425 degrees. Prepare butter crust pastry. Mix flour, sugar, cinnamon, and lemon rind in medium bowl. Sprinkle lemon juice over blueberries and stir into mixture. Pour into pastry-lined pie plate. Dot with butter and cover with lattice piecrust top.

Lattice piecrust top: Place 6–8 strips across fruit-filling. Take cross strip and weave it through other strips, starting in center. Fold strips back as needed. Continue weaving lattice until desired result is obtained. Trim edges of strips on lattice crust and fold lower overhanging pastry crust edge up and over. Seal edges and flute with fork.

Cover edges with a 3" strip of baking foil to keep from burning (remove foil for the last 15 minutes of baking). Bake until crust is lightly browned and juices bubbling, approximately 35–45 minutes.

NOTE: Oven temperatures vary. Check pie after 30 minutes and continue accordingly.